Re<sup></sup>

'I adored this book! A sweeping love story that takes us from the end of the Second World War to present day in both Scotland and Estonia.' *Books By Bindu*

'This is a beautifully told story of three lost souls making the best of the life they have.' *Grace J Reviewer Lady*

'I loved this book because the beautiful quality of the writing drew me in and held my attention completely. By the end of the book I had been so captivated by the stories of Maria, Angie and Jaak that I was extremely moved. Elegantly wrought into a beautiful narrative that is part history, part love story, part tale of endurance and suffering and part love letter to Estonia. A meticulously researched, beautifully written sage of identity, people and love in many forms. Don't let this book pass you by.' *Linda's Book Bag*

'The descriptive quality of the author's writing made me feel as if I was there: in the forest of Estonia, holding my breath as I hoped the Russian soldiers didn't hear me; in the cancer centre, waiting to find out if my treatment was working; in the grimy Edinburgh flat, frantically rolling a spliff to try and calm someone's temper. It was an immersive experience and sometimes I was glad when the perspectives changed so I could breathe a little easier. One of the most compelling books I've read this year and I feel privileged to have read it. Whilst the subject matter isn't always easy, it's a beautiful story which challenges readers to look beyond the surface of those they see in life.' *Bookycharm*

'Wow this book is breath-taking. I was completely captivated from start to finish as the stories of three characters – Maria, Angie and Jaak unfolded. I loved the settings of Estonia, Scotland and Siberia and I learnt so much about Estonia's history and hardships. The author writes with such beautiful skill and knowledge and it is clear the country is close to her heart. The way their lives are interwoven is wonderful and I thought the whole book was a beautiful love letter to Estonia. The Unravelling of Maria is in parts funny, tragic and epic and I thoroughly recommend it.' *Lena – Jera's Jamboree*

'There is a lot happening in this novel, but Curlew balances the many strands with skill, and it was refreshing to read a story with such a wide scope. It feels unfettered, imaginatively daring, boldly taking in grand themes of war, loss, memory and illness as well as the smaller, everyday moments of connection that build up a friendship.' *Elspells*

'Sometimes you can feel, through the writing style, how an author has put so much of themselves into their work. This is definitely the case here. Strong research and knowledge combined with characters written from the heart make this an absolute gem of a book.' *Herding Cats*

'A beautiful, emotional story that will touch your heart.' *Rajiv's Reviews*

Also by this author

Dan Knew
Don't Get Involved
To Retribution


Writing as Fiona Curnow
Before the Swallows Come Back

The Unravelling Of Maria is a work of fiction

# The Unravelling Of Maria

F J Curlew

This one's for you, Mum
x

# PART I

# Chapter 1

## Maria
## June 1993

I clambered out of the window, mumbled to myself, cursing at the stiffness of my old legs, held on tight to the knotted sheets and slid my way down ungracefully, most likely comically. My room was only on the first floor and really, such a means of escape was not necessary, but I wanted to do it *properly*. This was something I would do only once in my lifetime. I had to make the most of it.

Once safely down I took a quick glance back at the building, blew it a kiss, took a deep breath, picked up my handbag, and tip-toed across the lawn to the row of pine trees that hid the grounds from the road. I felt like a rebellious teenager sneaking out of the house to meet an unapproved of boyfriend or some such thing. It was so exciting and peculiarly familiar. Ah yes. That time. So long ago. Leave it be. I had no time for dilly dallying around in memories that were of no use to me.

My feet reached the gravel of the drive. Crunch, crunch, crunch. It was noisy. Too noisy! I might wake them. Alert them to my escape. Allow capture. That simply wouldn't do! *Slow down Maria. Slow down.* I stepped back onto the grass and padded softly along it until I reached the gate. It was locked. Of course it was.

I knew it would be and had come prepared. The keys I had stolen from the drawer in the front desk were gripped tightly in my hand – master key for the windows, master key for the bedrooms, master keys for the exits. I could have caused utter mayhem had the mood taken me, locked and unlocked doors and windows willy-nilly! Of course I had no time for such unnecessary frivolity.

I was shaking as I tried to slip the key into its hole, resulting in ineffective fumblings, the key at the wrong angle, its aperture evading it, my frustration threatening to get the better of me, be my undoing. Let me tell you, the desire to curse at my ineptitude had to be kept tightly under control! I held my tongue, clasped one hand around the other to steady the shake and tried again. Yes! The clunk as it turned. The squeak of the rusted hinges as they were forced into action, when really they shouldn't be. Nothing ever happened at night in this place, except, of course, death. The dying conveniently waited until nightfall before slipping off their mortal coil, or so we were led to believe. It was enough to make one fear falling asleep!

My instinct was to hurry away, but I knew I mustn't. This had all been so meticulously planned with every single action gone over, and over, and over again. The plan was faultless and it was imperative that it be followed. I had promised myself that. There would be no being silly, no indecision. Follow the plan and all would be well. I locked the gate behind me and allowed myself a chuckle as I turned my back on that place for the last time. What on earth were they thinking anyway, putting me in an institution such as that? The damned cheek of them.

'For my own good indeed. I'll show them what's for my own bloody good!'

Had I just said that aloud? Oh dear, I hoped not. I certainly hadn't intended to. I paused for a moment to listen, just to make sure that no-one's attention had been drawn, suspicions aroused. Thankfully, I could hear nothing untoward and all seemed well, so with little hesitation I continued on my way.

The lights of the building faded (those confounded spotlights that never allowed darkness; never permitted the deep wash of night to bathe one to sleep. I hated them so!) until all there was to guide me was the path of the road. A small, single-track greyness twisting and turning its reptilian way through the hills and forests of the Scottish Borders. Finally I was enveloped by a dark so dark I imagined that I could feel it. It was a living, breathing entity. There was no sound either, other than the occasional creak of a tired old tree, the soft pad of my footsteps, the gentle puff of my breath, the vexatious click of a complaining knee cap. *Yes, well, you can just stop that right now!*

I couldn't remember when I had last felt such a quiet. It was blissful! No longer the coughing and spluttering, whispers and groans of near strangers. The squeaking footsteps of the staff on the nasty linoleum floor. Their laughter, complaint, secret meetings – oh yes, I knew what they got up to and I'll say no more of that! – flushing toilets, buzzing lights, other people's lives intruding on mine. God, how I hated it. But now, now there was only me, my plan, my journey. Everything was ahead of me now. What an adventure!

There was a walk of some seven miles along this quiet little road until I would reach the junction. There I would meet the main road. It was imperative that I had reached it and was well on my way before daybreak. I knew that I could do it. It had been easy enough practising, as I had walked around and around the

3

grounds, counting my footsteps, estimating distance covered, building up my stamina, the odd mumble as I walked; a display of possible insanity and no questions had been asked. No harm was being done and no attention required. That suited them fine. Little did they know! Sometimes I even managed a quickening of pace – almost a run – if I were far enough out of the sight of the prying eyes of the staff; of other nosy inmates. Inmates! When did I become an inmate? Ludicrous! Well, no longer. Unchained! I had had my fill of that place. At last my unravelling had truly begun.

I was counting my steps as I went so that I would know how I was faring. I had estimated that two steps were, as near as dammit, a yard or thereabouts, one thousand, seven hundred and sixty yards to a mile, therefore approximately three thousand, five hundred and twenty steps. Of course that was rather fiddly to work with so I rounded it up to four thousand, thus leaving room for tired legs and smaller steps, stumbles, and any other complications that I might happen upon. I estimated that in twenty eight thousand steps I would have reached the main road. It sounded like a lot; an awful lot, and if I hadn't walked it over and over and over again, in the grounds, I might have doubted that I could do it at all. Three hours. That was what I had allowed myself. Three hours.

There wasn't time to stop and notice what was around me. The scent of a summer night, pine sitting heavy on the air – such a comfort I always find – the earth rich with green, the essence of green; of life itself. There would be plenty time for such things later on. That night it was all about speed and stealth. I imagined that I were a spy. It was wartime. I had been captured and was now escaping. It was peculiar how there was something real about that thought, that scenario.

Something familiar. Why couldn't I remember? I shook my head at my predicament, my lack of memory. All I had was the feeling, the knowing that I came from Estonia and now I would return. Four thousand and twenty. No. Two thousand and forty. Confound it! How easy it is for numbers to slip through one's mind. I checked my fingers. Four curled in. Yes! Four thousand and twenty one, four thousand and twenty two...

I stopped dead, froze like the proverbial startled deer. There were many of them in these woods. I had seen them from the window of my room, watched them high-hoofed and dainty; but flighty, scared creatures always on the alert, always fearful of something. It felt very much as if we were kindred spirits at that moment in time. I was convinced that I had heard the sound of a car. Yes. Lights were suddenly picking out the trunks of the trees. Little shadows jumping out onto the road. I took a sharp intake of breath and prepared to leap into the ditch at the side of the road. Of course I had no idea of what might greet me there, but I had no option. Leap I must! A pain shot up my arm as I landed. The squelch of mud, cool water. I didn't move, didn't cry out, just squeezed my eyes closed and held my breath. I heard the car getting closer, not slowing, music pumping out of its windows. Something modern, mechanical, just ghastly! It drove on by, the noise drifting into the trees and away.

'You silly old woman!' I mumbled, and laughed at myself.

I was drenched and covered in mud. 'Oh, deary, deary me. What a frightful mess!' I whispered to the dark.

I hoisted myself up. A slight panic. Something was missing. My bag! Where the devil was it? I couldn't do without that. My maps, my drawings, my money, my passport. Everything was in that bag! I tried to stare through the blackness, but it was useless. I could see nothing. Absolutely nothing! I sunk back down on my hands and knees and patted at the ground around me, the squelch of mud as my fingers groped through it. At least I thought it was mud, but one could never be certain, not in that darkness. I didn't pause to think of what else it might have been, as I simply had to find that bag! The condition of my hands, my fingers, were an irrelevance.

I hadn't dropped it somewhere else, had I? *Think Maria. Think!* Muddled. Everything was so muddled. Confound it! *Pull yourself together. Focus!* There had been a car. I had seen the lights. Yes. And then I had jumped. And the bag? I racked my brain, sifted out the unnecessary, the foolish thoughts that raced through my mind when I was disconcerted. *The bag. Focus on the bag,* I told myself. Yes. It had been over my shoulder. I was quite sure of that. I could even feel the weight of it as I replayed the jump in my mind.

'Oh dear. There are just some things one can't plan for I suppose,' I whispered to myself. 'It has to be here somewhere. The most important thing is not to panic, Maria. It doesn't do to panic.'

I stretched a little further afield, guddling around in the muddy murkiness. My fingers caught something. Yes! I was quite sure it was the strap. I tugged at it. There was a peculiar sucking squelchy sound as the earth released it and the sudden change in force made me fall back into the muddy water once again. An involuntary squeal escaped from my mouth. I allowed myself a quiet chuckle at my predicament. Whatever else, at least I now had the bag clutched tightly in my hand.

I clambered up the side of the ditch and back onto the tarmac of the road.

'I must look like an absolute tramp! Oh dear. That will never do. Or perhaps it will? I could pretend that I am an old lady of the road. Yes! I rather like that. If anyone should question me I am an old lady of the road. Ha! That will no doubt confound the lot of them!' I said in conversation with myself.

The thought of my sudden change of persona amused me enough to dilute the cold, and the damp, and the realisation that I had absolutely no idea of how far I had come. I didn't have the foggiest idea of how many steps I had taken but had the feeling that I had been walking for some considerable time. The junction was close. Surely.

I picked up my step and strode purposefully on, playing my new scenario over in my head. Perhaps I had spent my entire life wandering. Yes, just wandering around with absolutely no purpose whatsoever; with no commitments, just me and the road. Kind people would have offered me food at their doorsteps. Perhaps I had foraged through the countryside, picking apples and berries, wild garlic, sorrel, and dandelions. I might have slept in barns of straw; on luscious moss in the depths of dark forests in the company of nature, of animals, of wildness. I smiled. This was so much more fun than counting steps.

Finally, with great relief, I came to the T junction and the main road. I should turn left and head south. That much I remembered. No need to check my notes. There was no traffic at all. Well, at such an hour, of course it was deserted. I knew it would be. That was the whole point!

# Chapter 2

## Angie
## July 1987

'Oncology?' I asked the nurse, who was trotting along in her squeaky white shoes, an her uniform that was way too clean to be true. How is it they always look so immaculate when they're dealing wi blood an sickness an disease?

She gave me that look. Water off o a duck now. Look through. Look past. It doesnae matter. Only this time I couldnae. Aye, I know, I know. Pinned eyes. That look that says junkie. I know that you know, but I'm here an I need yer help, aw right? Then she smiled. It was genuine an warm an I liked her. Just then I liked her. I couldnae help but wonder how many drugs she could get her hands on, though.

'Have you got your appointment letter?' she asked.

'Aye,' I said, handing it ower to her. It had been gripped that tight in my hand that it was aw crumpled.

Her eyes narrowed as she read. 'Right you are, love. Just along there. You'll see the signs.' More smiles an softness as she pointed the way.

I wondered if it was training, that niceness, that *I understand*. Or was she always like that? Was that her? Really her? Couldnae imagine life letting ye be like that.

I started walking along the corridor. That smell. Death an chemicals. I wanted to puke; to turn around an run out, pretend that none o this had happened. Cancer, for fuck's sake. As if I didnae hae enough shite to deal wi wi'out that. Thanks man, yeah. Nice one, God. Cheers pal!

When I had first heard, everything was a blur. Their words didnae make any sense. Nothing stayed in my head. Just cancer. Buzz, buzz. Cancer. Demons an blackness. Aye. Then I thought about it. Chances were I'd be dead soon enough anyway. The smack, the drink, some punter getting too rough, some other fucker trying to steal my shit. People like me die aw the time an it doesnae matter. So, aye, I had cancer, an that was shite, but I might get through it, I might get clean.

Deke had laughed at me when I'd said about the rehab, about getting clean. "You're such a dreamer," he'd said in his posh voice as he bubbled the smack up wi a wee bit o water in a teaspoon. "I've no idea why you'd even try to stop, Babes," as he drew the murky liquid up through the needle. "What's the point?" as he tightened the belt around his arm, held one end in his mouth pulling it tight, slapped his veins an shot up. Sighed, head going aw soft, droopy, eyes closed. An I knew how he felt. An I knew it was brilliant. An I knew it was aw I wanted. An I shot up too. An we sat an gouched out for the rest o the day, or maybe it was night. No idea. Time blended. Days an nights. Weeks an years. One big fucking blended blur. It's just about survival. One fix to the next. Time? That was for folk that worked. Folk that had some shit to wake up for, to schedule their lives around. A reason. Mine was smack. End of. Get clean? Ha! Aye right!

I'd always been a bit wild, a bad girl. Well, it's no as if I didnae hae reason to be. Dumped by a mother that didnae care. Stood at the corner o the road. "You just wait there, doll. I willnae be a minute. Just getting you some sweeties, aye?" She'd disappeared. Left me standing there. Too scared to move. Too scared to cry. A car pulled up an I was whisked off to this big cold monstrosity o a place. Nuns. Cruel nasty women dressed in black spouting their Christianity at me. Punishment doled out for no other reason than "learning". Aye, right. I learned, so I did.

Ye get by though. Ye do what needs doing cos ye have no choice. At sixteen I was kicked out. I hated the place. Course I did. Couldnae wait to leave, but when it happened, Christ, there's me in this world that I knew nothing o. People. Strangers. It was terrifying. I'd go back to the orphanage at the end o the day an just stand an look at the place. It was the only home I knew. The only place that I felt I belonged. An now I'd been turfed out. Magic!

*

I saw the sign "CANCER CENTRE", got to the automatic doors, an almost turned right back around. It was easy enough to rationalise it. I mean, what was the point? My days were numbered anyway. No happy rosy shite for me, but I didnae turn back. Something made me walk right on through. A wrench at my stomach. Breathe in. Deal wi it. No questions. Just deal wi it.

The place was packed. People wi death written aw ower their faces: grey skin, hollow eyes. Nurses, doctors, orderlies, busy, busy, busying themselves. A volunteer offering cups o tea. Aye. That was gonnae help! Fuck's sake. I scanned the crowd. Force o habit. I could call it a skill. Sussing people out in a matter o seconds. Whose got what an how stupid are they, how casual wi their hard-earned cash, their look-how-well-I'm-doing accessories? How fit are they? Ye dinnae

10

want some super-healthy nut-job chasing after ye! Fat ones. Old ones. Easy ones. They were the best. But this place wasnae like that. Naw. This place was a different world. Weird. Made me aw on edge, like. Even more than usual.

I wanted to sit at the back. I always sit at the back, keep yer eyes on folk, know what's going on, but there was no seat. Just one right at the front next to some auld woman. I hovered, thinking I could stand, but then I'd be a target for the eyes o strangers; the common judiciary. Ach shite!

I walked across an she bristled. I could feel it, her distaste, but I was used to it. *Look lady, I only want a seat. Nothing else.* She smelled nice. Posh perfume. Expensive clothes. Course I was thinking she has to hae money. Easy enough to dip her bag. It was just sitting there, open, on the seat beside her. I wouldnae normally hae thought twice about it. No idea why I did. Something about her maybe? Something about being in there wi aw o those sick folk. It wasnae like a real place, a normal place. It just wasnae.

I scanned around the room again. There, on the wall, a whiteboard wi the consultants' names on them wi an estimated delay time. Two hours! I had to sit in that place out o a nightmare for two hours! It was like she'd read my mind.

'I know. It's an awfully long time to wait, especially in...well, in our circumstances.' She smiled in a resigned kind o a way. 'Would you like some tea? There's a machine at the back there. I'm sure it's pretty ghastly, but it might help to pass the time.'

I didnae know if I could deal wi this. She was gonnae be one o those auld women that just havered on an on an on about meaningless shite. Fuck's sake.

11

# Chapter 3

Maria
July 1987

One couldn't help but notice her. She looked lost. I'm sure we all looked somewhat lost in that place, but hers was a deeper kind of lost. It was as if something in her soul had been switched off. Very sad in one so young. I have to admit I was nervous – scared a little even – when she moved towards me. I had never been in close proximity to someone like that. I couldn't say for sure, but I imagined she was in her early-twenties. She had a spiky look to her; an aggressiveness, but she was pretty. Underneath all of the make-up and the attempt to look frightening, one could see that she was really very pretty.

It was peculiar how the Cancer Centre stripped away common assumptions. Barriers seemed to lift, odd bed-fellows struck up conversations. Well, I thought that was what I should do. It wasn't as if she could do any harm here, was it? A few pleasantries would help to pass the time. I had already tried to chat to the gentleman on my right, but I don't think he even understood what I was saying. I remembered that feeling of not understanding anything, of feeling like an alien. It was so very long ago, but feelings as strong as that, as painful as that, well, they stay with one eternally and pop back up at the most unexpected of times.

## Maria 1944

Her brain was screaming. She couldn't understand anything. What she saw. What she heard. Everything was an awful confusion of strangeness, wrong and unknown. She tried to scramble through the darkness in her head for something to hold on to. Pictures, words, anything that would make sense; anything she knew. But there was nothing. Simply nothing.

She could see people, but their voices, their faces, were all strange to her. There were beds. Rows of beds. A smell of disinfectant; a cleanliness so strong it felt dirty. She understood that she was in a hospital. The sick and the injured, groans and complaints. Urgent whispers. But why was she there? She checked herself, her fingers searching the surface of her body for a clue. There was a raised line on her forehead, evenly spaced bumps. Stitches? She surmised that she had been hurt somehow, somewhere. There were no bandages, no other injuries, just that constant screeching in her head threatening to drown her. One of the nurses noticed her sitting up and hurried across. Noise came out of the nurse's mouth. Unintelligible noise. The nurse smiled, checked the notes and left again.

She studied her hands. Yes, they were familiar, her fingers delicate and slender. She traced a pattern of moles that snaked around her arm. Those she knew. Those she understood. Those were hers. This was her. Her body was known to her. But her mind? Her mind was a stranger.

She didn't try to speak. The words of these people – nurses in crisp starched uniforms that snapped with each

13

step – weren't hers. She was sure of that as she listened, trying to understand the mood of what they were saying. The feelings she picked up on were soft, concerned, and she didn't feel as if she were in any danger. At least that was some comfort. Whatever this was, she felt that she was safe.

A few days had passed and still nothing had come to her. A nurse had placed some clothes on her chair, said something unintelligible and smiled, as she pulled the curtain around her bed. It seemed that she was supposed to get dressed. She ran her fingers over the material of the skirt. It felt like something of good quality. A crisp green cotton. There was a cream coloured blouse and a smart little jacket to match. The fit was good. Were these hers? Had she been wearing them upon her arrival? She slipped her feet into a pair of leather shoes and sat on the bed wondering what she should do. She didn't know why, but this didn't feel like her. Any of it. It felt awkward. Wrong.

The nurse came back and led her along the ward, through the swinging doors, to a corridor where a man was waiting for them. He smiled. She didn't smile back. She had no idea of whom he was.

'No papers?' he asked, looking her up and down whilst speaking to the nurse.

'Nothing. We don't even know who she is or where she's from.'

'A refugee?' He held a strand of her blond hair between finger and thumb. Stroked it. Stroked her cheek. Smiled.

'Most likely. She was found washed up on the shore, poor thing. We tried Swedish first, of course, but there was no response. It was the same with German and

14

Danish. Nothing. We did our best, but we can't have her staying here when she's not sick.' She shrugged her shoulders. 'She's a mystery, this one.'

'Right you are then. I'll see what I can do for her.'

He took her arm and gave it a squeeze that didn't feel friendly. It felt more like a threat. She looked back at the nurse for some kind of a sign, some kind of reassurance perhaps. Something that intimated that this was all right and she needn't be worried. The nurse disappeared around a corner without even a backward glance, no smile. Nothing.

She was put in a car and driven along strange streets to a large harbour. Massive cranes like iron skeletons, scratched at the sky. Colossal ships stood tied to the pier with mooring rope looped through immense rusted iron rings. Bunting flapped between their masts, chimneys stood tall in their middle. The gangplanks were busy with people. So many people. Children alone, adults, families. Some of them looked sad, lost, like her. Others smiled and waved as if in celebration. This felt familiar. This sensation. Boats. Water. Perhaps she was going home?

As they walked up the gangplank of one of the ships – the sound of their footsteps, the clamour of the people, the swirl of dark water beneath them – a dreadful feeling gripped her. It wasn't just fear. No, it was more than that. An awful dread. Loss. A pain that gnawed at her stomach.

Once their journey was underway it was simply awful. The weather was turbulent, the ship being tossed about amidst ominously high waves. Seasickness had struck many of the passengers. The smell of vomit permeated everything below deck. She sneaked up onto the upper deck where the sea air blew the badness away. The spray from the waves splashed onto her face and she laughed. The sound was peculiar. It was as if she hadn't heard it before; a stranger's laugh, someone nearby. She knew though, that it had come from somewhere deep inside of her.

As the ship ploughed on through the rough swell of the sea she clung on to the railing and stared into the vastness of the water. It made her feel so small; a tiny speck of insignificance. But there was something akin to a knowledge inside of her. Almost a memory. Almost. A feeling that she had felt before. This. Just this. She tried desperately to force something to come forward, something to show itself to her, but nothing came.

Despite the sadness that it now swelled inside her, she felt sure that she had, at one time, liked the sea, the water, the sound of the gulls shrieking above the noise of the engines. As she watched their swoops and dives into the water she found herself wondering where they had come from; where they were going to. Or did they just stay there, out at sea, drifting from one boat to the next, one swell to the next, one meal to the next? Did they know anything at all other than what they needed to survive? Just being for as long as they could until they were no more.

She stayed up on deck for as long as she could. People came. Some said things. She didn't know if they were talking to her or not. She didn't care. The gulls made more sense than they did. When it turned dark and all around was nothing but a heavy blackness she could still hear the gulls, see streaks of their white bodies swooping through the odd light that was escaping from the boat, then disappearing again into the obscurity of the night.

Nothing.

Eventually a hand grabbed her sleeve and pulled her back down below, angry words were said and she was put to bed amidst the smells and the sounds of strangers. She pulled her hands over her ears in an attempt to block out the noises, but they bled through anyway. The breathing of strangers, snores and whimpers. Whispers. She lay on her back staring at the bunk above her until her eyes became too heavy and eventually she lapsed into an uncomfortable sleep.

When they finally reached land the man took her arm again and led her down the gangplank. He was smiling at people, nodding his capped head. She stared through the docks, scanning the people, the places, desperate for something to cling on to. Something that said, yes, you belong here. Nothing came. No words, no faces, no buildings. Nothing. She didn't know what she should be feeling or how she should be behaving. Was she in danger? Should she call out; try to make her escape? To where? To what?

*

'Who's this then?' A large woman with a heavyset, serious face asked as she peered into the back seat of the car. 'Out you come then. Let's have a look at you!' she instructed, her tone brusque.

'No idea. No papers. Haven't had a peep out of her, maybe mute. No-one said. Anyway, she's all yours!'

'Right. And does she speak English?'

'Like I said, no idea.'

This was another language, but still not hers, still a swarm of strange unidentifiable noise.

An envelope slid from the woman's hand to his before he drove off again, leaving her with another stranger. It

17

was dark and there were no street-lights, just the odd streak of light escaping through cracks in the curtains of the windows. A pale glimmer from a weak, crescent moon. The building was a dark outline against the night sky with tall chimneys and a pointed roof. There was the feeling of countryside, of clean air, trees, and wildness. It felt like such a sharp contrast to the people, the building. She wished that she could slip away, drift into the trees and become one with them.

She wasn't allowed to linger and was hurried round to the back of the building: the squeak of a narrow door opening, the slap of their feet on concrete steps, a dimly lit hallway, a set of wooden stairs leading up two storeys to the top floor, a bare landing with three doors leading off from it, a dirt encrusted skylight above. The woman unlocked a white wooden door. There was a small room with a single bed, a wardrobe, a cupboard, and a curtained window.

'Right, this is you,' the woman declared, before retreating and locking the door behind her.

She sat on the bed, not knowing what to feel. The floor was bare apart from a small threadbare rug that sat beside the bed, under which there was a bedpan. She had no idea of where she was from, but she was determined that it wasn't somewhere like this. She didn't belong in a place like this. An awful panic set in her chest, leaving her short of breath. She stared at the walls, terrified of what might lie beyond them; of what this future might hold for her.

In the morning she was given some different clothes to wear. Awful, trashy looking things. The woman put make-up on her face, pinched at her body as if it were a thing; a possession of hers.

'You'll do. Looks like yours, you'll do just fine.'

1987

'So, is this your first time, dear?' I asked.

'Aye,' she replied. 'You?'

'Yes. It is all rather nerve-wracking, is it not? One wonders, doesn't one? Oh well.'

'Think I'll just get that tea, aye. Ye want one?'

'Oh, yes dear. Thank you so much.'

'Angie. The name's Angie,' she said, as she handed me a cup of tea and took her seat. 'Guessed you'd be a sweet an milky kind o a person.'

I laughed politely. She was wrong, but I didn't deem it necessary, nor prudent, to mention. 'Oh, what a beautiful name you have, dear. Maria. My name is Maria. It is so nice to meet you.'

We sat quietly and drank our tea. I didn't think that she was the chatting type, so I let her be, besides which, I didn't have to wait for very long before my name was called. I didn't hear it at first. There were so many people, so many distractions. I had heard something being called, but it had been muffled, and no-one had stood up. The nurse had called again, more precisely, more insistently, as if she were becoming just a little bit impatient. Well, one can imagine, can't one? It must be such a demanding job. Anyway, I listened that little bit more carefully.

'Is there a Thompson here? Maria Thompson?'

'Oh, my goodness, that's me,' I whispered under my breath, as I stood up and walked across to the nurse. My legs felt weak. 'Oh,' I mumbled, as a dizziness swept over me and I feared that I might stumble and fall as my legs gave way.

'Are you all right there, love?' The nurse asked. She subtly slipped her arm around my waist, supported me,

19

and smiled. 'You'll be fine. I know it can be a bit overwhelming at first, but we're all very nice in here.'

She patted my hand and led me to a small room, a brown paper folder tucked under her arm. I stared at it as it sunk in. That was me. That folder under her arm was who I had become. What I had become. Oh dear. I tried to listen; to take in what was being said to me, done to me, but it was all so unreal. I was a distant thing. Not me. Not the person I knew. I was left with no idea of what had been said to me other than that my treatment would begin within the following month or so, depending on the results of my surgery. It was altogether terrifying, but of course I would keep it buried. It was just another feeling that wouldn't show itself to the world. It was for me and me alone.

As I left the hospital I took a deep breath, held my head high, and smiled at the world. This was how I would be seen. This was who I would be.

# Chapter 4

Angie
July 1987

Christ I was glad when it was her turn an she tottered off wi the nurse. She'd begun to annoy me. I hadnae told her my name so as she could keep calling me, "My dear". My fucking dear! Who even talks like that anyway? I'd started getting twitchy. Needed a fix. Needed a drink. Preferably both. Nae chance! Shite! What was I thinking coming here wi nothing in my pocket? No back up. No wee bit o comfort. No safety. Who the hell did I think I was? Me straight, doing this? It crossed my mind to walk back out. Just get on wi life. But naw. I'd come this far. Sit an wait. Deal wi it.

'Just leave it, Babes,' Deke had said the night before. 'Screw them. Stay here with me.' He'd squeezed my shoulders, shrugged like it didnae matter. Like it was no big deal. I couldnae believe it.

'For Christ's sake, Deke! It's no like I've got the fucking flu!' I'd shrieked at him.

'I know, Babes.' He'd stroked my hair. Smiled. 'But those places, those doctors. This'll keep you right,' he said, as he swung his legs off the bed an reached for the works. 'Yeah. This'll keep you right.'

21

'You are such a fucking moron! Christ knows why I stay wi you.' I threw my glass o juice against the wall, enjoying the noise, the shattering. Wee pieces o danger aw ower the place.

'Oh, Ange,' he said, aw soft an concerned, like. 'Here Babes. Come on.' He held the syringe up, flicked it, pushed the plunger until a wee drop o magic juice, the essence o life, poked out the needle. *Ready for you,* it said. *Ready for you.* 'You go first, Babes?' He reached his arm out, offering me the works. 'Come on.'

Of course, I did. An I was fine for a while.

Time was when he'd've made sure I went. He'd've kept me straight, taken me there, sat wi me, held my hand, whispered wee jokes in my ear, made up silly wee stories about the other folk in the waiting room. Made me laugh at the world. That was how we'd started, way back then, wi a joke. A wee wise-crack.

\*

I'd been standing outside the orphanage, just looking up, wondering what to do, where to go, remembering hurt an pain, but missing it. How fucked up is that? Anyway, this guy walked up an said, 'Ah, and she waits for me still.' Quite a posh voice, like he'd been to private school. His hand was on his heart. He was grinning. It was a dead handsome face that said "smile."

I smiled, then checked myself. Said, 'Eh, what?' Wee alarm bell going off. So, he'd seen me there before. Been watching maybe. How stupid must I have looked? Suddenly I was nervous. Must have looked it too.

'Hey,' he said, putting his hands up, looking fake hurt. 'No need for that. I don't bite, well, not until I've introduced myself. The name's Derek. Deke to my friends.'

He grinned at me some more, raised his eyebrows. They were the kind that point up in the middle – dead cute – Nice eyes too. Soft an kind an dark, dark brown. They say a lot about folk, eh? Eyes.

'Would you like a drink? I'm buying.'

'Eh, aye, why no?' I answered, feeling brave, thinking he's aw right, feeling okay again.

We drank an laughed an it felt really good. Just sitting in a pub, like normal folk. Having a drink, like normal folk. It didnae matter where it was going. He was making me feel good an that made him special in my eyes. A couple o weeks later an I'd moved in wi him. I had a home. A place. I was real.

*

How did we slip into being this? Something so different. Life. Just that. A no way out kind o a life.

I'd almost done it too, the next morning. Stayed there. But naw. For once in my life I was facing up to what had been thrown at me. No running. No hiding behind that heroin mask. That secret place. It was like I'd been challenged to a fight an I was gonnae take it on. I'd deal wi this. I'd beat it. I'd swithered aw ower the place. Out the door – I'm gonnae do this. At the bus stop – naw, just go home. On the bus – doing it. At the hospital – go home. An there I was. What a screw up! I tried to focus in on people. They blurred in an out. The T.V. was on. Couldnae see what was flickering away in front o me. My head. Shite!

My leg was thumping up an down, like it does when I get twitchy. My fingers were threatening the shakes. *Christ. Call my name. Please call my name. I swear I'm gonnae run if ye dinnae call me soon.* I wanted to get up an just walk about a wee bit. Stretch my legs. But I knew they'd just lead me right out o there. I couldnae do that. I couldnae.

At last! 'Angela Baynes?' I jumped up like I was really eager. Like I was looking forward to this. Like,

23

yeah – party time!

Smiles. Soft words. Reassurances. "We're all here for you." "We're your team." "We're on your side." Did I believe them? Maybe, aye. They'd asked too many questions though. My life. My habits. I was as honest as I had to be. Spilled it out. Well, most o it. They talked about alternatives. Methadone. Rehab. Said it was aw about me now. I had to put myself first. I had to get myself as healthy as I could. Aye, well, that would aw be very nice, but what was the point when I knew none o it'd work? Been there, see. Done that. I'd get back home. There'd be a packet for me. A set o works. I'd use them. An moving out? That wasnae an option. No for the likes o me. I told them I'd talk to my GP. Promised I'd try, knowing full well I wouldnae.

When it came to talking about the treatment – what they were gonnae do to me – I blocked it out. They said I should have brought somebody wi me. Someone to help me understand. Someone who could remember everything for me. A bit o support. An who would that be then? Time was. Aye, time was.

## Chapter 5

### Jaak
### Estonia Summer1949

Jaak wasn't going to go through that again; being hauled away by the Reds, like last time in 1944. He had been twenty three, his whole life before him. He and Maarja, childhood sweethearts, the couple everyone envied. Meant to be, they said. Meant to be. What did that even mean any more? He had no idea. It was peculiar how everything, absolutely everything had changed. The meaning of words, the thought behind them. Familiar trite sayings had become meaningless. He struggled to make sense of anything these days; to hold on to anything that might keep him grounded, make him feel like there was a purpose, a point in living.

They had been planning their wedding for the following summer. It was going to be the best year of their lives. The war would be over, freedom just around the corner, and their lives bound together forever. How naïve they had been. Not just them, but the whole country. As the Nazis left, the Soviets marched in. One cruel oppressor in place of another.

Maarja's mother had already finished the dress. Of course, it had been wartime and everything was scarce so she had crafted it out of her own wedding dress. Old ivory silk and lace with some tiny white cornflowers embroidered on its hem, neckline and cuffs.

'Oh, it's simply gorgeous,' Maarja had enthused, twirling around in front of the mirror, the biggest smile spread across her face, her fingers trailing over the exquisiteness of the fabric, of the detail.

Her mother returned the smile, but weakly. 'I had wanted more for you. Something better, you know?'

Maarja hugged her. 'It is the most beautiful dress I have ever seen. I couldn't imagine anything better. I adore it!'

'What did I do to deserve a daughter like you?'

'Oh, silly!'

Maarja had been desperate to show Jaak, at least to tell him about it, but she couldn't and she felt as though she might burst. When they had met that night they had talked about the house they would live in. Jaak had already built it for them and it was perfect, he'd said, made of logs, two storeys high, a porch with a balcony above it that overlooked the forest, a garden full of trees and flowers with enough land for them to grow most of what they would need. Plenty of space for the children they would have.

But no, instead she had fled across the water with her family. He had been arrested with his, herded onto a train like cattle. The clatter of its wheels on the tracks. The shouts of soldiers at the station. The helpless cries of the children and their mothers as they were separated from the men in Russia and pushed into other carts, so very scared.

That awful journey. The whispers, if anyone spoke at all. Whispers of where they were headed to; of what would become of them. Would they ever see their families again? Touch their children's faces? Breathe the forest air? Walk the land that was theirs and had been their forefathers before them? The land they loved. Estonia.

He had been separated from his family, like everyone else. Terrified eyes staring across the space between them that grew longer and longer until there was nothing. No-one he knew; just him and a swarm of heartbroken strangers – all men. Silence. A silence so painful, so awful. Too awful for tears, for any emotion to be shown.

\*

He had spent five interminable years in Siberia. A land of such harshness. Heat and mosquitoes in the summer, an unbearable cold in the winter. Five long years of not knowing anything. But he had been one of the lucky ones. He had survived, been pardoned, and allowed to return home.

Home. Could he really call it that any more? His family were gone, presumed dead. His beloved Maarja on that boat. He had heard tales of boats having been torpedoed by the Soviets, sunk, lying deep on the bottom of the Baltic Sea. Yet somehow, despite all that he had heard to the contrary, he felt sure that she was still alive. Somewhere out there, the essence of her remained in this world.

He sat on the back doorstep of their house in Pärnu. Only it had never been theirs. Just his. His and his memories, his dreams. It was a dangerous way to live. So many people were lost, missing, dead, exiled, but he had to keep her alive in his mind. That way she could come back to him. One day she had to come back to him.

He checked his watch. It was nearly midnight, but caught in the haze of midsummer's white nights; that peculiar opalescent light that only belonged here. Right here in this little town that he loved, from where he could smell the sea and the forest; the scorched wood of the houses that had been baking in the heat of the summer's sun. The sweet heaviness of lime blossom, nature, life, all around, so rich, so plentiful. But now there was, once again, that smothering smell: soldiers, weapons, oppression. A bitter fear that he could taste.

It was time to say goodbye. He stood up and took in one last deep moment of his garden; the apple trees, fruit bushes but no flowers now. It wasn't the time for flowers. Tending anything delicate, creating beauty, had become an impossibility since his return from the gulag six months ago. Had it really only been six months? Like everything else, time had changed. It was difficult to measure, to understand. Life was no longer full of beauty and hope. It was simply about getting through one more day.

Many had believed that the West would live up to its promises; that the White Ship would come and set them free. But it didn't. The West turned its back on them and allowed them to be swallowed up by the Soviets as if they didn't matter. They didn't exist. No. If they were to be free again they had to do it by themselves.

Jaak ran his fingers along the wooden logs that made up the walls, across the rough stone that formed the foundations. He had to keep these exact feelings, these memories, strong and fresh and permanent. They would

28

not fade. He wouldn't allow them to. Memories of old Estonia would be locked away in his memory bank, stored, kept safe, for when they had won back their freedom. Now he would fight.

Johann came around the corner, exactly on the hour as arranged, and patted his shoulder. 'Are you ready, Brother?' His voice was hushed, serious, bearing little resemblance to the jovial boyhood friend, the constant companion of his youth. Now he was a man ready to fight and kill for his homeland; a knapsack over his shoulder, a rifle across his chest.

'As I'll ever be, Brother. As I'll ever be.' Jaak managed the semblance of a smile. The confirmation that they were now Forest Brothers and that this was what they had to do. It was right. They crept along the silent road and into the woods, into the forests, into places that they knew so intimately. Each tree: oak, ash, elm, birch, maple and spruce. Each trail; some man-made by hunters, children, foragers, lovers. Others carved by nature: moose and fox and deer, lynx and wolf and bear. They followed as the paths became less trodden, less obvious, until they had to stoop to find their way through the tangle of branches, leaves, and shrubbery. Wild blueberries and honeysuckle carpeted the ground at their feet.

He had lain there with Maarja – God, that seemed like a lifetime ago – with nothing but the sounds of the forest and the whispers of their passion to break up the night. They had had such dreams, such plans. Despite the war. Despite the darkness that had swept over their country, they would survive, have many children, grow old together. Estonia would be free and the world would be put to rights. Everything as it should be. Only now, nothing was.

29

# Chapter 6

## Maria
## July 1987

I really didn't know what to do when I got home from that first visit to oncology. It was as if I were in some sort of limbo. Everything felt so strange and unreal. I was surrounded by my own possessions in my own little house, all mine, chosen by me, but I felt so detached from it all. It was both peculiar and unnerving.

I hadn't wanted to stay in the Highlands. It wouldn't have been wise, and besides which, it had never been my home, Glenbirrie. Not really. I had lived there for over forty years but never truly belonged. And, well, circumstance saw to it that I had to make my getaway rather abruptly. So, yes, I had decided on a move to somewhere completely new. Whitewashing my life, one might say; the proverbial blank canvas.

This little place felt like it was mine the moment I saw it advertised for sale, and Aberlady suited me just perfectly; a delightful little coastal village in East Lothian with a shop, a post office, and a public house. Not that I would ever use the latter, but it seemed to give the village more of a gentle homely feel, a sense of completeness. I had the coast – mile upon mile of glorious sandy beaches, for the most part very quiet –

which was perfect. Long walks in places that I didn't know, but that felt somehow right. I was convinced that I had once lived by the sea. It was a part of me. The connection was strong and personal. Perhaps living here would be the start; would allow whatever lay hidden to resurface? Oh, that would be so wonderful!

My early life had become a forbidden subject as soon as I had married Andrew. Perhaps he was frightened of things unknown, of history. I didn't know. Perhaps it was all for my own good. What if I had been a German, an enemy? What if I had something dreadful lurking about in my history? It wasn't to be spoken of and that was that. The war wasn't long over and feelings still ran strong. I was tutored incessantly, given elocution lessons and taught to behave in a manner befitting a lady. I was saved and I was lost.

Andrew and I never spoke much about anything of any consequence. I knew not to ask of his first wife. She was left behind like my forgotten childhood. As for the life I had led before I met him – the life I knew about – I was only too happy to leave that well alone.

## 1946

She soon began to pick out words, to stretch them into something that had meaning. Days became weeks and this language filled her head. Her thoughts became English thoughts, but she kept her tongue still, as it suited her to be dumb, to listen and pretend that she understood nothing.

They had called her Dora. Dora Johnson. She knew that wasn't her real name and she didn't like it. One of the other girls was called Maria. That was beautiful, Maria. It sang to her, so she secretly took it. She listened to talk about people, places, things that had happened to

31

others, and used what she could, what she wanted. She stole magazines from the reception and pored through them in the quiet hours of early morning, in the secrecy of her room, making up her. Pictures began to form in her mind of who she had been, of where she had been. She practised, telling her story to herself, answering people's imaginary questions in her head, becoming Maria.

*My name is Maria. Yes, I am British. I know, I don't have the English accent, but I am living in Sweden in the war. My mother is Swedish, you see. And my parents say I would be safe over there. Yes. Because Sweden is neutral. Oh, no. My mother and father both had the most important jobs and they had to stay in Britain. They died. Both of them. The blitz. My grandmother lived in a very big house in Gothenburg. I had finery of all kinds. Beautiful clothes and everything I wanted. Even my own horse! Yes, I know. I was very lucky. Luckier than many other children of the war. But my grandmother had a sickness and they sent me back to Britain. Yes. It was very hard for me. I was so alone and scared. Britain was a very strange place to me. Not like a home at all!*

Sentences were added, details were filled, as the story became longer and longer. The conversations she had grew in complexity alongside her vocabulary. It was a very peculiar thing, to build one's own history like that, but it felt good to be somebody. It kept her sane, gave her a reason, a purpose; something to cling on to.

Life at Sunnington House was a succession of men and chores: uncomfortable, cold, and humiliating. That was how they kept order on top of the fear; discomfort and humiliation. She was there for so very many days. She had tried marking each day off on a piece of paper but had lost count; each mark a small line on the back of a picture of a wooden house that she was drawing. It was something she thought she remembered; something she thought she knew. She felt it important to have some record, a kind of structure, some piece of knowing, the foundations of her.

She had taken to stealing, not a lot, not enough to be noticed, and only from the men. A shilling from a pocket here, a sixpence there, it mounted up soon enough. She hid everything in a sock behind a loose skirting board that she had made looser. When the time was right she would find a way out of there. Of that she was sure. This couldn't be it. She wouldn't allow her life to be...this!

She couldn't truly remember not feeling like a stranger. It became easier as she got to grips with the language, as she began to understand the way of things. Who she was? How she came to be there? No, that hadn't shown itself to her. She had fought for it; wrestled with that place where her memories should lie, patiently waiting to be called upon, to spring into life, but nothing came. Nothing showed itself to her. She was floating in a pool of unfamiliarity, like a piece of wood adrift on a strange sea. The ever-present threat of it all becoming too much, until finally water-logged, she would sink, lost, forgotten. She had no choice other than to accept her fate, for now, and she did what she had to do, however distasteful it might have been. There was nothing else.

## 1987

But now? Now I was becoming me, whoever that might be. I had no-one to seek permission of for anything any more. Neither did I have anyone to seek comfort from. Not that comfort had been given by Andrew, but the thought, the possibility was there. Anyway, I found myself wondering what it might have been like if Andrew had been with me. Would it have made things any easier? I decided not and put the thought to bed. I would go for a walk along the waterfront, avoiding the peculiar potholes that peppered the grass down there. Their hidden depths had caught me unaware when I had first arrived and I had misjudged my step, slipped and stumbled into one of them. An unceremonious shriek echoed along the beach as my leg lost itself, thigh deep in dark, putrid water. The water stank and so did I! I had always enjoyed walking off the beaten track, but on this stretch of land I vowed that I would now stick to the path, such as it was. Sometimes it was little more than an indentation in the grass; sometimes nothing at all, if the tide had been high and the weather inclement.

There were two coastal walks that I loved. To the left, towards Edinburgh, if the tide was out, there was an immense expanse of sand. A not inconsiderable bob of seals often stretched itself along the water's edge. I would count them as best I could as I walked. Funny cumbersome blobs of fat on land, but beautiful elegant swimmers staring with their puppy-dog eyes in the water. I felt sure they were watching me! There were at least fifty at any one time, probably more, but my mind had a tendency to wander off and I would lose count.

Seabirds that I couldn't identify swirled, and dived, and shrieked all around. I decided that I should get a book, learn about the seals, the birds, perhaps invest in some binoculars, become a birdwatcher. It seemed to be a popular past-time down here. Fitting in, you see, mimicking, that was best. That was what I knew. That had been my life.

Sometimes the birds drifted about on the sea, so plentiful that there was a mass of white, like an enormous cloud covering the water, swelling and falling with the waves. When they took off, en masse, a cacophony of formidable sound, shrieks and screeches and cries swirled around, filled the air. Spectacular. Really most spectacular.

Rocky cliffs and peculiar walls of huge sandstone led up to Killspindie golf course, battered by the waves at high tide, but resolutely standing firm. I avoided the golf course with its manicured land and small clusters of men making their way around the picturesque eighteen holes. My purpose wasn't to be disturbed by people. To walk in solitude along the rocky beach was my ideal. If the weather were being kind to me I would sit on one of the small rocky outcrops whose tops were covered with soft springy grass, delightful sea pinks, orange lichen, clover and daisies. I could sit there for hour upon hour undisturbed by any other humans. It was glorious.

The other walk was to the right, towards Gullane, the direction I had chosen that day. At the far end of the village a little wooden bridge led into the bird sanctuary. My word, if you could have heard the noise! There were so many birds, all competing, it seemed; trying to outcry each other. It was simply splendid.

Trees and bushes grew at the most peculiar of angles due to the severity of the relentless East Coast wind. They reminded me of little old men with stooped backs. Shrubs and spiky buckthorn huddled together alongside a narrow track, the weaving together of branches overhead created a tunnel-like effect. I imagined that the track had been made by the feet of bird watchers and the paws of animals: foxes, deer, rabbits, even weasels. I had come within feet of all of them. My breath held. My step halted. Such a thrill!

Then there were the dunes. Tall grasses clinging into fragile ground. There was one steep dune with a path of sand in between the spiky grasses. I climbed up and stood at the top, my hands on my hips, a deep sigh as my eyes took in this most beautiful of places. The beach was magnificent, vast expanses of white sand, and not a soul – not a solitary soul in sight. A lone gull shrieked above me as it circled on the cusp of a pocket of air and whirled around, flying with the wind, turning against it, then with it again. It looked to me as if it were playing a wonderful game. Yes, I was momentarily envious of its sheer abandonment.

I breathed in the air as if I were breathing in this place itself. Filling my body with its purity; with the raw elements of life. I sat amongst the sand dunes, the grasses all around me swishing and swaying, whispering their stories of the sea, of wildness, and of timelessness. This was so very beautiful. As long as I fed on this I would survive. I had to survive. My story wasn't done. Not yet. And I would not be beaten.

A chill set in as the sun slid behind the sea and I knew I had to dash if I were to find my way back before it became pitch black. I felt the build of a slight panic, but I was used to places with no light pollution, to places of total darkness, and pushed it away. I didn't twitch at unidentified noises, nor did I look behind me. Focus on one's path; the way ahead. That was always best.

I reached home; the squeak of the hinge on the wooden gate, the gentle curve of the crazy-paved path that led through the garden heavy with flowers and shrubs all competing for supremacy with scent and blossom and foliage, the click of the lock on my front door. When I closed the door behind me that young woman – What was her name again? Angie. Yes, that was it – Angie sprung into my mind. I wondered what she was doing. How she was feeling. How very peculiar. I had barely spoken to her.

# Chapter 7

## Angie
## July 1987

Weird. I hadnae really thought about aw o that mortality shite. Well, ye dinnae, do ye? Sure, folk died. Folk I knew. Too many o them. But what really happened. Me. Me an death. Naw. Hadnae really taken it in. Processed it. But now I was an I didnae like it. Shrivelled, shrunken, eaten up by cancer. Shite! At least the drugs were my choice. O my doing, ye might say. But this was something else entirely. I knew what would happen. It would sit there whizzing around an around in my brain, unless I got myself out o it. Dulled. Sedated. Brain switched off.

I checked my pockets for some dosh. Pound coins are brilliant for that. Ye think ye're skint, but ye rustle around in pockets an linings an there ye go; enough for a wee swally! A couple in the pub, or a few more back at the flat? I fancied the pub. Being around different folk. Buzz, buzz, chatter, chatter. Time passes. Who knew? Maybe some kind soul would buy me one? Or I'd go home. A fix an a swally? Naw. No right now. No the day. The pub it was.

It was tea-time. Getting home frae work time. Aw these folk. Clean sparkly folk heading home. I got off the bus at the top o The Walk, no sure where I was headed, which local. There's a few o them an I have to be careful, aye; remember which ones I'm barred frae. Sometimes I stotter in, see, out o my face, needing something. Anything. Sometimes I get mouthy. Sweary. Folk dinnae like it. "Out, ye wee bampot!" was my goodnight a few times more than I'm proud o.

Just then I was sober. The line I'd taken earlier on was still keeping me level, just. I was as near to okay as possible, considering. I headed on down The Walk. Funny place that. Starts off quite posh: big flats, bay windows, nice shops. The further down ye get though, the grottier it aw becomes: restaurants, trendy bars an deli's become second-handies, bookies, cheap pubs an pawn shops. The pawn shops. Aye, they know me well an aw. Chored stuff needing shifted pronto. A rip off, but hey, I couldnae really complain now, could I? Blind eyes turned, swift transactions done, goods stuffed under the counter, cash stuffed into my hand, an we're aw happy. Except the poor sod I'd chored off o, but hey, needs must and they're more than likely insured. No biggie.

Anyway, I'm wandering off topic here. Normal state o affairs. I caught Big Davy heading my way out the corner o my eye. No wanting to be pestered into turning a trick. No the kind o company I was looking for just then – Christ, was I ever? No. Course no. Who would be, eh? Who would be? – I did a casual swerve into Iona Street. Zip around into Buchanan Street. Dodgy as fuck. Junkies, thieves, an desperation. Ignore it. Round again into Dalmeny Street an back out on Leith Walk. Dinnae look back, just saunter on like it's aw good. Can slip away frae anybody me!

Jeannie's'd do. Pretty sure I was okay in there. She's cool. The bar's a shite-hole. Blood stains on the floor, proudly left as a reminder that *no shit shall be taken here.* The place was nearly devoid o life. The juke box was belting out Donna Summer, "I Feel Love" – oh do ye, aye? – The same auld geezers sitting on the same auld seats, heads down, staring into their pints, ignoring the poor woman up on the tiny stage, twisting pasty legs around a pole in her bra an pants, gyrating. Doing her best, but failing miserably. Felt for her. At least what I did, I did in private, no up there to have the piss ribbed right out o ye by some waste o space tossers, some o whom were noising it up in the corner, well-wellied, chanting Hibs' songs. One o them clocked me; whistled me ower like I was a fucking dog.

'Come away an join yon lassie on the stage hen. A wee twosome eh?'

He licked his licks. Disgusting! His mates were egging him on. Shouting, leering, rubbing their crotches.

'Aye, well, ye'll find fuck aw down there!' I hissed at them. 'Low-lifes!'

'Right, you lot. Any more o that an you're right out o here, got that?' Jeannie called across at them. Shut them right up.

'No harm meant, lass,' the shouty one called across at me.

'Aye, right,' I said, keeping my back to him.

'What'll it be then, Ange?'

Great, I was getting served. I slipped onto the bar-stool, red plastic wi dirty nicotine-stained foam sticking out o the slash marks. Old fashioned dark wooden bar, scored to shit. Names an stains. Beer mats on their umpteenth use. Never wise to risk anything on tap. Ye never know what ye might pick up. A wee voddie an orange'd do me nicely.

I sat chatting about nothing to Jeannie. Big woman. Blond hair aw dry frae too much peroxide. Blue eye

shadow. Bright red lipstick stuck on her teeth. Always! –
How does she even manage that? I so want to wipe it off
every time I see it. Cannae help myself – Skintight pink
top, buttons undone obscenely low, massive cleavage
proudly displayed, gold crucifix getting suffocated. Wee
black Lycra mini-skirt, bare legs bruised an broken
veined. But she's a good woman. Lived through so
much shite you wouldnae believe. Still giving it large.
Good to hae on yer team. Happy for now she was on
mine.

A couple o drinks later an my cash had dried up. No
point in asking for credit. She doesnae do that. No
would-be punters to take up the vennel for a quick hand-
job. No wanting to do that anyway. A strange feeling
settled on me. I didnae know what. Just something
different. I wondered, just for a second, about that auld
woman. How was she doing? Where the hell that had
come frae, I'd no clue. No clue at aw.

Chapter 8

Jaak
Estonia September 1949

Summer had left and now autumn washed the forests in golds and reds, oranges and yellows. Trees thinned as their leaves blanketed the ground. Animals prepared for hibernation, gathering, hoarding, burying, digging. Soon the land would be whitewashed. Silenced. The Forest Brothers moved from bunker to bunker, keeping the risk of being found to a minimum. Hunting and foraging became more and more difficult as plants died back, berries withered, wildlife hid.

Deportations continued. Land and property were taken. Stalin's purges of the "bourgeois nationalists" left villages decimated as anyone with land, with money, with higher than average intelligence, was taken away and sent to prison or worse, to the labour camps of Siberia. Even teachers were considered enemies of the people. The Brothers fought on.

'Do you ever wonder about home?' Imre – the scout and youngest of their brigade – whispered to Jaak, as they were returning from a farm with supplies. 'You know, your old house? Your family?'

41

Jaak replied with a shake of his head.

'Never?'

Again, a shake of his head and a finger to his mouth. Never. It doesn't do. Thinking like that doesn't help anyone, least of all you, he wanted to say. He wanted to believe. Of course he thought about it. About Maarja. About the future they had planned. About that last night together in Pärnu.

## 1944

There would be no argument, no discussion, Maarja was to leave. Her parents had insisted, and although it killed him inside, Jaak had agreed. The time had come and the life they shared was over. They were to join the grey faces of the grey lines of the disenfranchised. So many people who had lost everything and were running into the unknown. Families that would sleep with a bag already packed, with their clothes on; even with their shoes on. When the time came they had to be ready. They would be given no time to pack. Children whose nightmares had been about imaginary monsters now had their nights filled with terror about the Reds. The slam of a car door. The thud of boots vibrating through the land. The rumble of trains filled with men, women and children who were being taken away from everything, from everyone they knew. No. Maarja and her family had to leave now, while they still could.

The house Jaak had built for them was to have been kept hidden from her until their wedding day. He had pictured her delight upon first seeing it, imagined her face as she took in each room, as she understood the time it had taken; the love that it had been built with. But now they knew that nothing could be planned for.

42

Nothing expected could be counted on any more. Every day, every hour was a danger.

Jaak and Maarja had decided that they had to spend those last few hours together in what should have been their home. He had tied a scarf around her head as a blindfold and guided her up the little track he had created that led to their house. They stepped lightly, almost tip-toeing, as if this were something illicit, her arm though his, tucked tightly in against his chest so that she could feel his excited breathing; their ears tuned in to the gentle sounds of the night. In the distance a different sound carried on the breeze. Soft thuds that lit up the distant sky. War. Strangely, deceptively beguiling. For tonight they wouldn't hear it.

He guided her hand so that she could unlatch the gate. Her fingers fumbled their way around the wood and flicked the catch open.

'Now Jaak, now! I need to see!' she squealed, like a child.

He laughed and untied her blindfold. Candles lit up the path through the garden. More candles stood in each of the windows. It was quite simply the most beautiful thing that she had ever seen. She stared, dumbfounded, her hands drawn to her face.

'Oh Jaak. It is...' Tears forced her to silence.

He took her hand and led her into the porch. They walked from room to room, blessing each one with words of love. Despite them both wanting to do more, they wouldn't. That was for after they were married. To do anything now would be wrong and it would suggest that this was it. The end. It couldn't be. Neither of them would allow it to be.

# 1949

Stealth was what kept the Brothers alive. Imre knew that, but this trip always left him too excited. The support of loyal locals who did what they could to help was invaluable and they had several who helped them, whether it be leaving food hidden in the forests or inviting them in to sit and eat. Food and spare clothing were left in prearranged drop-off points: a hollow tree trunk, the hole left by dislodged roots, an animal's burrow. The Brothers had enough support to keep fighting.

Some sympathisers invited them in to their homes to share their meals when they could. The Brothers would eat from one plate, use one set of cutlery, drink from one mug, so that there was no trace left behind, no casual mistakes that could could cost a life. Of course it would mean death if the locals were found out, but they wanted to play their part; to help in the fight, to cling on to the hope that their little country would survive. Today was one of those days. One of those personal connections that meant so much.

It was a house of only women, the men having been lost in the war; the father and his son. Imre could barely contain himself. He had fallen in love with Evi, the eldest daughter. It was the worst thing a soldier could do, but he had no control over it. No choice. His feelings had taken over, swarmed through his body, left him helpless, and during this visit she had smiled such a smile. Her whole face had lit up upon seeing him. She had stroked his hand as she passed the milk-can over. A soft and secret caress. At last he knew for certain that his feelings were reciprocated. When all of this was over; when they had sent their enemy packing with its tail between its legs, with fear in its belly, he would ask for her hand. She would become his.

Jaak and Imre trudged back through the mud. Heavy rainfall had churned up the ground, left it sodden, the going heavy, their footsteps cumbersome. That familiar squelch of mud sucked at their boots, creeping through the holes in the leather, drenching their feet.

The crack of splintering wood broke through the rhythm of their footsteps, through the gentle sounds of the forest. A scream. The scream of a woman.

'No! No, please!'

A gunshot split the air. The sobbing of the younger children. The screeching of crows.

'Christ, that was our fault! Someone must have seen us, reported them. Christ!' Imre whispered, his eyes wide with terror. 'We have to help.' He turned and bolted back towards the farmhouse. *Please let that just be a warning shot. Please!*

Jaak froze, his mind in turmoil. What should he do? What could he do? The Reds didn't carry out patrols of the countryside on their own. The Brothers were sure to be outnumbered. To go back would be suicide, but could he live with himself if he did nothing; if he left Imre to die alongside the others?

He couldn't call out. He couldn't change this. Any of it. Shit! They would torture Imre; bleed information from him before killing him. He didn't think he had a choice. He ran after him, trying to reach him with his thoughts. *Wait! For Christ's sake wait! You can't do a thing on your own!*

Whether Imre had heard Jaak's thoughts or not he didn't know. Of course such things were possible. People were capable of so much more than they were aware of;

45

so much more than mere existence, especially in times such as these. Times of desperation; of life and death. Imre glanced back over his shoulder and seeing Jaak closing in on him slowed, so that he could catch him up. They were well versed in talking without words. Eyes and hands were a much safer means of communication. Jaak grasped Imre's arm and squeezed tightly; *stay in control of yourself. Stay in control!*

They agreed to split up; one on each side of the little farmhouse. The stone barn that was attached to the wooden living area was the larger of the two spaces. The snuffle of cows and pigs rummaging through their straw and the scratching and clucking of hens gave out a deceptively peaceful, gentle sound. A thatched roof covered both. A trail of trodden earth led to the wooden hut that housed the toilet pit, another to the stone well, where a bucket swung idly from its rope in the ever strengthening wind. There was an orchard of trees that still bore some fruit: apple, plum, and pear.

An army vehicle sat parked on the dirt-track at the front of the house, its engine ticking over. Only one. That was encouraging. The driver leaned against it smoking. Imre crept, crouched, to the back of the Gaz 67 and whipped his belt around the soldier's neck. He squeezed the life out of him, the soldier clawing desperately at the leather, Imre watching as his face turned purple, his eyes bulged, and he was nothing any more.

Jaak was at the side of the barn, watching, waiting. When he saw the driver's body slump to the ground he edged around to the front porch, his gun ready, his senses on high alert.

'Just get rid of them. Make a statement. If you help these vermin, you die,' was shouted from within the

46

house.

'But she's too pretty not to have some fun with first.'

Jaak turned back and saw Imre charging towards the house. Training didn't matter now. All that he had been taught was beyond him. Beyond this situation. He was a thing wild. No longer sane. Barely human.

Jaak had no choice. Of course he would follow, do what he could, even though he was probably signing his own death warrant.

Evi's mother lay on the floor, a pool of blood creeping around her body. Evi held the other two children close to her, their faces pressed tightly in to her body. She stood silently, just staring, open-mouthed, at the soldier who was pointing a gun at her head.

Imre was screaming. No stealth now. Fear had become the best tactic. They were being attacked by a maniac. There were three Reds. They hadn't been expecting this. Imre charged at the one pointing the gun, pummelling him to the ground. The gun fell from the soldier's hand and slid across the floor. Imre was astride him. He pounded the butt of his rifle across the soldier's startled face. The gruesome crack of splintering cheek-bone.

Jaak took aim from the doorway and fired two shots in quick succession. He didn't like how much he enjoyed it, the taking of a life, but he did. It would have been better if it had left him cold. But no. He had enjoyed it. It almost made him smile.

# Chapter 9

Maria
July 1987

I decided that I had to pass my driving test. It was all well and good relying on public transport, but I wanted the freedom that having my own car would bring. I took one of those crash courses. Guaranteed to pass your test within seven days, was the proud boast. The instructor was obviously somewhat taken aback by my age, but I learned well enough and, much to my delight – and to his I might add – I did indeed pass within the promised week.

A few days later I noticed a card in the post-office window. I liked this little shop. In fact, I had a particular fondness for this little road. It was quaint, charming, with whitewashed buildings, tiny cottages and grander houses standing side by side. An ancient rough stone wall ran along one side of the road. More cottages of the same material nestled amongst their tidy gardens on the other side, centuries old, yet all in such perfect order. All showing that they were loved and cared for. It gave one a feeling of permanence, of perseverance, of survival.

The people in the Post Office had learned my name very quickly. They greeted me with a pleasant smile, chatted about the weather and suchlike. They even stocked special items if requested. For me it was Orkney oatcakes. I was rather partial to them, you see. Anyway the card read, "Car for Sale." I had decided that I should investigate.

'Good morning Mrs Thompson. And how are you today?'

'I am very well, thank you dear, and you?'

'Aye, fine! And what will you be after then?'

'Actually, I was wondering about the card in the window? The car for sale?'

'Oh, aye. That's young Andy from up yonder.' She nodded in the direction of the small council scheme on the streets behind. 'You can trust him, right enough. A fine wee mechanic, so he is. Shall I give him a call for you?'

'Oh, if you wouldn't mind, that would be splendid!' I enthused.

And that was that. Within the hour I had bought my first car. It was a very nice little Peugeot 205. A sporty looking little thing. Red and racy! It made me feel rather special. Young and jaunty!

'Aye. Just ye gie me a call,' Andy had said, as cash and keys exchanged hands and we shook on the deal. 'Any problems an I'll sort them right out for ye! No that there'll be any like, but, ye know. Aye?'

My little car! I was very pleased with myself. For the last forty years I had done little other than keep house, and even then I had had a housekeeper to do most of it on my behalf. I had never made any decisions about anything of any import. Indeed, I had seldom left the house and grounds, and if I had, it had always been in the company of Andrew. He didn't like the idea of me meeting people on my own. Quite what he thought I might do I really didn't know. Or perhaps he was more concerned with what I might say? Thankfully the grounds were expansive; acre upon acre of forest and hill. We also had a river and a loch. So much for one family, and we weren't even that. Much to Andrew's disappointment I was never able to provide him with the heir he so wanted. There was a time when I feared for my place. Might he get rid of me somehow, find himself a fertile wife? He never did and for that I was grateful.

Of course there was the gamekeeper and his wife and children, but I was instructed to steer clear of them. It wouldn't do to get into casual conversation, to become involved in any way other than as an employer. Sometimes I would find myself sitting high on the cliff above the loch, watching the children play their great games of adventure, as they scrambled about the water's edge, disappeared into the trees, the boat house. How I would love to have been allowed to join them, but I wasn't and I didn't dare to. I would keep my distance as instructed.

\*

So, there I was. In the space of a few months I had bought myself a rather lovely little cottage just outside Aberlady village, and now my own car. These were monumental, life-changing purchases. It felt, despite my age and illness, that life was just beginning. Once more I was learning about who I was, what I could become, but this time of my own choosing. No-one was directing me, instructing me, moulding me, controlling me. It was just me. After the initial trepidation of being entirely on my own I quickly grew accustomed to it, learned to appreciate it, and was now relishing it.

That very day I decided to grab the car by the wheel, as it were, be adventurous and drive along to Gullane. It was only a couple of miles away, but I had barely hitherto ventured out of the village (I didn't count going to oncology as something I did, choosing to distance myself from that whenever possible. It wouldn't sully my life. I wouldn't allow it to!) I had been used to staying close to home, familiar places, so anything else, such as this, was really quite an adventure. I had bought myself a map of the local area from the Post Office. They had very kindly marked out places of interest for me and explained the best ways of getting there.

The coastal road sliced its way directly through Muirfield golf course. It was quite famous apparently and held large international events, Opens and such like. One had to be mindful of golfers walking across the road with their clubs and accoutrements. There was such a severe bend in the road as one approached the course one had to slow done to almost a crawl anyway! I had just rounded the bend when I was struck by peculiar little flashes of light that splintered across the road in front of me. I was momentarily confused. Was I seeing things? Had something frightful happened to my brain – some other ghastly side-effect of this awful illness? I laughed at myself when I realised it was simply the sun glinting off the clubs of the golfers as they swung them in a powerful arc above their heads. The peculiar ping of club against ball had been similarly confusing. Such a lot of noise emanating from a small ball.

I kept my eyes peeled for the correct turning as I reached Gullane village. Following the instructions I had been given I drove slowly past the graveyard on my left, small shops on the right, and turned up the twisty little Sandy Lane; old stone walls, a pleasant assortment of traditional buildings from cottages to grand sprawling houses, although one could see little beyond the high walls. A quick peek through an open gate was all that could be managed. After carrying on into the car park I parked on the grass alongside the other cars, of which there were quite a few. I was somewhat disheartened as I had been hoping to find more peace and quiet. A slice of solitude with only the gulls to keep me company.

I followed the trail down to the beach. Again it cut through sand dunes and buckthorn. It was remarkably beautiful. A curve in the land created a large sweeping bay of sand. Waves rolled in and crashed themselves, spent, on the shore. Children squealed and jumped over them, running in and out as if in some splendid game of dare, or some such thing. I decided to turn away from the main beach and headed towards the rocks and cliffs at the far side.

The further I went, the quieter it became, until there was no-one there but me, at least no-one I could see. I clambered over rocks when they blocked my path, being very cautious of the seaweed that popped under my feet. It left an unexpectedly perilous slickness hidden beneath its slimy tentacles and fronds. I had almost upended myself when I first stepped on it, slipping ungraciously, my feet being unceremoniously swept away from me, arms and legs akimbo! I had squealed like a frightened child, grateful that no-one had witnessed my fall from grace. At least, I hoped no-one had! Well, I hadn't seen anyone so that was all that mattered. If one doesn't know that someone has witnessed one make a fool of oneself, then one hasn't, has one?

With each promontory, each outcrop of rocks that I successfully manoeuvred my way around, or over, I was rewarded with some new spectacle. Something secret and special, opening up just for me. It was as if nature were whispering to me once more, "You see? You see what I have to offer you?" as she had when I had begun to explore Glenbirrie. Hour upon hour had been spent drifting through magnificent forest, scrambling down crevices in the craggy rock face carved out by the tumultuous waters of the river. Indeed my favourite place had been a deep pool caught in the steep rocks where I would swim and lay and wile away the time in the solitude of nature. A deer would sometimes appear – I assumed it was the same one as it grew in confidence with each meeting until it was almost at touching distance. Almost. Our eyes had met and it felt as though she were trying to read me. Could she trust me? It seemed that she thought she could as the following year she came with a fawn in tow. It was such a splendidly, enchanting experience and I felt so very privileged!

*

I had walked along an assortment of smaller coves – some pebble, some shell, some sand. Me and the birds again. Just me and the birds. I had gone quite some distance, tracing the edge of the water, lost in a gentle swathe of an almost dreamlike state. Nature can do that to me. Pick me up and carry me off to a far off place. I came upon a steep cliff and paused, wondering if I should turn back. No, I had come this far and my walk felt somehow incomplete. I would carry on.

Twisting its way up the cliff was a track, barely identifiable as such, but a track nonetheless. To one side there was a steep drop down to the rocks quite some distance below. On the other side stood a seemingly insurmountable precipice. My way looked somewhat pernicious, but I persevered, clasping onto the tufts of grass for support, praying that they wouldn't let me down with weak roots or deceptive strength, and my word, was I glad that I had! My heart stopped. My breath faltered. I was dumbfounded. Stretched out in front of me was a pristine deserted beach, but I knew it! This place felt so much a part of me. It swelled me, filled me with its presence. I was drawn, pulled under the water, bathed with it in the gentlest of ways.

Helpless but still. At peace. Such an incredibly profound peace. I belonged here. But I couldn't. I couldn't even know the place. How could it have had such an absolute impact upon me?

# Chapter 10

Angie
September 1987

The last few weeks had passed by in a strange blur. No just the usual being-wasted blur. I'd tried to be good, just doing what I needed to keep me sane, functioning o a sort at least. Naw. This was a blur made out o being scared. Aye. Scared o the shit that was about to be shoved into me. How's that for a wee touch o irony, eh? Me scared o something being pumped into my veins through a needle!

Puking up wasnae a new thing. Feeling shite aw the time wasnae a new thing. Lucky me! Better prepared than my other chemo chums, aye. So what was it, this fear? I guessed it was the whole "It might no work" thing. Or maybe it was that once the chemo had started I knew I had to keep away frae sick folk, frae germs, or that could kill me too. Fuck's sake. Some chance o that round at my bit. Folk in an out aw day an night. Buying a bit. Scrounging a bit. "Let's go round Ange an Deke's an get wasted." It pissed me off something rotten, but it paid the way. Kept us in drugs. Wee bit dealing, wee bit hustling, wee bit choring, that was me. That had become us.

It was weird how it crept up on us, aw sleekit, like.

No tim'rous wee beastie. Naw. No poetry in our lives. This was more like a dirty disease. Aye, we both smoked dope. That was normal. Everyone did. We sold a bit, just to our friends, as a favour, like. Then to their friends. Then Deke's dad died. He had money, right enough, but it was the new wife's now. The bitch hadnae even told him his dad was sick. They could have at least said their goodbyes. Finished it aw wi soft words an forgiveness. But naw. The bitch kept it a secret an Deke only found out when he read about it in the papers. He was broken. I mean, they'd had this massive falling out – something about studying, university, the family line, aw that shit – hadnae spoke for God knows how long, but yer dad's yer dad, aye?

One o his mates came round wi a wee packet o smack. "This'll sort you out, mate," he'd said, as he tipped it onto a mirror and cut it into three lines. He rolled a fiver up, snorted a line and handed the note to Deke, then me. Oh, aye, it sorted the both o us right out.

*

I got to the hospital an tried to hold my head high as I walked through the doors o the Cancer Centre. No second thoughts this time. No wee niggles o will I, won't I? I was doing this, an I was beating the bastard. I checked in. Leaflets everywhere. Cancer this, cancer that. Nice smiles frae the nurses. Barely a glance frae the other patients. Aw stuck in their own private hell, I guessed. Most o them wi other folk too. Families an friends, an the likes. You could see them chatting away, trying to make it aw okay. Trying to mask the reason they were aw there. A wee bit o chitter an chatter, aye. That'll do it, aye.

So, I was there on my own. I could deal wi that. No biggie. I took a seat by the window. Fuck aw to see apart frae concrete, but that wasnae the point. It was something else. Somewhere else. Won't be long they'd said. Great. Couldnae wait!

I heard a posh voice an glanced ower at reception. It was that auld woman again. What were the chances, eh? She saw me an smiled, mouthing a wee "hello". A wiggle o her fingers in an almost wave. What was her name again? I tried really hard to dredge it up. It wasnae coming. If she sat down next to me I'd just hae to wing it. As if it mattered, Christ! Aw that mattered in that place was making it out again.

She tottered across the waiting room towards me. I say totter because that's what auld folk do, eh? But she didnae really. She had quite a stride on her for an auld biddy like that. She was looking better than she had last time I'd seen her. How was that even possible? Her white hair was up in a tight bun, make-up on – aw nice an careful, no slapped on like some auld folk do – a posh suit, matching shoes an bag. She could've been on the cover o one o they magazines for rich folk. House and Country or, Manor Houses and Gardens, Christ I didnae know the names. One o they sort o things that other folk read.

'Hello my dear. May I sit?' she asked, pointing at the chair beside me.

'Aye. Nae bother.'

'Angie, isn't it?' But she didnae wait for an answer. 'Yes. Angie,' she said, aw smiles an confidence. 'Such a beautiful name.'

I just smiled back an nodded.

'How have you been keeping? I mean, since the last time I saw you. In general, of course. Not the whole,' she looked up an made this weird circle wi her head. 'Well, you know. Gosh it is so difficult, isn't it? What does one say?'

'I'm aw right. Ye know. Considering.'

We both started to laugh. No a wee giggle. A right big laugh. Folk were looking, but we were just laughing, no really knowing why.

She slapped my leg. 'Oh, my dear, I am so glad that you're here. I rather like you.'

'Aye. Likewise,' I answered, an strangely enough, I meant it. Okay, I'd still steal off o her if I got the chance, but I'd feel a bit shit about it.

# Chapter 11

Maria
September 1987

I had been trying to take deep calming breaths on my way there. That whole Cancer Centre thing was just something I had to become acquainted with, but no matter how hard I tried, the panic still fluttered in my chest, like a little sparrow trapped in a chimney breast. It threatened to snatch away my ability to talk, to walk, to be...well, me. I had felt so nervous walking in, but I did my best to hide it behind a head held high, my shoulders straight, a smile fixed.

The whole place was awash with strangers; the crispness of nurses, the swathe of unfamiliar noise, dulled whispers from the other patients and their companions. There were couples and small groups of people; only a few on their own, like me. It did make me feel, well, alone! A little bit downhearted. It would have been nice, comforting even, to have had someone beside me. Just for that reassurance if nothing else. *You don't have to do this on your own. We're here for you. We love you.* And then I saw her sitting staring out of the window. Young Angie. A familiar face at least. I had something else to focus on.

I took my seat beside her, grinning, as if we were the

best of friends, at once feeling foolish and intrusive. What if she preferred to be left alone? What if the last thing she wanted was to have me sat beside her? But it was just the relief, you see. Thankfully she smiled back at me. Well, if you could call it that. The edges of her mouth curled up at least.

I asked her how she was and found myself all tongue tied and ridiculous, but we laughed about it – the whole situation; a splendid raucous laugh. I couldn't remember when I had last laughed like that. Perhaps I never had? Laughter had never really been a part of my life. The Glenbirrie Estate had always held a seriousness about it, a heavy presence that forbade frivolity. I must confess, that laughter felt so good: the relief of it, the expulsion of tension. But people were staring. *Oh gosh, how very inappropriate!* I chewed on my lips, averted my eyes from Angie's and controlled myself. That I was used to. Keeping my feelings hidden, controlling myself.

'So, my dear, are you here on your own as well?'

'Aye. Just little old me.'

'Don't you have a partner then? A boyfriend? A pretty young thing like you!'

Angie laughed, but not in a jolly way like we had just moments before. It seemed more rueful than joyous.

'I'm so sorry. That was rude of me. I don't mean to pry.'

'Nae bother.' She raised her eyebrows. 'I guess ye could say I've got a partner o sorts, but, well, he's no here is he?' She stared, a distance in her eyes.

'Oh my dear.' I took her hand and gave it what I hoped was a reassuring squeeze. It was cold and too slender, too fragile for one so young.

'Aye. I guess we just stay together the now because, well, we do.' She shrugged. 'No other half for you, then?'

60

'Oh no dear. My husband died.'

'Oh. I'm, I'm sorry.' She looked down at her boots. Those big clumpy things, Doctor Marten's, I believe they're called. Horrible ugly things. So unbecoming for a woman.

'That's quite all right. We...well, we weren't awfully close either, shall we say. I must admit, I am rather enjoying my new-found freedom! This,' I cast my eye over the waiting room. 'This was something of a disappointment, put rather a dampener on things, so to speak.'

I listened to myself, wishing I could suck the words back in. How stupid! It wasn't just the words. I worried that I was being too familiar, too chatty, too foolish and could feel a blush creeping up my neck. It was always my neck that turned red first. I could feel it pulsing, tingling, before any redness set in and worked its way up my cheeks, and then I became simply scarlet – almost the whole of my face an awful beacon of embarrassment. Andrew would poke fun at me if he was in a good mood, which was seldom. More often than not he was ill-tempered and quick to chastise. "It is so unbecoming," he would say, which, of course, only made matters worse. I didn't want to think about him just then. He wasn't welcome. I dismissed him from my thoughts.

'And your surgery? Did that all go to plan, my dear? No nasty surprises I hope,' I asked, and then instantly regretted it. My God! What a question! I really am as stupid as Andrew believed me to be. Yes. Stupid and insensitive! What if she had had some dreadful news? They had found more. Her prognosis was, well, not a positive one.

'Aye. As good as...Seems like they got it aw.' She shrugged and pulled a grimace of acceptance.

'Good, good.' I thought it best to keep quiet, not stumble over any more insensitive words.

The nurse walked back towards us from the reception, those awful folders under her arms. She looked at them and called some names expectantly. A young man rose to his feet and walked across to her, a forced smile glued to his face. Angie stood also.

'That's me then,' she said. 'I hope it aw goes well for ye, aye? Take care.'

They had said that the wait wouldn't be too long. I stared at the magazines, considered picking one up and flicking through it, but I had to pay attention, listen for my name. Besides which, one never quite knew who else might have touched them, read them. I didn't much care for the thought. Thankfully, I was called soon enough.

So there I was, sitting strapped up to that frightful chemotherapy contraption. The poison now drip-drip-dripping its way into my veins. A poison so dangerous that it had warnings plastered all over it. Skulls and crossbones. POISON. The nurses were clad in plastic aprons and gloves to protect themselves from it, and yet, here it was being pumped directly into my veins.

Such an overpowering smell of disinfectant, of chemicals, clung to the walls, the windows, the chairs, the machines; filled the recycled air. There was a fear so tangible that it hung like a blanket above the place. It smothered everything and everyone. The machines humming and clicking. A phone ringing. An alarm buzzing. The squeak of rubber soles on the linoleum floor. Soft words from the nurses. Heavy sighs from the patients. Time crept by so very slowly. It seemed interminable. Would that my life were so! We are such odd creatures, impatient, complaining about time, desperate for it to pass, and then, when it has, when life has begun to bid her farewells, oh, then we wish that we could get it all back. All of that wasted time. All of those precious seconds. Yes. Give them to me now.

They gave me a prescription for so many different pills, medications – anti-sickness this, anti-pain that, steroids. How was I going to manage to keep on top of everything? It was all so confusing. I left the hospital wondering just how awful it would be. Or perhaps it would be nothing? I would be one of those lucky ones like the young man who had been sat opposite me that day. It was his last visit, apparently.

'Is that it then, aye? Hasnae bothered me at all. Right as rain, so I am,' he had said with a big grin on his face.

The nurse had smiled back at him. 'Lucky you! I wish more people got through it all this easily. There seems to be no reason. For some people it is just easy. For others, well, it is not!'

She had an unusual lilt to her voice. I wondered where she came from. I didn't think Scotland; Eastern Europe somewhere perhaps.

'Aye, well, thanks lass.'

She put her arm around his waist and gave him a little squeeze. 'You take care of yourself, yes.'

'Oh aye, I'll do that all right. Dinnae take this the wrong way, but I hope I dinnae see you again!'

The nurse laughed and waved her farewells.

I could only hope, think positive. That was the thing to do! Chin up. As I walked back out of the hospital I straightened my back, switched the stoop into a stride, and reached my car with an improving attitude. I got a pleasant thrill every time I started her up and give the engine a gentle rev. That day was no different. Little things!

It had started to rain rather heavily. I switched the wipers on to full speed, so glad of my recent purchase. I would have been sitting on the bus for an hour or more soaked through. This had been such a good buy! As I pulled out onto the main road I caught a glimpse of a figure huddled under a tree that offered scant protection. I didn't allow myself to become distracted. The rain thundered on the roof, my vision of the road ahead was quite badly affected by it. I wondered if I should pull over somewhere; pause until the torrent eased? No. I had to learn to be confident in all situations. It didn't do to give up, give in. Not any more.

# Chapter 12

## Angie
## September 1987

It was chucking it down an there was no bus shelter. I was trying to get at least a bit o shelter frae the tree, but it had awready had a whole load o its leaves fall on the ground. No much shelter there. I glanced across at the hospital wondering about scooting back an waiting there till this eased off a bit. Naw. The less time I spent in there the better. Rather get soaked than breathe in any more o that place. Then I clocked her, didn't I? An I'm sure as hell she saw me. My new friend, Maria. Aye, right! Some friend. There she was tootling off to her posh house in her nice wee car. An me? Aye. Left standing in the rain. What else would ye expect? It was me. Angie Babe. I laughed at myself. No good shit ever came my way.

I decided on a smoke. Knew I shouldnae – my health an aw that – but let's be honest here, fags were the least o my concerns in the whole addiction category! I checked the packet. The last one. I took it out, dead careful like, pulled my jacket ower my head so as I could get it lit. I puffed an puffed at the tiniest wee bit o flame that had decided to tease me. Finally the fag was lit an I took a deep draw, my hand still covering it, keeping the rain off, right when some ass-hole decided it'd be a laugh to steer into the massive puddle that had sprung up by the kerb an spray me wi a bloody torrent o dirty water!

'Fuck's sake!' I screamed at them. 'Wankers!'

So, I was soaked through, as was my last fag. Wet an droopy like some guy's used cock. Useless. I chucked it in the gutter in disgust. Watched it fa apart, wee bits o tobacco drifting off on their own, mixing wi the leaves, disappearing. Aye, aw gone.

I got back to my bit an Deke came right out wi, 'Where the hell you been, Ange?'

No how are ye? Did it aw go okay? Can I get ye anything? Naw. None o the normal, nice, expected greetings.

'Big Davy's been round,' he added. 'Needs you to do a turn. Some client of his got a liking for you. Can't be pissing him off, Babes.'

'Babes! Dinnae you Babes me! You dinnae even know where I've been, do ye, eh? Fuck's sake, man!'

'That's why I'm asking!' he replied, aw stroppy an sarky. Like I was some idiot and he wasnae.

'The hospital, *Deke*. The chemo, *Deke*.'

He slapped his forehead wi his hand. 'Oh shit. I forgot. I –'

'Aye, ye forgot. Cos it's nothing, eh? Well, fuck you! Fuck Big Davy! Fuck the lot o ye!'

I stormed into the bedroom. The flat may have been a shit-hole, but I kept the bedroom as nice as I could, the bed made, my clothes folded, things in their right places. That was the one part o my life that I had control ower; that I could keep in order. It was important to me. If Deke really wanted to piss me off he'd move something; my wee ornament o an angel that had its special place beside my bed – had it for as long as I can mind. Think it was frae my ma. Cannae quite remember, no for definite, but that's what I decided on when I was wee and it stuck – my crystal that sat on the chest by the window, fragmented light, wee rainbows; my fuchsia that always flowered. Shouldnae, by all accounts, but it did. Anyway, move any o them an there was a good chance I'd go mental.

Everything was as it should be. I stripped off all o my nasty wet clothes an nashed into the shower. I'd have done it anyway, soaked through or no. Get the hospital washed off o me. Big Davy'd be back. I knew that. An I'd have to do what needed to be done. I knew that too. If it's someone asking for me that meant it would be a hotel, most likely, no the usual cars or back alleys. Woohoo! I was getting fucked in a hotel – cause for celebration!

But then, that day, I was so no in the mood. No that I ever am, but I do what needs doing. That day? that day was different.

# Chapter 13

Maria
September 1987

When I got to just past Prestonpans the rain suddenly stopped. The sky had streaks of blue breaking through it, getting wider and wider the further east I drove. I glanced, only for a second, at a spectacular rainbow that had burst across the water to my left. The blare of a car horn made me start and I suddenly realised that I was drifting across to the wrong side of the road! I righted myself quickly, gripped the steering wheel tightly and focused only on the road ahead. That was a close one! This whole driving palaver was a good deal more complicated than I had first thought. One didn't dare allow one's concentration to slip, even for a moment!

I reached Aberlady and did something rather peculiar. Instead of stopping at my little house, I drove right on by. I couldn't quite fathom why. I had been so looking forward to getting home, to making myself a cup of herbal tea, settling down in my recliner and just relaxing. Switching off from the outside world, from all that was happening to me. Letting it all slide off at the door. My home was my sanctuary and it wouldn't be sullied. Not if I could help it.

But no, something was pulling me on. I followed the

pull and it led me to the bents in Gullane. I knew where I would go from there. The car park was deserted, the beach likewise, apart from some hardy dog-walker. I stood and watched from the top of the dunes for a few minutes as the Labrador bounded into the sea, leaping at the waves and dashing out again, running about the sand in a huge circle before repeating the whole process over and over again! Such innocent pleasure that brought a welcome smile to my face.

Instead of walking down the hill to the beach I kept to the clifftop above the border of buckthorn. I was on the golf course which was also almost empty apart from a few golfers taking refuge under their enormous multicoloured umbrellas, even though the rain had all but stopped. Quite a spectacle really! I felt somewhat guilty, an intruder, but I doubted I was close enough for them to even notice me.

There were neatly cut squares of grass here and there with little flags protruding from holes in their centre. I skirted around them as they looked somehow precious. Tufts of unruly grass interspersed with small bunches of wild flowers – sea pinks, clovers and something dainty and yellow which I couldn't identify – caressed the edges of the cultivated course. A peculiar row of large concrete blocks stretched across its edge. They had been built in the war, apparently. I wondered again which side I had truly been on.

Ahead I could see the peninsula beyond which lay my beach. I left the path and hurried through the grass, past the gorse bushes and on to the cliff top, beneath which lay the bay. Despite it still being wet I sat down in the grass. It was thick and held a rather sumptuous springiness to it. The water was choppy and grey, reflecting the sky above it. I breathed it in; that peculiar feeling of belonging.

On that occasion I had decided to walk down to the sands. I slipped my shoes off, unpeeled my tights and left them on the rocks. The sand felt delicious between my toes. The trail my feet left were the only ones I could see besides those made by the birds that jerked their way along the water's edge. They seemed unafraid of me as I walked amongst them and made my way into the water. The cold bit at my skin, but I carried on in, hitching my skirt up and tucking it into my underwear, as I walked deeper and deeper. The waves splashed against me, the cold numbed my flesh, but in a splendidly invigorating way. It soon became apparent that a paddle wasn't going to satisfy me.

I hurried back to the sands, took off all of my clothes and scampered back into the water. There was no-one around to see, and to be honest I really didn't give two hoots. Not then. Not that day. The delight as I walked deeper and deeper, not caring, just not caring, spray on my face, waves breaking over me, around me, until I was out of my depth and had no choice but to swim. Right then, nothing else mattered. There was me, there were the birds, and there was the water. We were one. Beautifully, spectacularly one. And it was pure and clean and free. And I was someone else.

# Chapter 14

## Jaak
### Estonia September 1949

Jaak and Imre began dragging the bodies of the dead soldiers out of the farmhouse and hauling them into the Gaz. There could be no trace of them left at the farm. That would mean certain execution for the rest of the family – Evi and her sisters.

'Couldn't we let the girls come and stay with us?' Imre asked, knowing what the answer had to be, but asking nevertheless, as the last body was jostled into place on the back seat.

'Our life is not a life for them. You know that. Besides, their help here is invaluable,' Jaak replied, scornfully. 'We'll drive the car far enough away, crash it into a tree and set fire to it so that it will be seen as nothing more than an accident. The girls will stay here and work for the resistance, like always. Nothing will change.'

Imre found it difficult to disguise his disappointment, but he knew in his heart that Jaak was right. Their mission had to come before any individual feelings. Country before people. Struggle before freedom.

Evi and her sisters did what they could to remove all evidence of the abomination that had happened from their house. They scrubbed at the bloodstains with brushes and bleach until their fingers were raw. The stench of the bleach had soaked into the wooden floorboards, overpowering everything else; the air so heavy with it that it stung at their eyes, snatched at their lungs. The stain, whilst not obviously blood, was still there, staring back at them accusingly. Evi shook her head. She hated the feeling that this left in her stomach. Someone had been killed in their house. Their home. Death stained their floor – her mother's and the soldiers'. She had to pull on all of her strength to focus on what needed to be done, as her mother's body lay outside awaiting burial.

'Help me girls. We need to cover this,' she called to her sisters. It wasn't just for their own safety, but also to hide the constant reminder of what had taken place there. They worked in a peculiar silence as they shifted furniture and moved rugs around, trying to make everything look normal. No tears, no sobs, just a quiet acceptance of what fate had thrown at them. The marks were hidden, the smell would fade, the act wouldn't. There was nothing more that they could do. It would have to be enough.

Jaak started up the engine of the Gaz. It was good to be driving again, to feel as if he were in control of something. Their progress felt agonizingly slow as they followed the tracks that had been made by the Gaz upon its arrival. Once they drove off the farm track and out onto the road they might well come across another Soviet patrol. They would have to be vigilant. One kilometre out, or so, and the farm track met the road. It was little more than a dirt track itself, a single track road made up of compacted dust and dirt. They slowed to a

72

stop and Jaak cut the engine, staring left and right at the road that disappeared into trees in both directions. They would have to rely on their hearing to alert them to any danger now.

'Anything?' Jaak asked quietly.

Imre tuned his ears in to their surroundings. The hush of the countryside. The call of a crow. A reply from another. The creak of a tree. The rustle of the leaves. No engine. No marching feet. No Russian voices.

'No. Nothing,' he replied in a whisper.

Jaak switched the ignition again and decided to go in the opposite direction from that which the patrol had come. They were pretending that the search had continued, nothing untoward had happened at the farmhouse and the soldiers had simply carried on to the next property. He veered left into the forest.

They drove on in silence for five more kilometres, senses alert, but not for the beauty of their surroundings: the deep rich forest, trees so tall and proud, the wildlife that scurried and leapt through it. No. They were only focussed on human interference. A sign of their enemies. But little could be heard above the noise of the engine; little seen beyond the cloak of the trees.

They came to a sharp corner beyond which a small clearing opened up in the forest. There was a steep grassy slope downhill, ending at a collection of erratic boulders large enough to cause considerable damage to a vehicle. A small stream gurgled its way behind the stones, a heron stood elegantly on one leg searching for fish; beyond that nothing but more dense forest.

'You get out here,' Jaak instructed Imre. 'Help me shift these bodies, put them in the right positions and make a circle back through the forest. You can't leave any

73

tracks. You got that?'

'Sure.' Imre saluted and grinned as if this were a game. It was both endearing and infuriating at the same time, such innocence in a time of darkness.

Jaak sat on top of the driver. The feel of the dead body under him, still warm, was as distasteful as it was unnerving. It felt as if it might spring back to life and throttle him. He slammed his foot down hard on the accelerator, swerved into a skid and leapt out of the Gaz just in time. He rolled in the mud and lay on his back, staring wide-eyed as the vehicle careered onwards, straight into the boulders. The heron took off slowly and gracefully, crows shrieked angrily and flew up into the sky, swirling above the crash site. Jaak waited, watching, praying for a flame, a spark, something to ignite the vehicle.

Nothing was happening. It was dangerous to get close to the volatile vehicle, but he couldn't afford to wait any longer. He had no idea of whom, or what, might be within hearing distance, striking distance. There was no choice now but to run down and be that spark himself.

When he reached the wreckage he ripped a piece of material from one of the soldiers' uniforms and stuffed it into the petrol tank. He reached inside his jacket for the matches, closing his eyes in frustration at the dampness of the sandpaper. He struck a match against it. Nothing but a line. Again. Firmer. With more conviction. He had almost given up hope – almost begun to panic – when finally a match caught and the flame stayed long enough to set the material alight. When he was sure it would work – that the flames would make their way along the material and into the petrol tank – he bolted to safety, leaping over the stream and running further

74

into the sanctuary of the woods, away from the road.

It didn't take long for the explosion to rock the ground beneath his feet. Flames engulfed the vehicle, licking at the metal, splintering the glass. The stench of diesel and burning flesh. Foul black smoke spiralled up through the trees and into the sky, blending with the ominously dark clouds.

If any Reds were nearby they would definitely have been alerted this time. They would be on their way. He had to try to cover the footprints he had made. Disguise them. And quickly. He tugged at some bushes and snapped off a handful of branches and twigs, then retraced his steps and whipped away the evidence as best he could, leaving a scattering of wood and leaves as extra cover. His footsteps were deep, heavy in the mud, but he thought he had done enough. The profound darkness of nightfall was imminent and if the clouds kept to their promise of a heavy downpour, which they looked like doing, nature would help him on his way. He didn't imagine that there would be too much of an investigation anyway. It was a crash. An accident. Nothing more.

He could just make out the shadow of Imre twisting through the trees. One second there, the next second gone, at one with the forest, hidden by the girth of a tree-trunk. Only a flicker of a human form. They would meet up at the old windmill. The boy was impressing him. Following orders. Not doubling back to check on his sweetheart. The boy was strong.

# Chapter 15

## Angie
## April 1988

So, that was it then. Treatment ower an now it was just a waiting game. Aye, I'd felt totally shite, like having the worst hangover ever combined wi a nasty wee dose o smack withdrawal, but instead o it getting better as time wore on, it just got worse an worse for a whole week. I couldnae even walk up the stairs for that week. Didnae even get out o my pit. Couldnae eat. Didnae want to. Everything tasted like metal. Like auld cardboard. Disgusting. No, it wasnae an altogether strange feeling for me. It was shite nonetheless.

Anyway, the second week things got better an by the third I was almost a human being. But then it aw started again. Shite, shite an more shite. Didnae stop me frae needing to turn tricks, though. That bastard Big Davy wouldnae let me stop. The first week, aye. I was no use to anyone that week and he knew it. The next two though? Aye. Off you go Angie. Away an work. Fuck's sake! Even when my hair had started falling out; big clumps o it lying there on my pillow, an I'd shaved the rest o it off. "Turns some men on," he'd said. A sick woman wi a shaved head. Fuck's sake!

At the clinic they said I'd responded well to the treatment. They said my prognosis was good. Better if I could clean myself up. Ditch the bad stuff. How could I do that? I lived wi the bad stuff. I was the bad stuff. The bad stuff was shoved in my face, or in my veins. It was always there. I wasnae.

It had been a shitty winter, an no just for me. It was stormy, rainy, blowing a hoolie most o the time, an dark as hell. Folk walking along wi their heads down an their hands stuffed deep in their pockets. But the days were getting longer, the weather getting better, an I was alive. Getting better too.

Better weather meant that there'd soon be more tourists. Me an Deke would head on up to Waverley Station. Another form o income. Another layer o choring. Posh bags skipping ower concrete. Our eyes peeled, scanning. Foreigners wi loud mouths an fat wallets, vacant looks an bulging pockets. Aye, easy pickings. Deke'd give them directions an I'd dip their pockets, bags, whatever. "Thank you so much. Ain't you Scotch just the friendliest!" Oh aye, we were friendly aw right! Ye had to be careful, mind. There were bizzies everywhere, cameras too, spying on ye, telling tales. Sneaky bastards!

So, I was up for my next check-up. Every six weeks it was. Nail-biting time. Imagining pains an lumps time. I'd just come out. Should've been feeling aw happy. Aw clear again. Getting there. But it was just another day. Another shitty day. Nothing good to go home to. Christ, I was so sick o it aw. What was the point? Really? What was the point? It'd be easier if they'd said, "Sorry Angela. It's bad news." But they didnae. That way out didnae appear to be coming my way.

I heard her calling. 'Angie! Angie dear!'

Hadnae seen her since that first day o treatment last

year. Hadnae thought about her much either. The odd "I wonder how that auld woman is?" as I was sitting in the chemo chair or lying on the radiotherapy table. Strange thoughts fly through ye in those places. Yer head's that full o fear that anything else is welcome. Ye bring it in, dwell on it, hold it for as long as ye can.

Anyway, I thought about ignoring her, picking my step up, but I didnae. Fuck knows why, but I turned around an waved, waited for her to catch me up.

'Hello my dear!'

She had this big beaming grin spread across her like seeing me was something special. Weird!

'Aye. Hi.'

'I don't want to ask, but I do want to know. You've been on my mind such a lot, you see. How are you my dear?'

'Aye. So far, so good. Aw clear. You?'

'Oh, that's marvellous! Simply marvellous! Listen, I was just going to go for a cup of coffee and a slice of cake. A small celebration of food tasting like food again! It would be so much nicer to have company. Would you care to join me?'

'Eh...'

'I'm buying, of course. My little treat.' She linked arms wi me an squeezed, still smiling, like we were best buddies. 'Oh, come on dear. Just for me!'

'Aye. Aw right then. Aye, that'd be nice.' What else was I gonnae say. Me? Turn down a freebie? Aye, right!

'Could you recommend anywhere? I don't really...' She got a wee bit flustered. 'I don't really know this place terribly well, you see.'

I can spot a liar a mile off. Oh aye, going for a coffee were you? I doubt that! Anyway, I tried to think o somewhere posh an pricey. She had money. Why no? We settled on The Laigh on Hanover Street. Walked past it a few times. Smelled it. Coffee an home baking. One o those places that I wouldnae normally step foot in for fear o being turfed right out again, but things were different now, aye? I was wi posh-woman here.

We got in her car. Funny thing for an auld woman to have. It was more a boy-racer type o car. Aw flash an chrome an shit. A racing stripe, bucket seats, the lot. Nice enough though. We parked on Queen Street Gardens. Close enough.

# Chapter 16

## Maria
### April 1988

It was quite a shock when I saw her. That beautiful hair, all gone. How very sad. Her eyes had unbecoming dark rings around them. It was the first time I had seen her without make-up as well. Nothing to hide behind. She had a baseball cap pulled low over her brow. Her jacket – that awful big leather one – hung off her. She had been thin before, but now she looked so very sick. Emaciated. I chatted and smiled and looked beyond; imagined the girl behind that awful sickness. I didn't want cancer to be what now defined me and I thought that she deserved the same courtesy.

Life can be so very strange. The Laigh of all places! As Angie and I turned down the steps into the basement she hung back, kept herself behind me, as if she were hiding. I stepped through the door and was instantly taken back half a century. The place had barely changed.

### Maria 1949
The train had slowed, the whistle shrieked, and she had arrived.

'Waverley Station, Edinburgh. This is Waverley Station,' the loud-speaker had crackled out.

80

She watched and waited until everyone else had alighted, scanning them for any tell-tale signs; for anyone else looking around, trying to spot her, pick her out from the crowd. There was no-one that she recognised and more importantly, no-one that seemed to recognise her. Had she really done this? Escaped? It would seem so.

She stepped gingerly on to the platform and slipped in to their flow, just a fellow traveller, one of them. But then they began to disperse, heading off in so many different directions. There were different exits and so many people. It was all noise and strangeness. She stopped and looked around, trying to make sense of where she was, in this vast cavernous space of metal and glass, steam and noise. She felt giddy, her head spinning, her step faltering.

'Are ye all right there, lass? Ye're looking a wee bit lost, so ye are.'

It was a policeman. His smile was warm and friendly. His accent very hard to understand, but she managed. She did what she had learned to do. Mimicked him.

'Yes, a wee bit lost.' She forced a smile in return.

'Where is it ye're headed to then?'

'Um...' Of course she had no idea of where she was headed as she looked around for clues, a sign, feeling foolish.

'Princes Street, is it? Most folk coming up from down south head up that way.'

'Yes. Yes, Princes Street.'

'Aye, right ye are then.' He pointed across the station. 'You want to be heading up yonder. Waverley Steps. Mind an hold on to yer bonnet, lass. It's gey windy up yon steps! Blowing a hoolie, so it is!' He turned and waved.

81

She waved back and walked amongst her fellow travellers feeling better, more like she had a purpose. She wasn't lost. But, of course, she was. Utterly!

Suddenly, as she made her way up the steps, such a strong wind blew at her. She guessed that gey meant very! Her bonnet began to lift off her head and she slammed her hand on it just in time to keep it in place. The wind caught at her skirt, at her jacket, whipped her hair across her face. She squealed, one hand attempting to keep her skirt from lifting up, the other, her bonnet from escaping. A group of boys laughed, nudging each other. Carefree. Happy. She envied them.

Seventy-two steps later and she was on Princes Street. It seemed very grand. On one side there was a row of expensive looking shops, on the other a large park set in a valley with an abundance of trees and shrubbery, on its far side a steep hill with rather grand looking buildings cutting their way through the skyline, flags fluttering – something official she assumed. She just stood and tried to take it all in: the buildings, the people, the buzz of a large city.

She realised soon enough that if she were to look more normal, to belong, she would have to move, copy them, become one of them. She walked along Princes Street, beside the park, past a large, impressive art gallery with great pillars all the way around its exterior. She paused for a moment at a junction. Which way now? Up the hill towards the buildings she had seen from the park or across the road and towards what looked like the continuation of the park. She decided on the latter.

At the far side of this section of the park there was a castle; a real live castle atop steep cliffs of black rock. She walked through the entrance wondering if anything could be more impressive than this! She found herself at a clock set into the ground that was made entirely of flowers. She thought it the most beautiful thing that she had ever seen; so very delicate with thousands of flowers telling the time. The precision that had been taken, the planning that had been involved; it was quite mind-boggling. This must be a special place, she decided. As she was standing, staring, lost in a reverie, a cuckoo poked out of a box and sang. She laughed aloud, unable to help herself. It was so unexpected, so frivolous, and so beautiful.

'Delightful, isn't it?' a man's voice said quietly behind her.

She wasn't sure if he was speaking to her or to someone else, so she ignored it. She didn't know the way of people here yet. It was best to keep quiet and not draw attention to oneself. She wished that she hadn't laughed.

'Do you know there are twenty-five thousand flowers in that design?'

She realised that he must have been talking to her as there was no-one else around. What should she do? Be friendly, of course. *I am Maria and I am friendly and confident and I have nothing to fear. Not now.*

She turned and smiled. He was tall and distinguished looking. He lifted his fedora to reveal smartly cut hair peppered with grey that matched his well-tailored suit.

'Oh, have you counted all?' she asked.

He laughed and cocked his head. His grey eyes twinkled, but she sensed a sadness behind them. The laugh felt detached from the person somehow.

'No, no, my wife used to love this place. We would come here whenever we were in town. After she died I made it my mission to find out every last detail. There was no cuckoo then, but she would have approved, I am sure.'

'I am sad for you.'

'There is no need. It was a long time ago.'

'The war?'

'Yes. The war. Come. Walk with me.'

She stepped back. Nervous. Fearful. Men were not to be trusted.

'It's all right. I mean you no harm. It's just rather pleasant to have someone to walk with for a change. Would you?'

She had to start anew, to become the person she wanted to be. The new her. This person would trust, would live without constant fear and suspicion. His sad eyes finally convinced her and she accepted.

'You're not from here, are you?'

Her skin prickled. 'Yes. I am Maria, and I am from Edinburgh,' she replied defensively.

'Really? You don't sound it.'

She regurgitated the rest of her well-rehearsed story about Sweden and her parents. This was the first time she had said all of it out loud; said the words that she had been practising in her head for so long now. He seemed to believe her. At least he listened as though he did. His face said he did, and he didn't ask any questions that made her think he knew that she was a liar.

They had reached the end of the gardens and she had learned a good deal about Edinburgh. He had told her all about the Ross Bandstand, the castle, and the gardens. Her brain was like a sponge, soaking in all of this, building memories, creating history.

'Well, Maria, I have probably bored you quite enough by now,' he stated.

'Oh no! It has been very interesting,' she answered, truthfully.

'Really?' He cocked his head and narrowed his eyes slightly making him look very serious. 'I wonder, perhaps we could meet when there is a concert on? It really is most impressive: the castle, the gardens, and beautiful music. Or dancing? Do you like to dance?'

She didn't know what to say, what to do. This man seemed nice, but then so many of them did, at first. How very different everything had become so very quickly. She knew nothing, absolutely nothing about any of this. About here. About normal. Was it normal to ask a young woman to go to a dance with a stranger?

'I am so sorry. I fear I may have overstepped my mark. I have just so enjoyed your company. Forgive me, please. If you think you could, I will be here at two thirty on Saturday.' He raised his fedora, nodded at her. 'Good day, Maria.' He turned and walked off.

She didn't know what to think, more importantly, what to do! Evening was slipping into night and she had nowhere to stay; no idea of what she was going to do with herself. This hadn't gone to plan at all. Her intention had been to find a cheap hotel or a guest-house, and settle herself in before looking for work the following day. She would have to hurry. Even now, darkness frightened her and she didn't know why, but her fears were the closest thing she had to a memory of her old life and in a strange way she enjoyed them. Perhaps they would lead her out of the mystery of who she really was?

She took a deep breath, gathered her resolve, and walked purposefully on, as if she knew where she were going. As if she had every right to be there. *I am Maria. I am from Edinburgh.* It didn't feel like it, as doubt and worry clawed at her. The people at that awful house had called her Dora, but that wasn't her name. She knew that she was somebody else, but she had no idea of who that might be; of where that person came from. She didn't know anything. *This sort of thinking won't do! Pull yourself together.* She tried to convince herself again. *I am Maria...*

She had walked beyond the shops and out of the city centre. The sky was turning dark, but a tinge of the lightest of hues of pink and blue still clung to the air and lifted her mood, stroked her fear away with a gentle brush. She turned right and onto a pleasant looking side-street of three storey houses, quite grand, with pillars and large windows and hefty doors. Shadows now stretched across the entire street, blending into the gloom of the onset of night. She glanced casually up and down, not wanting to look lost, hoping to find a sign that said, "Bed and Breakfast" or "Guest House" or "Rooms for Rent." Anything!

Finally she came to a rather severe looking building with a sign hanging in its window that read, "Vacancies". She climbed the steps, forced her best confident smile through her apprehension, and pressed the brass bell. It clanged along what sounded like a large empty space. A sickening knot caught hold of her stomach. This was too grand for her, surely?

'Start as you mean to go on,' she whispered to herself. But perhaps not tonight. She heard footsteps, turned and darted back down the steps but wasn't quite quick enough.

'Yes? Can I help you?' a voice called out from the narrow space that had opened up between door and frame.

'Oh. I am looking for a room. The sign.' She pointed and smiled.

'Come on then,' the woman gestured her closer with a beckoning finger. 'Let me have a look at you.' She studied her with squinting eyes and a distrustful frown. 'Just you is it?'

'Yes, I am alone.'

'And how long will you be staying for?'

'I, I'm not sure.'

'One night then and we'll see. Can't be having any old Tom, Dick or Harry lodging. I run a respectable house,' she added pointedly, her eyes scrutinising Maria's entirety, slowly, critically. She clicked her tongue against her mouth and ushered her in, talking all the while. 'No men. No visitors. No noise. No entry after ten.' She stopped and checked the clock. 'Just in time. You're lucky! Money up front. Breakfast at eight sharp. Any questions?'

Maria wasn't given time to open her mouth, let alone answer.

'No. Good!' She made her way behind the heavy wooden desk, opened a large leather-bound notebook with a flourish, held her hand out. 'Identity card?'

Maria felt as though she were a balloon and someone had just begun to let the air out. 'I, I didn't think we needed them any more. I threw mine away.'

'Oh, did you now? You could be anybody. That foreign sounding voice of yours.' Again, the eyes narrowed, asking questions, raising concerns.

'My name is Maria...'

She repeated her story, adding more detail and more emotion than before, encouraged by the woman's softening expression and less severe stance. This was becoming a skill; words tripped lightly off her tongue, reinforced by confident eyes and a strong stance. The lies were now becoming reality. If she believed her own story, so would others. The room was more expensive than she had bargained for, but it would do for now. It was a start.

Her room was on the second floor. Its large windows looked out onto an open area. She couldn't make it out in the gloom – a shadow filled space, perhaps a garden, seemingly silent. The furniture in the room was made of a dark, heavy wood. It smelled old and was somehow comforting. She ran her fingers over everything: smooth wood, rich deep carpet, a heavy quilted bedspread, crisp cotton sheets. It was all so luxurious, and for one night it was hers. She would enjoy it. Take full advantage. Dream a little.

*

Saturday had come and she had plucked up the courage to meet Andrew in the gardens, as he had requested. As they stood at the entrance to the Ross bandstand the sky had suddenly blackened: a crash of thunder, a flash of lightning, rain coming down in a torrent. Andrew held his umbrella over her and smiled. The rain clattered on its taut fabric, drowning out his words. Streams of water fell all around them.

'Perhaps we should seek shelter?' Andrew repeated, almost at a shout.

'Perhaps we should,' she had replied, smiling, nodding to ensure she was understood, not knowing if this was appropriate or not, but feeling, well, relieved somehow.

'Come. I know of somewhere close by.'

They rushed across Princes Street – a smell of horses, the rumble of trams – and up Hanover Street, over the brow of the hill, past a large statue of George IV, bronze and imposing. They ducked into a basement. It was small and dark with perhaps eight or nine round wooden tables with four chairs around each. The welcoming aroma of coffee and home baking filled the air, bringing an anticipation of tingling taste-buds.

Andrew ushered her in in front of him, though she would have preferred to walk in his shadow.

'Quick, quick, in you go!'

He shook his umbrella before he stepped inside, closed it and set it in the holder at the door. She noticed the ornate silver handle, the rich dark wood. As she took him in, everything about him suggested money. She couldn't for the life of her fathom why he had chosen to show her a kindness when everything about her clearly said poverty. It wasn't possible that he knew what she was; whom she was running away from. She decided to ignore her trepidations for now and accept his kindness. Perhaps there were simply good people out there? He shook their coats and hung them on the stand, grinning all the while.

The waitress seemed to know him. She smiled a warm welcome. 'And what will it be today, sir?'

'A pot of tea and some cake, I think.' He turned to Maria. 'Does that sound agreeable?'

*Agreeable* – what a strange word, she thought to herself as she worked out its meaning, as she had to do with so many of the words he used. He was so very different from anyone she had met before. She repeated new words over and over in her head, making sure that they stayed. She would remember them. She would become more like him. Even though she had only just met him, he was making such an impression on her.

'Yes, that would be agreeable,' she replied.

He smiled, seemed to bite back a laugh. She hoped that she hadn't done something foolish, said the wrong words, done the wrong thing. She returned the smile and tried to suppress the blush she could feel creeping its way up her neck.

The cake was divine. His word. She stole it. She loved the sound of it, the feeling it left in her mouth. Divine! As they chatted she let him do most of the talking. He seemed to know so much about everything. When he asked about her, the answers she gave were brief, nothing beyond the story she had made for herself, the character she had created. She had to remember everything, ensuring she didn't make any mistakes. It wasn't easy and she couldn't let her guard down. A few words about herself and then another question to him. She was getting good at this.

## 1988

'Thanks,' Angie said, as she wiped her mouth with the back of her hand leaving a trail of chocolate across it.

I must have stared at it because she suddenly looked a trifle embarrassed and snatched at her napkin, rubbing and rubbing at the smear of chocolate. How like me! How like the girl I was so very long ago. Awkward and nervous.

'You're no frae here then, Edinburgh?' she asked, still rubbing at her hand, not looking at me as she spoke.

'No. No dear I am not.' I smiled.

Seemingly content with the cleanliness of her hand she put the linen napkin back on the table and our eyes met again.

'Lived here aw my life, so I have. So where is it ye're frae then?'

I took a deep breath, toying with the question; toying with what answer I should give. I had been holding this lie inside me for so very long. Pretending that I was from Edinburgh, that I had been sent to my grandparents' home in Sweden during the war. But I didn't feel the need to perpetuate that myth with this girl. With Angie. Perhaps it was the sickness, perhaps it was just this girl. Whatever it was, I decided to tell the truth and it felt quite marvellous.

'Well, here's the rub. You see, I don't actually know.'

'You're kidding, aye?'

'No dear.'

'How come?'

'Well now, where to begin? I had amnesia. Well, no, I have amnesia. I woke up forty-odd years ago, in a hospital, with no memory whatsoever. I didn't know who I was, where I came from, anything. The most terrifying thing was that I didn't understand anything either. Whatever language they were speaking, it most certainly wasn't mine! The war had just ended and there was so much confusion around: refugees, orphans, widows. You can't imagine, my dear! So many lost souls.'

'So, ye're foreign then?'

'It would appear so!'

'An what happened? I mean how did ye end up here, like?'

'Well, fortune smiled on me, I suppose. Eventually. I met a man and he, well, he looked after me.'

'Yer husband?'

'Yes dear. Andrew, my husband.'

When we had arrived the cafe had been quiet, but I realised that it had suddenly become busy. Every table was now occupied. There were people all around us. Strangers talking, listening. There was a buzz of noise and I felt a flutter of panic. The walls seemed to be closing in on me, suffocating me. I felt hot, flustered and yes, scared. I wasn't comfortable in there any longer. It was time to leave.

# Chapter 17

## Angie
## April 1988

She went aw weird on me. Called for the bill. Paid. Left her tea an cake sitting there, unfinished. I couldnae make out what was going on, but whatever, we were out o there.

'Goodbye dear. I –' she called back, as she rushed off to her wee car an drove away.

I was left standing there wi no idea o what had just happened. I hadnae said anything, done anything wrong. I thought she must've seen someone that she didnae want to see. We all hae our secrets, aye? Even posh folk. Naw. Especially posh folk! Shame cos I was just getting interested. Anyway, at least I had a few quid in my hands now. She'd left a hefty tip an I'd swiped it as we left. Ye have to take yer chances when they show themselves to ye, eh!

I thought about going home to Deke. Someone to share the good news wi. Someone to talk about it aw wi. Aye, I'm okay. Still okay. But that wouldnae happen. There'd be people. There'd be a hit. There'd be a load o bullshit. People talking about nothing. "Yeah man" this, an "yeah man" that. How good was the gear? Can you no gie us a bit more? Aye, bullshit, bullshit, bullshit.

That wasnae what I wanted. No what I needed either. Naw. I decided instead to nip in to Oddbins, buy a couple o beers, head on down to Princes Street Gardens.

It was nice down there, an I was taken right back to when I was a wee lassie. One o the few memories I hae o my mum that are decent. We'd come for a wee trip, a picnic in the gardens, a look at the flower clock. That was my favourite, see. A magical wee place where the flowers told the time an a cuckoo popped out o its wee house on the hour. She'd timed it just right so as we'd get to see it. "Cuckoo" Squeals o delight frae me. A grin an a wee squeeze frae her. Cheese an ham sandwiches, Irn Bru, an doughnuts, aw o my favourites. Everything that I loved right there that day. She wasnae even that drunk. A wee bit, but no so as it embarrassed me. No so as folk stared or tutted or turned away, pretending we werenae there.

That had been the day before though, eh. The day before she dumped me. It was like she had wanted to leave me wi one decent memory. Aye. She'd done that aw right. I clung on to it tight, night after night. My mammy loved me. Once upon a time she loved me.

I tried to find her again when I got out o the orphanage. Deke was aw, "Are you sure that's a good idea, Babes?" An I was aw, "Aye! I need to know Deke." I wasnae even that sure the name she used was real. Carmen, she'd called herself, Carmen O'Donnell. No date o birth. No record at the registrar's. Nothing. I was too young to know the address. Somewhere up by Arthur's Seat was aw I could remember, an no the posh bit either. I thought it had maybe been Dumbiedykes cos it just felt familiar an I was pretty sure I used to nip across the road an play in the park at the bottom o Arthur's Seat.

Deke was really sweet back then. He chummed me,

walking aw around places that I thought I remembered; people that I thought might know: the corner shops, some random folk out in their garden that looked like they were maybe the same age as her, the lollipop men. Nothing ever came o it. "Sorry hen, no idea." It was like my ma hadnae even existed. I guess that's what she wanted though, eh?

'You've got me, Babes. You've always got me,' Deke had said softly in that deep sexy voice he had. 'We're family now. Just you and me.'

'Aye,' I smiled up at him, feeling his arm around my shoulders, aw protective an manly an gorgeous. Aye. That was Deke. That was us. That was then.

When we'd moved in together it was aw just pure magic. I couldnae believe what was happening. Me, Angie, wi this gorgeous guy who'd do anything for me. We bought things for the flat to make it ours, no just his. "Whatever you want," he'd said. We got most o it frae John Lewis's – nothing cheap like – aw good stuff: dried flowers an brass candlesticks, some classy prints, Van Gogh's "Sunflowers" for me – aw bright an beautiful – Monet's "Water-lilies" for him. He said that the blue matched my eyes. A new duck-feather duvet, white Egyptian cotton sheets, cos that's what I wanted. Aw clean. Aw new. Aw ours.

He was a guitarist. Played session for some big names an got decent money for it. We were doing aw right. The flat was in Stockbridge – nice, cool, trendy part o town: deli's an wee boutiques an artsy cafes an pubs that folk wi posh voices hung out in. I'd still pinch myself every now an again. I mean, there were always girls hanging around him – of course there were – giving him the eye, an a lot more given half a chance! But he wanted little old me. An it was aw beautiful for a couple o years and then, well, then Lady Heroin strolled in an took ower. Stripped us o everything. We just got up an left ourselves in another life. Aye. Another life.

*

I'd settled myself down on the grass under one o the big trees right in the middle o the Gardens; my back against the trunk, my face towards the castle rock. Trains rumbled by, kids ran about screeching, squirrels came right up close wi their wee twitchy tails wanting a bit o food. Some folk fed the birds. Fights between crows an sparrows an seagulls. I just sat there for hours, sipping at my beer, no wanting to get drunk – that was weird – watching it aw, doing nothing but reminisce, until I had nothing left.

## Chapter 18

### Jaak
### Estonia Spring 1953

At last the snows had begun to melt; to creep back into the ground with the strength of the bright spring sun. Winter had seemed interminable, so very cold and harsh. Finally the earth began to come alive again. You could feel it, smell it, taste it, as nature changed, as life returned. A viridescence clung to the air in scent and taste. The palest of greens danced on the tips of the trees, ready to burst into splendour; to transform the world into a place of colour and warmth and beauty again.

A rumour had swept through the forests and farms. On 5th March Stalin had died. The world would truly change; not just the physical one, but the mental one as well. The terror he created would be over. Surely. An amnesty was being given to many of the prisoners; sentences cut, gulag populations thinned. An amnesty was also to be offered to the Forest Brothers. After so many years of hiding and persecution, could it really be over?

Jaak, Johann, and the remaining Brothers – those who hadn't been picked off, fallen foul of their enemy's bullets over the years, or sent to the gulags – were sitting together outside their bunker. Serious conversations were being had. They, like the other brigades, were discussing what to do; how to react to the amnesty. Many of them had families to return to. They could be fathers and lovers, husbands and sons again. They could go back to their land and sow the seeds of their labour. It had been so long and they ached for it.

There was a sense of guilt for giving up after so many years of struggle, but really, what effect were the Brothers having? They were so hugely outnumbered. The immensity of the Soviet Union against them, little Estonia, now, officially, not even a country any more. Now they were a republic of the USSR. The flick of a pen across paper and it had been done. The Molotov-Ribbentrop Pact had been made. Their fate decided. Not by them. Not a decision taken by the people of Estonia. No. They were a chip to be bartered. A deal to keep peace. Really? Was that really their fate? Yes. It seemed it was.

The Brothers had taken more lives than they had lost, slowed the enemy down, been an annoyance, but their numbers were dwindling. It was becoming futile and they had their own lives to lead: a bed to sleep in, a wife to hold, parents to provide for, children to teach. They could do that now, if with a heavy heart.

Jaak and Johann held a different point of view. They had both seen the worst of the Soviets first-hand. Lost their families. Parents, grandparents, uncles and aunts had been annihilated. They were both the only survivors from their families that they knew of. The way of the Forest Brothers had become their lives, their raison-d'être. The Reds were still their enemy. That much hadn't changed. It could never change. Not until their land was theirs again. Truly free.

'We stay and fight?' Johann asked. His gaze held by the scurry of a beetle across the rotten bark of the fallen tree they were sat upon.

Jaak spat on the ground. 'We stay and fight,' he confirmed. 'There is no way I'm going to walk back out there and be told what to do, how to do it, by some damned invaders. Screw them! Estonia will be free!'

Johann smiled and took his friend's hand tightly in his. 'Estonia will be free!'

The moment Imre had heard about the amnesty he had rushed through the forest to Evi's house. He wasn't waiting any longer; couldn't wait any longer. He reached her door breathless, dripping in sweat despite the chill of the spring air. He ran his fingers through his hair, swiped at his face in a vain attempt to clean it, picked at the shoulders of his jacket. It wasn't necessary. She had seen him at his very worst over the years, but this was the most important moment in his life. He had to try.

He knocked on the door, sheepishly, his nerves jangling, his thoughts haywire. She opened the door and smiled. Despite all of his planning, the speech he had prepared flew out of his mind the minute he saw her. He could barely remember a single word of it.

'Evi,' he grinned, staring deeply into those eyes that were so impossibly blue, clasping her hands between his, embarrassed at the dirt and grime that encrusted his fingers. He grimaced, blew out a heavy breath. 'Will you marry me? I…I know I don't have much,' he stuttered, his words falling over themselves. 'Well, I have nothing.' He screwed his face up. His expression desperate. 'But I love you. I adore you. And I will look after you. And –'

She silenced him with a kiss.

\*

'She said yes!' Imre sang to himself, to the trees, to the heavens, as he raced back from the little farmhouse, tripping over the tangles of new growth at his feet, desperate to share his news with the Brothers. They would be so happy for him. He just knew they would.

A shout rang out through the trees. '*Stoy!*' (Halt!)

Imre hesitated briefly. Surely he must have misheard? There was an amnesty. It was all okay now. He ignored it and carried on delirious with love and anticipation. He would tell the Brothers, relish in their congratulations, pack the little he had, and run back to her. To Evi. The most beautiful girl in the world who had agreed to become his wife! Imagine! His grin was fixed, his eyes moist with tears of joy. His heart was thumping in the very best of ways. He wondered if one could die of happiness; if his body just couldn't survive the immensity of this joy. Of course, one could die of grief. That was well known. But joy?

The metallic click. The harsh crack. The sickening thud of a bullet sinking into its target. The screeching of birds taking off in fright.

Jaak and Johann heard the shot piercing the silence of the forest; heard the birds screech. They exchanged anxious glances. It could be a hunter. A farmer. But they both felt it. Something had gone terribly wrong. When your lives have been so entangled – as dependant upon one another for survival as theirs had been – a thread ran through you; a fundamental connection, and you just knew. Something sinister had enveloped the camp. That cloak of fear that they both knew so intimately hung over them again. Another life was in danger. A life significant to them.

Peetr had already said his farewells and headed in the opposite direction from the sound of the gunshot, towards his home in Mustla. He would be far away by now, well out of earshot. It could only be Imre. There was no hesitation. Of course they had to find out what had happened, help in any way they could. They were Brothers. The boy had grown into a man in their company. He had alerted them to danger on so many occasions, saved both of their lives. Perhaps there was still a chance, although they both doubted it. They could hope for that little while longer. Believe in a life that they feared was no longer of this earth.

They crept through the forest. Birch trees and pine, deceptively beautiful. Silence apart from birdsong and the rustle of newly sprung leaves in the gentle spring breeze that promised summer. It took them fifteen minute to swipe their way through the trees, shrubs, and undergrowth before they reached the track which led to Evi's house. An unnatural silence. Jaak suddenly stopped dead, closed his eyes. He couldn't bear to look, nor could he turn away. Their young compatriot's body blocked the path in front of them. He had been stripped. Left there, naked. The ultimate humiliation. You are nothing. There is no point to you.

'*Stoy!*' (Halt!)

And there was no point. Not now. It was surrender or die. Death was never the right option. Surrender? No. Not that either, but as long as they were alive there was a chance of something. More shouted instructions. Jeering. Mocking. There was no point in protesting, in pointing out the amnesty, that this shouldn't be happening. These Red brigades were a law unto themselves. They did as they pleased. Jaak and Johann did as they were instructed and lay face down in the mud. Jaak clenched his hands in the soil and squeezed. The smell of the earth. The scurry of insects.

# Chapter 19

## Maria
## November 1988

It was deep autumn: cold, windy and dreich. I hurried along the walkway, not looking at anything other than the ground, on my way to the now very familiar Cancer Centre. Its doors hissed themselves open for me. I smiled at the receptionists as I passed my appointment card over, was checked in, and took my seat. I liked to take the same seat, if it was available. The one by the window.

I always hoped that I might see young Angie there, but I never did. So many of the same faces – people I shared an illness with, had a peculiar connection with – but not her. I felt so guilty about the way I had left her that day at The Laigh. It was so very rude. What must she have thought of me? I had a burning desire to offer my apologies, to make amends, but mostly, of course, I wanted to make sure that she was well. She seemed like such a vulnerable soul, despite all of her bravado, and she had touched me in the most unexpected of ways. I couldn't quite define it. It didn't feel maternal or sisterly, but it was deeper than the comradeship of simply being a fellow patient. I did believe I truly cared about her for some unfathomable reason.

Of course – even though the weather was foul – after my appointment I would go and spend time at my beach, as I now believed it was somehow fundamental to my survival. I was just manoeuvring my way around the roundabout at the top of Leith Walk when I decided to pull in and pick up some delicacies from Valvona and Crolla's delicatessen; that little slice of Italy in the centre of Edinburgh. Such a wonderful shop! The aroma of coffee and distant places, a distant time. Staff were clad in old-fashioned aprons and equipped with equally old-fashioned manners and charm. Ah, it was heaven! I could spend hours perusing the cheeses, olives and cold meats from the chilled counter; the pastas, oils, breads, and wines from the shelves that stretched to the ceiling. A lovely chunk of Parmesan, a blue Brie, some herbed olives, a nice bottle of Barolo, and some splendid crusty bread filled my bag as I left the shop to the ubiquitous *"Ciao Bella!"* It was both charming and flattering. I did enjoy it so!

I was just about to drive off when I glimpsed a commotion of some sort. Peering through the murk and greyness of a foul Edinburgh evening in late November I tried to focus. There, amongst the shadows of the tenements, picked out by the dull glow of the street-lights, two figures were in some kind of a tussle. I hesitated then looked away. It was none of my business. But as my headlights swung across them I saw her. Angie. She was being pushed against the wall by a large thuggish looking fellow; her face staring up at his. I had no idea of what might be going on, but it certainly wasn't anything good.

What should I do? I had never been in such a situation before. I hardly knew the girl after all. It was her affair, not mine, surely. But no, something made me stay. I sat there, my headlights glaring at them, making a display of whatever might be going on. The man turned around and glowered at me; such a vile, vicious look on his face. I pushed my hand on the car's horn with as much ferocity as I could muster. It blared loudly and persistently and I must admit I was rather enjoying it!

The door of the public house on the corner opened and a couple of people came out to investigate what was causing the commotion. More stopped in the street. It seemed I was drawing attention to myself and, more importantly, to the stramach playing out in the glare of my headlights. The man pushed Angie back against the wall, his finger in her face, anger spewing from him and he strode off, a nasty air in his wake.

# Chapter 20

Angie
November 1988

I couldnae believe it! It was her, Maria, who had gone
an shone her lights on us. Blasted her horn. Big Davy
had nashed off as soon as folk started looking. Noticing.
Christ knows what she was thinking. Ye dinnae mess wi
folk like him an get away wi it. He'll only come back
twice as hard. At least he didnae know that I knew her. I
could plead innocence – *Naw. No idea who she was
mate. Some busy-body. No idea at aw.*

I was watching him an watching her, praying that she
wouldnae make a move until he was well out o sight. It
was like she'd read my mind. Knew the score. She just
sat there an watched. Waited till he was gone.
Everybody else had turned away, got back on wi their
own shit. I straightened myself up. Dusted myself down.
A discreet wee nod o recognition at her an I was about
to head off. He'd get me again in a few minutes. Nae
point pretending otherwise.

Only she didnae drive off, did she! She pulled up just
around the corner an opened her door.

'Angie! Angie dear,' she called in a loud whisper.

I should've moved off. Walked away. Pretended I
didnae know her, but I jerked my head up the road an

she understood. It was freezing an the wind was howling away, making the rain slash into my face. It was bloody awful. Naebody hanging around there that didnae need to be. I figured a wee bit o shelter would be good. I caught her up an jumped in beside her.

She wasnae like I thought she'd be. No full o questions. No full o sympathy. I couldnae make her out. No one bit!

She just smiled an said, 'Where to dear?'

'Eh.' I stopped. Thought. Aye, where to? Big Davy had only been putting the frighteners on. No been working hard enough. No been moving enough gear. No been pulling enough punters. Christ!

'I've been sick Davy! Really, really sick, ye know?' Well, I had been. Okay, I was feeling fine, well, as good as, but ye milk it, eh? I mean, I just felt different, is aw. I just wanted something else. Anything else. 'Ye cannae expect me to – '

'Oh, aye I can. Just you watch me sweetheart!'

*

Anyway, where to? Aye, where to? Course I was gonnae go back to Leith. Junction Street. Get her to drop me there. Close enough but no too close. I gave her directions an we headed off down The Walk. She slowed down a bit an looked at me.

'You know, if I can help dear; if there is anything at all I can do, just let me know.'

'Aye, well, it's no that easy, is it?'

'Sometimes it is, dear. Sometimes it is.'

She turned back an watched the road, thank Christ. Her driving wasnae the best.

'When one puts one's mind to it. Well, you know,' she added.

Nuh! Nuh I didnae know. She had no clue. There was nothing she could do. Nothing I could do. My life was shit, an that was that.

'There was a time when I was in a very nasty situation. Unpleasant men, rather like your friend, I imagine, well, they kept me prisoner; forced me to prostitute myself.'

If she hadnae been staring at the darkness through the windscreen she'd've seen my chin hit the floor! Was I hearing this right? There's this posh woman aw wrapped up in smartness an wealth an she's telling me she was a hooker! Was she having a laugh at my expense? Telling some stupid story? It didnae seem so but...

'How come? I mean. Christ!'

'Well, do you remember me telling you about my memory loss?'

'Aye. Course.'

'And my husband?'

'Aye.'

'Well, there were a few years in between them you see; between my waking up and my meeting Andrew, you see? And during that time I was living in a brothel. Kept under lock and key. Used. I worked for them for quite some time, pilfering money when I could. A few pennies here, a few pennies there soon added up. The clients didn't notice. I felt I deserved it! Don't you dear?'

'Christ, aye!' I could just picture her doing it an aw. There was something, I dunno, something gutsy about her. Like she could get away wi murder. 'An ye got away how?'

'Well, I had planned it over many months, years actually. Finally, late one night, when I believed the time was right, I waited until the last light had been switched off and the house was sitting in silence. Gripping my shoes in my hand I tiptoed down the stairs in my stocking-feet so very slowly. One step. Listen. Breathe.

108

Another. Listen. Breathe. It was agonizing because I was so desperate to run, to bolt my way out of there. To change my life into something bearable – assuming there was such a thing, but you see dear, I knew I couldn't run. One hurried, ill prepared step and the whole game could be over.

'I knew which steps on the stairs creaked and avoided them as best I could. A cough broke the silence. The squeak of a bed followed. I froze, praying that there would be no footsteps. I waited, hardly daring to breathe. Can you imagine?'

She glanced ower at me, her eyebrows raised.

'Aye, an the rest!'

She nodded her head an flicked her gaze back to the road.

'I was nearly there. A quick dash across the back hall and on through to the kitchen. I didn't dare use the lights and had to trust to my instincts; to what I had practised when I could. There were only a few occasions when I had been able to actually walk this through. Our movements were so controlled, you see? I had played this entire scenario over in my head though, practising and practising, again and again. I knew there were six paces to be taken before I got to the office. On the wall to the right sat the key cabinet. That was the most dangerous part. I had to break the glass to get the key to the back door. I used my shoe, wrapped in a towel.'

She laughed just a wee bit an mimed hitting at something in the air. I was hooked, so I was!

'Aye! And?'

She smiled an carried on. 'A firm but gentle tap. It wasn't enough. A harder tap. It was no good. I would have to make more noise than I had anticipated; than was safe. The bedrooms were quite far away. If I were quick enough, didn't make any mistakes, I could make

109

it. I remember exhaling, taking a hefty swing at it. The glass finally shattering, shouting its way across the stone floor. Again and again and again. Oh my dear, the noise! So unbearably loud. I reached in for the key. It was easily identifiable because it was so large and chunky. My fingers snatched at it, curled tightly around it and I fled.'

We'd stopped at the lights. She stopped talking, sort o stared at me as if she'd forgotten who I was. Weird like.

'I'm sorry dear, am I boring you?'

'Naw! No at aw. This is pure brilliant.'

An it was. Someone else's life. Someone else doing mental shit! I thought about me. I'd done nothing like that. Hadnae stood up for myself like that. Hadnae decided enough was enough an made a run for it. Naw, no me. I'd just let everything happen. It was like I'd sunk into this cess pit o a place that was mine an I'd just stayed there. Just treading water, staying alive. Just. Fuck's sake. What a waste o space.

'That day at The Laigh. Do you remember?' she asked.

'Aye. When you did a runner!'

'Quite dear! And, I do apologise. I had wanted to tell you then but–'

The lights had changed. The car behind flashed its headlights at us.

'Oops!' she said wi a quiet laugh an pulled away again. 'You see, I believe that when people like you and I meet – people who have shared experiences – there's an understanding. Something deep and primordial. I felt it then and I feel it now.'

She turned to look at me. 'Do correct me if I'm wrong but, well, am I?'

'Eh. Naw. No that far off the mark.' Cos, aye, I'd felt

it too. Something a wee bit weird. A wee bit different.

# Chapter 21

## Maria
## November 1988

I had surprised myself, getting rather carried away in the telling of my story. I wasn't used to having company, you see; to just chatting to someone, and I found it all a bit peculiar, but there I was, going back to places I hadn't visited for such a very long time and sharing them. My memory of that time came back instantly. From the moment I began telling Angie I could actually feel everything, see everything. It was as if I were reliving it all. And in a strange way it was also new to me. As the story unfolded I too was learning about my past. The past that had been so deeply buried all those years ago.

I worried that I was perhaps boring her. An old lady wandering off amidst her memories. She assured me that I wasn't and her face also confirmed that. It appeared I had something interesting to tell. I continued.

'Well, I bit my lip as a piece of broken glass sunk itself into my foot. I balanced myself against the wall and winced as I pulled the shard out of my flesh. It sent a burning pain rushing up my leg. I could feel sticky warm blood. There was no time to do anything about it. I ran back through the kitchen, fumbled for the keyhole, and unlocked the back door. Lights had been turned on and lit up the garden. I didn't dare look back. There was no point, you see? I just ran and prayed that I had enough of a head start. There was shouting behind me. Furious voices. I knew that my escape had been discovered.

'I clambered over the high back wall – old rough stone that left ledges, indentations, foot holds – avoiding the front gate and the driveway. That would give me more cover, more time, a decent head start. My knees were grazed but that didn't matter. Once over I hurriedly pulled my socks on. I knew that I had blood on my hands. A good deal of it. I pushed my feet into my shoes and closed my eyes to the pain. There was probably still glass in there, but I had to get away. Rise above it.

'That house had been all that I had known. What lay beyond was a mystery to me. I had heard talk of "town" and it didn't sound like a far-off place. The soft hush of the town's night-time lights in the dark confirmed the way. There was no moon and I had no light. It would have been a giveaway anyway. The darkness, for then, was my ally.

'After I had scrambled through some waste ground, perhaps an unkempt garden, I came to a road and I followed it, keeping myself hidden behind the hedgerow that stood tall on either side. The town wasn't as far as I had first thought and it didn't take very long at all to reach it. I guessed fifteen, perhaps twenty minutes, but time is a difficult thing to master in such situations, when one is fleeing for one's life! A low rhythmic thumping rumbled through the silence. It was drawing closer like a mechanical beast. A terror gripped me; swept through me. Oh, my dear, you can't imagine! I wanted to scream, but I didn't know why. That chugging had been something awful, somewhere, somehow. I fought to hold on to my thoughts, to control them, to calm my breathing. I had to be rational. It was a train. Just a train. Surely that was a good thing. It was nothing to fear. Anonymous, fast, travelling long distances. It would suit me very well.

'I had no idea of the cost, but surely I had more than enough to take me far away from there. Would it even stop in "town"? My God, I didn't even know where I was, never mind who I was. I should have tried to find out more. Leaving like that without any knowledge of...anything.'

We were being summoned to a halt by more traffic lights. The street was simply awash with them! Stop start. Stop start. I much preferred country driving. I took the opportunity to look across at Angie. She had twisted around and curled one leg under herself. Her face was lit up by the red of the lights. The click-click of the pedestrian crossing. The pitter-patter of the rain. The swish of the wipers. The hum of the heating. A blur of rain-smudged lights drifting into the distance. Peculiar, unreal, other-worldly.

'So?' Angie asked, snapping me out of my reverie.

The lights had changed and I pulled off again.

'Well, I really wanted to find a place with enough light for me to check my foot. It was throbbing angrily and horribly painful. I didn't want to wait for sunrise, though it was mid-summer and that would come soon enough. I wanted to be gone by then. To be untraceable. Hidden. Someone else. Someone of my own making.

'There was no choice but to walk along the pavements for the last few hundred yards or so. I felt so obvious. Such an easy target. Barely anyone else was around. Houses. People asleep in their houses. The odd car. I hurried on, praying that none of them were looking for me. A thumping heart as they drew close. A

114

breath held. A blown out exhalation of relief when they drove on by.

'Finally I had reached the station. I ran up to the door, and pushed at it, anticipating escape, but it was locked. I looked around, quite desperate, in search of some place to hide. On the other side of the car park I could make out some bushes. They would do. I dashed across, took cover and hid, crouching in the soil amongst the foliage, waiting for the arrival of whoever might work there. A car swooped in, circled around, stopped. It sat there idling for a while. I didn't dare look; if I couldn't see them they wouldn't see me, like a child! The click of an opening door, the sound of footsteps getting closer, then retreating again. Some mumbled utterance and they drove off again. I could breathe! After an awfully long time, so long that my legs had become stiff, a woman finally arrived and opened up the station. I gave her a few minutes before walking in.

'Where. Where is the next train going?' I stammered out. That wasn't good enough, but the transition from words in my head to words from my tongue was a difficult one. My accent must have been awful. My words stuck. I could feel my face redden, my legs weaken. But she smiled.

'She looked me up and down. I didn't like that, but I had become used to it. People often looked at me like that. Like I was a strange thing. An oddity. "Edinburgh," she answered. Perfect! She stamped a ticket and handed it to me, still smiling. Her smile had reverted to being soft and friendly and I became wrapped in its warmth, if you can understand that.'

'Oh aye,' Angie replied. 'I get that.'

'I limped out of the station buildings, my ticket clenched tightly in my hand. This was it. I was going somewhere of my choosing. I was terrified and excited and it was all so very new. I was me, Maria. It hadn't said that on my identity card, but I had taken great pleasure in tearing that into little pieces and discarding it. I didn't need one any more and I could be anything I wanted to be. Maria had somehow felt right and so it was. I had officially become Maria.

'Steam billowed out of the train. The noise of its engines, its brakes, the screech of its whistle. All over-powering, deafening. My knees buckling at that feeling again. That distant unidentifiable fear. You know, I still have this inexplicable fear of trains. Anyway, the train seemed to take an age to finally come to a halt. I gripped the handrail, climbed hesitantly up the steps and looked left and right. A long corridor. A row of doors that opened up into compartments. People sitting in them. Strangers. Strangers staring. I carried on, hoping to find an empty compartment, a space just for me. There wasn't one, but I did find the toilets. I crept in and locked the door. The smell was none too pleasant, the seat splashed on, but I sat down anyway and washed my foot as best I could. There were indeed small pieces of glass hiding amongst the skin and they were difficult to remove. My nails were long and strong and I was able to use them as tweezers, in a fashion. I did the best I could in the circumstances.

'I plucked up the courage to open one of the compartments and sat down, not looking at anyone, trying to be inconspicuous, invisible. Perhaps I should smile, say something? I didn't know. Best not, I decided. I squeezed myself into the corner of the compartment, my head turned towards the outside, my body barely visible to anyone walking along the corridor. Were they even still after me? Was I worth anything to them? It wasn't as if I were the only girl that they kept there.

'The train rattled on through towns and cities I didn't know. The further we travelled the more I began to allow myself to let my guard down, to relax, to take in the scenery. I would absorb everything and store it in my new self; my new memories. Flat land became hillier, wooded; the trees denser, taller, beautiful. The light, the sky, somehow felt more familiar the further north we travelled. There was a crispness, a clarity to it that whispered a sense of belonging. Edinburgh. I couldn't wait. I would be there soon. My name is Maria. I am twenty four. I am from Edinburgh.'

# Chapter 22

Angie
November 1988

She took her eyes off the road an turned an smiled at me.

'Which way now, dear?' she asked.

We'd reached the bottom o The Walk. I should've got out then, but I didnae want to. No until she'd finished her story.

'Eh, take a left. It's no far now.'

She was silent for a bit. The clicking o the indicator, the hum o the fan heater, the patter o the rain. I let her drive right on past my road-end an got her to pull in at the school on Junction Place.

'So what happened then?' I asked, when we'd parked up an she'd pulled the brakes on.

She put her hands on her chest and looked up at the roof o the car. 'Oh my dear, you can't imagine the fear. If they had caught me, well, it doesn't bear thinking about! But here we are!'

'Aye.'

'I was lucky, I suppose.'

'Did aw right for yerself, but?'

'Perhaps.'

'An yer memory? That never came back then?'

'No. No it didn't. I met Andrew, we married, and I had to become this estate owner's wife. This new person, and so it was.'

'Ye must wonder though, aye?'

She just raised her eyebrows. 'Oh, enough about me, my dear. What about you? Who is Angie?'

I squirmed a bit. What could I say? Compared to a story like that? The truth? Aye, why no? Didnae matter, did it?

'What you see is what you get. Junkie, waste o space, nothing to tell.'

'Oh, come now. That's not what I see. We all have our stories, don't we? Our secrets. We all do foolish things, but we learn, and we move on, and we are never ashamed of who we are or how we got there!'

'Ye think, aye?' No so sure about that myself. My middle name could be ashamed. But hey, I figured she deserved a wee bit frae me. 'There's no much to me, like. Orphan. Well, no really, but dumped by my ma when I was four. Brought up in an orphanage. Kicked out at sixteen. Met Deke, my man. Drank too much, but it was a laugh, eh? Then we got intae drugs. That wasnae such a laugh. Do whatever needs doing to get what I need. Turn tricks. Steal. Aw the things they tell you about junkies, that's me. Aye.'

'You see, we're really not so very different!'

*Oh aye, we are. Whole different ball game! Shouldnae've said that. Shouldnae've said a damned thing. Switch it back. Switch it away.*

'Do ye no want to find out? I mean, yer roots? Aw that stuff. Ye must want to know, aye?' I asked.

'Yes dear, I do, but it's so very difficult. What if I don't like what I find?'

She turned her head away an sniffed. I thought maybe she was greetin an I felt aw awkward an guilty. I

119

reached for the door.

'Wait a minute dear,' she said, as she leaned ower an opened up her glove compartment. A wee light came on an picked out a wad o cash. Like hundreds, maybe even thousands o pounds. It was in neat wee bundles aw tied up wi rubber bands. Christ's sake, you dinnae leave that kind o money sitting in yer car, do ye? No folk like her. No a little auld woman like that. That's asking for trouble, so it is. She fumbled about amongst it an pulled out a pen an a wee yellow post-it-note. She wrote her name, her number, an address on it, an pushed it into my hand.

'If there is ever anything I can do. If you're ever in any sort of trouble. Anything at all. Or if you just want a chat or to go for a coffee or a drink. Anything at all. You just give me a call. Will you do that for me, dear?'

'Aye, right,' I said, thinking, as if? She'd never want to speak to the likes o me again. No now that she knew.

'Do you promise me, Angie?' she said, squeezing my hand, staring right into my eyes.

'Aye. Aye, I promise.' What else could I say?

# Chapter 23

## Jaak
### USSR Summer 1953

They were taken to Tallinn in trucks full of other prisoners: civilians, enemies of the State, threats to security. Most were unaware of what they were supposed to have done. Some simply had land, had wealth, had an education, came from a family of substance. In Tallinn Jaak and Johann lost sight of each other, neither knowing where the other might be. Now it didn't do to wonder, to hanker. They had both been through this before. The inevitability of their fate. It was purely survival from here on in. Nothing else.

Jaak was herded on to a train and taken across the border into Russia and then on to Moscow. From Moscow they travelled north – far north – spending days cooped up in a cattle car designed for animals or carcasses, not humans so tightly packed that they could barely move, barely breathe. It was summer now and the heat of the sun sucked away the oxygen the prisoners snatched at. Their bodies stank: sweat, filth, and fear. A vicious concoction from which there was no relief. There was no toilet, just a small hole in the corner of the carriage which reeked of human waste; more and more of it as the journey continued. They were in darkness, apart from shards of light which broke tauntingly through the wooden slats, momentarily blinding if they caught your eyes; seared across them like a branding iron.

Jaak wasn't sure which was worse; to be like him, aware of the hell that lay ahead, or to have to imagine, to wonder what might be in store when they finally reached the labour camp they had been assigned to. He knew that the further north they travelled, the worse their conditions would be.

At last the train stopped and they were hurried out. The political prisoners, criminals, traitors. Russians, Ukrainians, Latvians, Lithuanians, Estonians. People of no value. Limbs ached. Legs refused to behave. It was as if they had a mind of their own. They would wander, swerve. Some men stumbled as they were jabbed at with rifles in an attempt to speed them up, to intimidate them.

A young man walking in front of Jaak was silently crying, made evident by the shudder of his shoulders. He was fighting it, trying to cling on to whatever dignity he could muster, but it was more than he was capable of. His feet tripped over each other and he fell, lying helplessly in the dirt.

'*Vstavay*!' (Get up!) '*Sobaka*!' (Dog!) was screeched at him by the guards.

Jaak stooped forward to help him up, grabbed his jacket and pulled him to his feet. 'Stay up lad, for Christ's sake!' he muttered as purposefully as he could. As discreetly as he could. No eye contact. Nothing beyond the minimum.

The boy gathered himself, pushed himself. 'Sven,' the youngster managed to force out, as he looked up beseechingly at Jaak. 'I am Sven.'

His legs were barely able to keep pace with Jaak as he anxiously tried to make a connection. Jaak ignored him. Humanity was not allowed to show itself here.

Half of the prisoners were ushered towards a collection of dismal sheds which served as housing. Jaak and several hundred others were led in the opposite direction. They were travelling on, first by truck, packed together like sheep bound for slaughter, kilometre after interminable kilometre, bumping along roads which barely existed. Their journey then continued by boat; their destination Kolyma, in the very far north of Siberia. A place so far from anywhere that escape wasn't even a worry for the guards, let alone a possibility for the prisoners.

The sun barely set at this time of year and nature was in a rush to bring forth all of her blossoms and berries. The continuation of life. The mountains that stretched around the camp were blushed with the red of lingonberries. Mountain briar cloaked the earth with delicate flowers and perfume, a peculiarly tender scent in this harsh environment where everything else smelled wet, musty, almost unpleasant. Vines clung tightly to their surroundings, their tendrils clambering, gouging, stealing life, smothering. Larches stretched, green and luscious, soaking up the precious daylight. Mosquitoes massed in clouds so thick that it felt as if they might suffocate you; so many of them swarming like a poisonous gas into your mouth, up your nose, making you gag and choke. The prisoners covered their mouths and noses as best they could, with arms, hands, sleeves, lapels. The guards hung face nets from their hats.

The camp itself was something entirely different. An

123

alien place. Grey and dismal despite the colour all around. Places such as these could never be anything but ugly. Over the entrance hung the inscription, "**Labour is a matter of honour, a matter of glory, a matter of valour and heroism.**" Jaak cleared his throat as he glanced at the familiar quote. It had hung over the last camp he had been sent to when he had been separated from his family that first time. A knot caught in his stomach at the memory. He knew that there was no honour to be had here.

A long low building housed their beds and little else. Row upon row of bunk beds. A hierarchy had already established itself. The criminals were at the top. The lords of this manor. They were physically strong and good workers and that was all that mattered here.

Jaak lay down on his bunk. He knew the importance of sleep. There was never enough time for it to fully rest you, and you had to do your best to grab it when you could. All that he could do now was get through each day. The world outside no longer existed. It was this camp, this day, this hour, this minute, and nothing else. He knew that if he were to survive, it had to be this way. A switching off of everything else. Every memory, every feeling, everything human had no place here. Maarja. Her face. Her touch. Her smile. He desperately wanted to follow the image. The dream. Live it for one final moment. No. He couldn't allow that. He sent her away. Humanity had left.

# Chapter 24

Maria
December 1988

I had watched the arrival of the pink-footed geese.
Thousands of them swarming in, in relentless waves,
screeching overhead in a great "V" until breaking into
mayhem, dropping and lifting again, swirling and
spinning, before landing clumsily on the ground. It
amazed me that so many of them could manoeuvre
through one another without collision. The bay was
smothered in them, their cries almost deafening. I trod
lightly as I walked along my usual track at dusk, not
wanting to disturb them but yearning to be amongst
them. There was something magical about them, and it
was so uplifting. If the weather permitted I would wrap
myself up in layers before heading down and sitting on
one of the rocks that stood proudly in the boggy grass.
Listening. Just listening as the tumult slowly slipped
into waves of sound that gradually lessened, cries
becoming whispers, until the geese settled down for the
night and fell finally silent. Then I too would wend my
way home, satisfied, grateful.

And so the days and weeks passed, my time spent on
beaches, in woods. I had indeed picked up a book on

local wildlife, and a pair of rather splendid binoculars had come my way through a chance encounter with a birdwatcher who had offered me the use of his old ones. It was pleasing how some people formed a group; a connection made through their love of nature. My fellow birdwatchers would smile and nod and offer pleasantries. Some would helpfully point out unusual sightings – an egret here, a tern there – and I was fast becoming something of an expert. I took photographs and made sketches of birds, trees, seaweed, anything that took my fancy.

When I wasn't out amongst nature I would be wrapped up in my little cottage, a log fire burning, the wash of flames reflecting off the polished wooden floor, highlighting my scattering of Persian rugs. I would sit in silence just looking at my world through uncurtained windows – dusk settling on the bay, clouds rolling in from the sea, the moon glinting on the water if it was calm, or splintered shards fracturing across the waves in a storm; birds, always birds.

December was suddenly upon us. Fairy lights and decorations lit up windows and doors. A jolliness clung to the village. Smiles and warm greetings were offered from neighbours and strangers. We had never "done" Christmas at Glenbirrie, as Andrew had said it was commercial poppycock and was to be ignored. But this year I felt like doing something: decorating, joining in, being happy and frivolous. I decided I would drive in to Edinburgh to buy some decorations. Before leaving I argued with myself. Perhaps it was a mistake? I wasn't sure of where to go, after all. Where did one even buy Christmas decorations? Was there such a thing as a Christmas decorations shop? *Oh, don't be so foolish*, I chastised myself. It would become obvious. Of course it would! All would be well. It might even be fun. And off

I went, before I had managed to change my own mind once more.

I had only just recently convinced myself to venture beyond the village to do some shopping. It was all so new to me, you see. I had spent a lifetime of having everything done for me, of barely leaving the estate so I wasn't used to this at all. Edinburgh. Princes Street. People. Everywhere there were people. The streets were jam-packed with bodies jostling and rushing. I felt uncomfortable, even panicky; I had an urgent need to seek refuge from the mayhem! A building I recognised caught my attention. Jenners. It was right there. Grand and imperious, made of red sandstone, Gothic and glorious. Caryatids stood proudly supporting the pillars of the building. Ornate stonework adorned the exterior. Swirls and curls, goddesses and lions. Window displays were festooned with decorations. I stood, staring at a memory.

An angry complaint from a stranger and a jostle from another broke my reverie. It seemed I was causing some annoyance. I composed myself and walked in through the stately entrance.

I wandered through the building to the grand hall, trying to avoid getting in the way of people. They all seemed to know where they were going, what they were doing. My fingers slid along the wooden balustrade as I made my way up the stairs of the three floors. Waterfalls of fairy lights cascaded down them. A Christmas tree stretched from floor to ceiling. White lights. So simple yet so overwhelmingly beautiful. I couldn't help but stand and stare. The girl I had been all those years ago was still so much a part of me. She took me back to the last time I had been in this building some forty years ago.

## 1949

Andrew had taken Maria to Jenners a few weeks after they had begun courting. Of course she had walked past the shop frontage many a time, glanced longingly at the clothes in the windows; the beautiful extravagant things that she could never hope to own. But now, here she was, walking through the doors as if she were a woman of substance. Her clothes, despite being the best that she owned, felt shabby and commonplace. A wave of embarrassment washed over her as she was sure that everyone could see that she didn't belong; that she was a cheap fraudster. But she was with him. Well, she was walking in his shadow, but that was fine. She understood.

He strode through to the ladies' department and introduced her to one of the assistants.

'I would like you to kit this young lady out in something akin to that.' He gestured towards one of the manikins. 'Yes, that would do nicely, and another two or three outfits of a similar style.' He smiled, confidently. 'And all of those accoutrements you ladies like so much. Anything she might need. The entire kit and caboodle!'

'Yes, sir. Of course.' The assistant bowed slightly as she spoke. 'If you would like to follow me, madam.'

Maria returned soon enough, laden with bags and carrying the biggest smile, to find Andrew sitting in one of the armchairs reading his copy of "The Times". He glanced up at her and cocked his head, grimaced more than smiled.

'My dear, why don't you pop back in and dress with what I have just purchased for you. You don't really want these old rags now, do you?' he suggested, tweaking distastefully at her old dress, her cardigan.

'I, I suppose not,' she had replied, sheepishly, feeling

that she should have known. Of course she should have. She was such an embarrassment! That nasty blush was shouting from her neck, crawling up her face. *Oh God!*

He had smiled at her, shaking his head slightly, seemingly amused. 'I am sure this nice young lady can dispose of your old garments for you.' He looked expectantly across to the sales assistant.

'Yes, sir. Of course.'

When Maria returned his look was approving as he crooked his arm for her to take. 'Well now, don't you look splendid!' he said, patting her hand, and at once she felt accepted.

'Thank you so much. They are beautiful. Everything is so beautiful!'

In truth they weren't to her taste. They were plain and smart and boring, but undoubtedly expensive. A beige silk blouse, a fine woollen suit, also beige, light brown shoes with a strap and a low heel, a matching handbag. They did make her feel special though. Someone. If not her, at least someone of import. Someone who had a right to be here. Someone who belonged on his arm.

\*

They had just finished tucking into the most delicious lunch of poached salmon, sautéed potatoes, and creamed spinach followed by cranachan with fresh raspberries for desert. It was all so luxurious.

'Marry me,' Andrew had said, quite out of the blue, as he poured her another glass of white wine.

'I...I beg your pardon?' She was sure she hadn't heard him correctly. It was barely more than a whisper after all.

He put the wine bottle down and took her hand in both of his, staring deeply into her eyes. 'I think we should get married. What do you say?'

'I...Oh gosh!'

They had only known each other for a matter of weeks, but did that really matter? This would mean security. Belonging. She would be safe. But she wasn't whom he thought her to be. How was she going to get around that? She had no documents, no birth certificate, Maria simply didn't exist! Alongside the excitement of being asked, a panic set in. She would be found out and everything would slip away.

'Just say yes. That's all you have to do.' He stood up, walked around the table so that he was beside her, got down on one knee. 'My darling Maria. Will you do me the honour of becoming my wife?'

Heads began to turn. Other customers were watching. Everybody was watching. The waiters had stopped serving. A silence of expectation clung to the dark oak panels, the luxurious crimson velvet curtains, the crystal chandeliers, the linen clad tables, the silver cutlery. Quite how this would all pan out she didn't know, but for now, for this moment it would be a fairy-tale.

'Yes. Yes I will!'

He smiled, stood up, and kissed her hand. A ripple of applause and soft laughter trickled around the room. They embraced.


1988

I felt dizzy. The memory. The time. Yes, that was it. Just the memory. I grasped at the handrail. Swooned. A hand on my shoulder.

'Are you all right?' a young man with a badge asked.

'I...yes...I am so sorry. I just. Yes, I am fine.'

He led me to a chair and sat me down. 'Let me get you some water.'

130

# Chapter 25

Angie
December 1988

Christmas was busy for us, me an Deke. Just like the shops up town, folk were wanting to stock up. *Aye, just a wee bit to get us through, eh.* Students, folk wi good jobs, folk that were just normal. Proper lives. They were round our bit buying, stocking up. Me an Deke were businesslike. Packets o smack an bags o weed an dope, aw ready an waiting. Everything a wee bit light, a wee bit more cut than usual. Crushed sugar, flour, it didnae matter. Folk didnae know any better. The regulars, the junkies, they were just desperate. You could get away wi any auld shit at that time o year. Things dried up, ye see. Dealers shut up shop. We were smart. We planned. Well, Big Davy didnae leave us wi much o an option.

We'd had folk round aw bloody day an night. It had been relentless. I wouldnae mind so much if they'd just do the transaction an go on their way. But naw, they didnae understand that this was a business, no a fucking community centre. Anyway, by two in the morning we had finally managed to shunt the last straggler out the door.

'Fuck's sake. This is pure mental!' I grumbled at Deke as I collapsed beside him on the settee.

'I know, Babes,' he said, taking my hand, pulling me in close, slipping an arm around my shoulder, kissing my head.

I looked up at him, a wee bit alarmed. This wasnae normal. No any more it wasnae. 'What's going on Deke?' I asked, thinking he'd done some shite an he was about to own up.

'I've been thinking.'

Or he's gonnae dump me. Chuck me out for some other woman, someone more like him. 'Aye?' I said, trying to keep my cool.

'How long have we been together now? Eight years?'

'Aye, something like that.' *Aw Christ, here it comes!*

'Do you remember, way back before this.' He glanced around the tip o a room screaming to be cleaned. 'You know, back when we were clean. Clean and happy.'

'Aye. Course I do.'

He pushed me away from him. Grabbed my shoulders tight. Stared hard in my eyes. 'Let's do it, Babes. Let's get clean. You and me both.'

I swallowed hard. This wasnae what I had been expecting at aw. 'An what's brought this on then?' I asked, my voice aw squeaky.

'You. Me. The way it's been since you got sick. It's shit. All shit and I am so sorry.'

He started greetin. Tears rolling down his face. Christ, he was serious. My head was spinning. Thoughts running away aw ower the place. This was huge. This was fucking massive. It wasnae a yes or no thing. I didnae know what to say. Course I wanted to get sorted. Course I did, but shite. This was huge! I'd tried before an fallen flat on my face. He'd never tried. Never even mentioned it. If we both did it?

'Come on, Babes.' He wiped his nose on the back o

132

his hand, swung his long legs around an walked across the room to the desk, pulled open one o the drawers, sat back down wi a leaflet an stared at it a bit, biting at his lip, aw nervous an twitchy like, glancing across at me. Then he gave it to me. Put it in my lap. I picked it up an read. Clouds House, it said. A picture o a big country mansion. Testimonies frae folk. Famous folk that had been there an come out the other side.

I sat quiet for a bit, spinning the leaflet around in my hands, the thoughts around in my head. 'Aye but, it'll cost a fortune.'

'No,' he answered. 'Well, yes, but I can sort it. We can do this, Babes. We really can.'

I was scared. I was scared as fuck. But I wanted it. I wanted it so bad. 'Aye! Aye, let's do it. Me an you!'

He went into the kitchen, came back wi two sets o works aw ready to go. 'Can't go cold turkey right now, can we?'

Naw. Naw we couldnae. Course no.

The next day it was as if that night hadnae happened. Nothing said. Nothing. He got up an headed straight out wi'out a word. Maybe he was off booking something? Maybe it was aw gonnae be sorted in secret? He'd come home wi tickets an everything. *Ready Angie Babe?* Maybe, aye? Maybe?

He got back in the evening. Dark as shit nearly aw day. Darker now. He sat down on the settee, held his arm open for me, but something didnae feel right. There was an anger an I was scared, but I sat down anyway. Ye do, aye? Do as ye're telt. He squeezed my shoulder real hard, so that a pain shot down my arm, across my back. I winced. *Naw, naw, naw.*

He didnae hit me. It was just words. Nasty wicked words that cut like a razor. Sliced their way through everything that was decent. The threat was always there, though. Always that menace. Always expected a doing at some point. He'd snap an I'd get it. But I knew he wasnae like that. No really. That just wasnae him. No Deke. He wasnae one o those sort o guys. Big an strong an powerful, but soft as a wee puppy inside. That's what I loved about him. That softness. Even through aw the shite I knew it was still there. That softness. I mean, when ye've had that, been that way, ye cannae just lose aw o it. It doesnae just go. No aw the way away. That was what I thought.

He whispered right up close to my ear so that I could feel his words. 'So, who the fuck is he then?' He pushed me back an jabbed me in the stomach wi his finger.

'What? I–

'Don't you dare!' Jabbed me again, eyes crazy. 'I know. I know you were with him.' Jab. 'I know you got into his car.' Jab. 'I know you weren't working.' Jab.

I was panicking. *What the hell's he talking about? What's going on?* Then it clicked, aye. Big Davy. He had seen me get in Maria's car. He must've known. Christ, things just got worse. 'You mean up at Elm Row a few weeks back?'

'I mean up at Elm Row. A few weeks back,' he answered slow an nasty an sarky.

'It's no a he, it's a she, Deke. Just a women frae the Centre. The Cancer Centre. We chat, that's aw.'

'Oh really? Do tell.' He grabbed my chin an twisted my head around. 'Come on then. Tell me what you *chat* about!'

Flecks o spit flicked onto my face. He'd lost it. Completely lost it. Paranoid as fuck. Always has struggled wi it, an I didnae get why. It should've been me that was the jealous one, no him. He's the gorgeous one wi aw the women after him. Had to fight them off, stand my ground when there were women around, so I

134

did. Slip my arm through his, rest my head on his shoulder, aw possessive. *Aye. He's mine. Hands off!*

Sometimes he tipped ower the edge, like he was doing right then. Cocaine did that to him. Too much o it made him wiry. Volatile as shit. He must've been wi Big Davy, cracking open some new coke, pure stuff, strong stuff. I needed to get him back. *Say something. Say anything. Sort it!* I was stumbling, blurting.

'She, she's called Maria. Auld woman. Just blethers away to me, aye. Posh too. Christ, you wouldnae believe the money! Keeps a big wad stashed in her car. Working on choring a bit. Easier than turning tricks, eh? Ye dinnae like me turning aw they tricks, eh no, Deke? Eh no?'

He just stared. Wild eyes.

Shouldnae hae said any o that. Shite!

'So where is this cash then, eh? Show me.' He held his hands out. Screeched. 'Show me!'

'I havenae. Couldnae. No yet.' Then it was me that was greetin. Sniffling away like a wee lassie. 'I've got her address, though.' I stuffed the post-it-note she'd given me that night into his hand. 'See?'

I reached for the Rizlas, skinned up, keeping my eye on him aw the while. My hands were shaking. *Stop it, stop it, stop it.* He was pacing, checking out the window, looking back at me, pacing. The one thing that would calm him down was a joint. A decent one. I flicked the lighter, burned the edge o a nice piece o Gold Leb till it started to smoke. I breathed it in. Calmed me down. Better. He was still pacing, muttering nonsense. Noise, no words. Awfie, scary noise. I crumbled the hash into the joint, rolled it up. Fingers no so bad. No so shaky. Tore the edge o the fag packet off, rolled it up to make a roach. *Come on, come on, come on.* Slid it into the end. Twisted the top. Bit the wee bit o paper off. Lit it up as I walked across to where he was standing. Handed it ower.

'Here Deke, honey. Here.'

He took it. A deep draw. Held it far down in his lungs. Blew out a huge plume o blue smoke. Softened him just enough. Edges bending. Untangling. He sat down again. I wrapped myself around him. The veins in his neck were thumping. 'Come on Deke, honey. It's just me an you. Always just me an you,' I whispered, kissing his neck, stroking his hair, nibbling on his ear. 'Me an you.'

Normal folk would fuck. Roll on the floor an fuck. Me an Deke? Me an Deke shot up. But it was okay. We were okay.

# Chapter 26

## Maria
## December 1988

My decorations were up. I must admit I rather liked it. There was a joyfulness to everything. The sparkles and greenery. I had even gone the whole hog and invested in a rather splendid Christmas tree, so tall that it almost reached the ceiling! It came to me in a pot, which was rather clever. I could just pop it in the garden and use it again the following year. Of course it was from a local chap recommended by my friends in the Post Office. What a splendid little shop! Quite what I would have done without them I don't know. My life would certainly have been the poorer for it.

Now that my decorating was done I didn't really know what to do with myself. What did one do at Christmas? I had decided a short while back that I should invest in a television. Andrew had never been a fan and it hadn't really occurred to me before then, but with not feeling quite up to par and, perhaps being just a little bit lonely, I thought it might be prudent. Something to help pass the long dark nights of winter. There was such a splendid choice! Nature programmes, fascinating documentaries, films, and of course, current affairs. I had little knowledge of what was happening in the outside world. My life had been quite extraordinary in its seclusion from everything and I felt like it was now my duty to keep myself informed; up to date.

I had just settled down to watch the news at six when I heard something of a commotion outside. People were in my garden and they were singing! What on earth? I tossed my blanket aside, hurried to the front door and pulled it open. A semi-circle of adults and children, some of whom I had seen before in the village, were standing there, holding lanterns and singing the most beautiful Christmas carols. I felt so very privileged. What a lovely thing to do. Upon leaving I was given a card with a name and address on it.

'We're having a little village get-together this evening at eight. Do come!'

Well, you can imagine my predicament. What was "a little village get-together"? Did one dress for such an occasion? Should one bring a gift? I assumed so. Evenings at the Glenbirrie Estate had always been formal, even when it was just the two of us – Andrew and me – which it usually was. We seldom had official visitors other than during the hunting season. He would host parties of men dressed in tweed. I was expected to keep myself out of the way unless called upon to smile and hold polite conversation. A memory crept up. That day when I realised; when it all made sense.

## 1953

The East Wing was Andrew's private domain, a part of the house that Maria was forbidden from entering, besides which it was always locked. But that day, as she walked past the formidable oak door that led to that forbidden place, there, jutting out from the brass lock was the key! It seemed as though Andrew had forgotten

138

it. How could one resist such a temptation? She glanced around the hallway, up the grand staircase, listened intently. There was nothing. She tried to turn the key, but the door was already unlocked. Slipping her fingers around the cool metal of the handle she pushed; the door clicked open. She slithered between door and frame, closing the door again behind her.

The place should have been empty. Despite knowing that Maria tiptoed along the corridor feeling somewhat contrary: more dark oak doors with brass handles, flagstone floors, raw stone walls, portraits of Andrew's ancestors, grand and proud. It dawned on her how peculiar it was that she hadn't known about any of them. He had never mentioned family, and now these people, these strangers adorning his walls, were her family too, at least in law. She wondered if it were perhaps down to her heritage, her unknown background and he was ashamed of her. No. That didn't make any sense. He had moulded her, made her acceptable, a lady in behaviour and title. Surely, if she were someone to display proudly to his friends, his family should also be accepting of her?

An iciness clung to the walls, to the floor. Not the chill that always sat in this house – such an old large space that never really felt warm – but something more, something different. A shiver crept up her spine. She was about to turn around and leave; pretend that this had never happened. It didn't feel right and she regretted having disobeyed him, having gone against his strict instructions never to enter this wing. It was his house after all. His domain. She should not have intruded.

She had just turned to retrace her steps when she heard a noise; a peculiar noise. The door at the far end of the corridor was slightly ajar and the room beyond, she

139

guessed, was the source of whatever it was that she could hear. She turned back and crept along the corridor to its far end, checking behind herself as she went, pausing at each door and stopping to listen. When she reached the door that stood slightly ajar she pressed her back against the wall and held her breath, listening. The sound was now unmistakable. It was the sound of human copulation! Someone was copulating. She thought at first staff; one of the gamekeeper's family. No. One of the participants was Andrew! She recognised the timbre of his voice, the noises that he made during intercourse.

She was caught in a quandary – a dreadful one. If she were to look she would find her husband in flagrante delicto. Was that really what she wanted? No it wasn't, but if she didn't look she would never know who he was with. It wasn't that she was jealous – there was no love between them; she was quite sure there never had been – but she felt threatened and had to know who her rival might be.

Holding her breath she craned her neck around so that she could just see in. The curtains were closed but an amber light shone from the bedside lamp. She could make out heavy furniture, a four-poster bed with its covers tossed to the floor, and on that bed, Andrew. That was no surprise, but as she focussed, her eyes adjusting to the soft light, she could see that he wasn't with a woman, but with one of his male friends. Flesh on flesh. Bodies writhing. Whispers. Groans. It was soft and loving and beguilingly beautiful. So this was lovemaking as it should be; something she had never experienced before, never witnessed. Lovemaking. She couldn't look away. The noises began to climax with the bodies. This intrusion upon his private life had become too much. She turned

140

and ran.

Now it all made sense. Everything. Why he had chosen her, a person of no consequence, a person with no history. Why their coming together was cold – nothing more than a performance. Why none of it mattered to him. Quite the contrary. She was his charade, his ticket to respectability. It didn't matter to Maria either. He was her security; her reason to be allowed to stay in this country. *I am Maria. I am from Edinburgh.* It had become apparent that if she were to remain as such she would have to keep quiet, protect him and his dark secret which would lead to shame, mockery and imprisonment, were it to have been revealed. No, she wouldn't do that to him, to them. What would be the point? But should she tell him? Let him know that she knew and that she would never breathe a word to anyone else? That he was safe. That they were safe. No, not that either. She would carry on as if nothing had happened.

## 1988

I decided that I should indeed dress for the occasion; make an effort. I had left Glenbirrie in such a state of fluster that I hadn't taken very much at all. A rushed suitcase. Little beyond the essentials really. It seemed I had nothing suitable, nothing festive, or special in the slightest. Oh dear! Perhaps it didn't matter. No, of course it didn't. I was being silly. An attractive scarf to wrap around the crew cut that was taking an eternity to grow out – oh how I missed my long hair, the feel of it on my shoulders, down my back, the gentle soothing massage of the brush – a spray of Chanel, and an application of lipstick would do the trick.

I checked my reflection in the mirror and stared at myself as others might. They would ask questions, want

141

to know more about me. There was too much. Too much to hide. Too much I really didn't care to divulge. I had had a lifetime of pretending. It had to stop, but I had no idea of how to do that. How to begin to tell the truth. I stared at my unnaturally thin body – the result of the chemo-therapy, the inability to eat very much of anything – my clothes too loose, too boring. Not me. I picked at them, tugged at them. No. This was not how I wanted to look any more. Yes, I would get healthy. I would get better, but I would also shop. A complete change of image was required. If I were to learn who I once had been I would have to discard all that I had become. I would have to demolish the new building to uncover the old. Carry out an architectural dig on myself as it were.

As I stood there in a state of flux, Angie slipped into my thoughts. Dear Angie. The peculiar girl with whom, it seemed, I could be honest, I could expose myself to, at least to some degree. I realised that I missed her. How I wished I had said more than just, call me if you're in trouble. I could have asked for her number as well, made it more obvious that I simply liked her, enjoyed her company. But perhaps not. Perhaps that was foolish thinking. Why would a young thing like her possibly want to be friends with an old woman like me? It was just circumstance that had thrown us together. We were both sick. Cancer patients. It was hardly the basis for a friendship, nor for any form of a relationship.

I wouldn't go to the get-together. It would be easier to make up an excuse. I was old and I was sick after all. I felt sure that it would be understood, accepted, if I were even to be missed at all. I turned the lights off and sat upstairs, in the back bedroom, from where I had a view of some of the village. I imagined the goings on at the get-together: couples chatting, small groups forming, glasses being filled. I wasn't sure if I even wanted to be a part of that.

A crash distracted me. Breaking glass. It sounded frightfully close! I wondered if there had been a car accident and dashed to the other side of the house from where I could see the road. As I peered through the darkness I noticed that the interior light of my car was on. I focussed. There were figures in my garden! It seemed I was being burgled, my car ransacked! I wasn't having that!

# Chapter 27

## Jaak
## USSR Summer 1953

Jaak was awoken by the harsh clang of the bell. It was five o'clock, but the sun was already high in the sky. Night time bore little difference to day at this time of year. He and the other prisoners silently slipped into line. They took the tools they were given – pickaxes, shovels, wheelbarrows – and traipsed along the track to the mines. Gold. Mining for gold, but barely clothed, barely fed, barely human. They had to meet their quota, even though it was so very difficult to do for the strong and healthy, let alone the sickly, weak men most of the prisoners had become. Failure to do what was expected of you could mean execution; your body tossed onto a truck then buried in a pit with others whose crime had been not being strong enough.

Rations were meagre. Coloured water they called soup. A chunk of bread. It wasn't enough to keep hunger at bay, to settle restless stomachs. The weakest drifted painfully away until they were of no use and were disposed of.

Jaak was swinging his pickaxe with all the strength

he could muster, his hands blistered and bleeding. Sweat trickled down his brow streaking the dirt, leaving his face scarred, blurred.

'Hello,' a young voice chirped, totally unbefitting the time, the place.

Jaak turned to his side. It was that boy again. The boy from the journey. He had survived thus far. That was good.

'Sven,' Jaak acknowledged, nodding. 'Still alive then.' He turned away and continued to swing at the relentless stone.

'You never told me your name,' the boy said.

'Jaak. I'm Jaak.'

'Estonian?'

Jaak paused and glanced back at Sven. He kept himself to himself. It was safer that way. He didn't like anyone knowing anything about him. Knowledge could be used against you. Keep yourself as an insignificant shadow. That was best. He narrowed his eyes in reply.

'I thought –' Sven continued but was cut off mid sentence.

'Lad. Keep quiet. Do your work.'

Sven sighed. He was desperate for help, for a mentor, for a friend. Since that first sign of kindness, that helping hand, he had hoped it might be Jaak. The gangsters had already begun to show an interest. He was both young and good-looking, with finely chiselled cheekbones, gentle eyes, and a softness that could be described as feminine. They would take full advantage soon enough and there was nothing he could do about it. But he wanted one person. Just one person to trust.

He made sure that he stood in line with Jaak on the march back to camp. It felt safer. Conversation was allowed there, though most were too tired to bother. Sven persisted.

'My mother was Estonian.'

'Was?'

'They shot her.'

Jaak nodded. It was brutally commonplace and barely worthy of a mention. He went against his better judgement and continued the conversation.

'Where was she from?'

'Narva.'

'And you?'

'Narva too. My father was Russian, so that was my first language, and now I have no-one to speak Estonian with anyway.' He shrugged.

'Keep it that way. We speak Russian if we speak at all. It's safer.'

It made Jaak feel like a traitor, burying his heritage like that, but it was for the best. Here, be like everyone else. Don't stand out. Blend in. Every day was the same. Get up. Work. Collapse into bed and hope that you will live to see the following day. There was so much he could explain to Sven, warn him about, but perhaps it was best not to know. Find out for yourself and maybe have longer to be optimistic. Imagine that there might be a way out. Something easier. Something better.

With each day that passed the pain deepened. The hunger became more acute. Sickness was inescapable: malnutrition, scurvy, tuberculosis, and fevers. The heat sapped everything from you. Mosquitoes and lice constantly crawled over your skin, sucking at your blood, making a redness so angry and painful; food for the infections that sat waiting, taking hold, growing. The ability to carry on was like a numbness. A dull numbness that only just kept you alive.

Sven would still seek Jaak out, still try and force conversation. The effervescence he managed to exude in spite of it all reminded Jaak of Imre. He hoped that they wouldn't share the same fate.

'What is it you did then?' Sven asked.

Jaak allowed himself something akin to a laugh. 'Article fifty eight. Life sentence. You?'

'Article fifty eight as well. I don't even know what that means. They never said what I'd done.' He shrugged. 'It was just article fifty eight. They beat me until I signed a confession. I didn't even read it. Just signed. A man can only take so much. Ten years. But I'll see it out. I'll get home.'

'I'm sure you will, lad. I'm sure you will.'

It didn't take long for the change to happen. For men to slip into something else. Something beastly. Three weeks, perhaps four for the strong of mind, the resilient. The relentless labour that racked bodies, beatings that scored skin and shattered souls, hunger that stole flesh and all things human. They were no longer men. Creatures of the gulag.

It was even taking hold of Sven. Jaak could see it in the weight of his body, the stoop of his shoulders, the hollowness of his eyes. There was no sparkle left. No youth. Barely a glimmer of the young man who had arrived at the camp only a few months ago. He had been taken, used, on top of everything else. Every day was just torture. Yes, he had more food than most – gifts from the gangmasters who took their pleasure in him – better conditions, but he would rather not. He would rather just be a man.

'I can't do this, Jaak. I can't,' Sven whispered, as he

shuffled alongside Jaak on the way to the mine. 'I'm going.'

'Going where?'

'Leaving. Walking away. Going. Just going.' His voice was cold, detached.

'Talk like that will get you killed. Quiet lad.'

There were people all around. Guards, prisoners, everyone was a danger. Don't trust. Don't be afraid. Don't ask. Simple rules of life out there. Simple. But Sven persisted.

'Will you help me? You know stuff. I know you do.'

Jaak couldn't tell why, but his intended non-compliance came out as, 'Will you listen then?'

'Yes!' Sven's heart began thumping. Life coursing through his veins once again. A glimmer of hope had opened itself up to him like the first star appearing in a dark sky. Perhaps he had a chance.

'Tonight. At dinner. The edge of the forest. Quiet now.' Jaak glanced around. No-one seemed to be taking any notice of them. The guards were focussed on the stragglers, jabbing at them, snarling at them. The prisoners kept their gaze to the ground, oblivious to everything but their own survival.

Jaak was true to his word. He was there, waiting as agreed. They slipped silently into the forest, dark and dense. Jaak's sentence was life and life here was short. He had nothing to lose. Perhaps that was why he was going along with this. It didn't matter. It really didn't matter. But Sven did have options. He could, if he was lucky, survive his sentence, have a life to lead.

Despite being far enough away from the buildings of the camp not to be heard they spoke in whispers, as if the trees themselves could betray them.

'You can do this, lad. Ten years might be cut to five. You could make it home. Get yourself a girl. A beautiful Estonian girl.'

'No,' Sven replied resolutely. 'My mind's made up. If you're with me, that's great, but if you're not I'm going anyway.' He looked Jaak square in the eye so as there would be no misunderstanding; no uncertainty of his determination. No room for doubt. 'And...' He lowered his gaze to the ground. 'Christ, and the things they...Christ! I'd sooner die on my feet than live on my knees.'

Jaak understood. Of course he did. He had been through it himself on his first stint at the gulag.

'Right. Right you are. But if you want my help you need to wait. Get through winter, and at the first sign of spring, that's when we'll leave. If you just wander off into the wild now you'll die for sure. There's nothing out there but wilderness, and in the winter, less than nothing. The cold will kill you in under a day. You need to plan. You need to know where you're going. You need to learn how to survive. Get through this winter, okay?'

Sven closed his eyes, battling with the visions of what lay ahead, battling with the tears that he could feel welling up. This wasn't what he wanted to hear, but it made sense. Of course it did. Six months. He had to get through the next six months. He wasn't sure if he could.

Jaak put his arm tightly around Sven's shoulders and squeezed them reassuringly, as a father might to his son. He hadn't intended to get involved. Involvement in this place meant pain and loss and grief. He didn't want that. Not again. But here he was attaching himself to someone else. Caring when he shouldn't. He should have said no. No to everything. He should have ignored the boy. Told him to be on his way. Told him to leave him alone. Why hadn't he? Was it just that the boy was an Estonian too, or that he was young, that he reminded him of himself, of Imre? Was this payment for a life he could have, should have, protected better? Saved? Perhaps.

Winter had come all too quickly; autumn barely showing itself. A flicker of change in colours, the sudden falling of leaves, and it was over. The darkness and pain of winter lay upon them. It was like hell itself. Men shuffled, barely able to move in the cold that snipped at their bones; souls snapped up at the same time. Frozen people barely alive. Fingers stuck in the shape of an axe handle, unable to straighten, to do anything other than chip away. Searching for gold. Bodies would simply fall at the mine-face, like lights being switched off. Nothing any more.

Jaak knew it would last for half a year and more. The light would creep back. Daylight, for what it was worth, would stretch itself, rolling back the overwhelming darkness of winter, but it wouldn't bring any warmth. Not for agonising months. The snow would stay, metres thick. They would bear the pain of frostbitten fingers and toes, blackened flesh, numbed, dead. New prisoners would be shipped in to replace those who had passed away, been executed, or simply given up. Life there would leave you if you didn't fight for it.

A constant stream of human beings replaced the dead as if they were broken machinery. For amusement some of the guards would send a couple of the prisoners out into the vicious cold without any clothes. Bets would be made on who would die first. Less than dogs.

Keep your head down. Work as hard as you can. Don't argue. Don't catch anyone's eyes. Don't. Just don't.

*

It was difficult for Sven not to show any excitement as the days grew longer and the heavy darkness of night was pushed back again. Soon. Soon it would be over. He would walk out and just keep walking. He had followed every instruction. Instructions from Jaak, from the guards, from the criminals. It didn't matter. Nothing mattered apart from seeing this out. Getting through the days. Building up his bag of supplies, little by little, crumb by crumb. His affiliation with the criminals at least served a purpose now. He had access to so much more than the other prisoners, than Jaak. An army lighter. Some cans of pork. A knife. Vodka. Little by little and never from the same person twice. Sven whimpered as he returned, one more time, from the forest where his swelling bag lay hidden. He was desperate.

He felt a prod in his back. The whisper of breath on his neck.

'Keep moving. Don't say a word. Don't look round. Walk!'

It was Jaak, but why was he behaving like this? Was he betraying him, saving himself by handing Sven over? No. He wouldn't do that. But this place. This place made everyone sub-human. Eyes staring like the eyes of starving wolves.

'Pick your bag up. Move it.'

Sven didn't hesitate. Didn't question. He had to trust Jaak. Without that he had less than nothing.

They were heading away from the camp. Once they had clambered through the barbed-wire fence that stretched around the perimeter of the official camp border and were through the surrounding woods, there was only wilderness. They both stood for a moment and stared at the vastness of it. It was breathtaking and even in their state, in their desperation, they could appreciate it.

'Sorry, lad,' Jaak whispered with a nudge to Sven's ribs. 'I couldn't have you knowing anything, getting excited, giving it away. The twinkle of an eye is all it takes.'

'I thought...Christ, I thought you'd turned on me! Bastard!'

He was annoyed, but he was grinning. The thrill of finally being on their way was far greater than any disappointment he held at not being trusted to be a man.

'Keep your ears pinned, your eyes peeled, and your voice a whisper. Only speak if you have to. Got it?'

'Yes sir!'

The air was so pure. The sky held the most brilliant blue. The sound of running water was all around them as the snows melted and formed streams, rivers. The crackle of breaking ice. Freedom. This was the smell of freedom.

Despite wanting to take the quickest way home, the shortest route to get them as far away from the camp as possible, they stuck to the curves and twists of the trees, keeping themselves hidden, their footprints less obvious, less able to be tracked. From here on they would travel at night as much as possible. Not only because it would keep them hidden, but it was also coldest then. Even in spring, temperatures at night could fall well below zero. Steal the breath from you. It was better to be moving.

Summer was creeping in, but with it there was little chance to hide. There were only a few hours of darkness now and that would become nothing soon enough. The white nights of June and July would leave them exposed. They had to move as quickly as possible in the darkness that offered itself to them.

As they travelled on Sven was struck by the total nothingness. There was no sign of human intervention. No buildings, roads, telegraph poles. Nothing at all! Now the compass made sense. He had been nervous stealing it, but without it they would never find a way out, especially in the dark confusion of the heavy forests where a man could walk, unknowingly, in never ending circles.

South. They were heading south. Not west as Sven had assumed. Home was to the west of here, but south was the safer journey. They would need to find clothes that didn't shout gulag. Papers of some sort. A story. A believable story of how they happened to be wherever they were found, because found they would be.

# Chapter 28

## Angie
## May 1989

It didnae happen, the whole rehab thing. Course it didnae. Why would it? Why would my life turn around into something even half decent. Naw. Winter crawled on by. Same-o same-o. I could tell by the way that Deke looked at me I shouldnae ask. Shouldnae make him feel any worse than he did. Sometimes ye just shut up. If the time was right, if he could do it, he'd do it. Cannae force it. Nae point. Nothing works if it doesnae come frae inside o you. Naw.

'Off to the clinic, Deke, I called, trying to sound cheery.'

'Oh. Oh, right Babes. Yeah,' he said, scratching away at his arm. 'Angie,' he added as I was opening the door. 'I love you, Babes. I really do.'

'Aye,' I answered. It still melted my heart. Just no so much.

My appointment was at two. Always the same day, near enough the same time. The stair door squeaked closed behind me an the sun blinded my eyes. I squinted an turned the corner. The sky was aw pure blue. A wee bit chilly, but no bad. No bad at aw. I checked the time an decided to walk. I could get most o the way there along the Water o Leith, aw leafy an green an somewhere else. Super shitty to super posh. Folk wi houses wi big windows. Aye. Deke didnae like me walking along the river by myself. Said I might get mugged, attacked. Said it was dangerous. Like I really gave a shit!

Anyway, it was nice. It really was. An I took the time to see it. To really see it. I was usually just nashing somewhere on a mission, picking up, dropping off, working, but when I had the clinic I got the whole day. Just me. I liked that. A wee bit peace an quiet. I wasnae wasted. Just calm. Just okay. Didnae even hae a fix. A wee line, that was aw. An it was good. Sometimes, when the world wasnae snipping away at me, it was okay, an I could look at stuff an appreciate it. That day was like that. I could see the trees, an the water, an the tall, tall buildings, an the cliffs, an the auld, auld walls covered in moss. I pressed my fingers into it – aw soft an squishy – an I smiled.

It was Deke that had brought me here that first time. I didnae even know the place existed. That sneaky wee swathe o countryside creeping right through the centre o the city. Seemed like a lifetime ago. Still as clear as day though. Something I have that no-one can take away. That feeling. Sometimes I just needed it. The memory o me an him when it was aw just special an beautiful an, *"How lucky am I?"* We'd walked along that same path. We'd stopped at that same wall. He'd picked me up an placed me on the moss. It felt like a throne. Me a princess. It felt bloody brilliant.

*

'I love you, Babes,' he said, his arms tight around my waist, my legs wrapped around him. He beamed at me, then he turned around so that he was facing across the water at the massive wall o rock. 'I LOVE THIS GIRL!'

he shouted so loud that the words bounced back at us, echoing down between the cliffs an the tall buildings an sinking into the trees.

I laughed an gave him a wee playful slap to his shoulder. 'Shh! Folk'll hear.'

'And that's the whole point,' he said, grinning. 'I want the whole world to know.'

He picked me up, spun me around, an around, an around. I shrieked an laughed aw at the same time. A beautiful wonderful feeling that lives wi me forever. Then he shrieked too as he lost his balance an we fell ower, tumbling to the ground, rolling our way down the embankment, landing in the water. The sunlight danced through the leaves, sparkled on the water. I was on my back. Drenched! He was on top o me wi his arms outstretched either side o me. The water was freezing, but the sun was warm, the feeling between us intense, like we were on fire.

'Christ I want you so bloody badly right now,' he whispered as he looked right deep into my eyes. 'Fuck,' he breathed. He pulled me up, water tumbling off o me, off o him. He glanced around. 'Come on,' he said, pulling me back to the wall.

He leapt ower, held his hand out for me, pulled me ower too. It was aw rocky an mulchy an there were nettles an brambles an auld dead branches covered in moss. We didnae care. He took his jacket off an laid it down on the ground for me to lie on, like I was this special, delicate person, an we had the best sex ever. Maybe folk could see us frae their big windows. Maybe folk could hear us as they walked on past. It was so slow, an so quiet, an so dangerous, an so beautiful, an there was no-one else in the world right then apart frae us. Me an Deke.

'So?' he asked, when we stood up an he was trying to

get aw the crap out o my hair. Leaves an twigs an bits o moss an weeds. 'Are you mine? All mine?'

'Aye,' I answered. 'Course. Course I am.'

He picked some blades o grass an braided them into a string an tied it around my ring finger. Kissed it. 'There,' he said. 'It's official now.'

I laughed, threw my arms around him.

Still got that wee string o grass pressed between the pages o my copy o Lord Of The Rings. Felt right to me somehow. One o they books, eh, that just takes ye right away frae it aw. Lets ye believe in magic, just for a while. I never did get the gold one he'd promised. Sort o slipped by like everything else. Aye.

*

I realised soon enough that someone else was there. A posh couple in Barbour jackets an wellies – like they were out in the country proper – came strolling around the corner wi a Labrador. Too fat, it was, waddling away. Some folk! Anyway, the man was staring at me, a look on his face, like I was something scary, something dangerous. The woman had turned away, her nose high in the air. I smiled.

'Morning!' I said, as if we were on the same playing field, as if I was the most normal person in the whole world, as if I wasnae greetin at the memory. At the loss o everything. As if.

The man grunted something an they walked on by. I drifted off an suddenly realised I was at the Dean Bridge. The bridge that folk jump off o when they've had too much. When life's just got too shit. It's no that high, but high enough. I pulled Deke off o it no that long ago. He was off his nut. Screaming about aw kinds o messed up shit. I'd be better off wi'out him. The world would be better off wi'out him. Aye, well, no on my watch. An then, the thought grabbed me. Climb up,

jump off. Aw done. What difference would it make?
None. None whatsoever. I doubt if anyone would even
notice. No really. No more than a quick thought on a
lonely night when a wee bit o relief would've been
good.

# Chapter 29

## Maria
## May 1989

They were becoming quite normal now, yes, quite commonplace, my trips to the Cancer Centre. In a peculiar way I rather enjoyed them. I think it was the familiarity of them, the normality of them, the acceptance of them. There would be the slight trepidation as the day drew closer. The day itself when nothing else would settle in my thoughts other than what was about to be done to me. What lay ahead. The friendly greeting from the receptionists. The scanning of the leaflets and posters as the time ticked by and one sat and waited anxiously, hopefully. All of the faces. Many of them now familiar, but not people one would say hello to. A smile of fellowship would suffice. A nod of acknowledgement. One's name would get called and one sat in the consultant's room, smiling as best one could, as one got checked, poked, and prodded. Then that elation if one got to leave with another all clear. Six more weeks of survival.

Of course there could be bad news, but one shouldn't dwell on such things. No matter what they said about the perils of my age, my prognosis, that beastly disease was not going to get the better of me! I'd be damned if it would!

I was glad of the appointment this time around because it had forced me to leave my little house. I had become rather reticent, you see, since that unpleasant incident at Christmas time, the burglary. Even my home had become somewhat sullied, but at least if I locked the doors securely, if I was careful, it didn't feel so bad.

The neighbours had been wonderful, appalled that such a thing should happen in the village. Word had spread like wildfire and people came – people I didn't even know – and they brought little gifts: cake, some home-made pies, even a bottle of malt whisky! That was my nearest neighbour, old Archie. He was rather fond of coming in for a wee tipple. I think he might have had other intentions, but at my age. Really! I can't imagine why one would even want to.

Anyway, I had been very well cared for. My shopping done, my garden tended (also by Archie!) the doctor would pop in when she was passing, just to check up on me. How very decent! And then there was the dog. They had agreed that I should have a dog for protection. It needn't be a large ferocious thing, just so long as it barked. Most burglars would be put off by the barking of a dog, apparently. I was left with little choice in the matter. It seemed that somebody knew somebody whose dog had had a litter of puppies. Border terriers. Feisty little things. I rather liked them. They still had one puppy. It was the runt of the litter that had been left behind as all of his brothers and sisters tootled off to their new homes. That also suited me. Something of a reject, not quite right. I thought he might fit in rather nicely.

I had a modicum of trepidation about my visit; about meeting this little dog. I did so hope that we would take to each other. They say that, don't they? That there can be this instant connection between dog and owner. A knowing. I really wanted that to happen to me. That instantaneous unconditional love. How wonderful! I needn't have worried. As soon as his owners opened their front door to me this little chap came bounding across, sliding on the wooden floor, and jumped up at me, his little tail beating ferociously, excited yips escaping from him. Without a word of a lie, I held my arms out and he leapt straight up into them, licking and licking at my face. My heart was simply exploding.

'Bad boy! No!' the owner reprimanded. 'I'm so sorry,' she continued as she moved to take him from me.

He snarled at her and returned to licking my face. This little dog was mine! What a wonderful thing; to instantly meet something and fall so terribly in love.

'Oh, he is simply adorable,' I enthused.

'Yes, well! As you can see he only bears a passing resemblance to a proper Border Terrier. Some genetic throwback, the vet has assured me. Somewhere in his lineage there has been a bit of a mix-up!'

Apparently his legs were too long, his tail too short, his colouring slightly wrong with too much white on his head and shoulders. I however, could see nothing other than pure perfection!

'Can I take him home with me now?'

'Yes, yes, of course. He is a wee monkey, mind you. Don't you be putting up with too much of his cheek. He'll be running rings around you soon enough. You need to show him who's boss from the get-go. Isn't that right, Archie lad?'

I laughed. 'Is that what you've called him? Archie?'

'Yes. It seemed to fit!'

I took out my purse. 'How much is he?'

'Oh no. Put that away,' she said. 'There's no charge.' She gave me some food, his bed and a blanket that smelled of his mother, some toys, put his leash and collar on, and we were off. It was the most splendid of feelings, to be walking along the pavement with a little dog trotting in tow. My little dog. I kept looking down at him, smiling. He kept looking up at me, an eager sparkle in his eyes, his little tail erect and proud. Oh, I was in love! Of course I couldn't leave his name as Archie! There were many ways in which the human Archie could interpret that and they would all be wrong.

'How about Albie? Would that do? Albie!'

He looked up at me and wagged his tail. Yes Albie would do just nicely.

\*

I had felt rather guilty about leaving Albie at home alone, but the garden was secure and Archie had kindly fitted a cat flap for him so that he could get in and out as he wanted. He would be fine, I convinced myself.

I still didn't feel quite ready to drive so I had booked a taxi. Extravagant perhaps, but I wasn't up to travelling on buses either. I was still walking with a stick, you see. It was so very frustrating, but I had been told to err on the side of caution. Don't do too much. Don't risk further damage. Very well. I would follow the advice I had been given, albeit reluctantly!

I glanced around the waiting room. Young Angie hadn't been there on my last visit, even though I had switched my time to try and make them coincide – my appointment and Angie's. The old gentleman with the enormous growth on his neck just sat self-consciously looking at his feet. How awful for him. The woman with him – I had assumed his wife, but it could just as easily have been his sister, a friend – was chatting away, but he was ignoring it, ignoring everything, I thought. The young man with no flesh left on him. A shadow. All that life ahead of him, perhaps no longer his.

I hoped that nothing untoward had happened to Angie. Of course, there was no reason to assume that her appointment time would remain the same, but one did see so many of the same faces, I was rather hoping. Sadly, there was no sign of her. "Our" seat was empty, so I took it anyway, taking my time, sitting down nice and slowly, allowing the arms of the chair to take my weight. I hoped the wait wouldn't be too long as I wanted to get back to Albie. The thought made me smile. Having something to care for, to worry about, to miss.

I hadn't noticed Angie's arrival until she sat down beside me.

'Hiya!' she said, quite breezily.

'Oh, hello dear. How lovely to see you again.' I squeezed her hand. 'Lovely!'

She did look well, certainly better than she had the last time I had seen her. Her hair was growing back rather nicely, and she had it styled in a boyish kind of a way which rather suited her. Gave her a lightness. She looked somehow cleaner, brighter.

# Chapter 30

## Angie
## May 1989

I surprised myself at how pleased I was to see her sitting there aw on her tod an I went straight across an sat down beside her. She wasnae looking so well though. Her face was pinched, like she was a wee bit feart o something. There was a scar on her face that I hadnae noticed before. She'd always had the one on her forehead, but no this one. It still looked new, an fresh, an angry. An she had a stick. I had to ask, eh!

'You're no...I mean. The stick? The scar? What's that aw about?'

'Something of a stramash I'm afraid, dear!' she said, rolling her eyes, tossing her head back.

'Aye? What happened then?'

'Oh, it was on Christmas Eve, can you believe it? One would have thought...anyway, some thuggish types smashed their way into my car, right there in front of my house! I had my lights off, you see. I assume that they thought there was nobody home. Well, I heard the smash of glass outside, hurried across to have a look out of my window, saw what was happening, rushed downstairs and charged out of the door, shouting at them. "What the bloody hell do you think you're doing? Get away from there! How dare you!" I was simply furious! You can imagine. I brandished my garden spade at them, making as much noise as I possibly could, swinging it towards their heads!

'You're kidding?' I could just picture her doing it an aw. Brave as fuck, like!

'One of them leapt at me, pushed me to the ground, and kicked me. Yes! Kicked me!'

My eyelids felt like they had glued themselves open an there was a sickening knot tying up my stomach.

'Well, they ran off with a considerable sum of money and left me prostrate on the ground and my little car rather badly damaged. One of the thugs had caused this,' she said, fingering at the scar on her face wi shaky fingers. 'And the fall, well, it caused a rather nasty fracture to my leg, hence the walking stick!' She jiggled it in the air, almost hitting me wi it. 'I've been somewhat laid up since then.'

'Fuck's sake. I am so sorry. That's awful, so it is. Awful! Did they get away wi it then? The bizzies no catch them?'

I was asking, hoping that they had. Hoping that it was just some local junkies, or stupid teenagers, or some desperate parents needing money for Christmas. I know what that can do, see, desperation.

'No dear. I'm afraid not. They got clean away. It was dark, you see, and I live on the edge of the village so no-one saw anything. They were just a nasty shadowy presence. Oh well.' She shrugged an pulled an odd wee face. Crumpled. Hurt. 'C'est la vie! I suppose.'

She breathed out real heavy an scrunched her head into her neck, hunched her shoulders like she wanted to disappear. I felt sick as fuck. This was just wrong. Even for me, this was wrong.

'Our lovely policeman has taken up the habit of

popping by to check on me as well. He doesn't think there's any chance of catching them now,' she added.

I knew fine well there wasnae. No a chance in hell.

'You know dear, a thought just occurred to me. You should come.' She reached ower an grabbed my hand, squeezed it, but lightly, looked right in my eyes. 'Why don't you? Come over for a visit. I'm sure you'd like it. Fresh air. The seaside. It would be lovely. Do. Do please. It would make me so happy.'

What could I say. I owed her that much, eh. 'Aye. Aye, I'd like that.'

She beamed this big smile at me an I'm sure I saw her start to tear up. *Naw, dinnae dae that. I'm sure as hell no worth that.* She sniffed a wee bit, sort o shook her head as if she was shaking away whatever had grabbed on to her.

'Splendid! Oh, and you can meet Albie. I'm sure you two will get on like a house on fire. He is simply adorable!'

'Eh, Albie is?' I asked, thinking, she's no gone and got herself a man, has she?

She laughed, slapped my thigh. 'Oh, my dear. No, no, no. Nothing like that. He's my dog. My little Albie boy.'

I laughed back, relieved, but I didnae really know why. Why it should matter. But it did. I would have worried that she was being used. That she was being taken advantage o. There was this innocence about her, see. Easy for some fucker to take her for a ride. Aye. Dead easy.

When I got home I was raging. I slammed the door shut. Screeched at him. 'Deke! You evil fucker!' He was sitting on the sofa wi Big Davy. Some deal going on. I wasnae giving a fuck.

Big Davy smirked. 'Aye, nice to see you too, doll.'

'Fuck off!' I snarled at him. 'Deke! In here now!'

166

I stormed off into the bedroom, expecting him to follow. When he didnae I walked back out. They were laughing, weren't they? Laughing!

'Off ye go, Deke. You be a good wee boy. Dae as yer slapper tells ye.'

He got up, aw sheepish like. Embarrassed. Came into the bedroom, Big Davy's eyes an his sneer following him.

'Angie Babe. Come on now. There's no need for that.'

'What the fuck have you done?' I said, really slowly, making it clear as anything how angry I was.

He put his hands up. 'No idea what you're talking about, Babes. Davy's just dropped off some new gear. Uncut. Come and get a fix. That'll sort you out.'

'It's no about that, Deke. Everything's no about that. Fuck's sake! Aberlady. My friend. The auld woman ye robbed. But ye didnae just do that, eh? Oh Naw. She only gets beat up as well. Christ's sake! She's an auld woman! A really decent auld woman!'

'Oh that...'

'Aye, that!'

'It wasn't me, Babes. Swear.' He put his hands up again, aw submissive. Stepped towards me like he was gonnae gie me a hug. Wasnae having that! I pushed him away.

'Wasnae you, eh? But you know what I'm talking about, aye? How come, eh? How come?'

'I just mentioned it. Just in passing, like.'

'You're a fucking ass-hole Deke! Fuck off!'

# PART II

# Chapter 31

## Jaak
### Estonia Summer 1964

Jaak bent down to scrape up a handful of sandy soil and let it trickle through his fingers.

'Smell that?' he asked, as he stretched his hand out to Sven, lifted the soil to his nose. 'Home!'

His face held the broadest of smiles and he was exuding happiness, a joyousness that Sven had never seen from him before; didn't even know that he was capable of. The dour seriousness of the past decade had slipped off him as casually as he might have discarded a coat, or a jacket.

Their pace lifted in the knowledge that their journey was finally coming to an end. Rest and relative safety were beckoning them. To their left Scots pines stood thick and tall, still and silent; their scent heavy in the late summer air. On their right there was luscious deciduous forest; birch, maple, aspen, with yet more pines towering majestically above everything else. They were surrounded by the sound of insects buzzing and scurrying, swallows swooping, feasting on them, a beautiful mesmeric dance of life and death.

Jaak paused. Around the next corner stood his house. Such a peculiar feeling of dread and elation washed over him, a knot squeezed at his stomach. This was his land, his home. His. He had cleared the earth, stripping the felled trees of their bark in preparation for making the logs that would become the walls of their home. He had spent day upon day digging a hole for the well, lining it, building the surrounds and hanging the bucket on its hoist in readiness for the day when he and Maarja would use it for the very first time. He had made the stone foundations, built up the logs, secured the steep roof, fitted the windows. Friends and family had dropped by, helping as and when they could. Finally the house had been decorated inside and out, all without Maarja getting a sight of it.

He couldn't wait to see the look on her face when she finally laid her eyes on it; what he had built for her, for them. He was a quiet man and boasting and bragging had never been a part of his character but, back then, he had been so proud of what he had achieved that he was fit to burst. He knew that she would love it.

And now he was back here again. This wasn't how any of it was meant to be.

Maarja. He had let her slip back into his thoughts as the months had turned into years; as their escape from the gulag had become more and more of a reality. No-one would be looking for them. Not now. They would be presumed dead. All they had to do was be smart, be careful, and they would reach home. And so they had and it was terrifying. He wanted to laugh, to cry, to scream, to do everything a man possibly could, and yet he didn't want to do a thing. Perhaps to be stuck here in this moment of possibilities, in the not-knowing, would be best. He clutched on to Sven's arm, seeking support, reassurance, something.

Never before, through all of their travels, had Jaak shown anything other than strength. He was the leader. The man who knew. The man who had kept them safe, alive, trudging through snow and ice, battling against wind and rain, setting traps for rabbits and birds, stealing army uniforms from dead Soviet soldiers, convincing others they came across that they had become separated from their unit; creating stories and lies that had kept them from execution, from starvation, from death. But now? Now he had lost every semblance of strength.

Sven had read the situation, putting his hand firmly on top of Jaak's, squeezing in confirmation. He was here for him. This would all be okay. As their eyes met a tear escaped from Jaak's. He swiped at it.

'Right!' he said, drawing on the memory of the man he knew himself to be, speaking with both conviction and determination.

They walked along the little dirt track, its edges heavy with wild flowers – poppies, daisies, grasses, shrubs. So little had changed. The sky was so very clear, so blue, so unbelievably beautiful. No other sky in the world looked like this.

And there it was. The walled garden, the fruit trees, the well, the stone foundations, the wooden walls, every inch that he knew so well, yet he didn't. Not now. Nothing had changed and yet everything had. There were shoes lined up by the porch. Someone else's shoes. Jackets and coats hung from the wooden pegs that he had carved. Someone else's jackets and coats. The door opened.

173

'Yes? Can I help you?' A stranger, a woman speaking in Russian.

'I used to live—'

Sven stepped forward, butted in. 'We had friends who lived in this house, perhaps ten, fifteen years ago? We hoped that they might still be here?'

'This is my house,' Jaak mumbled to the gravel at his feet.

The woman folded her arms across her chest, looked distastefully at Jaak and Sven. Drew closer. Stared.

'There is no ownership of property any more!' she growled.

Sven stepped back, tugging at Jaak. They had to leave, and quickly. 'Sorry to have bothered you.'

Jaak stood, open-mouthed, unable to move, to comprehend. Of course he knew that things had changed, that property had been taken and given to others to live in, but somehow he had never anticipated this. Not here. Not his house.

Sven tugged at him again, whispering. 'We need to move. Come on.'

As soon as they had turned the corner and were out of sight Jaak slumped to his knees, fell forward on the sweet grass and sobbed. It was dangerous. He wasn't thinking. They couldn't draw attention to themselves like this.

Sven glanced around anxiously, took hold of Jaak's shoulders, pulled him up.

'Come on man! You need to hold it together. Do you know anyone we can trust? Anyone we can go to? Come on Jaak, I need you to be strong, to get us out of this.'

Jaak lifted himself up and swiped at his clothes, straightened himself. 'Sorry lad, I just..I was hoping for something else. Not that.' He tossed his head back towards the house. His house.

Sven smiled. 'Lad! It's been over ten years and I'm pushing thirty and you still call me lad!'

Jaak allowed himself a smile in return. 'You'll always be lad to me, lad!'

They slapped each other's shoulders and headed into Pärnu town. Trees still lined the road, but they were interspersed with more and more houses, until human impact was greater than that of nature. Surely there would be someone here, a place he remembered, a face he recognised. Of course he thought of Johann, but he was scared of what he might discover. His family home would more than likely have been taken over as well. He may well have died in the gulags. Maarja's house? If her family had survived. If she had survived. If her grandparents were still alive. All of that was possible, but did he have the stomach for any of it? A decade of escape, perhaps six or seven thousand kilometres had been travelled, and now that he was home he felt utterly lost again.

They heard running feet approaching from behind. A voice called out, 'Hold up there! Wait a minute!'

They paused, both unsure, breath held, pulses racing, before turning around and facing whatever was coming their way.

'Is that really you? Jaak!'

'Johann? Johann!'

They stood and stared at each other neither believing what they were seeing; what fate had allowed. Both of them had survived and returned. Stories like theirs just didn't happen, but this one had. They embraced, took each other's shoulders, stepped back a pace, stared some more.

'We thought...I thought you were gone. I would never have taken your house otherwise, but it was going to go to some strangers. I thought it better to be me.'

'Of course, Brother. Of course!' Jaak raised his eyebrows questioningly. 'And the Russian woman?'

Johann grinned sheepishly, looked at the ground and back up again. 'Tatiana. My wife,' he shrugged. 'But she's a good woman.'

'She's Russian!' Jaak replied coldly, distastefully.

'A lot has changed Jaak. An awful lot. We've all had to move with the times. Adapt.'

'But you, with a Russian, after...after everything?'

'A woman, Jaak. Tatiana is a fine, strong woman who has done me the world of good. If it hadn't been for her – well, I might not be here at all. When I returned, I was barely alive. You understand. I know you do. I was sick and weak and she nursed me. She cared. She cares still. My home had been given to someone else and she, she helped me. Without the help of her friends in the housing department I would never have been allowed to stay here.'

Jaak grunted in reply before adding, 'And...and what of Maarja? Her family?'

Johann simply shook his head. There was no need for words. Everything had gone.

'You're welcome to stay here. Both of you.'

Making sense of this was an impossibility – living with the enemy – but he had to survive. Johann's offer for them to stay with him and his family was accepted, however awkward it all seemed. Whose house was this? Who was in charge? Did Jaak have to seek permission before doing something in this house? Yes, it seemed he did.

Learning about the new way of life, the rules they had to follow, the acceptance of a superior power was so difficult. Neighbours couldn't be trusted any more. Family couldn't be trusted any more. Even children were not to be trusted. It made Jaak baulk to witness Johann's children heading off to school with their Pioneer's uniforms, their red neck ties proudly displayed, the bile they spouted upon their return about the glorious Soviet Union, their great leaders, the enemies in the West.

How had this come to pass? Jaak struggled with everything that was around him now. The house, its occupants, the children of his closest friend and Brother speaking in Russian, behaving as if they were good little citizens of the Soviet Union. Russification. Everywhere. Russification. Even here. Even in what had been his. An influx of Russians, their language, their ways. Estonia was in danger of dying. Of becoming nothing but a memory.

*

'I'm leaving Sven,' Jaak announced quietly, as they walked along the beach, huddled against the biting cold, their layers of clothing making movement stiff, stilted. Winter had taken hold again and the world was washed in white; the sand hidden beneath thick snow, the sea frozen in great sweeps and waves stretching out as far as the eye could see. White. Nothing but white. And utterly deserted. There was something about this that they both enjoyed. Perhaps it was the memory of what they had fought their way through as they trudged across Siberia after they had escaped the gulag. Perhaps it was simply the challenge; man versus the elements – something that they both knew so intimately. The beach walk had become a ritual irrespective of the weather. Perhaps due also to the knowledge that here they could talk honestly, openly, without fear of being overheard, reported.

'This is killing me,' Jaak continued.

'I can see that,' Sven confirmed.

'I've been speaking to that woman, Tatiana. She's as keen for me to leave as I am. Her contacts at housing have come up with an apartment on Kooli. Someone died apparently. Anyway, if I want it it's mine. What do you think?'

'Why not?'

'Oh, I'm definitely taking it, I meant would you like to share with me? Until–'

Sven cut in before his friend had the chance to continue. Now was as good a time as any.

'I've met someone, Jaak.'

He didn't really know why he had kept this secret from the man who had been like a father to him for so long. The man who had taught him how to survive anything. It felt somehow as if he were letting him down.

'Her family approve and they've said I can move in with them as soon as we're married. I –'

Jaak grinned, slapped Sven on the back.

'That is great! I'm so happy for you. Well done lad!'

And he meant it, but he was also rather taken aback. Secrets had been kept even from him. That hurt. He was also somewhat apprehensive of being on his own again after such a long time. Sven was like family to him now. Or at least he thought he was.

'I...we would like you to be the *Pulmaisa*,' Sven said.

'It would be an honour!'

Okay. The most important job at the wedding was to be his. The overseer, the organiser. He was family after all.

*

Jaak had settled into his new solitary life, busying himself in his work at the sawmill. Sven was very content in his married one. They kept in close contact through them both being in the local choir. Singing would not stop. Their weekly beach walks would also continue as they shared their thoughts on Estonia, what it had become and how it might somehow return to being the country they remembered from their childhoods. A free nation. It was now such a distant memory, but one they both felt they had to talk about, rekindle, keep alive. They shared thoughts and words that could not be uttered in public. They trusted each other completely.

There was always the shadow of rebellion. The singing in quiet places of Estonian songs. The clinging on to their culture through discussion, memories shared, history remembered. Everything had to be done with such caution, your confidantes chosen with the utmost care. Soviet spies were everywhere and one just never knew. Song festivals had continued to be central to the culture of this new Estonia, but the songs were to be Soviet – a celebration of the Soviet Union – with a sprinkling of "approved" Estonian songs in amongst them, to keep the populace quiet.

Jaak and Sven made the journey to the song festival in Tallinn every five years. As with everyone else it was those few precious Estonian songs that they went for. They would sing the Soviet songs because they had to. That was the price they paid for being allowed to gather as a nation and sing their own songs. And what a feeling that was!

It was 1969 – the Song Festival's one hundredth birthday. Of course this was going to be an emotional event and it had to be handled carefully. The authorities were wary of the possibility of passions rising too high; of this becoming more than just a song festival. There was a buzz in the air, an expectation. Jaak and Sven stood amongst the thirty thousand singers and musicians who filled the stage at the *Lauluväljak* – the immense amphitheatre which was the song festival grounds. As the programme drew to its conclusion there was one more song that everyone wanted to sing.

'*Mu Isamaa,*' (my fatherland) the audience called. '*Mu Isamaa on minu arm!*' (my fatherland is my love) The choristers joined in. They were demanding that they should be allowed to sing their outlawed national anthem. The crowd, the singers, everyone.

Jaak and Sven stood tall, smiling, calling, their hearts swelling with the sound. The choirs and the crowd stood their ground and they sang and there was nothing that could be done about it. Despite being instructed to leave the stage, they refused. They sang. The audience sang. The brass band was ordered to play in an attempt to drown the singers out, but one hundred instruments could do nothing against over one hundred thousand voices singing as one.

This was dangerous. It was too big, too powerful. Something had to be done. Finally, the authorities allowed the music's composer, Gustav Ernesaks, to take his place as conductor on stage and lead the choirs and the audience, through one final official rendition of their anthem. It was an attempt to save face, to pretend that this had been their intention all along.

The feeling that was sweeping uncontrollably through this immense and joyous crowd was electric and everyone could feel it. Estonia's spirit had survived. The

Singing Revolution had begun. What now, the country wondered? What now?

*

It was 1987 and Gorbachev had come to power as leader of the Soviet Union. He had begun to implement change. The introduction of *Glasnost* and *Perestroika* had meant that voices were permitted to be heard. A loosening of tongues that had been bound for so many years. People began to voice their opinions, to tiptoe towards something different.

In spring of that year plans to begin phosphorous mining in northern Estonia created uproar. The environmental damage that would be caused was unacceptable to the Estonian people. To protest about environmental issues wasn't thought to be such a problematic issue, after all, Soviets cared about their environment too. Students and young people gathered and demonstrated until finally the plans were given up. The mining wouldn't be allowed to proceed. They had won. The first social victory had been achieved. People power.

The seeds of political dissidence had been planted, quickly taking root and continuing to grow, building with each month that passed. On 4th June, 1987 young people had gathered in Raekoja Plats, (Town Hall Square) Tallinn, to listen to the music of Aarne "Korsten" Meensalu and Tanel Vainumäe. The music carried on until the early hours of the morning. The musicians promised to return the following night. Word had spread like wildfire and a huge crowd turned up, spilling out of Raekoja Plats. Rita Mägar, the director of the Recreational Parks Directorate, authorised their use of the Song Festival Grounds and ordered the workers to prepare the grounds for the concert.

The crowd walked from the Old Town to the Song Festival Grounds and gathered there every night for a week to sing, despite attempts from the militia and the KGB to stop them. Punks and young people were singing national and old Estonian songs, but also songs that were anti Soviet.

The following year Sven met up with Jaak. They were heading up to the "Old Town Days" night-time concert in Raekoja Plats, Tallinn. Jaak had been sceptical. It was for young people. Perhaps he was getting too old for such things.

'Look what happened last year,' Sven had enthused. 'It was massive! And more importantly, it was defiant. Can't you feel it, Jaak? The air? The people? Something's happening; something big and important. This will be more than just a concert. I am sure of it!'

Popular singers and bands performed. Estonians were singing in Estonian about Estonian issues. Once again voices swelled. People swayed like a great tidal surge. More and more of them. Perhaps now...Perhaps now...

'I have to let Sirje know!' Sven called excitedly. 'She has to be here. The children need to be here! Every Estonian needs to be right here!'

As word got around more and more people turned up over the next few days until there was an ocean of people all swaying, singing, *"Estlane olen ja Eestlaseks jään."* (Estonian I am, Estonian I shall be.) Hands held high, joined as one. Musician, Papp Kõlar drove by on his motorbike with the Estonian flag fluttering above it. Another flag appeared in the crowd, then more.

'Did you bring it Sirje, Did you?' Sven asked excitedly of his wife as she found him in the crowd.

She smiled. 'Of course I did!' She unfurled their flag, as did hundreds of others.

Sven kissed her, took the flag and joyously hoisted it above them. The old woman standing next to them stared up at it, her face wet with tears. So many tears and such joy.

Outlawed Estonian flags that had been hidden in people's basements and barns, cellars and attics, were now being raised high and proud. Singing had become their weapon, their power. A sense of unity, of possibility, had enveloped the Estonian people once again.

# Chapter 32

## Maria
### 23rd August 1989

It was yet another glorious day. I so loved the clarity of the air here, the quality of the colours, the sky bleeding into the sea. Such a vibrant blue it took one's breath away. I had taken Albie out for a decent walk along the waterfront, but he was never quite satisfied, never tired, despite all of the scrambling over rocks, charging around on the sand in pursuit of some poor unsuspecting seabirds, swimming about in the water after a stick, a piece of seaweed, a feather, something imaginary; at least to my eyes!

I had been so looking forward to this day. Angie was coming. My first official guest. Of course there had been Archie and the policeman and the doctor, but they didn't really count as guests, did they? Anyway, it was important to me that the day was the very best it could be. My house had to be in tip-top condition. Not that I felt the need to impress, no. It was simply important to show that one cared; that one had made that extra effort, I believed. Of course I doubted that Angie would judge, cast aspersions on my house-keeping skills, but that was irrelevant. I was determined that my little house would sparkle!

However, it appeared that Albie had other ideas. He leapt after the duster, ratting away at it as if it were a prize catch! *No!* or *tch!* or *bad boy!* had absolutely no effect. A waggle of my finger in reprimand was simply seen as an encouragement. I had resorted to a game of throw the ball, have a quick dust, throw the ball again, ad infinitum! As for using the vacuum cleaner, well, young Albie believed that the machine was some sort of vicious beast and it was his duty to see it off. The corners of my vacuum were scratched to pieces by his little razor-like teeth!

As I cleaned and checked it suddenly dawned on me that my sitting room was rather sparse of decoration. There was my recliner, a small table and two chairs, my window-seat where I spent many an hour gazing out at my view, which was spectacular, but inside – in here – it was perhaps rather unfriendly, lacking ornaments, pictures, and such like. There were signs of dog to be seen everywhere but little of human, of me. I began to panic. Perhaps the place felt cold. Perhaps Angie wouldn't feel comfortable. Isn't it peculiar how it takes a situation like that, seeing one and one's world through the eyes of an outsider, to have a clearer view of one's circumstances?

I had done my best, even carefully selecting an assortment of flowers from my garden to display in a couple of china vases I had picked up in a lovely little shop in North Berwick. They always cheer things up don't they? Flowers. I may have gone somewhat overboard, eventually filling another two large jugs with roses, cornflowers, poppies, and daisies – a profusion of colour and scent – and placing them on the windowsills.

I stood, looking around, still unsure, but at least it

was cheery now – it would have to do. I had promised to be waiting at the bus stop for her so that she wouldn't get lost. Unnecessary, of course, as my instructions had been quite explicit, and the village is hardly a place in which one might get lost. That aside, one only had to ask for the old lady who had been robbed and anyone could point the way. But that wasn't the point. It was nice to have someone to welcome one, I imagined. That feeling of wretched loneliness and fear that I had experienced upon my arrival in Edinburgh all those years ago had never truly left me.

I checked the time on my wristwatch. Gosh! I would have to dash if I were to be at the bus stop in time. Mind you, one never could tell. The bus was liable to arrive ten minutes either side of its scheduled time. I knew I hadn't missed it as I had been keeping an ear open for the distinctive sound of it trundling past my garden. One last quick glance around the room. Yes. It was presentable. I thought it rather pretty actually, with all of the flowers. I straightened my skirt, draped my best floral scarf around my head, over my shoulders – I had become rather adept at this – slipped my lipstick across my lips, squeezed them together to ensure an even coating, and reached for Albie's lead.

He knew something exciting was happening. They can sense things, can't they, dogs? He was yipping and spinning in excited little circles.

'Come here, Albie,' I urged softly, trying to calm him so that I could clip his lead on, patting my thighs in soft encouragement. He was having none of it, the little rascal!

In exasperation I scooped him up and rushed out of the door, carefully locking it behind me. I smiled at my garden as we hurried through. Such an array of colour and scent. It really was rather splendid, even if I do say so myself. Much to the consternation of Archie, who was something of a gardener, I had simply thrown packets of wildflower seeds all over the border, in gay abandon. They had taken, flourished, and to my eye were simply beautiful; as near to being as nature intended as I could manage. Archie had tutted and shaken his head, instructing me that I should have planted this here and that there – chrysanthemums, begonias, dahlias and such like – but I was delighted with what I had done. He could inform me on how to tend the roses, but as for the rest, that was up to me!

I strained to listen to the traffic as I craned my neck, checking left and right. One had to be careful, especially at that time of year. Young people in an excited rush to spend the day at the beach. Tourists not knowing the way of things. Locals who assumed they knew the road and therefore had no need to drive carefully. I nipped across and walked up and down the stretch of grass that separated the waterfront from the road as I waited. I found standing still for any length of time to be something of a problem these days, a bit of mobility being the more comfortable option. It was easier, you see; less demanding on my rather racked body. That nasty illness and its treatment had certainly taken their toll. Add to that the beating I had taken, well, let's just say I was not at my best! But one perseveres, doesn't one. One perseveres. The bus came and I held my hand out to stop it. I couldn't see anyone standing which was peculiar. The doors hissed open.

'I am so sorry. I am expecting someone, you see. May I take a peek?' I asked of the driver.

'Aye, but quickly, mind. I'm running late as it is.'

I felt such a fool as I checked the heads of the passengers and realised that she wasn't there. My face had turned its customary shade of scarlet.

'I am so sorry for the inconvenience,' I said rather quietly as I retreated. 'So sorry.'

I decided to wait for the next bus. They ran every thirty minutes so the wait wouldn't be too long. There were an assortment of benches one could sit upon if one so desired, and there was the view of the bay – the waves lapping, the birds swooping and chittering – one could never tire of that, so it wasn't a problem. I decided against that option however and half a mile or so later found myself at the rather grand Luffness Estate. Peering behind the old stone wall surrounding the grounds and the house beyond I wondered if it, like Glenbirrie, were a place of secrets; a place of hidden unhappiness and foreboding. A place of imprisonment.

I don't know how long I had been standing there, caught in a rather gloomy reverie, but the sound of a passing bus snapped me back to the present.

'Oh dear, Albie. I do hope we haven't missed her!' We made our way back to the village as quickly as we could, my eyes on the lookout for some lost soul, only there wasn't one. Perhaps she had already found the house and was waiting? Perhaps she had been and gone? No. I hadn't been that long, surely. I checked my watch. No.

There was no-one at my house so I decided to take a bit of a walk along the main road through the village, just to make sure she hadn't nipped in to the local shop, or taken a seat at the bus stop heading back into Edinburgh. There was no sign of her anywhere.

'Well Albie, it looks as though it will just be you and me for afternoon tea. What a shame.'

I returned home and decided on some gardening to settle me. My heart had sunk and I was in need of some of nature's therapy.

# Chapter 33

Angie
23rd August 1989

I was going to go. I really was but, well, I got on the bus an I thought about her meeting me aw smiles an happiness. I thought about seeing her walking along the road wi her stick, going in to her garden, her house, knowing that it was aw my fault. I'd fucked up an she'd paid for it. Naw, I couldnae face her. I skipped off the bus again at London Road. Walked through the park, aw trees an posh folk wi their designer dogs, an a few chancers eyeing folk up, looking for an open bag, an easy pocket. Easy to spot them when you've done it yerself often enough. Aye. I was clocking them, thinking, that's my life. Just that. Aw fuck!

I wandered along the paths that twisted up the hill through chestnut trees so thick an full that there was no sunshine getting through. In the shade it was chilly an I shivered, but I sat down on one o the benches anyway. Hadnae been there two minutes when someone had parked himself beside me. 'Got any gear,' he whispered. I turned an looked at him. Didnae recognise him at aw. Gave him a look, shook my head. Is that what I am? Is it that fucking obvious that even strangers can see it? I guess so, eh? Angie the junkie, the dealer, the dirty waste o space. Aye.

I walked off sharpish an crossed ower the cobbles o Royal Terrace. Massive houses wi their own private stairways, all arches an *stay outa my house* railings wi pointy tops, an brass knockers, an private parking. Residents only, aye. A car shrieked its horn at me – get out o the way! I jumped. Hadnae noticed it. No need for that, Christ's sake. I put my middle finger up, pulled a face at the bastard as he drove on by in his blacked out windowed BMW. Fuck you mate! Wouldnae want to see in even if I could.

I dipped in between the hedges, past the church, an up Calton Hill; the back o they big houses aw hidden behind a wall that's twice the height o me, an some. I climbed aw the way to the top o the hill. No that far, but far enough, an steep enough to snatch the breath frae ye. Up at the top I clambered up onto the National Monument – like our own wee Acropolis standing up there. Half finished way back in the time o long dresses an gas lights, an left that way, so it was. Folk wouldnae cough up back in the day. Wouldnae pay for it to be finished. Scotland's Disgrace or Scotland's Pride, depending on yer politics. Deke says we should be proud. Says that it's a finger up to Thatcher an her pals. Anyway, up there ye can see for miles, the whole o Edinburgh, Fife, East Lothian. Up there ye're distant, separate frae everything. At least that's how I felt and I didnae want to go back down. Back amongst aw o the shite. I stared across it aw an my eyes settled on where I should've been. East Lothian. Heard about it. Never been there. Never been anywhere really. Seldom left east Edinburgh! I looked back to Leith. My place. Didnae feel like it. Nothing felt like it. I was like this mistake. This piece o nothing that didnae belong anywhere. That didnae do a thing worth shit. Felt shite.

*Why no, eh? Why the fuck no?* I checked my watch, hoofed it back down the hill. Magic. The lights were red, the wee man green, the beep-beep-beep shouted across the street, an the 124 was sitting waiting for the lights to change. There were folk standing at the bus-stop. I'd be fine. I'd catch it. I was aw out o breath. My legs were hurting, my chest thumping. The doors were just closing. I banged on them. 'Hold up mate!' Thank Christ he was decent. He smiled an the doors opened, an I showed him my ticket, an it was aw okay. I parked myself at the back, next to the window. Stared out, watching for nothing.

Dunno why but that song that Deke used to sing for me – Tom Petty, "Refugee" – that was sitting in my brain going around an around. I first heard it when we'd just come back frae trying to find where I used to live an I was aw sad an feeling useless an he sat me down an strummed away on his guitar an he sang. Funny that, how songs sometimes mean everything. They speak just to you.

*

'That's what you're like, Angie Babe. My little refugee. It doesn't need to be that way, you know. I'm here for you, always. You know that, right?' He'd smiled an put his guitar down an wrapped me up in his confidence. In his everything's fine hug. In his you're mine breath.

'Aye,' I answered, an I meant it. Me an him.

'We're family. Just me and you. No need for anyone else.' He laughed. 'Besides which, both of our other families are shit! Just forget about them. They don't matter one iota. Angie and Deke. That's all Babes. That's all.' He kissed my eyes an I felt just brilliant.

'Aye.'

*

It became our song. No the stereotypical love song. No aw soppy an undying love an aw o that, but it was ours. It was us.

A fly crawled up the window. I watched its legs, its feet, its attempt to cling on. A wee bit wind. It was gone.

An suddenly I was there. Aberlady. "Just out of the village," she'd said. "Two sharp bends and the stop is right there. You can't miss it. Right on the waterfront." I looked out at the posh wee houses, in the posh wee village, at the flower baskets an trimmed hedges an cleanliness. Aye. That's what I noticed. It was aw clean an sort o sparkly. Like it wasnae real. Like it was frae the movies. An I felt sick. I felt stupid. I felt like carrying right on through. The bus went around the first corner. She was right. You couldnae miss it. The bend was so sharp that the bus had to almost stop to get round it. I breathed in aw o that doubt, pushed the bell. The second bend. The bus stop. I stepped out, saying cheers to the driver.

The air. The air was different. Aye, clean, even though the road was quite busy. Ye could smell the beach, the seaweed, the birds. I had a wee look around, trying to get my bearings. Wee houses, some grass, water, trees, no much. No much at aw. Couldnae see Edinburgh either. Good! "Walk past the last house," she'd said "And then turn up the little track and that's me." I found it easy enough. Her wee dog must have smelled me. It was bark, bark, barking away at me before I'd even got there. I could hear her too.

'Albie! Quiet now! Quiet!' in a no serious but pretending to be kind o a voice.

I smiled. I felt better. This aw felt better. I reached the gate. A mass o flowers. A tiny wee bit o grass wi a metal table – one o they nice ones wi fancy tiles on top – an a couple o matching chairs on it. Everything else was just flowers. She was on her knees picking at weeds, her hands in thick rubber gloves, a streak o mud across her face. A posh scarf was wrapped ower her head like she was something out o one o they auld-fashioned movies, aw graceful an special, like Sophia Loren, or Audrey Hepburn. I liked those auld movies, so I did. Took ye away, ye know? She looked up an beamed at me. That was just lovely. A great big happy-to-see-me smile. When had I last had one o them? A while back, that's for sure.

'Oh, my dear, I am so very glad you made it. I wondered, you see. I thought perhaps...Well! Never mind any of that. Do come in.'

# Chapter 34

## Maria
### 23rd August 1989

Well, you can imagine my surprise when Angie did turn up after all. Of course I was delighted as I had so been looking forward to her visit. It had felt somewhat awkward at first; not the easy chat we had shared at the Cancer Centre or when we had met in Edinburgh. Perhaps it was because this was my home and there was no longer an even-footing to stand upon, that anonymous commonality we had shared before. Now this was me in my world and I could see that she felt somewhat uncomfortable in it.

'I think tea in the garden, dear. Don't you? It is such a beautiful day.'

'Aye, that would be grand,' she said, with an attempt at a natural smile, but I could sense that it was forced. She was looking around as if she were nervous of something or someone. I hoped it wasn't me. Oh dear.

'Would Earl Grey suffice?' I asked, breezily, taking off my gloves, adjusting my scarf, trying to mask what I had picked up on.

'Eh, aye, I guess.'

I wasn't sure that she had quite understood. Her look

was quizzical, but I didn't want to embarrass her, so chose not to seek clarification. I must confess it was something of a relief to escape to the kitchen for a few minutes. When I returned with my tray, little Albie was sitting on her lap, quite the thing. She was scratching him behind his ear, smiling, whispering to him. How splendid! What a clever little chap he is!

'Barry wee dog you've got there,' she said, at last meeting my eyes and smiling.

'His name's not Barry, it's Albie, dear.'

She scrunched her eyebrows together in question then laughed. 'Eh, no. I know that. Barry means great, fine, grand.'

Of course I began to blush, but I didn't think it mattered. We laughed. Both of us. Heartily! And that was that. Whatever had been held up between us had disappeared. I was so relieved. It seemed that this would become the pleasant experience I had envisaged after all.

'Make these yerself, aye?' she asked, as she tucked into one of my little cup-cakes, crumbs tumbling down her T shirt, her left hand stroking them off.

Oh, if only she knew! I had spent hours making them. Batch after batch until I was satisfied. Baking was rather new to me, you see, and they had to be right. Just so. Some things are important.

'Yes, I did dear. Do you like them?'

'Aye!'

'Barry?' I asked, with a grin.

'Barry!' she confirmed.

We both laughed again.

We chatted about Aberlady – the birds, the sounds, the way of life – under the bluest of skies, reflected on the still, still sea. Sometimes Aberlady can be so breathtakingly beautiful and I was happy that it had been one of those days; that Angie had seen it at its finest. It is such a delight to be able to share beauty.

As is custom in this part of the world, the weather began to turn, the sky filling with clouds, a chill settling in. I had suggested moving inside.

'Have you ever been to the wee pub up the road there?' she asked.

'No. No, I haven't. You know,' I confessed, 'I have never even been inside a public house.'

'Ye're kidding me, aye?'

'No, my dear.'

'Do ye fancy it?' she asked, her eyebrows raised expectantly.

'Well, I...Oh why not!' I slapped my thighs in affirmation and we headed off. I felt somewhat guilty as Albie's little whips of disappointment at being left behind echoed in our wake, trailing off as we rounded the corner. The click of the cat-flap and subsequent silence set my conscience to rest. I imagined he would be settling in his bed in the kitchen. Good boy!

As soon as Angie had opened the door to the public house and ushered me in I had wished that the ground could simply swallow me up. Oak beams ran along the ceiling and the whitewashed walls, there was a scattering of tables and chairs. A sturdy wooden bar took up a fair amount of one corner. A couple of men stood there, leaning against it, chatting, drinking from large glasses of what I assumed to be beer. I had no idea of what to do, where to go. Does one smile at strangers? Does one sit at a table and wait for service? I recognised a couple of the faces, people I had passed in the street, stood behind in the local grocers, perhaps even said good morning to, had the occasion presented itself.

The young lady behind the bar smiled and said, 'Hello!' in friendly greeting, lifting some of my apprehension. I smiled in return.

'And what'll it be?' she asked, her expression changing as she noticed Angie behind me. Her smile momentarily dropped then lifted again as she turned her attention back to me.

Well, I didn't have the foggiest! 'Angie?' I asked, turning to look at my companion, 'What'll it be?'

She smiled and her eyes scanned across the mind-boggling selection of bottles that stood behind the counter. 'Eh, a wee bottle o Becks for me.'

'Two wee bottles o Becks,' I echoed, smiling.

A television whispered from the wall, the tables glowed with a wash of blues and reds, a blurred reflection. The news was on. I knew because I recognised the presenter. Such a nice young man. It felt as if I knew him personally, he had become such a frequent voice in my life, a guaranteed smile at six o'clock. The report was showing a stream of people standing in a line along the side of a road, hundreds, no thousands of them. Men, women, and children. They held their arms aloft, joined together, flags fluttered amongst them. Blue, black, and white. My body felt as if it were on fire. I clutched at my chest.

'Oh! *Mu Jumal*!' (my God!)

'Eh?'

I felt a tug on my arm. It was Angie. I couldn't tear my eyes away from the television. I was transfixed.

'What did you say?' I heard her ask.

'I...nothing...Did I say something, dear?' I replied, not diverting my sight from the screen.

The reporter had gone silent as the camera swept along the road, the people. I could just make out that a song was being sung. The words, the song, they were a part of me. They were me and I was them. I stood and I sang.

*'Sa oled mind ju sünnitand ja üles kasvatand; sind
tänan mina alati ja jään sull' truuiks surmani; mul
kõige armsam oled sa mu kallis isamaa!'* (You have
given me birth and raised me up; I shall thank you
always and remain faithful 'til death; to me, most
beloved, you are my precious fatherland!)

I could see nothing but the people and their beautiful,
beautiful flags, hear nothing but the song. Faces. A face.
It was there and then it was gone. And suddenly the
report stopped. Some other news. Something else. I felt
bereft. Suddenly empty. Suddenly missing something so
utterly vital. An ache in my heart. Tears streaming down
my face.

# Chapter 35

Angie
23<sup>rd</sup> August 1989

I had no idea what had happened, but it was just massive. There was this change in her. I wondered for a moment if she was mental. Just this crazy auld woman an I hadnae known about it before. She'd made a right fool o herself, standing up an singing like that, though. Would've been aw right down my bit, but I guessed no there. It wasnae a randomly standing up an singing kind o a place! Folk stared an muttered an nudged each other. Someone laughed. Fuck them!

She was just standing there looking aw lost, aw confused, her face soaking. I felt rotten for her, so I did.

'Maria. Let's go. Come on,' I said quietly, guiding her away an out the door, leaving a dirty look for them. She was greetin away like she wasnae gonna stop. It was painful, so it was. Thank Christ her house was only two minutes away. I slipped my arm around her waist an managed to get her to put one foot in front o the other until I got her home. Even that wee dog o hers jumping up an yipping an spinning in wee circles didnae bring her out o whatever it was she was stuck in. I clapped the dog. Sat Maria down. Made her a cup o that smelly tea she likes. Still she was greetin. This wasnae right. I was worried for her. Thought about phoning for the doctor, calling on a neighbour. Something. Then the greetin turned to sniffs an she was just staring.

'Maria? Are you aw right there? Should I maybe get someone?'

She sniffed, pulled a hankie out from her sleeve and dabbed her face wi it.

'No dear. No, I'm fine. Really. It was just. I know, you see?'

She grabbed my hand and squeezed it that hard it almost hurt. Stared at me.

'That place, that language, that song. I know them all. Did you catch it? The name of the country. Anything?'

The wee dog jumped up an sniffed at her face. She smiled, let go o me an gave him a cuddle.

'Eh. Some place near Russia, I think. There was some demonstration about independence. That's aw I got.'

'My dear,' she clutched at her heart. 'I do believe that is where I am from. Such a feeling. Such a terribly strong feeling. But it was so very sad. I...oh...'

Her head drooped an I didnae want her to lose it again.

'Here. Drink yer tea. It'll do ye good, aye?'

'I am so sorry. Such ridiculous behaviour.' She grabbed my hand again. 'Can you forgive me?'

'Dinnae be daft! It's brilliant! Ye're gonnae find out who ye are. That's dead brilliant!'

'Do you really think so, dear?'

'Aye. Aye I do.'

I said I'd stay the night. Watch the ten o'clock news wi her. Help her find out more. This time she was ready, a pen an some paper on her lap, wee Albie at her side, her eyes fixed on the screen. The Baltic States, it said.

She stared, dead quiet, an her eyes welled up, but it was okay. This time she was okay.

Anyway, I stayed an got the best sleep ever. Course I'd brought a wee bottle o methadone wi me. Knew I couldnae get by wi'out it. Kept it hidden frae her though.

I heard her pottering about in the kitchen when the birds were still singing away at the morning. It must have been hell of an early. I checked my watch. Half six! Couldnae remember when I'd woke up wi the dawn – gone to bed wi it, aye – but hey, there it was!

'Where would one go to find out about such things?' she asked, as we were sitting in her garden eating breakfast; a fresh fruit salad: strawberries, raspberries, blackcurrants, aw frae her garden. Oatcakes an chunky whisky marmalade an fresh coffee. A wee change frae Frosties, that's for sure!

'Eh, about that place ye mean?'

'Yes.'

'The library maybe?'

'Oh, I don't have one here dear. I simply don't have the room!'

I almost laughed, but I managed to stop myself, swallow it down. What kind o a life has she had? 'The public library. Up town.'

'Oh! I had no idea there was such a thing. How foolish of me. Of course, dear. Of course.'

She was always doing that. Putting herself down. I thought I was bad, but her? even worse. Strange. I'd a thought wi everything she had, money an the likes, she'd be aw confidence, like her voice; like the way she walked, but naw. I wondered about what had really happened to her. I wanted to ask, to find out, but this wasnae the time.

'I'll chum ye, if ye like? To the library, aye?'

'Oh, would you, dear? That would be splendid.' She clapped her hands in front o her chest like she was a wee excited lassie.

'Aye, Course! Nae bother!'

I wanted to tell her. I wanted to tell her that it was my fault she got robbed. I wanted to tell her that I had that bottle o methadone in my pocket. I wanted to tell her that I didnae want it. I wanted to get shot o it aw. Get clean. Aye. Get a life. I wanted to tell her aw o that. It wasnae the right time for that either. She was on this huge high about what she'd seen last night. The Baltic States. I had no clue where they were, even. Just near Russia somewhere. I guessed up north as well, cos o the whole weather thing – It's Baltic, so it is – an aw that.

But then I thought, fuck it. There was never gonnae be a right time, was there? I blurted it aw out. The whole lot. She didnae move. Didnae flinch. No until I'd finished. She stood up an I thought she was gonnae turf me out. Call the bizzies on me. But naw, she just came ower an hugged me. For ages an ages she just hugged me an it felt bloody brilliant. It stretched right through me. My body felt it, but more than that, my head felt it.

'Well, it seems that we both have a monumental journey ahead of us dear, doesn't it? How splendid that we can do it together.'

I wasnae sure what she was meaning, but it felt good. Aw o this felt so good. 'Aye,' I said. 'Aye.'

# Chapter 36

## Jaak
## Estonia 1989

It was the 23$^{rd}$ of August, 1989, the fiftieth anniversary of the signing of the Molotov-Ribbentrop pact – the casual dismissal of a country's right to exist extinguished with the swish of some foreigners' pens. All three Baltic States – Estonia, Latvia, and Lithuania – claimed that the pact had been unlawful and as such, the annexation of the Baltic States into the Soviet Union illegal. A mass demonstration had been planned.

'Are you ready?' Sven called, as he, his wife, his children and Jaak stood at Johann's door.

How good did that feel? It was like a calling to arms, to revolution, but a peaceful one.

Johann came out, a knapsack slung over his shoulder, his boys, now grown into men, in his wake. 'I have never been more ready for anything in my life!' he answered, his Estonian flag poking out of the corner of his bag. They shook hands firmly.

Johann held his hand out to Jaak. Their eyes met as hand gripped elbow. That old greeting of friendship and more. Despite their recent history, their disagreement over Russians, and in particular Johann's choice of wife, that connection was still there.

'Brother!' Johann said with a grin.

'Brother,' Jaak replied, returning the grin.

It had been too long and this felt so very good.

Johann's wife, Tatiana, stood in the shadow of the hallway, watching, distant, listening as their excited voices trailed off in a language she didn't understand, couldn't speak. Of course she knew why they were doing this, perhaps even understood, but she couldn't approve, be a part of it. She was Russian and this whole Singing Revolution felt as though it were against her and her people. Although, in truth, she felt neither Russian nor Estonian. A strange separateness had settled between her and any country. It was unnerving. Uncomfortable. It was becoming more and more apparent that Estonians didn't like her – didn't want her here – as dirty looks were cast her way. She felt as though her marriage and everything that had defined her were now at risk.

But she wouldn't join the counter demonstrations either. That Russian voice wasn't hers. The language, yes, the words, no. Interfront held no interest for her. Her comrades had suggested that she join, that she come and let her voice be heard. Estonian independence, if it came, would alter their way of life – could cause problems for them – and they should demand it be stopped, halted before it began. But no, all that she wanted was to be allowed to continue with the life she now knew: Johann's wife, mother to his children.

She envied Johann and the rest as they strode joyfully up that track, with the anticipation of something wonderful, spectacular ahead. For her? No. She was fearful. This feeling was new to her and she didn't like it. She closed the door and settled herself at the kitchen table with a cup of coffee. The creak of the chair, the scattering of home-made rugs on the floor, the small window that framed a piece of land she had grown to love.

'For how much longer?' she whispered to herself, her eyes catching a spider in its web as it eased its way across the silken threads, spinning and stretching, spinning and stretching.

*

'Can you believe this?' Johann exclaimed, as they walked along the main road that carried on down to Latvia and Riga, and further south to Lithuania and Vilnius. People. People everywhere. Over one million people – Estonians, Latvians, and Lithuanians – who all held hands as they walked until an unbroken chain had been created across all three countries, all declaring that they were not Soviet. The illegal Molotov-Ribbentrop Pact would no longer define them as such. They sang, they smiled, they all felt it.

'This is it, I tell you. Freedom shall be ours!' Jaak called in joyous anticipation. His heart fit to burst.

'Freedom!' Sven and Johann and hundreds, thousands of others chorused.

'Wherever you are Maarja. Wherever you are, know that you are here with me,' Jaak whispered to the sky.

They started to sing because that was what they did. That was who they were. Of course the song spread, voice to voice, heart to heart, soul to soul.

# Chapter 37

Maria
May 1990

Young Angie had very kindly agreed to accompany me on my first visit to the Central Library. It was somewhat daunting for me to be in a place of strangeness amongst so many people, and she understood this. It had taken rather a long time to organise – she was busy or I was poorly – but finally, there I was. The first major step on my path of discovery, or so I hoped. I was quite happily driving again, but Angie didn't want me to pick her up. Instead we were to meet at St Giles' Cathedral on The Lawnmarket.

My word! When I got there the place was jam-packed with such an assortment of people. American accents, Japanese voices, cameras clicking and video contraptions filming away at the most ordinary of things: buses, lampposts, black taxi-cabs. I had never imagined, let alone been amongst, such a commotion! Such was the density of the crowds that I had to push my way through to reach the cathedral, feeling very awkward in so doing! *Excuse me, excuse me. I'm so sorry. Do you mind if I just squeeze past.* Crowds, bustling, pushing; more fear that was almost, almost a memory. Oh, I did so wish it would come to me.

Anything. Anything at all beyond these feelings. The fear.

Ever since that first awakening when I had watched the news report in the Aberlady Inn, seen the flag, sung the song, I had been trying to force synapses to make their connections, neural pathways to form and bring something to the fore. Surely images would now show themselves to me. Memories would drift back. But nothing seemed to work. I had feelings, nothing more. What good was that? I felt that I had some connection with Estonia. I felt that something awful had happened. I felt a terrible loss. That day's visit, I believed, might be of such great importance. *Please let this open my history up to me. Let this show me, me.*

Finally I found myself at the correct steps of the cathedral. There were several, you see, and I had been instructed to wait at the ones nearest to the Heart of Midlothian – a heart shaped pattern on the ground made out of cobble stones that apparently one spat in for luck. Of course I would never dream of doing such a thing – Even here there were too many people, but at least I had the cathedral wall to my back which was offering me some semblance of security – a safety buffer – and I had a viewpoint from where to keep my eyes peeled for Angie. Cobble stones and historical grandeur spread themselves out before me. The magnificent arches and pillars blackened with time. A hint to Edinburgh's past, about which I knew a considerable amount. I may not have been permitted to leave the grounds of Glenbirrie, but I could do so in my books! A well-travelled reader, one might say.

'Fucking tourists!' Angie mumbled. 'Christ, I forgot how much I hate it up here!' She cocked her head and smiled. 'Hi!'

'Oh! Hello dear. Yes, it is rather busy, isn't it!'

'Right, let's get out o here!'

It seemed that she was just as apprehensive as I was, looking around nervously, pushing her way through the throngs of people, checking behind to make sure I was in her wake. Thankfully the library was only two minutes away and the sudden change in atmosphere palpable. Chaos to order. Unfathomable noise to utter silence. And for me, comfort. Books meant safety, books meant learning, books meant escape.

## 1957

'I really don't understand the problem,' Andrew had said. 'You have everything you need right here.'

'Yes, yes of course I do but –'

'But! Aren't you grateful? Aren't you content with all that has been given to you? Don't forget how I found you. The situation that you were in. There are many. Yes many, who would bite their hands off to have been blessed with all of this.'

He gestured around the hall where they were standing. The dark oak panelling, the stone floor scattered with exquisite Persian rugs, the grand ornate staircase reaching up to the first of three floors. And with it all a smell of time, of permanence, of power; rich and heavy, sumptuous and oppressive.

'This house, the grounds, the horses. My God woman, you want for nothing. Absolutely nothing!'

'I know, and I am extremely grateful. I am sorry. Forgive me.'

He drew her to him, kissed her head and said, 'We'll say no more about it then.'

Of course, it was true. She had little to complain about living a life of luxury as she did, but she felt like a prisoner. A porcelain doll kept in a cabinet. She knew

208

nothing of where she lived beyond the grounds. She had no friends; no contact with the outside world whatsoever. As the years drew on her frustrations grew. She pretended otherwise but in truth she wanted so much more. A life. Conversation. Human interaction. She began sneaking into the kitchen and chatting to Catherine, the housekeeper. It was forbidden, but for her it was necessary. That smidgeon of human contact kept her sane.

1989

'Where might one find literature about the Baltic States?' I enquired of the woman behind the library counter, feeling rather brave and knowledgeable.

She very kindly led us to the appropriate aisle. We had only been there for a few minutes when Angie, quite out of the blue, piped up with, 'Eh, look, I'm sorry, but I have to nash. Cannae hang around. Ye're aw right now though, aye?' she whispered.

'Yes dear, of course. Thank you.' I was somewhat taken aback, but I had learned to expect some peculiar inconsistencies from her. A sudden change of heart. 'But I really want to talk to you. Will you call me? Soon?'

'Aye. Aye,' she replied, as she hurried off. No smile. A look of, I didn't know, fear perhaps, certainly trepidation of some sort.

I did worry about her so, and I had resolved to do my utmost to lighten her burden, but there was nothing I could do right now. I focussed on the task in hand. The Central Library was the most magnificent of buildings, its ancient walls imbued with such knowledge. Such learning. Of course it reminded me somewhat of the library at Glenbirrie where I had spent so much of my time, lost myself in a world of books; books that reached so high there was a ladder that spun around the room on a metal thread, allowing one to access the highest shelves. I would pull it around from one side of the room to the other just for the sheer enjoyment of doing so. Simply because I could! I had run my fingers along the spines of Steinbeck, Wilde, Stevenson, Hemingway, Kafka, Chekhov. All names that I hadn't known. All stories that I could fill my head with; drift away with books; places and people, real and imaginary. It was bliss, and it was approved of. Andrew's wife should be knowledgable of literature, of classics, of the English language.

But this, this was so much more! I spent hour upon hour in the reference library, seeking out everything to do with the Baltic States. I would devour the history, the culture, everything I could possibly find. I borrowed what I could and headed home.

Albie was quite delirious upon my return. The poor little chap was leaping and yipping and spinning around even more than usual. Such was his excitement that he dribbled a little trail of urine across the kitchen floor, looking up at me apologetically as he did so, expecting chastisement. I felt extremely guilty at having neglected him so. It was well past his walk time.

'Oh Albie,' I said, bending down to stroke him. 'I am such a bad mother!'

I lay my treasure of literature on the counter and clipped his lead on, indulging him in a longer than usual evening walk. The tide was high, leaving the beach non-existent. The rocks were mostly covered and rather treacherous, so we took the high golf course route. Albie bounded and charged and leapt at the gulls and crows that seemed to be playing a game, teasing him. To his delight he found several lost golf balls – one of his most treasured activities – to add to his already excessive collection. I would have to find a means of recycling them, perhaps surreptitiously dropping them on the golf course when Albie's attention was elsewhere.

By the time we returned home the birds were settling on the water. The sky was tinged with pink. The sun sinking behind the sea lit up the water with a fiery orange. Once again my breath was taken from me by the sheer beauty of this place. I inhaled deeply, grateful. Yes. Now I was grateful. And so excited! My future, my past, were perhaps opening themselves up to me at last.

After we had both eaten I settled into my recliner with the books by my side, a notebook that I had purchased for this very purpose on my lap. It was blue and the pages within were beautifully crisp and pristine, trimmed with gold. I almost felt guilty writing the first words inside. The Unravelling Of Maria, I wrote in a bold sweep. Yes! This would be my unravelling in the very best of ways. At least I hoped that it would. I set the notebook aside and closed my eyes, that tinge of trepidation there again. Albie leapt onto my lap, licking at my nose, wagging his little tail.

'What a wonderful little chap you are,' I said to him. He insisted that I pet him as I read. I will confess that little insisting was required.

I had found much about the Baltic States. They included three countries, Estonia, Latvia and Lithuania. The political history of the area had been full of turmoil; the Molotov-Ribbentrop Pact, the war, the many countries that had ruled over them, invaded them, most recently the Soviets, then the Nazis, then the Soviets again, but I learned little about life there; about the people and the general way of things. It was now a part of the USSR, kept behind the iron curtain, kept secret. I wanted more. I wanted to see films, documentaries, photographs, to hear the spoken word. No. I wanted to go there. I wanted to step on Baltic soil and feel that I belonged. I wanted to know me. If I do nothing else in my life, let me do that. Allow me to live long enough for just that.

# Chapter 38

Angie
May 1990

I'd felt a bit shitty leaving her like that, but the place just gave me the creeps. Too much space. That musty smell. Something weird about it. An when I'd spotted the fucking Drug Squad acting aw casual at one o the tables, well, that was get-out-o-there time. I wasnae carrying much, but enough to get me lifted. Enough to get me sent down. Its no like it'd be my first offence. No slap on the wrist for me. Wasnae about to risk the jail. Plus I had somewhere to be an she'd be fine wi aw the books an students an folk saying *shh*. Never took kindly to folk telling me to *shh*. I nipped out an nashed between the traffic an across the road, hiding myself behind a pillar. Sure enough, the DS had followed me out. *Shite!*

They didnae pull me up in the library which, I guessed, meant they were wanting to follow me. My mind was racing. Maybe someone had grassed on us. Someone who knew I was on my way to see Malky D frae Leeds – Gear to sell; a new contact for Big Davy; a nice big bust for the DS – Couldnae make sense o it. Deke, or Big Davy? Surely no. Maybe someone's got a big mouth. Maybe Big Davy's got a woman an he's blurted something out. Trying to impress her. Trying to be the big man. Naw. None o that made sense.

Course, big change o plans then. I wasnae about to walk into whatever it was that was going down. No softener frae me before the deal was done. No this time! I needed to disappear. Weave into the crowds o tourists. Duck down a wee bit. Squeeze around an past an through. Hoof it down the cobbles, around the corner into Cockburn Street, an down the steep narrow steps o Fleshmarket Close. Careful, careful. Dark an slippery. Tall ancient tenements dripping wi dirt an grime, green slime clinging on to walls made black wi murky time. Tourists looking aw about, "Oh gee, ain't this just the cutest?" blocking the way. *Can you no do your stopping an chatting an taking photies somewhere else, aye?* I almost knocked one o them ower an got a dirty look an a *tut*! Really? My town. Fuck off!

By the time I got to Waverley Station I'd lost them, the DS, but the place was always full o bizzies so I still had to be careful. Keep my eyes peeled. Ducking an dodging. Christ! What must it be like to hae a normal life? To no be looking ower yer shoulder aw o the time. To no be scared. To no be running an fucking hiding. To no be ready to do anything just for a hit. Just for that release. That nothing else matters. Just that. To just be ordinary? To no be me. No idea.

I got home an aw hell was breaking lose. Deke screeching at me, Big Davy calling me a stupid cow.

'What was I meant to do, man? The Drug Squad on my tail? Would ye rather I led them to yer guy, aye? Would that be better for ye, aye?'

Course, I knew better. Cannae gie that man cheek an no come off the worse for it. Wallop! A slap right across my face that stung like hell. That was gonnae bruise.

'Yer punters like that an aw, aye? Girls wi bruises,

aye? Is that a thing?' I should've kept my mouth shut. Course I should've. I knew what was coming.

He smiled that nasty dirty, ye're-gonnae-get-fucked smile. Aimed a punch at my stomach. Breath gone, almost blacked out, an my legs gave up on me. Boots landed all ower me when I hit the deck. Again an again. Wished I could pass out. No feel it.

'You need to get her sorted out. Mouthy wee cunt!' Big Davy hissed at Deke, before putting the boot in one more time.

I just lay there curled up in a ball, groaning, until I heard the front door slam shut. I wasnae gonnae greet. Naw. Hurt like hell. Aw ower it hurt like hell, but I sucked it in.

'Angie Babe,' Deke muttered as he knelt ower me. 'Are you all right?'

I looked up at him an I just felt sick. Just felt, what the fuck use are you even? What the fuck use are you?

He reached out for me. Tried to check me ower. How hurt I was. Looked at my face.

I turned away. 'Just get away frae me. Right now I hate ye.' An I meant it. We'd had our problems, sure. We'd had a whole load o shite come our way, but who just stands an watches as his woman gets kicked to shit? Deke does. Aye, Deke does that. I crawled off to the bathroom. Filled the bath up wi water so hot that it was almost painful. I slipped in, a little at a time, a little at a time, until I was covered an the heat was smothering the pain.

I hadnae planned to. Wasnae thinking really. Just did it. The next day I called her. Maria.

# Chapter 39

Maria
May 1990

I was worried about her. She hadn't sounded like herself. I'd questioned her, but she said she didn't have time to talk. She had asked if she could come and stay with me for a day or two. Well of course she could! I did insist that she didn't bring any drugs with her. Her methadone, yes, that was prescribed, and, of course, I understood that she needed something to tide her over. I had been researching that as well, you see, drug addiction. The poor girl, it sounded simply awful.

Archie had come to see me and, to be honest, I really wasn't in the mood. I had so much research to do, but he was only being kind, after all, so I welcomed him in and offered him a cup of tea. It was far too early for his customary tipple! We chatted about this and that; the weather, gardening, local gossip (which I had little interest in, but it seemed one was supposed to take heed of such matters!) Well, after a short while he cleared his throat, wriggled slightly in his chair and piped up with the following!

'Yon lass that I've seen you with.'

'Young Angie, you mean?'

'Aye, I guess so. The one that was in the pub yon

day,' He looked down somewhat awkwardly, seemingly embarrassed, before continuing. 'Yon day you got all upset.'

Oh dear. Even though it had been some time ago, it would appear it hadn't been forgotten. I imagined everyone talking about my little episode. Casting their own judgements. Me being the subject of village gossip!

'Yes Archie. I remember it well,' I said, straightening my back and shoulders, raising my head, not allowing any sense of embarrassment to creep in.

He sighed heavily. 'Aye, well, folk like that. Well, what I'm saying is you need to be careful. A woman like you and a girl like that. Well.' He shook his head, a rather disdainful smile on his face.

'What exactly are you trying to say Archie?'

'She's trouble. Her sort are trouble and I wouldn't feel right if I hadn't done the right thing and warned you. Folk talk, you know? Folk talk and word gets around and we think that you should...you should distance yourself from...well, from her and her sort.'

Well, let me tell you, I didn't take too kindly to his attitude. I could have feigned taking heed, but no! Enough of pretending to be something I am not. Enough of the restrictions and burdens placed upon one by society and its simply ludicrous judgements. She was my friend. My one and only true friend, and I was having none of it!

'Archie, I understand that you mean well, but I am perfectly capable of looking after myself, of making my own decisions, of choosing my own friends. I hope that young Angie will be staying with me as my guest and I trust that, should you meet, you will be civil. No, you will be courteous and gentlemanly!'

As I made a blatant display of checking the time on my wristwatch, I could see him twitching, as if there

217

were a wasp trying to settle upon him, such was his discomfort.

'In fact I am just about to go and collect her, so if you don't mind.' I rose and he followed suit.

'Oh Maria, I haven't offended you have I? It's just...well, I care about you. I meant no harm.'

'I'm sure, but if you don't mind.' I gestured towards the door, just falling short of ushering him out. The cheek of the man!

I decided that Albie should accompany me. He liked Angie and it was apparent that the feeling was reciprocated. I didn't know what it might be that was troubling her, but I now knew that the affection of a dog could lift one's spirits better than anything else. As I reached for the car keys Albie had retreated to his customary place, lying on his bed in the kitchen alcove, with the saddest of eyes following me, anticipating being left on his own, making sure I was aware of just how cruel I was being.

'Not today, Albie lad. Today you are to be my special chaperone.'

The delight on his little face when I called him over and clipped his leash on! It was simply splendid! Of course I had taken him to Gullane and North Berwick and Yellowcraigs. In fact we had completed our tour of all of the local beaches several times now, but he had never gone in the direction of Edinburgh before and it wasn't his walk time, so he knew that something quite extraordinary was happening. He had leapt into the passenger seat and sat, alert, his eyes fixed on the road ahead, as if he were my navigator and my guardian, as well as my trusted companion. A low growl crept out when some stranger had the audacity to peer through the window at him as we waited at the pedestrian crossing in Longniddry. How dare they! I stroked his little head and laughed.

'You splendid little chap.'

It seemed that he became somewhat apprehensive as we drove into Edinburgh, rather like I did. The busy streets, the heavy traffic, noise and people everywhere. One had to be on one's guard at all times. I knew my way to Valvona and Crolla's well enough and Pilrig Church, where I was to pick Angie up, was only a little bit further down Leith Walk. I found it without any problem and turned into Pilrig Street in search of a safe parking spot.

It struck me as quite extraordinary how quickly the place changed. One minute we were amongst tall grey somewhat gloomy tenements and the next, rather splendid houses, in which one imagined people of some substance might live. I crawled along, seeking out an appropriate space, glancing up at the rather pleasant three storey buildings with bay windows, gardens, rather grand entrances. I was suddenly startled by the blast of a car horn. The chap behind me overtook recklessly, his middle finger raised at me as he passed, whilst his lips mouthed words which I am quite sure were profanities!

'Oh Albie. The boorishness of some people. The utter boorishness!'

Such was my upset that I almost stopped there and then, not caring about the obstruction that might be caused. Thankfully a space showed itself to me almost immediately and I parked up. I checked my wristwatch. We were early and there was time for Albie to have a little walk around the park, which cheered him up no end, although his little hackles raised themselves upon the approach of any strange dogs or people. He barked at some young men. I didn't chastise him as I was sure that his senses were spot on. Dogs know things, sense things, that we just don't.

219

Albie must have caught the scent of Angie because suddenly his little tail began to wag and his ears pricked excitedly. Sure enough, there she was just rounding the corner as we approached the church. She was hunched, her head covered with a hood and she was limping. What the devil?

# Chapter 40

## Jaak
## Estonia 1990

Jaak and Sven had been to Tallinn for another Popular Front meeting. Something was happening; something monumental, and they needed to be a part of it. The Supreme Soviet of Estonia had declared that Estonian would become the official language of their country once again; that Estonia was sovereign. Not independent. Not yet. But it was so close. There had been discussion about identity cards. They no longer wanted to be identified as Soviet citizens. They would be Estonians once again and perhaps this was the way to do it. If enough people could register as Estonian citizens their little country would have to be recognised as such. Legitimised. Surely!

Estonia would be an independent nation again with the right to determine its own future, to govern itself, to be free. It was dangerous; of course it was. They were still dealing with the might of the Soviet Union, despite all of the changes that had been allowed since Gorbachev came to power, despite *Glasnost* and *Perestroika*, it was still the Soviet Union, and it remained mighty. The new

Estonian identity cards had been nicknamed tickets to Siberia, as anyone who had one was at risk of being sent to the gulags, but despite that, the trickle had become a flood as more and more people turned up to register. The danger didn't concern them so much now. Their number had become too great. The entire Estonian population couldn't be rounded up and sent to Siberia.

'Why do you stay single?' Sven asked as they walked up Toompea, their Estonian identity cards now proudly in their possession.

They had just reached the top of the hill, from where they could see across the whole of Tallinn, with its Hanseatic spires, the remains of its medieval wall dotted with circular towers and their pointed roofs, its orange and red tiles, the tall tower of the town hall with *Vana Toomas* (Old Thomas) standing proudly atop in bronze, the imposing spike of the Niguliste church spire, and beyond, the Gulf of Finland.

'I've got Sirje and the kids, Johann has Tatiana and their family. And then there's you, all by yourself when there are so many beautiful women to chose from. After all of this time and you've never said why.'

Jaak blew out a deep breath. 'There'll never be anyone else for me. I just couldn't,' he shrugged. 'That's just the way of it.'

'Who was she then, this woman who completely stole your heart?'

Jaak smiled. 'Maarja. I built that house for her, for us...but...the Soviets had other intentions.'

'Did they kill her, then?'

'You know, lad, I don't know. She left way back in 1944.' He gestured out towards the Baltic Sea. 'Out there. Somewhere out there.'

Out there was the unknown. Out there were possibilities. Out there were dreams. Out there were nightmares. Out there.

## 1944

Jaak had travelled from Pärnu to Tallinn with Maarja. It was from there that her boat would leave. He had walked with her to the docks. Nothing was said. They held hands more tightly than ever before. That electricity still flowed between them, but now it was stilted, menacing, wrong. Everything that had been beautiful was warping, contorting itself into something unbearable.

When they finally reached the docks there were people everywhere clutching on to the little that they could carry. Jaak watched, disbelievingly, from behind the barrier as Maarja and her parents showed their documents to the guards on duty, his throat so tight he couldn't swallow; could barely breathe.

They were ushered through and made their way onto the ship. Maarja hesitated, looked back to where Jaak was standing, staring. She waved, covered her mouth with her hand, not believing what was happening. She couldn't do this. Not yet.

'I'm sorry. I'll be straight back. I promise,' she called to her parents, as she pushed her way back down the gangplank.

'That's not wise, miss,' a sailor said, reproachfully.

'One minute.' She put her hand on his shoulder. 'Please. Just one more minute.'

She didn't wait for his approval, nor did she heed her parents warnings.

'Maarja! No! Please. No! There's no time! It's too – She

223

ran back for one last touch, one last breath.

Jaak was there and then he was gone. She stood on tiptoes looking desperately from the gangplank to the crowd and back again. Then she saw him. He was being pushed backwards by the soldiers; back with the crowd of those being left behind. She forced her way through calling, 'Jaak! Jaak!'

He was shouting back at her, but she couldn't make out his words – 'I'll wait for you Maarja. Forever. Now go! Go!' – She stumbled and fell. Feet trampled on her blue coat, trampled on her blonde hair. She could see nothing but feet, boots, shoes. Was this how it would end? She would be trampled to death by her own people; her escape the loss of her life. Finally a hand reached down through the madness and pulled her to her feet. The stranger smiled. It was the first smile that she had seen in days.

'Are you all right, miss? You need to mind your step out here. Dangerous, so it is.'

'Thank you,' she managed to reply. 'Yes, yes I'm fine. I'm looking for someone.'

'We all are, miss. Good luck!'

There was a sudden swell of noise. A gunshot. A strange concoction the likes of which she had never heard before. People were standing, waving, shouting, crying, hugging, falling to their knees. The gangplank was being pulled up. There was no time to think. This was the most awful decision of her life and she had no time to think. She bolted back to the ship. Grabbed on to the railing of the gangplank.

'I'm sorry...I,' she stammered at the sailor.

'You're all right. On you come now. On you come.'

She had no words. A swathe of something terrible

swept through her. What had she done? She stood amongst the other travellers. Silence, hats off heads, tears streaming down faces, staring back at their land. The whisper of words they knew so well. *"Mu Isamaa, mu önn ja rööm."* (My fatherland my happiness and joy) Their national anthem. It spread from voice to voice, person to person, heart to heart, soul to soul, swelling into a tide. A tragic choral tide.

The spires of the old town stood proudly; visible for so long before slipping, painfully slowly, into the black waters of the Baltic Sea. Gone. There was nothing left to see apart from the flare of explosions that lit up the sky above Tallinn in a sickening terrible orange. The fighting was drawing closer by the minute. Everything was disappearing. Everything.

Confusion. Fear and total confusion. She was straining to make sense of any of this. Fighting to hold herself together. There were no lights allowed on the boat. They had two enemies out there. Both the Germans and the Russians were liable to torpedo them, to bomb them. Darkness. Total darkness. And a terrible, terrible fear.

*

Jaak's sleep had been tormented with thoughts of what might have happened to Maarja. Was he wrong about her survival? Had she sunk with that ship? Did her body lie at the bottom of the Baltic Sea, trapped in the mangled wreckage? A thousand scenarios visited him in dreams and nightmares. More often than not he woke up in a panic, sweating, trembling. Her face had been falling through the blackness of the sea. Her smile slipping from her and turning into a scream. Her hands reaching out, desperately clawing at the water, trying to reach him. Sinking and disappearing. And then she was gone.

225

Nothing.

# Chapter 41

## Angie
### May 1990

I'd taken the bus. Wouldnae normally. Waste o money and it's no that far, but I was hurting an I was nervous an I just wanted to get there quick. To be in her wee car an safe. That's how she felt to me. Safe. I got off the bus at Albert Street. A quick scan o The Walk, up an down. Couldnae see anyone I knew. My leg was sore, my stomach too, an my head was thumping. I'd taken a line before I left – no for the wanting; for the needing – it helped but didnae sort me. No enough. It's only a two minute walk, but it must have taken me five. I got to the crossing, pressed the button, waited like a good girl for the green man – no because I do that, just because I couldnae walk fast enough to skip safely between the cars like normal.

I couldnae help but smile. The minute I turned into Pilrig Street, there's her being dragged along by wee Albie who's aw waggy tails an happy yips. How cute is that? She was smiling, but she was frowning too, her eyes aw drawn together. No surprising really. Knew I looked as bad as I felt.

'My dear girl,' she said, aw soft an concerned like. 'Whatever has happened to you?' She put her arm around my waist. I winced. 'Oh. Oh dear. I am so sorry. Why don't you just rest against the wall here and I'll fetch the car. It's just down there.' She pointed a wee bit down the road.

'Naw. I'd rather walk wi you, if it's aw the same, aye?'

'Of course, dear. Of course. Can you manage?'

'Aye.'

When I was sat in that wee car, her dog on my knee licking away at my face ever so softly, an we were driving out o town, it felt so good. Like some massive weight had been lifted off o me. She didnae talk, just drove real quiet, like she knew that was what I needed. Quiet.

When we got into her house she made me sit in that recliner o hers while she boiled some water, made some tea, dabbed away at my bruises an cuts wi something that stank awful but felt really good.

'When you're ready, dear. When you're ready,' she said.

She just let me be, an that was special. No need to talk, to explain, to justify. Just to be. That was aw I had to do an I couldnae remember ever feeling like that before. I wasnae hungry, but she made me eat a bowl o soup.

'There's nothing like a good bowl of home-made soup to lift one's spirits,' she said.

Aye, well, maybe. I downed it in spite o myself.

'I wonder if, perhaps, a doctor should have a look at you?'

'Naw, no doctor. I'll be fine.'

'If you're sure, dear.'

I wasnae, but I didnae want to go near any doctors. No just then. I hurt worse than I'd ever hurt before, but I didnae want a doctor wi her questions an her looks.

Maria has this way o getting me to open up to her, so I did. Told her the lot; the DS, the beating, Deke. She listened, like she does, just quietly. No looks. No judgements. Just listening.

'I have a plan, dear,' she said. An it was my turn to listen.

'I've been looking into things – remedies, cures, treatments and the likes – talking to people that know about such things. Anyway, the crux of the matter is, I would really like to help, if you'd let me. If you're ready?'

I didnae know what to think. Are ye ever ready? Did I want out o the cess pit that was my life? Aye. Could I see anything beyond it? Naw. No the now.

'What were you thinking then? Help how?' I asked, curious but no that hopeful. I mean, what did she really know?

She took my hand an smiled. 'Well, it just so happens that I have been going to see a couple of holistic healers, for my own purposes, but never mind that for now.' She made a funny wee gesture wi her hand. A sort o "pff" wi'out the sound. 'The point is, they are good people, Jenny and Stewart, who tragically lost their own daughter to drugs, and now they like to help where they can. You know. To try and prevent such tragedy in others. Anyway, should you be willing, they'll take you in their charge for six to eight weeks, or longer if need be. Support you as necessary. What do you think?'

'Eh, I. I dunno. It's a lot. I mean. A lot to get my head around, ye know?' I didnae even know what holistic was. Didnae want to seem stupid so didnae ask.

'Why don't you sleep on it and if you want to, we'll discuss everything tomorrow. All right?' She squeezed my hand an smiled in a soft, reassuring, no pressure, kind o a way.

'Aye. Right ye are.'

I was hoping for a sleep like the one I'd got that last time I'd stayed here, but it wasnae happening. My mind was just going mental, spinning an spinning things ower. Big Davy? Would he let me? Naw. What good's a girl wi'out a problem? To him, no use at aw. Need to do it on the sly. Then there's Deke? Aye, it's aw shite the now, but that's just because o the smack. That's no him. An if I could get back him, auld Deke, that man...But ye cannae think like that. I know ye cannae. Smack doesnae care about what-ifs. Doesnae allow for what-ifs. I've had the talk before, see? At the doctor's, at the methadone clinic. "It has to be about you now Angela. No-one else. You can only think about getting yourself clean. Better. Back on track." I've heard aw the words. I know aw o that, but. When I think back to before aw the shite. Me an him. We were pure magic. An I melt an I want him. An then, there's last night when he just stood an watched. An I was feeling it aw again. Every punch, every kick. An I was thinking, *Aye. Maybe aye!* But it's no that simple, is it? It's never that simple.

I didnae know how long I'd been in bed for. Ages it felt like. Sweating an tossing an fretting an doing it aw ower again. Then I heard the door squeak open. Wee paws going clickety-click on the floorboards then pad, pad on the rug, then a weight on the bed an he was lying down at my feet. Wee Albie. I knew he got locked in the kitchen at night. I knew this wasnae normal, wasnae allowed.

I sat up, wincing at the pain, an patted the covers. 'Hey, wee one. Come on then.' I could feel him slithering up the bed, nudging at the covers an creeping down behind my back an it was the best feeling in the world. I smiled an reached my arm behind me an clapped him, his wee soft head nuzzling into my hand.

Then I heard the creak o a floorboard outside in the hall. The click o her door closing.

# Chapter 42

Maria
May 1990

I decided to leave her to have a nice long lie in the morning. Trying my best to be quiet I opened her door and whispered, 'Albie.' He trotted out and followed me downstairs. I let him out into the back garden so that he could relieve himself and sniff around, as was his custom. I imagined that he was checking the smells of the night. Had anyone, or anything been here? Did he have protecting to do, perhaps even chasing? He seemed to take the task very seriously with intense sniffing and staring through the plants, the bushes, and beyond! I settled myself on the back doorstep with my coffee and watched his endeavours.

It was a just a tad on the chilly side, the sun not yet at full strength, so I popped back into the kitchen to fetch a cardigan and wrapped it around my shoulders before sitting down again. As I sipped at my coffee I noticed that, towards Edinburgh, clouds were gathering and I wondered if they would reach us. It was surprising how often they left us alone, as if we had our very own microclimate; a little bubble in which to live.

It was almost noon when she finally surfaced. The swelling on her face was subsiding and the colour changing to yellow and green. She smiled and winced, lifting her hand to her bruised cheek.

'Morning. Is it still morning?' She looked up at the kitchen clock. 'Oh wow! I guess I needed that!'

'I guess you did. How are you feeling? Better I hope?'

She sighed heavily. 'Aye, much. Thank you.'

But she looked absolutely frightful. I did my best to pretend otherwise; to be as normal as possible in the circumstances.

'Good, good. Coffee?'

'Aye. Please. That would be grand.'

'I've left some literature there for you. You can have a little read, if you like, while I'm out with Albie. Unless, of course, you're feeling up to a walk?'

'Eh, no. No really.'

'Right you are then. I thought not. We'll see you in an hour or so. Come on Albie.' I jingled his leash and he came trotting over to me in his ever exuberant manner.

We had barely reached the curve of the bay when suddenly the sky darkened and ominously large drops of rain splattered onto the ground. I glanced up at the seriously moody and extremely threatening sky and decided that it would be prudent to make a dash for it, and dash we did! The drops became a torrent within seconds and by the time we got home we were both absolutely drenched! Thunder rattled the windows and lightning streaked the sky. I towelled Albie dry first and then myself.

Angie was sitting on the window-seat looking out at the rain-washed landscape, the leaflets on her lap.

'I love storms,' she said, without taking her gaze away from the window.

'Oh, I do too, dear, just so long as I'm prepared for them!' I replied, as a trickle of rainwater slipped down my back and made me shiver. I slapped at it and gave my head and neck another going over with the towel.

I didn't want to ask her, but I was rather keen to know what she thought about the whole rehabilitation scenario. To be honest I desperately wanted her to agree. Perhaps it was that she reminded me of that frightened young woman I used to be. Or perhaps it was that she had reached me; I felt that she was a friend, a person in whom I could trust, despite Archie's warnings to the contrary.

'Sorry,' she said, turning to face me. 'I'm being so rude. I was just getting lost in thoughts, ye know?'

'Yes dear, I do. I spend a good deal of my time sitting right there doing just that! I'm going to make myself a nice cup of tea. How about you? Can I tempt you?'

'Aye. Grand. Cheers.'

Albie was hovering around her feet, looking up pleadingly and I could read his intentions. Although I had done my best he was still wet and dirty and somewhat smelly. 'Bed Albie.' I instructed and pointed to his cushion. He threw me such a look of disdain before trundling off disappointedly and curling himself up into a little ball. I covered him with his blanket to keep him warm and encourage him to stay put. When I returned from the kitchen with the teapot and two cups Angie was in tears. I was rather taken aback, none too sure of what I should do. Maybe it would be best to step back into the kitchen, pretend I hadn't seen, and leave her to settle herself? No. I carried on through and set the tray on the table.

'Sorry,' she sniffed and wiped her face with her sleeve. 'It's...aw o this.' She glanced down at the leaflets, out at the rain. 'It's just so much. So much to take in, aye?'

'Well, of course it is, dear, but sometimes one just

has to grab the bull by its proverbial horns and do what must be done!'

'Aye. Maybe. But it's no just me, is it? There's Deke.' She looked out of the window again before turning back to me. 'So when? If I went, when would it be?'

'I think the sooner the better. Strike while the iron is hot!' *Such a fool – cliché after cliché.* 'I called them yesterday and they told me that they indeed had a space. We could get you in today, or tomorrow,' I answered hopefully.

'Christ! My head's buzzing.'

'I don't mean to rush you, dear, but perhaps now, considering everything that has just happened, is a good time.'

'I dinnae get it. Why ye're doing this. I mean, why would ye?'

'I'll be honest with you. I had wondered that myself, and I think there are many reasons, but does it really matter? I have money, you have need. What harm can there possibly be in helping a friend?'

'Aye, but –'

'And there is something you can do for me.'

# Chapter 43

## Angie
## May 1990

*Oh right. Here it comes*, I was thinking. Something I can do, aye? Always something. I didnae know what to expect. What could she possibly want o me? I couldnae believe it when she piped up wi what she did.

'If this is successful, and you feel up to it, you know, with all of the cancer and everything else. If everything goes to plan, why don't you and I go on a little adventure?'

'What are ye meaning?' I asked, no sure at aw. I mean...

'The Baltic States! Let's go together. Wouldn't that be splendid? What do you think?'

'Aye. Aye, maybe. Why no, eh?' Right then I wasnae sure. How could I be? But I said it anyway. Who knows?

'Why not, indeed!'

'But I need to sort things. I need to go back an sort things first.'

'Are you sure that's wise, dear?'

'Naw, but they'll come looking if I dinnae. They know where ye bide. They know.'

*

236

I went back to Leith late that night, an it was like the last twenty-four hours hadnae happened. I sat wi Deke an we got stoned, just like normal. Well, it was going to be the last time eh! Thank Christ there was no Big Davy an he wasnae expected till the morra. Just a few hours to pretend. No big deal. I could do it.

I hadnae gone to sleep. My head was buzzing, thoughts aw ower the place. I just lay there waiting an waiting until I was sure Deke was well out o it, snoring away, an he wasnae gonnae wake up. I slipped out frae under the covers, got dressed real quiet, found what I needed in the cupboard. Put the note I'd written on the table so as he'd see it soon enough.

*Deke,*

*Sorry but I'm away. Too much going on here for me to handle. I've found someone else. Says he'll look after me. That's what I need. He's from the States. I'm going there with him and I'll not be back. I hope you get yourself together. Won't forget you.*

*Angie*

*x*

Blunt, impersonal, enough room for him to hate me. That'd be best. Hate me Deke, an move on.

'Done!' I whispered. The carrier bag gripped tightly in my hand. No as if it had been difficult, like. Fuck aw to sort out. Fuck aw to pack. Sums up my life. Aye. The sum o my life. Fuck aw. I wasnae sorry to leave that; aw o that behind. Nasty little place, an a nasty little life, crawling wi damp an disease an other people's shite.

He was still lying there. Deke. Greasy black hair sticking to his face. Sallow an sickly. No the guy I fell in love wi. Nothing there. Could be dead. Could've choked himself right out o here. Didnae care any more. I didnae check. No this time. Heartless bitch? Maybe. He'd got totally wasted – right out o his head. Guess he was feeling guilty, an so he bloody should. Helped though. Meant that I could do it. Creep out – Good at that. Doing the deed. Creeping out – I tiptoed to the door. My feet sticking to the grimy carpet made a sound like Velcro. The type that's barely holding anything together. Quiet enough though.

I reached the lock. Took a deep breath. Held it. Turned the key so, so slowly. Slipped the bolts. Like a fucking fortress that place. Christ! Last thing, slid the chain. It was like that game I used to play as a kid. Operations or some such shite. Ye touch the sides an ye're out. Ye're dead. Only, I sure as hell wasnae playing any game.

Anyway, I had one hand on top o the other, trying to steady myself. Stop the shaking. Still had a hangover, see, even though I'd been careful, sneaky – one drink for his two, a wee puff on a joint, nae needles, just a wee line. I've got pretty good at pretending like that. Looking like I'm drinking, using, but no doing it. At least no aw o it. No like I used to. If it was there I'd down it, fix it, snort it, smoke it, pop it, no matter what. If it got me out o it, it was mine. But right then? Well, then I was trying. I really was.

So, there I was, a bit o a hangover, but nothing really. Capable. Aye. I clutched the wee brass ball o the security chain. Couldnae hae it clunking against the door, like. That last wee hurdle couldnae let me down. Wake him. Screw the whole thing up. Okay. I held my breath. Okay. Done it. I took a last glance back at him. A wee panic. My stomach turning ower. A stab in my chest. *What the fuck Ange? You can do this*. I slipped out the door. Pulled it to, so, so slowly. I wanted to slam it. To run. To shout. "Fucking aye!" I said it in my head instead.

The tenement stank o piss an puke tinged wi dog

shite, but that's aw right. Home's home, aye? But no for me. No any more. I slipped along the landing an down the tenement stairs. Broken glass littered the second floor. Used needles huddled in a corner. Could easily hae been mine no that long ago. I'd been good, though. I'd been trying. Nae needles. Promised, so I did.

The old guy frae the top floor was passed out in a heap in front o the stair door, a can o Special Brew clenched in his grime covered, purple hands. I nudged him out the way. He grunted as he toppled ower an his head cracked on the cold stone floor. The thud o a Friday night special. I should've stopped an checked, like usual, but naw. No this time.

I couldnae risk running yet. Folk running early in the morning here get noticed. We dinnae run for fun or fitness, see. No like in the salubrious bits o Leith wi the trendy warehouse conversions. Posh accents an poncie cars, coffee shops an pricey bars, more Michelin stars than folks wi jobs in our street. Jogging? Aye, right! We run to get away. Hoofing it along the road in a hoodie equals criminal. Equals desperation.

So I hunched my shoulders, dropped my head, hoodie up, eyes down, like normal. It was dead early. The sun's light was just breaking up the wee bit o night sky I could see through the dirty bleak tenements on either side o the road. I guessed folk were still in their beds. Most o them anyway.

Out on the main road. Great Junction Street. Then I ran. I ran like the bizzies were after me. Like I'd just done some massive scam. Like it was the only thing I could do. I hoofed it down to the bus stop, limp an aw. Jags o pain were shooting about aw ower the place. Ignore them. Run. Couldnae help myself. Had to try. Slow down now. Be normal. One o them. Dinnae draw attention to yerself. Heart pumping. Breath struggling.

Fuck knows how I could run at aw. But I could. Should've been dead. But I wasnae.

The lights o the bus sauntered along like no-one's in a hurry. Aye, take your time, pal! Right ye are! I checked the number o the bus. Aye. Good. Heading up Leith Walk, just like me. I hopped on aw casual like, ignoring everything. Stuck the right coins in the machine. Took the ticket. 'Cheers pal,' at the driver, no eye contact. I nipped up the stairs even though it hurt my leg. Like to see what's going on. Who's about. No that it matters. No-one gives a shit anyway. Stuck ups or low lifes doing whatever. Something an nothing. Just getting through. Aye, well, me? Me, I was out o there. Going somewhere. Aye! Going somewhere. I could feel myself smile, but it was weird. Like the smile wasnae mine. Like I didnae deserve it.

I stuffed my hand into the pocket o my biker's jacket – aye, it was nearly summer. Aye, I'd get aw hot an sweaty, but that was me. That was what I wore. That was my safety zone. It curled me up in it. The weight o it. The smell o it. Years o getting by in it. Making it. Anyway, in that pocket I felt the packet. That little square o paper that took me away; that killed me an saved me aw in one brutal shot. Obliteration. It was that last couple o grams I'd saved, just in case. Skimmed wee bits off an stashed them for emergencies. Might hae needed it to keep me straight. Help me think. But ye know what? Naw. I didnae want it. Didnae need it. Decided to dump it down the back o the seat. Right there. Right then.

I shuffled it in my hand, an twisted it around in my fingers. Hesitating. No quite letting go. What was I doing? I'd kill for this stuff. Probably have. I glanced up. There was this guy an he was staring at me. Or maybe he wasnae. Maybe he was looking through me.

Off somewhere else. Whatever. I slipped the packet back in my pocket. Just for then. Just till I could ditch it safely somewhere.

Doubts. Brain scrambling. Nothing good was coming into my head. I looked past the staring guy, out the window. Daylight. People on their way to work, shuffle, shuffle. My eyes were wet. Tears. An I had no clue why. Fought them away. No welcome. No any more. I'd started feeling a bit shite. Flaky. Wired. Aw the stuff I didnae want. Couldnae believe I was doing it. Fuck me!

# Chapter 44

## Jaak
## Estonia 1990

Pärnu was a small and quiet town. The antithesis to the capital city of Tallinn. Yes, it was home, but it wasn't what Jaak wanted or needed at that point in his life. He had had enough of feeling like a ghost. Of feeling haunted. For him, Maarja was Pärnu and Pärnu was Maarja.

He had moved to Tallinn to be nearer to the centre of political change: the large gatherings, the concerts, the meetings. If anything were to happen it would surely begin here. Here he had a reason to be passionate about something. To be able to yearn for something that was here and now and feasible – the return to independence for this little country that he loved. Nothing could ever replace Maarja in his heart, but this created a new space that swelled and flourished and helped him feel like he truly belonged somewhere. Here. Now.

It was May 1990 and the Estonian Supreme Council had declared that the flag of the Soviet Union would no longer fly over official buildings. The blue, black, and white of the Estonian flag would be the one to fly. The

Russians were furious. Feeling threatened, they demanded that their voices should be heard. Interfront protesters massed at the government buildings at Toompea, broke down the gates, tore down the Estonian flags, replacing them with the flag of Soviet Estonia, and stormed their way in to the courtyard.

It felt like a coup was happening in Tallinn; that Estonia's newfound strength would be swept away from them once again; that everything that had been building would be broken down. Crushed, once again.

Jaak was in his kitchen. He stood looking out of the fifteenth storey window of his flat in Väike-Õismäe. It was one of the huge Soviet housing estates that had been built since the occupation and bore no resemblance to the Estonia that he had been hauled from all those years ago. It was cold, concrete, inhospitable, but it was a roof over his head. At least he had a view. From here he could see the housing blocks built in a circular design that spread out towards Harku Järv – the tree-lined lake with sandy beaches – and further, the Baltic Sea. To the west and south, forests and to the east the streets of Tallinn. The twists and turns of the old town and the uniform lines and squares of the estates that had grown up around it.

The whistle of the kettle snatched his attention and he turned back to face the kitchen, twisting the knob of the cooker to off, he picked up the kettle and poured the water into his mug, wincing slightly at the near burn of his fingers. He stirred his coffee and walked towards the balcony. Before he reached it he was stopped in his tracks by the sudden change in tone on his radio. It crackled an announcement. The voice was that of the chairman of the council of ministers, Edgar Savisaar. This must be something important. Jaak turned the volume up and listened.

"The Supreme Council and the Estonian Republic's Government are calling the people to protect the government building in Toompea."

What the hell was happening? The announcement continued. The voice urgent, yet remarkably calm.

"Interfront gangs have surrounded Toompea castle and are attacking. I repeat, Toompea is under attack!"

'Good God!' Jaak said to himself. Without a pause for thought he called Sven. 'Have you heard, man?'

'Yes! We're on our way!'

Jaak hesitated for a second. Should he call everyone he knew? No. No need. They would know. He had to get to Toompea and he had to get there fast. As he ran out of the door he snatched his flag and his keys. He pressed the button for the elevator, again and again. It was taking too long. He decided that the stairs would be the smarter option. He took them three, four at a time all the way down and headed to where his motorbike stood.

On his way he bumped into his neighbour, Tiiu. She had tried her hardest to befriend him, invited him round for a meal, for drinks, engaged him in conversation, but it was difficult. He seemed to be such a private man. Still she had persevered.

'Jaak!' she called, ran across to him, grabbed his arm. 'Are you going? To Toompea?'

'Of course!' he replied.

'Take me. Take me with you,' she pleaded urgently, gesturing at his pillion seat.

'On you come.'

She wrapped her arms around him and held on tight as they sped towards the city centre. She guiltily enjoyed

244

this feeling. Being so close to him. Actually touching him. Holding him. The scent of him. The drive was only ten minutes or so. She wished it could have been longer, but also couldn't wait to get there, to defend her government, her country. The closer to the centre they got, the more people they saw on the streets. These weren't people going about their ordinary business. These were people like them. People hurrying to defend Toompea; to fight for their freedom. There was a determination on their faces. Not the soft smiles of the song festivals. No. This was altogether a different feeling. This was dark and serious.

At the square outside the parliament buildings the people formed a throng. Thousands of fists were pumping to the fervent beat of their voices demanding, *"Vabadus! Vabadus! Vabadus!"* (Freedom! Freedom! Freedom!) Jaak and Tiiu had ditched the bike and joined them. There was a tension in the air. If this turned violent the Soviet army would be called in and once that happened there would be bloodshed. Still more people came. More fists raised. More voices calling. Jaak waved his flag as he shouted for his freedom. Tiiu held on to his arm. No-one knew what would happen, but they were there and they were staying.

The Interfront protestors were trapped by thousands of Estonians who now surrounded Toompea, shouting *"Eesti! Eesti!"* (Estonia. Estonia) *"Vabadus! Vabadus!"* (Freedom. Freedom) Shouting and shouting, the crowd growing thicker and thicker as was the tension in the air. It felt like it could snap. Break. Shouting, insisting. Freedom! Eventually the crowd made a pathway along which the Russian Interfront demonstrators could retreat. As they left shouts of, *"Välja! Välja!"* (Out! Out!) were

245

cast at them.

The Estonian Popular Front leader, Marju Lauristin announced, "Dear people, thank you. We were sure that if you came to help us that you would do it in the way that you did. With your intelligence, your songs and your heart. That is when we are at our strongest. Thank you. Thank you. Thank you."

Cheers. Applause. Singing and swaying. Singing and swaying.

Jaak worked his way slowly through the crowd, scanning the faces for Sven, for Johann, for anyone else that he recognised. So many people were now smiling, singing, swaying. He felt, like every other Estonian, as though a great victory had been won that day and he wanted to celebrate. Who knew how long this would last; what the Russian retaliation might be? Along with that joy at having succeeded here there was also an undercurrent of trepidation.

Jaak had almost given up searching through the sea of faces when he felt a tap on his shoulder.

'Hey there, old man!'

'Sven!' They shook hands. A strong powerful shake. 'You made it!'

'Damned right I did!'

'No Johann then?'

'No. He called. He's not well. Couldn't make it.'

'I'm sorry to hear that.'

'Oh, it's nothing serious, just, well...' he shrugged. 'And who's this?' Sven asked, smiling at the good looking woman by Jaak's side, her arm linked though his, a look of tenderness on her face.

'My neighbour, Tiiu. I gave her a lift.'

'Uh-huh. Well, it's a pleasure to meet you Tiiu. I'm

Sven.'

'I've heard about you,' she replied with a shy smile.

Sven raised his eyebrows at Jaak. 'Oh have you now? All good, I hope.'

She laughed. 'You're the one he calls lad, aren't you? A peculiar name for a grown man such as yourself!'

'Enough of that!' Jaak cut in, looking from one to the other. 'From both of you!'

He knew what Sven would be thinking, putting two and two together and making a hundred, imagining romance.

'I'll leave you two together,' Tiiu announced.

'Don't leave on my account!' Sven protested.

She waved as she walked off amidst the swarm of jubilant people. One couldn't feel lonely at a time such as this!

The men spent that night in Jaak's apartment reminiscing, drinking toasts to everything that was important to them, but mostly to independence.

Tiiu lay in her bed wishing she wasn't alone. She wanted to feel jubilant with him. With Jaak.

Chapter 45

Maria
September 1990

A howling wind. Ghastly vertical rain pelting directly into my face as if the gods themselves were hurling needles at me! Little Albie took one look and dug his heels in. He wasn't about to step into that and made his decision perfectly clear by trotting back to his bed and lying there with a look that said "No!" I laughed and let him be.

'You be a good boy, Albie. I won't be long,' I said, as I gave him a farewell treat; a little piece of home-made liver cake which he simply adored. Although, I must confess that the making of it was rather ghoulish! I closed the door behind me, dashed along the path and found refuge in my car. It was only an hour's drive to the holistic centre; a charming, tranquil little place in the middle of nowhere, surrounded by trees and nature. The sea was on its doorstep. All things that were good for the soul.

I was greeted warmly, as always. This was my sixth, and final visit for the purpose of visiting Angie. Of course I had been many times for my own reasons, but that was a different matter entirely. I did believe that they might just have saved my life with their treatments and potions and wisdom. I certainly felt a good deal better than my situation warranted! And now it seemed that they had set Angie on her own road to recovery as well; a new lease of life for both of us.

They had kept Angie isolated for the first six weeks – strictly no visitors allowed – and I had been to visit each weekend since. I always brought news of what I had been doing: the weather, walks, gardening, research. Albie's antics were best received! I must confess that sometimes I made things up just to amuse her. I had been advised to keep everything light. She had a good deal to process, to recover from. They would concern themselves with the serious conversations, I was to be light relief. That was fine by me, however there was a good deal I would like to have discussed. Our future expedition was, naturally, foremost in my mind and I was quite desperate to know if her intentions had changed; if we were still going to be travel companions. I so hoped that it would all work out, but for now I had to wait. Give her time. Let her adjust to the new Angie.

And there we were. She was being released. Jenny and Stewart were extremely pleased with her progress. She was doing well and they had high hopes for her continued success, but this was only the beginning, the first step. Her road was a long one and she would have to continue to be strong if she were to get through this; to leave her addictions behind.

Of course I was nervous, worried, but I tried my best to mask it; to be warm and relaxed and welcoming. She did look well! There was colour in her cheeks, her hair shone, and her eyes sparkled. Quite a transformation.

I had bought some new clothes for her. Nothing too different from what she was wearing – jeans, one of those hooded tops, a leather jacket – but they were new, and I hoped, acceptable. It's always so difficult knowing what to do, what not to do. One doesn't want to cause offence, does one? But I did think that this new beginning deserved to be dressed up, smartened just a tad. As I'd been shopping for Angie I also splashed out on a change of look for myself. There was a multitude of bright colourful garments on offer and I so wanted to shed the drab expected garb of a woman of my age; a woman of my class. After quite some time spent perusing and debating with myself and asking the advice of the very pleasant young shop assistant I had added colour; I had added fashion with a sprinkling of rakishness and I rather liked it! I rather liked the new me!

'I'll put them on later, aye?' Angie said, taking hold of the bag and smiling.

I hoped that she understood the meaning behind them. That visit, that I had taken to Jenners with Andrew, so long ago, suddenly jumped into my mind. My own embarrassment; feelings of inadequacy, of foolishness.

'Oh my dear, I haven't offended you have I? I didn't mean anything by it.' I was stuttering and wittering on as my neck turned red. 'I just thought the new you might like a change, that's all.'

'Ye're aw right. No offence taken. Just itching to get away, is aw. Excited!' She grinned and raised her eyebrows, but I thought I could sense something else, an anxiousness, trepidation perhaps, but that was only to be expected.

'Good, good,' I replied, doing my best to keep my concerns well hidden.

We said our goodbyes to Jenny and Stewart. Strong hugs and soft words of reassurance for both of us. Once we were in the car the weight of whatever had fallen over us strengthened. It was uncomfortable. Worrying.

'Ye didnae bring along Albie then?' Angie asked, with obvious disappointment, as she strapped herself in to the passenger seat.

'No dear. He absolutely refused to set foot into the foul weather!'

'Wee monkey!'

'Yes. Rather. I'm sure he'll be leaping all over you when we get home.'

Of course, there I was assuming that she would be coming back to Aberlady. Nothing had been said to the contrary, but perhaps she had other plans. Perhaps that was the reason for her anxiety. She was reticent to tell me that she had other plans. But surely not. She couldn't be thinking about going back to her old life. To Deke and that beastly man. I didn't want to ask for fear of the answer.

'Aye. Fair looking forward to seeing him.' She put her hand on my shoulder – the lightest of touches. 'No offence like!'

'None taken!'

We both laughed and the air lifted and it felt like it would all be all right. Thankfully the rain had stopped and the drive became much easier. I was anxious to get home as quickly as possible. A police car suddenly appeared behind us, its blue light flashing. I pulled in to allow it to pass, but it came to a stop in front of us. How very peculiar! I wondered if I had been speeding. Easily done when one is excited and nervous and overly chatty. Oh dear.

Young Angie was obviously tense, her knuckles white as she gripped onto the seatbelt. Well, one can imagine, with her history she may well have reason to be! I had heard about her run-ins with the bizzies, as she called them. I was well aware of her criminal record, the prosecutions for drug possession, for prostitution.

The officers stepped out of their vehicle and strode across to us. I opened my window and smiled, as best I could.

'Good afternoon,' I said pleasantly.

'In a hurry are we ma'am?'

'I am so sorry officer, was I speeding?'

'Step out of the car please.'

I did as I was told. It is always best to be as charming and compliant as one can possibly be when dealing with officialdom.

He peered in at Angie. 'Both of you.'

I could sense something very dark from her.

# Chapter 46

## Angie
## October 1990

Aw Christ! The packet. The fucking packet was still in my pocket. Two grammes o a Class A, an there's me just out o rehab. Fucking brilliant. You couldnae make that shit up! What the fuck was I gonnae do? And then I looked at them. Looked at them closely. The one peering in the window wi a nasty smirky grin on his face was Jenkins, formerly o the DS.

'Well, what have we got here then, eh?' Jenkins snarled.

Course he'd recognised me. It was him that busted me the last time. Bastard. Only it didnae stick cos he'd fucked up an there he was, demoted to traffic duty. He must love me! Course I was desperate to be mouthy. To call him out for being the corrupt piece o shit he was. To make fun o him an his new career. I was about to open my mouth, but I remembered what I'd been taught. The new me. Count to ten. Inhale, exhale. Slow an easy. *I'm here, this is me, an everything is okay.* Only it wasnae was it? Aw the mindfulness in the world wasnae gonnae get me out o this one if he checked my pockets. *Fuck! Fuck! Fuck!* Nae choice. Nae choice at aw! As I stepped out I slipped the packet onto the floor, hoping he wasnae looking at me, at my face, at the fucking dread he was giving me.

'Angela Baynes!' he said, smirking, delighted.

I forced a smile. 'D.C. Jenkins. Oh, only it's no now is it?'

*Oh right! Gone and done it now Angie. Stupid, stupid, stupid! Five minutes out on yer own an ye're fucking everything up awready. Aye, what a star!*

'Pockets!' he snarled.

I obliged, emptying them, pulling the insides out so that he could see they were empty, holding my arms out for a frisk. Knew the drill.

'Excuse me! What on earth do you think you are doing? You have no right!' Maria chipped in as I was turned to face the car, my hands on the roof.

'Oh, I think I do ma'am. Known drug dealer speeding away from a police patrol car. I think that gives me just cause. Don't you?' He grinned at his mate. 'Check the car.'

'Young man! That is my vehicle and I'll have you know–'

'Step away from the vehicle ma'am, if you please.'

His pal was giving the car a right going ower, looking through the glove compartment, the pockets on the doors, poking his fingers down the back o the seats, flipping the backs forward, leaning in, shining his torch under them. He stopped, an I knew. I just knew. He straightened himself up wi that nasty arrogance that they have when they know ye're screwed. They've got ye an there's fuck aw ye can do about it. He grinned at me.

'And what might this be?' he said aw light an breezy an sarky. He handed the packet ower to Jenkins by the tips o his fingers as if it was infectious.

'Still on the hard stuff then Angela, eh? Looks like heroin to me.'

His bizzie buddy nodded in confirmation.

'Young man, the heroin is mine,' Maria piped up.

'Is that right, aye?'

'Yes it is, I'll have you know!'

'Oh, we've got a right one here! And who might you be?'

'I am Lady Thomson, formerly of Glenbirrie, and I demand that you take me in, or whatever it is that one does, and let this innocent young lady go. This is my car. My heroin. And it has absolutely nothing to do with young Angela here. I was merely giving her a lift, and that is that.'

She was standing there, hands on hips, a massive attitude. I had no clue what was going on, but she kept arguing away wi them, insisting the smack was hers. I didnae want her doing that, but I didnae want to go inside either. Lady something or other! She'd kept that one quiet. Maybe she knew folk. Maybe she could pull strings. Maybe I should shut up an let her get on wi it.

'What are you doing with class A drugs?'

'I'll have you know that I have terminal cancer! I am in such terrible pain a good deal of the time that sometimes the medicines that the good doctors at oncology prescribe simply don't stand up to muster, and on such occasions I rely on heroin to tide me over.'

She looked ower at me. My mouth was wide open. Course it was. This was pure mental. Things were aw zipping through my head that I didnae want to be there. She'd lied to me. Been lying to me for ages. Lied about who she was. Lied about the whole cancer thing. What the fuck? I had trusted her.

'License?'

'It is in my handbag, on the seat there. May I?'

Jenkins nodded at his pal who reached in and got her bag. As he was opening the zip she cleared her throat,

255

loudly.

'I beg your pardon, young man. If I may?' she said aw strict an confident an do-as-I-say, holding her hand out.

Jenkins shook his head.

His mate opened the bag an rummaged through it, till he found the license. His eyebrows lifted.

'Right enough! Lady Thomson it is.'

'As I said!'

Maria snatched at the bag o heroin, plastering it wi her prints. 'And this is mine too! Do with me as you will, but this innocent young lady is to be left out of it, do you hear? Or is it illegal to be in the company of someone who has hidden some class A drugs about their person? I think not!'

I'd never seen the bizzies so clueless. So confused. She held her hands out, her wrists together.

'Cuff me!'

'Eh, I don't think that'll be necessary, ma'am. In the back of the car, if you don't mind.'

She turned to me. 'Angie, use your keys. The house is yours. Look after Albie for me, won't you dear?'

'Aye, course!' I said. What else could I say? The lying bit was shite an I didnae get it, but she'd done this for me. Got herself in trouble wi the law for me. An it was big trouble. I watched her head droop as she sat in the back o the car an they drove off an I had to pull myself together. Wipe the tears away. Look after her wee dog. Christ!

I felt dead awkward when I got back to her bit. Albie was going nuts, leaping up an making his cute wee noises, but he kept nipping behind me, expecting her I guessed. Looking for her.

'I'm sorry, wee man, it's just gonnae be you an me for now.'

I took him for a quick walk an then wondered what to do wi myself. Course I was curious. If she'd kept the cancer an the title away frae me, what else? I was desperate to have a wee gander around the place – check things out – but I just felt super awkward. I didnae want to touch anything, open anything, move anything. It was weird.

They said that I should take it easy. That I shouldnae challenge myself; put myself under any stress. Well, that one was panning out just fine!

# Chapter 47

## Jaak
## Estonia 1991

In January of 1991 Soviet soldiers killed fourteen Lithuanians as they tried to protect their TV tower in Vilnius – it was imperative that they keep control of their media – hundreds more were wounded.

"They just opened fire on them. My God!"

One week later six demonstrators were killed in Riga, Latvia. The Soviets were trying to halt this independence movement and they were prepared to kill innocent civilians to do so. They were moving murderously up through the Baltic States. Estonians believed that they would be next. In preparation they began building blockades around the capital. Huge blocks of concrete were placed across the roads. Jaak helped where he could. They waited.

Jaak spent more time with Tiiu, each sharing their concerns, their fears. What would become of their little country now? After everything that had happened; the freedom they had stood for, sung for, marched for, dreamed of. Would it all be for nothing after all? No.

They wouldn't allow it to be. Estonia was rising and it would not be crushed again. Over those weeks and months, those heartfelt discussions, they had become friends. Good friends. Each trusting the other.

Gorbachev was in trouble. He had suggested creating a collection of semi-independent republics, sharing a common presidency and military. Perhaps that would offer enough of a taste of freedom to calm things down; a means to pacify the protestors? Soviet hard-liners were appalled and they arrested Gorbachev and staged a coup on the 19th of August.

Soviet soldiers were immediately sent into Estonia to quell resistance. There were tanks in the streets again, fear in the people, again. Estonian political leaders were advised to get their families out of Tallinn and away from their homes. The first thing that would be done would be an attack on the families of important people. Get the families to catch the leaders. To force them into submission.

*

"This is a nightmare. The old days have returned."

"Our streets are no longer safe. Our future. What of our future?"

"What can we do? What more can we do?"

*

Crack troops were flown in from Russia. They set up around Tallinn. A ring of Soviet soldiers had them locked in.

*

"This is awful What is to become of us?"

*

The TV tower had to be protected to keep broadcasts in the hands of Estonians. This was what had caused the deaths in their neighbouring countries, but there was no choice. The tower had to be held, despite recent history, despite what they knew would happen soon enough. Two young policemen were charged with protecting the tower from inside. They couldn't fail. To do so would mean an end to free broadcasts. An end to truth. Hardline Soviet propaganda would take its place. All would be lost.

As the Soviet tanks crept ominously forward, the Estonians ringed their TV station with trucks. Of course they knew all about the might of the Soviet Union. They knew what they were up against, but they would fight. No matter what, they would defend this. They would defend their Estonia.

Meanwhile, the Supreme Council and the Congress of Estonia debated their country's future. What should they do? It was a historic meeting because never before had the factions come together. Not like this. Something legal had to be voted for. A solid footing written in law. Not words, not songs. Law.

Finally, after many hours of debate, at 23:02 on Estonian television, the country witnessed that most longed for announcement. Estonia's independence had been restored. Legally they were an independent nation once again.

*

"What a feeling! What a feeling that was!"

*

The Soviet soldiers were ready. The two policemen inside the tower now knew that they were defending an independent country. Their independent country. They were expecting an attack early in the morning and as dawn approached Soviet tanks rolled in. The leaves on the trees trembled. Estonian civilians formed human shields around the tower, staring in the face of the tanks. The eyes of the soldiers. They stood, arms linked. Defiant. The policemen inside the tower drew strength from the crowd, from the restoration of independence. They threatened to blow up the freon gas that was held in the tower. Everyone in the immediate vicinity would be killed.

The Soviet soldiers didn't know what to do. They hesitated. Their way was now unclear. Their own country was in turmoil. Their future uncertain. Gorbachev was under house arrest. The coup leaders were under arrest. Boris Yeltsin was now in charge. He ordered the Soviet troops to retreat. And they did.

Sven, Jaak, Tiiu, and thousands of others applauded the two policemen as they walked out of the tower.

*

"Such a feeling. Such a beautiful, beautiful feeling."

*

'Heinz Valk was right,' Jaak said to Sven, his arm over his shoulder, as they walked away from the TV tower. '"One day, no matter what, we will win!" And we have! We have! Can you believe it, lad?'

Sven laughed. 'Yes, old man. We have.'

They walked all the way back through Tallinn, taking their time, breathing in this new air. This freedom. Talking easily and freely. A softness to everything. It felt like they were floating, such was the height of their spirits.

Yeltsin went on to declare that Russia was also seceding from the Soviet Union. Within days the Soviet Union had collapsed with each of the remaining countries seceding as well.

Around the world Estonia was finally recognised as an independent nation once again. Soviet icons were pulled down. Great bronze statues of Stalin and Lenin lay toppled on the streets, a metal noose around their necks. People celebrated as they fell. Was it really finally over?

## Chapter 48

### Maria
### August 1991

I don't know what I had been expecting really, but I was confident enough that I would fare better than Angie. The powers that be would show leniency towards an elderly lady of impeccable history, surely! And Angie? What a cruel twist of fate that would have been; to have gone through the whole rehabilitation process only to be arrested for possession of a drug that she had turned her back on. She told me later that she had completely forgotten about it until she saw that horrible drug squad chap. It had been in case of emergencies when she left her flat. Well, one could understand that, but it did leave me in something of a pickle!

I thought it best to treat being arrested as some kind of an adventure, a temporary foray into the darker side of life. It wouldn't last for long, of that I was sure. I had given Angie instructions on which solicitor to contact on my behalf. Dalglish & Dalglish would have my liberty secured in a flash.

The policemen in charge of my detention were pleasant enough, perhaps somewhat bemused, as I smiled and chatted throughout the entire imprisonment process – fingerprinting, having my photograph taken,

263

giving my statement in the interview room (I'll confess, that was something of a thrill, and I felt as if I were a character in an Agatha Christie novel, or some such!)

'Sorry love,' one of the policeman chappies said. 'It's lock-up time now. Get some sleep if you can. You'll be up in court in the morning.'

So there I was, in a cell. The smell was rather ghastly: sweat, disinfectant, stale alcohol. One could only imagine what my fellow inmates might have done to get themselves locked up in here. It didn't bare thinking about. There were profanities abound, let me tell you! Furious incoherent rantings. Young Angie's language could be rather colourful at times, but this, this was something entirely different, what I could make out of it at least. Of course the bed – I use the term loosely – was frightfully uncomfortable and I couldn't help but think of whom might have slept there before me. Someone unsavoury, of that I was sure. Sleep simply wasn't going to come. In fact I couldn't even bear to lie down. I spent the night pacing and perching on the edge of the bed, pacing and perching.

I must have looked frightful in the morning as they led me to the courtroom. Everything about me was dishevelled, I wore no make-up, my lovely new clothing was crumpled and crinkled, not to mention the bags that had taken up residence under my eyes.

As I stood in the dock listening to what was being said about me, watching the judge intently, trying to read the situation, gauge the feelings emanating from her, my heart began to sink. Nothing went to plan! Not a single thing. Despite my look of innocence, despite the strongest of protestations by Mister Dalglish senior, the judge, confound the woman, said that I should be sent to a secure hospice for my own safety! Unbelievable! My own safety indeed! She deemed that I couldn't be trusted to look after myself appropriately so it had to be done for me, securely, in a hospice full of dying people of dubious backgrounds.

It was simply ghastly. Oh, the accommodation was fairly acceptable, considering – a large stately home affair, though not as grand as Glenbirrie, which I suppose was more akin to a castle than anything else – I had a room to myself, with a window overlooking the garden. It was clean and reasonably comfortable. There were grounds, enclosed within a huge fence, that one was permitted to stroll around, making it feel less prison-like. Pine trees surrounded the entire place, which I did so appreciate. Their scent always lifted my spirits. Even there. One could look up at the trees, beyond the fence, beyond the incarceration, and imagine.

But how I missed Albie, my little house by the sea, my little car. My freedom, so long yearned for, finally found, and then snatched away again. Forty years of feeling imprisoned in a stately home in the middle of nowhere, and there I was again. Such a cruel trick for life to have played upon me!

And then it was Angie's turn to be visiting me. I so looked forward to her visits. They were such a relief. A lapse from the madness that surrounded me. I could tell that she was doing well. Once one knew the signs it really was very apparent when someone was under the influence of that nasty dirty drug. She clearly wasn't. Albie was also thriving. They wouldn't allow him into the building itself, but it was permitted for him to be in the grounds and they were, actually, rather pleasant. A much nicer place to chat to one's visitors than cooped up in a room being overheard, spied upon! And we had secrets to share. Oh yes!

Now it was Angie who would tell me amusing little

stories about Albie – I wondered if she too elaborated somewhat, just to bring more laughter into such a sombre setting.

'Oh, and can ye guess who keeps popping in to check up on me?' Angie asked.

'I would imagine that might be Archie?'

'Aye! He's a nosy old git, that one!'

'Aye! One could say that. Has he been...friendly?'

'Oh aye. It's nae bother. Asks about ye aw the time. I think he's got the hots for ye.' She grinned at me in a cheeky, suggestive way.

'Oh, I know dear, but really, I have no inkling for men and love and such things. Once upon a time, yes.'

'Wi yer husband aye?'

'Oh no dear. There was never any love there. Our coming together was purely functional. I craved the security he would bring and he was desperate for his wife to provide an heir. That was my function, you see, only it never happened.'

'So, ye've never been in love?'

'Oh, I am convinced that I once loved someone so very deeply. I run that first news clip I saw over and over in my mind and I can feel it. I can touch the feelings. I can sense the person. The flicker of the tiniest memories. A hand held. A cheek stroked. A strand of my hair being tucked so delicately behind my ear. But I never see a face, a person, a place. I only have these feelings. It is so very frustrating to know that it all sits somewhere deep in my brain, waiting to be unlocked, but that key, that key refuses to show itself to me.'

'Aye, well, maybe soon enough eh?'

'Oh I do hope so. And I am so very grateful to you for this. For your visits, looking after everything for me, plotting our great adventure.' I squeezed her hand so that she could feel my sincerity, but I think she knew

266

anyway. 'And I am so very sorry about keeping the state of my health from you. It was wrong of me, but I so wanted you to be accompanying me on my adventures for the right reasons, not out of pity. Can you understand that? More importantly, can you forgive me?'

'Aye, aye, nae bother. An anyway, I'd've been in the jail, for sure. I'd have been her again. Junkie, hooker, dealer. It's you that's made me this, an well, it's me that should be thanking you.'

'Quite a pair, aren't we?'

'Quite a pair!' She nudged me, grinning. 'He asks about yer health too, by the way, Archie, an I've no idea of what to say to him. I mean is it a secret?'

Of course what I had said to the police and the courts was true – one couldn't pretend about such matters. My diagnosis was that this nasty disease would be the end of me, but one has to put up a fight, doesn't one!

'Oh, I don't mind dear. The chances of me seeing him again are miniscule. And we have much more important issues to discuss, have we not?'

She laughed. 'Aye, we do! And...' she unclipped her shoulder bag and removed some brochures – ferry companies, travel advice, road maps, in short how to get to Estonia.

'Splendid!'

'Oh, an I found this.'

It was a book. "A Little of All These" by Tania Alexander – "An Estonian Childhood." Oh My! That would be devoured and who knew, perhaps memories sparked?

# Chapter 49

## Angie
## August 1991

I felt rubbish when I left her there, but it seemed she was coping fine. She had a big smile for the things I brought her: brochures, an books, an the beginnings o a plan. Something to take her mind off o where she was, what was going on. I was fair chuffed wi myself too. I'd done well, organising stuff, picking up the right bits an bobs an doing it aw while staying out o Edinburgh – old haunts, bad places – keeping to my new routine, staying in her wee house an looking after it aw, an, of course, wee Albie. Me! Looking after something! Me! Looking after myself! Wouldnae hae believed it a year back, but here it was.

Albie went mental when we went to visit her. He sat on her lap an wouldnae budge, snuggling right in tight, his wee head around her neck. It was dead cute, so it was. I was a wee bit jealous!

I'd felt properly shite watching her doing what she did. Taking the blame; taking the rap for me. That was something special. Something really special. An finding out that she was terminal. Fuck's sake! I just had to do it – stay straight. Of course it was for me. That's what they kept telling me. "You have to do this for yourself. You

268

can control that. You can't control anyone else." Fair enough. I got that. But I could also be doing it for her. It was good for me anyway. Kept me busy. Kept my mind occupied. Trips to North Berwick, to Haddington, to Dunbar, searching through second-hand books, libraries, travel agents. That was important for me too. Finding out. Doing stuff. It aw made me feel better about me. About life. Yeah. Seems I had one after aw an it wasnae aw shite.

She was full o saying that the cancer wasnae gonnae beat her. No yet. She was taking some sort o potions that Jenny an Stewart frae rehab had been making for her. Whatever it was she was looking good on it. But wee towns are wee towns, aye? an there's only so much ye can get there. I thought I should maybe nip in to Edinburgh. I had the car. I didnae need to go anywhere dodgy. It wasnae like it'd be easy to recognise me either. I looked different. Smart. Clean. I walked different too. I could feel it. Taller. Straighter. Aye, different.

'What do ye think Albie? A wee trip in to town, aye?' I took him most places wi me too. Didnae feel right being away frae him. He was like my adopted bairn. Anyway, in we headed. I'd planned just to find a place to park as close to the Central Library as possible. Nip in, ask some questions, nip out again. Easy aye?

I got parked in Chamber Street right opposite the National Museum. That was something else I could remember about my ma. On good days she took me in there an I got to press aw o the wee red buttons that made the machines spark into life. Trains an mines an engines an cars an boats, all frae way back. Lights would come on. Wheels would turn. It was pure magic an I loved it!

She didnae come around wi me. Ma. She just sat at the ponds wi the goldfish an waited till I'd done my tour. I knew see. I knew exactly how long I could spend wi'out getting a slap on my arm for being late, for making her worry, for being selfish. I pressed aw o my favourite buttons, stared at the stuffed animals wi the scary starey eyes, sighed at the magical sparkly crystals, an zapped around wi the Van der Graaf generator, then skipped down the marble stairs imagining I was a princess an this was my palace. It was so beautiful, ye see. So beautiful that it was easy to pretend.

'Right you!' She'd yank at my arm an I'd be back down in my reality.

*

A wee look inside wouldnae matter, would it? Just a peek for auld times' sake. I skipped up the stone steps, pulled open the hefty wooden doors, smelled that smell – polish an people, auld things, new inventions. That smell I liked, cos o the memories I guess. I breathed it in, felt wee again, glanced up at the ceiling, three storeys high, glass an arches an curling metal. It was like a work o art. A painting. Another world.

I walked around the entrance hall in a great big circle, looking up, hearing my step on the marble floors, the squeal o kids larking about, the voices o grown ups – some whispering softly, like they were in a church, others loud an brash an full o knowledge that they had to share wi everyone. Okay. Much though I was enjoying it, I couldnae stay. Had to nash.

Wee Albie had curled himself up in his blanket an was fast asleep. Good! I nipped into a newsagent's for some ciggies when the rack o international newspapers caught my eye. Maybe eh? Maybe! I pulled out an American one. The New York Times. A quick flick through. Would ye credit it? A story about Estonia declaring independence! How cool was that? She'd love it. Maria.

'You buying that or what? It's no a library, hen,' the shopkeeper called at me.

*Jeez!*

'Aye. Aye I am. Just checking first.'

'Aye, well, you can check after you've paid!'

'Sell much do ye?' I asked, aw sarky, as I handed the money ower.

Christ, it was a lot for a newspaper. It wasnae like it was my money, but still! Anyway, it would probably be worth it.

'I would've bought more. I would've bought the whole flipping lot if ye'd been decent,' I called back as I walked out the door, the wee bell chiming my departure, quite pleased wi myself for no going off on one, for no swearing at her.

I knew Maria had read enough about the history. What she wanted was what was happening right now. This was perfect! No need to go into the library after aw. I sauntered back to the car, chuffed wi myself. Maybe the shop in Aberlady could order them for me? Save me having to go in to town. Aye, it set me on edge, going there, an that wasnae good for me. No then. Keep it simple. Keep it easy. Keep it safe.

I could hear him, couldn't I? the minute I turned into Chamber Street. Wee Albie was going off on one, barking away like mental. He was leaping about. Folk were staring. Shit! I ran up, unlocked the door, jumped in. He wasnae stopping. Wasnae calming down. Wasnae even saying hello to me. Just barking an barking an barking, an his wee teeth were bared an he was snarling an snapping like he was some vicious guard dog.

'It's okay Albie. It's okay,' I said aw soft an soothing, but it wasnae working. We'd been getting on fine, but right then I had no clue what I should do. I thought about clipping on his lead an taking him for a wee walk.

But naw. He'd lost it. That might be dangerous, an I wanted out o there, so I drove off.

'It's aw right, wee man. It's aw right,' I kept saying, ower an ower, clapping him when I could.

I drove along, scanning everybody, checking, hoping it was just that someone had got too close, maybe tapped on the window to get his attention, to say hello, maybe frightened him. Some kid thinking he was cute an winding him up. But there. Standing, casual as ye like, at the top o the steps going down to Guthrie Street, fucking Big Davy. He was grinning. Staring at the car an grinning. Fucking, fucking, fuck.

# Chapter 50

## Jaak
## Estonia 1992

'I'm here to claim my property back,' Jaak announced to the clerk.

'What?' she replied, in Russian, a scowl across her brow.

Jaak sighed, tried to force a smile to his face. *Even now. Even now I have to speak in Russian, God damn it!* Begrudgingly he repeated his request in Russian. Tiiu had warned him about this as they had talked it over. She was good at this sort of thing; had a way with bureaucrats, with damned authority. She had offered to come with him but he worried. He worried that she was getting too close. Too close to being more than a friend. And he wouldn't. He just wouldn't allow anything like that to happen. It wasn't as if he had misled her. Right from the start he had told her that he wasn't available. She knew that.

'We'll need evidence from you. Proof of your prior ownership. Identification. Then we can look into it for you.' The woman barely glanced up at him, barely acknowledged his existence.

'Look into it? I built the place. Every stone, every log. I built it. Do you understand?'

He didn't want to lose his temper, to be rude, but this was all too much. Johann had taken possession of his parents' house, which left Jaak's little house sitting there, empty, waiting for him. He was afraid that someone else might move in, lay claim to it, but he didn't want to move back himself. Not yet. Not until there was no doubt it was his; legally and forever his. Even then he wasn't sure. Yes, he had to own it, but to move in? Alone? He wasn't yet convinced. It would seem as if he were accepting that Maarja had gone. Forever gone. He had kept her with him for so very long now it would be impossible to leave her behind; to finally say goodbye. Perhaps now that Estonia was free, now that there was no iron curtain, no us and them, nothing to prevent her return, perhaps now she would come back into his life?

*

Jaak watched from his apartment as the light faded, as the trees shed their summer clothing, as winter cloaked everything in snow, as spring leapt in again with all of her glory, and it was summer once more. There was nothing quite like an Estonian summer. Old women stood on the shores of Harku Järv, their toes in the sand, their arms stretched high in worship of the sun, allowing every pore of their bodies to soak up everything she could offer. Higher, higher, stretch to the sun. He stared over at the Baltic Sea as it sparkled in the sunlight, the bluest of blues. He knew it was beautiful. He could see it and touch it but not breathe it. Not quite.

'Where are you Maarja, my love?' he whispered to the sea.

There was a gentle knock at his door. He recognised it.

as Tiiu's. He had been expecting her to call on him. It was mid-summer's day, *Jaanipäev*, and one of Estonia's biggest celebrations. She had insisted that he should join her, celebrate, enjoy himself. The day was beautiful and she wouldn't allow him to hide himself away from it amongst his books and his journal. He had taken to writing his memoir. Every day, without fail, he would add a little bit more. Sometimes a memory, sometimes a thought, sometimes a dream. As his memory began to falter he felt the need to create a written record of his life, of himself; something that time couldn't snatch away from him. As he got to his feet to answer the door he acknowledged that Tiiu was probably right. There was no point in wasting a day such as this. It should be celebrated. Enjoyed. Who knew how many days he had left?

Tiiu smiled when he opened the door, cocked her head to one side, invitingly, her outstretched hand offering a bag of food and some cans of Gin Long Drink.

'I see you leave me no choice!' he said with a grin.

'No choice!' she replied. 'We are all going to my summer house. You have to come!'

'And who is all, exactly?'

'My family, some friends. They won't eat you! Come on.'

Many Estonians had a summer house. Most were simple wooden affairs, hidden away in the forests, that had been in the family for decades. As they rode out on Jaaks motorbike, within minutes there was nothing but a single-track lane that cut through forest. Leaves were fluttering in the breeze, shadows trickling across the road. Erratic boulders stood on the grassy verge dense with wild flowers. Tiiu tapped Jaaks' shoulder and

275

pointed towards a barely visible track that veered off to the left. More trees and then, finally, a clearing. Set amongst a field of cornflowers stood the little wooden summer house.

There was already a gathering of people he didn't know sitting around a fire as yet unlit. This would be a night of eating, drinking and merriment. Tiiu would make sure that he enjoyed himself. And he did. The company was fine, the conversation light, the alcohol flowed freely, the air was full of the scent of barbecuing – sausages, shashlik, chicken.

A few minutes before midnight Jaak crept away, slipped through the trees and down to the beach, gathering sticks as he went. He built his own small fire and lit it, as he had done every year since his return to Estonia.

'For you Maarja. Happy birthday!'

He stood and watched the smoke drift up into the sky. That peculiar light that wasn't light and night that wasn't night. Further along the beach in both directions, glimmers of other bonfires flickered. Excited voices floated across the water, shrieks and laughter as people jumped over their fires to whoops of encouragement. Jaak knelt down by his and watched until the twigs had burnt their way to ashes before heading back to the party. Tiiu had been watching from just beyond the treeline. She felt helpless. What could she do to fight against a ghost? She hurried back to the house, settling herself back by the fire before Jaak returned.

# Chapter 51

## Maria
## October 1992

Well, as soon as Angie had told me about what had happened – about that awful man – I knew we had to take drastic action. It was far too dangerous to leave things as they stood. Who knew what that beast might do were he to find her again?

It was such a shame that her visit had been dampened as she had brought such a wonderful gift of that newspaper all the way from America with such uplifting news. The Soviet Union had collapsed; the Berlin Wall had come down, and Estonia was free! There were photographs too; jubilant photographs the likes of which I had never seen before. I scoured smiling faces, places, searching for recognition, for familiarity, for a sign. Nothing leapt at me other than that feeling. I knew that something about this country was reaching out to me from every picture, every word.

Of course we had to set our plan into motion sooner rather than later. There were several reasons. Angie's precarious situation, my ill health (although I was still determined that I would not be beaten!) and my desperation to find my way home. We had settled on next June. It quite simply couldn't be done any sooner. There was so much to arrange. Albie's inoculations against rabies; ours against a multitude of possible sicknesses. That was rather tricky, but I had my own doctor and he was bound to keep his oath of secrecy so could do nothing to stop me. Inoculate me he must! I was sure he simply thought of me as some crazy old woman and that suited my purpose perfectly! Passports had to be procured, the necessary documentation gathered, witnesses found to confirm we were who we claimed to be. It was all rather complicated, but we would manage. Or rather Angie would. I was sure of that!

I had insisted that Angie become my power of attorney as it was imperative that she had access to my finances so that she could do all that needed doing, book our passage, pay for all that needed paying. The salary I paid her was for her alone and it wouldn't do for her to be out of pocket on my behalf. I had no children, no family – well, none to speak of – and I felt it right that she should be the person to have control. The Thomsons – those relatives that I had barely met and certainly not done so formally – had made their position very clear when Andrew had died. I was to leave. They would fight me tooth and nail to deny me the inheritance of Glenbirrie. If only they knew that I wasn't in the least bit interested in that place. After what I had seen I feared for my own life. That was all that was precious to me. Life.

## 1986

The telephone had rung that morning and left Andrew in the most frightful of moods, far worse than usual. Maria imagined that his frequent foul temper had something to do with him not being able to be himself, to love whom he wanted to love, at least not in public. Their life was a sham. She knew that, and she so wanted to let him know that she knew. It was all right. He could be what he was and she would never tell. Perhaps then he would have been a happier man.

She never did and she so wished it had been otherwise. Had she not been such a coward things might have been quite different, or perhaps not, she reminded herself at such times of self-chastisement. Since that first time she had witnessed his act she had kept her eyes open for signs. Signs of affection with other friends, glances of intimacy, assignations of secrecy, but there had been none and she believed he was in love with that one man. How heartbreaking it must have been for him, for them.

'Maria, I need you to stay in your rooms today,' he instructed. 'Whatever you hear, whatever you witness, do not interfere. Do you understand me?'

'Yes, of course, but—'

'Confound it woman! Just do as I say!'

She did as she was bade and retired to her wing. From her sitting room she could hear the crunch of tyres on gravel, the closing of a car door, but no-one entered the house. The front door thumped closed and she hid behind the brocade curtains, peering out as inconspicuously as possible. She could see two women, one very old, in a wheelchair, the other much younger, pushing her. They were going along the path that led to the woods. Of course she knew that place like the back of her hand; every inch of it. It had been her refuge on many an occasion. That secret place where she could disappear into the comfort of the forest with nothing but the companionship of nature. She grabbed her coat and hurried out after them, taking a different path, but close enough to hear, to follow, slipping from tree to tree. One shadow to the next.

Voices were muffled by the trees, but anger trailed in their wake. She was desperate to know what was going on, but dared not get any closer than she was for fear of being discovered. She followed their trail all the way to her pool in the river. They were stood on the very rocks that she had lain upon so many times before. She had always thought it her private place. It appeared that she had been mistaken.

'Andrew! I have not thought of you as my son since I discovered your disgraceful sexual proclivities, as you well know!'

'Your son I am, mother, and Glenbirrie is mine. This.' He cast a disparaging hand in the general direction of the younger woman, not removing his glare from his mother. 'This spawn of your own sexual misgivings, has no right to any of it, and neither, for that matter, have you.'

'Your father would—'

'Don't you dare!'

'You killed him! Your ways killed him!'

'Oh, I think not. I think your little affairs were far more effective a means of assassination. Mother!' He spat his words with such venom. Such hate.

His mother drew her walking stick out from beside her legs. 'Beast!' she shrieked and swiped at him. The stick caught his head. He stumbled and began to fall backwards, clutching at his face, blood spilling through his fingers, dripping on to the rock beneath his feet. His legs gave way and he fell, his head clattering horribly against the rock.

'You need to make sure of this!' his mother whispered

to her daughter.

The woman hesitated then kicked Andrew towards the edge of the rocks and the water far below.

He groaned.

'Finish him!'

Maria couldn't bear to watch any longer. To do nothing would be as good as murder. She had few feelings for him, their life together hadn't been a good one, but he was a human being. A man.

'No!' Maria screeched, as she ran out from the cover of the trees. 'No!'

They turned towards her, shock on their faces, then stared at each other. A nod of the old woman's head and Andrew's body had been forced over the cliff's edge. A heavy splash and he was gone. Maria threw her outer garments to the ground, kicked her shoes off and dove in. The shock of the freezing cold water was familiar to her. In fact she had always enjoyed it, the invigoration, the thrill. This time it rushed to her senses, clarifying, concentrating her thoughts. She surfaced, scanning the black water, frantically trying to see something, anything of him, but there was nothing. She swam under again and again searching for him, swimming deeper and deeper with each dive. Finally she snatched at some material, his clothes, him, but he was so heavy and her breath all but gone. She could do nothing without first resurfacing. She swam back up, inhaled deeply and swam down again. This time she was better prepared and using all of her strength she finally managed to pull his limp body to the surface and swim downriver until she reached a piece of the bank that was low enough for her to clamber out onto, hoisting his body after her. She turned him on his side, checked his pulse. Nothing.

'Help me! Somebody help me!'

She thumped his chest, forced his mouth open and breathed into it, growing more and more desperate, but trying to keep a rhythm, do it properly. It was futile. He was gone. It was to be her word against theirs. She would agree that he had stumbled and fallen or else they would blame the whole thing on her. They would say that she had wanted his money. She had pushed him. She had killed him. What else could she do? She left. As quickly as she could she left Glenbirrie, and all that it was, behind her.

# Chapter 52

Angie
June 1993

I'm no gonnae lie, it was tough an I was anxious as hell.
I had to keep going till June. Jeez that seemed like such
a long way away. I couldnae get my head round it when
she made me her power o attorney. She was awready
paying me a wage, like looking after her house, her dog,
was a proper job. I now had access to her bank, use o
her cheque book, the lot. Even her house would be mine
if anything happened to her. That was just mental! No
that long ago I'd've been taking full advantage. Out o
my face the whole time, easy peasy! The best stuff too.
Clean. None o that cut-to-pieces shit. But naw, seemed I
was a different person an it felt so very good, if just a
wee bit terrifying. Anyway, my biggest worry for those
few months had been Big Davy, or anyone else frae my
past clocking me.

Maria said I should trade the car in. That was what he
had recognised an it should be disposed of. So that's
what I did. Drove into the garage wi one car and out wi
another (Mental!) It was a lot safer, an I felt a good bit
better. I still stayed home most o the time though.
Safest. I'd figured that if her car wasnae seen; wasnae
parked there any more, he might think she'd moved

house, or at least that I wasnae there. An really, why would I be? It would be a bit wild, eh? Someone like me shacking up wi someone like her. Borrowing her car? Maybe, at a push. Living wi her? Naw. No way.

I was dead glad to hae wee Albie; he was a great wee guard dog. Anyone came near an he'd give it laldy! I never told him to be quiet. No once. For the first week or so I didnae sleep much. Too on edge. Too jumpy. Thank Christ I didnae hae access to any gear or that would've been it. Too easy to fall back on old habits in tough times. I knew that an I kept it right there in my head aw the time. "Move on from it, Angie, but don't forget." Aye, that was sound advice. I liked who I had become. I liked the life I had. I was even quite happy about Archie's nosy visits. Even invited him in, made him tea, said he was always welcome – I know, eh! But he was. For then. An extra layer o safety. Funny, cos I'm sure he thought that he was keeping an eye on me for Maria's sake, no for mine. Anyway, he lived almost next door so he'd have heard anything, known if anything dodgy was going on, an I was glad o that.

I'd walk for miles along the coast wi wee Albie. Seemed like he knew which way he wanted to go each day, different tracks, different directions. That was fine by me, letting him choose. He knew secret places, wee hidden away spaces. He'd trot along, his nose to the ground, maybe get the scent o the rabbits; see them zipping back into their holes, run for a bit barking away, but he'd always stop, look behind at me, come trotting back looking dead pleased wi himself. Cute as fuck, like!

That was something else I'd never done, walking just for the sake o walking, even in the shittiest weather. On dark winter days wi nothing but the howl o the wind whipping up the sea, heavy clouds black as thunder, we still walked. Me an that wee dog. Of course, he needed it, but I could feel it was good for me an aw. It kept me busy, it tired me out, helped me sleep. Same for him too. He let me know about it soon enough if he hadnae had a big enough walk, zipping about the house, making a nuisance o himself until I got the message an took him out again.

But there was something new an, I dunno, special about that whole thing. That nature thing. Watching it, listening to it, learning about it. It was like I hadnae seen it before. No really. An it aw helped. The dog, the place, the trust. Aye, it aw helped.

We got through winter well enough. Spring came. Longer days, more sunshine, softer weather (well, most o the time!) slower walks. Time to just sit an watch. Sit an rest. Sit an wait. At last it was June an I was itching to be off. Nice though it aw was, I couldnae quite settle my nerves. No until I knew we were away. Done!

I had everything we needed. Told Archie I was off on holiday, gave him spare keys, asked him to keep an eye on the place. Of course he was well chuffed. One o those guys. You know the type – needs to feel important, needed. That last night I was up to ninety. Couldnae settle, counting the minutes until it was time to set off. I watched the telly, made some coffee, walked around the house, ower an ower an ower. Wee Albie was always right there at my heels. I guessed he knew that something was up. He could sense it. Plus there were the two packed bags. One for me an one for her. Seemed that she'd got rid o most o her auld clothes. New trendy ones in her cupboard. Nice stuff too. Funny, I'd done the same but I'd smartened up, she'd smartened down an we met somewhere in the middle.

In the end I couldnae wait. I was meant to leave at three in the morning. It was only two, but what did it matter really? Just so long as I got there at the agreed time it would aw be fine. I could drive a bit slower, take a detour – wee back-roads. I clipped Albie's lead on an out we went. It was dead quiet, no a light on, let alone a curtain twitching. The whole place was fast asleep. Wee Albie must've sensed it too – the need to be quiet thing – there were none o his wee yips. I tried to close the car door as softly as I could, but even that sounded so loud, the click echoing away down the sleeping street. I took one more look behind me at that house. Just sat there for a minute, staring, remembering. My wee sanctuary o goodness an well, just being different mostly. Someone new. Someone I didnae know I could be. I couldnae help but feel like I'd dirtied the place somehow though, bringing my badness to it. But that was wrong-thinking. Ditch it!

'Okay,' I whispered to Albie, who had been really good, just sitting there quietly waiting. 'Time to go!'

Final check – passports, tickets, paperwork, bank card, cheque book, keys, money. Aw there. An that was that. We were off! The roads were dead quiet too. Hardly anyone about. The odd flash o a passing car, the rumble o a truck, but it was mostly just us. I smiled at wee Albie who was driving along wi me, staring out o the windscreen, swerving his wee body in anticipation o the corners. What a dog, eh? What a champion wee dog!

I'd driven that route often enough when I'd been to visit her, so I wasnae worried. We'd get there easy enough. Plenty time. Plenty time.

## Chapter 53

### Jaak
### Estonia June 1993

The process had been long and arduous, but finally Jaak had the paperwork. The little house in Pärnu was to be his again. He called on Tiiu. It was only right that she should join in his celebration, after all, she had played a large part in securing its return. He knocked on her door holding a bottle of *Sovetskoye Shampanskoye,* (Soviet Champagne) in his hand. He suddenly realised that this was the first time he had actually called on her. They had been friends for three years now and he had never knocked on her door, or been inside her apartment. He felt somewhat ashamed of himself, but theirs was such an unusual relationship. They were friends, but there was always that danger of it becoming something more and they were both aware of it. They both knew that, had circumstances been different, there was enough there to build something from.

'So, there we have it! My house is mine once more.' He looked to her and grimaced, placing the keys in the centre of the kitchen table. 'And now what do I do?'

'What do you want to do Jaak?' she replied, picking them up and fingering them, caught in a reverie of her own. A different time. Different histories. A different ending. 'I mean, what is there to keep you here?'

There! She had laid it out, offered him that last chance to give her a reason, something to cling on to.

He sighed heavily. 'Honestly, now that everything has been won; we have our freedom, our independence, and I am an old man…there is nothing. Nothing apart from you.' He looked at her, eye to eye.

She held her breath.

'And I have to be honest. You know where I stand. You know this could…we could never. It's not fair of me.'

A lump caught in her throat. She bit her lip and held back the tears she could feel building. Stop it. Stop it. Stop it. Friends. Let us part as friends.

'So you are leaving then?'

'I think so, yes. But let's drink to friendship; to the very fine person that you are.'

'Oh Jaak. You fool!' she said with a forced laugh, nudging his arm with her hand.

They smiled at each other, held hands across the table and raised a glass to each other.

'To friendship!'

'To friendship!'

'And, of course, you'll come and visit me.'

'Of course! It's Pärnu. Our summer capital. Just you try and stop me!'

That's not what she felt though. It was all too painful. How she wished that just for this one night he would stay with her. Lay beside her. Perhaps even – No. This would be goodbye.

As the alcohol softened them, loosened them, they

laughed about the dourness of that Russian woman at the ministry for housing, reminisced about the call to help protect Toompea, the Singing Revolution, the Baltic Chain. Things that would remain in their hearts forever.

Of course, she would have something more. Her love for him.

*

The following weekend he took the train back down to Pärnu. It was so very slow, trundling its way through forests and fields, but that was how he wanted it to be. A gradual slip back into the softer, slower time of Pärnu. Would it feel different now? Now that he had his home again. Now that he belonged again. He was worried, nervous, but also excited and he wasn't sure why. Yes, there was his house, but it wasn't that. Something else had crept into him, awoken in him, but he couldn't identify it.

Finally the train pulled in at Pärnu station. He stepped off and breathed in the air: forest and sea and the scorched wood of a hot summer's day. He didn't want to go straight home. Not yet. He took his time and strolled in to the town centre and on to Rüütli Street, small and narrow and friendly. The two storey buildings pink and white and green, wooden and brick, crumbly, in need of repair, just like himself. *Yes. Just like me!*

He suddenly felt tired and a little bit shaky. Georg's cafe was right there. He took a seat outside and waited. Composed himself. Breathed. As he sat and watched people stroll by, some of whom were probably known to him, former schoolmates, neighbours, now strangers, he wondered about why he felt like this; what was making him so apprehensive, so nervous. It wasn't too long ago that he had lived here, in his little apartment on Kooli, and yet...and yet this felt so very different.

He went inside and returned with a coffee and a bowl of redcurrant *kissell* – a childhood memory of sweetness and summer. Picking berries with Maarja and her mother, their fingers stained purple with the berries' juices, playing hide and seek in the woods, long, long days on the beach with nothing to do but swim and rest, swim and rest. It was beautiful.

He decided that instead of taking the shortest route home he would walk down Mere Puiestee, (Sea Avenue) in the shade of the abundant trees, past the grassland, the park, and on to the mud baths. From there he followed the track to the beach. He stood, hands on hips, breathing in the air, the atmosphere of the place. The last time he had been here, he and Sven would talk in quiet, concerned voices, aware of the ever-present threat of the Soviets. Now? Now he was free to be whatever he wanted. To speak his mind. To be himself. Yet he wasn't. Not quite. That piece of him was still missing. As he walked over the sand he imagined that he was holding her hand. She was leaning close into him. They were so very happy. Maarja.

# PART III

# Chapter 54

Maria
June 1993

Well, I had made my escape! I had reached the main road, as planned, and sat there, waiting, in the small, rather unattractive concrete hut that sufficed as a bus shelter. A peculiar thing to find away out there in the middle of nowhere, but there it was and I was glad of it. Perhaps there was a settlement nearby that I was unaware of. Yes. That must have been it.

I could hear the rain beginning to patter on the roof. At first it was gentle, rather pleasant, throwing up rich summer smells as it settled on grass, leaves, blossom, but then it became louder and heavier until there was an immense clattering. The enjoyment, excitement, of my adventure began slipping away as the cold crept in. I began to shiver. That wasn't good. It was important that I kept warm and I decided, despite my state of fatigue, that it might be wiser to pace up and down inside the shelter rather than sit on the cold concrete bench. There was only space for two paces and turn, two paces and turn; it was frustratingly ineffective! I attempted star-jumps instead. They had enforced keep-fit sessions in that awful place and now I was glad of the experience, the knowledge. Yes, I could do star-jumps with some degree of proficiency!

So there I was, an elderly woman, covered in mud, jumping up and down in a bus shelter! I almost wished there had been someone there to witness the lunacy. I'm sure it would have offered much amusement. However, I was utterly exhausted and my star jumps soon became a limp struggle, more of a damp squib than a shining star, but I pushed on through the growing blisters, heavy muscles, and shortening breath.

At last I heard the approach of a car. Its headlights lit up the forest on the other side of the road as it turned the corner. It slowed as it approached the shelter. *Dear God let this be her.* I waited, with bated breath, leaning back into the shadows, keeping out of sight – one couldn't be too careful in such a situation – but curiosity got the better of me and I popped my head around the gap in the shelter. As I stared out all I could see were headlights glaring at me, everything else was blackened by their brightness.

A panic overwhelmed me and I felt faint. I clutched on to the frame of the shelter. I didn't recognise the car, its shape, anything. Everything about it was unfamiliar. I was quite certain this wasn't Angie as the flicker of its orange indicator flashed across the black of the tarmac, the white of the bus shelter. There could be no doubt. I had been found out. Some busybody must have noticed, reported me. I felt everything drain from me. Every last bit of hope, of strength. Everything. As I slumped to the ground I heard the car door open. I didn't look, not wanting to bear witness to my captors.

The thought of going back there was simply unbearable. I didn't think I could survive it. The initial humiliation, the whispers and sniggers of the staff, of the other inmates. The sleepless nights and tiresome days. If I were to allow them to take me back I would be under constant scrutiny, perhaps even confined to my room, locked up. That really was more than I could bear. I would die. I was sure of it. There would be nothing else for it but to submit; to give up and drift away as was expected of me.

But could I make a dash for it? Let them think they had caught me, I was fully submissive and then perhaps shoogle myself free and run? There was forest all around. Trees and wilderness and darkness. I could lose them. Out there, right then, age and fitness were an irrelevance, surely. It would be my determination that would win the day. I would beat them, like the sickness, like the Thomsons, I would beat the lot of them. I will be free to end my life as me! Yes. I will be me. My name is not Maria.

I was just preparing myself, alerting my senses, tensing my muscles, readying myself to make a dash for it – what was there to lose anyway? – when suddenly the most glorious sensation came upon me. Paws clambered all over me and a little tongue was lick, lick, licking at my tears. 'Oh Albie!' I blurted out between the most undignified snufflings of desperate crying. The car. Of course. Angie had exchanged the car. I knew that. Why hadn't I remembered? That sort of foolishness would not do. It simply would not! It was imperative that I remained focussed, that I kept my mind fresh and alert. Above all, it was imperative that I remembered.

'Oh my God! Are ye aw right?' Angie asked, in a peculiar half amused, half concerned kind of a way. 'The state o ye!'

Meanwhile Albie continued leaping about all over me, licking at my face, yip-yipping in his most special of ways.

'Oh, I am simply splendid now, my dear. Simply splendid!' I held Albie close and whispered in his little ears. 'Albie, Albie, my darling little man, I am so very happy to see you! You have no idea.'

Angie reached her hand out to help me up. 'Ye're soaked through. Best get ye changed, aye?'

'Let's just move dear. Hit the road, as they say.'

'Aye, right, but–'

'I'll be right as rain soon enough, if you'll pardon the pun! Just drive dear, if you don't mind.'

With that we drove away, the wipers thrashing across the windscreen at full pelt. It was pitch black and the conditions extremely hazardous, but we were in a hurry and young Angie drove as quickly as one dared. That awful scenario was not going to be allowed to become reality. We would escape and there would be no turning back.

# Chapter 55

## Angie
## June 1993

I couldnae believe the state o her. Jumped into a ditch, she'd said, a big grin on her muddy auld face. But despite it aw, or maybe because o it aw, she looked more alive than I'd seen her in ages, maybe even than ever. Aye. Than ever. The weather was just pure awful. Chucking it down. I hadnae driven that much, an never in the middle o the night in conditions like these, but we were in a hurry. I'd given up worrying about Big Davy, or any o his thugs being after me. No-one had been on my tail. I was sure o that. Now it was just Maria an the bizzies we had to worry about, but I doubted we did really. No yet. Probably no at aw. I mean, it wasnae as if she was Scotland's most wanted, eh?

She stretched out an turned the radio on, wanting to catch the local news.

'I doubt that anyone even knows yet, let alone cares, but best to err on the side of caution,' she said. 'Escaped criminal that I am!' She clapped her hands like a wee excited lassie.

'Aye, Bonnie an Clyde o the Borders!' I joked.

She grinned. 'Of course, you are now an accomplice. Aiding and abetting a convict.'

297

'I am that!'

'You know, I am so very grateful. This.' She did that wee circle thing wi her arms again. 'I could never have done any of this without your help.'

'Aw naw. Dinnae start greetin on me, please. No need for that.'

She just sniffed an smiled an I felt a bit shite for saying it, but I was nervous an sometimes I spoke rubbish when I shouldnae.

We'd had the heating on full blast to warm her up, dry her off, an it was roasting, the glass getting aw steamed up. I opened up my window a wee bit, just to help clear it. The rain had stopped at last, an the sky had started changing, the black fading into grey wi bits o pink an red sneaking through. It was pretty, right enough, but more important, it made driving easier. I could put my foot down a bit more, get us away. We'd taken the A7 through the Borders an were just about to hit the M6.

I'd wanted to stop early on so as she could get cleaned up, but naw, she wasnae having it. No till we were right down in England, she'd insisted. We were both knackered, both in dire need o a sleep, but we trundled on anyway. We suddenly hit a thick mist that was sticking to everything an I could hardly see what was in front o me. Had to slow right down again. I just managed to make out a sign for a service station. I asked what she thought an finally she said yes. Grand!

We pulled in at Southwaite Services. Hardly anyone about still. Truck drivers mostly. I looked across at Maria. What a state! The mud had dried making her face look like she was half lizard. Her hair was caked in it. Dirty dreadlocks. She was pure mingin. She must've caught the look on my face.

'Oh dear, do I really look so awful?'

'Aye. Aye ye do!' I answered.

'A lady of the road?'

I laughed. 'Aye, something like that, though less o the lady! They'll turf ye out before ye even get in the door.'

I got her a clean coat an one o her scarves out o the bag I'd packed for her an we nashed across the car park. Wee Albie was standing staring out the window, none too happy about being left. We wouldnae be that long anyway. He'd be fine. We found the Ladies quick enough, aw bright lights an mirrors, an, thank God, empty. She stopped an stared at herself before bursting out laughing. A huge big belly laugh. Course I joined in. Ye cannae no when someone's laughing away like that. Infectious, eh?

'Oh my lord!' she said, when she had finally got a grip o herself.

It took a whole load o scrubbing an rubbing to get the mud off o her. The taps were those stupid automatic things that turned themselves off after ten seconds which didnae help matters. Anyway, eventually she was respectable enough an we left the mud splattered sink behind us an made for the cafe. A couple o full English breakfasts later an we left.

A quick pee an a wee explore for Albie, then we tried to get a bit o shut-eye in the car; the front seats down as far as they would go. It was comfy enough but it still wasnae gonnae happen.

'Well, I don't know about you, dear, but I am far too excited for sleep. My brain simply won't allow it.'

'Aye. Me too.'

But that wasnae quite the truth for me. For me it was nerves. This was just massive an I wasnae so sure any more. When we were talking about it, aye. When I was getting everything organised, aye. It kept me focussed.

Kept me on track. Kept the demons away. But now? Christ! I mean its me, Angie Babe. Smack-head, junkie, waste o space. This shouldnae be happening to me.

An what about when we got there? Estonia. What was I meant to do there? What if she snuffed it an I was left aw alone in this weird place where I knew nothing an no-one? What then eh? Sure, she had this destiny. She had this thing that she had to do. What about me though? Maybe I was too quick to jack it aw in. Maybe I should have stuck wi Deke. Helped him get better. Stayed the same. Just no done a runner like that. Christ! What a bitch, eh?

But then new me stepped up. I was better than that. I deserved more than that. It's no like he gave me much choice. *Remember that Angie. Remember him watching you getting beaten to shit,* I said to myself. Aye, I remembered him no lifting a finger, no saying a thing like, "She's my woman. Leave her alone." Like, "What the hell man. Get out!" Like, "Fuck off Davy! You lay another finger on her and I'll"– Aye right. I remembered.

It was as if she knew. As if she could read my mind.

'You know dear, it will all be fine,' she said quietly. 'You'll see. And I am so very grateful to have you here.' She reached across an squeezed my hand real tight. 'I am so thankful to have met you. I could never have done any of this without you.'

'Aye, but you wouldnae hae ended up in that place back there wi'out me either!'

'Oh, but that is an irrelevance. We are here, and we are on our way, and it is all rather special. I shall be eternally grateful to you no matter what. From the very depths of my heart I thank you, Angie.'

Aye, well, then it was me welling up. Me almost greetin. Christ, what a state! I sniffed, pulled myself together, talked to her, cos that's what I did wi her. Talked. Told her about the doubts I had been having about leaving it aw behind, leaving Deke behind. She listened, like she did. No judgements, just listening. An it got better. I felt better. I could do this. I really could.

As we headed south an the sun sneaked up an the mist lifted I put my foot down again. The traffic had picked up an we became just one o many. Insignificant.

# Chapter 56

## Jaak
## Estonia June 1993

The sun was sinking behind the Baltic Sea, washing everything in soft golds, the sky a pale, pale blue reflected in the still water. The beach was almost empty now. A few lovers strolled along the sand hand in hand. A middle-aged couple were sitting where the grass met the sand, silently taking in the beauty that lay before them. Jaak sat and watched as well. He ignored the whining of the mosquitoes, left them to their feasting, and waited, watching until the last of the sun had disappeared. His legs were stiff and tired as he tried to stand. His health was failing him, but he wouldn't check, go to see a doctor. He was old and that was that. Nature would take its course, as it should.

He turned his back on the beach and followed the little track through the grass that skirted the woods and led on to his home. Even though it was after midnight, it wasn't quite dark. The peculiar light of white nights cloaked everything. It was almost ghostly as he walked beside the hushed trees, the soft moon counting each one. Bats flitted silently through the air. The sound of his footsteps were all that he could hear. Even the swallows had settled and gone to bed, having had their fill of mosquitoes. He had a walk of about half a kilometre. There were no other buildings, no houses, just him and the trees. He was in no hurry as his fingers trailed over the tops of the long grasses heavy with seed, that rattled softly against his touch. A whisper.

He could hear her laughter – Maarja – as he watched the memory of her running in front of him. Her long blond hair flowing behind her. Her smile taunting him. He had caught up with her, grabbed her hand, pulled her close. She had feigned trying to escape, squealing in mock fear. He had kissed her. Her mouth softened and replied. They became one as they leaned against the trunk of their tree. The weeping birch that had been their secret place for as long as they could remember, its branches drooping almost to the ground, offering them a hideaway. They had carved their initials in its bark and sat there until morning, watching the sky lighten, the sun rise, whispering stories to each other, sharing their dreams. He had walked her home, as always, heading back to his house with a smile on his face, a skip in his step. He had felt like the luckiest person on earth.

His fingers ran over their initials. He traced each letter, ML JS, and the heart in which they were contained. "For ever," she had said as she had carved his initials. "For ever," he had replied as he carved hers. He had held her hand as they both created the heart. They had only been sixteen, but they knew even then.

He lingered at the tree. 'Forever,' he whispered into the night air.

When he reached the wall of his garden he stopped, remembering his return from Siberia all those years ago. This would be different. His home would be empty and he could do as he pleased. As he walked along the path that cut through his garden he could tell that it had been well tended, sense the abundance of flowers and fruit and vegetables. He was thankful for that. They were little more than shadows, but he could feel what they were. How different was this from what he and Maarja had planned? Not much. Not so much at all.

He fumbled in his trouser pocket for the keys, gripping them tightly in his hand, hesitant, perhaps even fearful. When he walked through this door what would he feel? How would he react? He turned the key slowly in the lock, a soft pleasing clunk, took a deep breath – old smells, sun-parched walls, dust, lives once lived – and stepped through the threshold, closing the door behind himself. He slumped to the floor and wept.

'Oh Maarja.'

# Chapter 57

## Maria
## June 1993

What a palaver it was. Motorways! Such a frightful experience. An interminable noise, people driving far too quickly than was prudent – than was the law – and having the audacity to beep abruptly at me for keeping to the speed limit! Well I never. Such anger. Such impatience. Let me tell you, I didn't care for it in the slightest! Not one jot! I had taken my turn driving and almost instantly regretted it. It really was rather stressful and not in the least bit reminiscent of my leisurely jaunts through East Lothian. However, time passed quickly enough and the miles with it. It was quite a relief to finally reach the A120 and know that we had no more motorways to endure and that we would soon reach our destination of Harwich.

We arrived with some time to spare and after checking that we knew exactly where to go – the ship was in our sights – we took a stroll around the area close to the docks. It was none too pleasant, but we didn't dare to venture far away in case we got lost, which I thought rather amusing considering the journey we had just undertaken.

Little Albie was enjoying being exposed to so many new smells and spent a considerable amount of time lifting his leg and marking his territory. Quite how such a little bladder could contain so much urine was simply beyond me, and how he managed to control it even more so. Oh for such bladder control!

At last it was time for us to take our place in the queue of cars waiting to board the ferry. As we inched forward I felt such nervousness which heightened the closer we moved to the ship, to escape, to freedom, and reaching its climax as I handed over our documents. Palpitations, a dry mouth, trembling hands, which I tried desperately to hide behind smiles and feigned normality. "Lovely weather." Soft smile. "Yes, just off on a little holiday." Excited grin and coquettish slant of the head. "No, no, he doesn't bite." Fake laughter and a carefree tossing back of the head. *You won't, will you Albie? Please don't!* Behind these social pleasantries my brain was churning over thoughts of the law. How did the police operate? Would they immediately send details of escaped prisoners to all of the port authorities, the airports and such like? Were we in imminent danger?

My erstwhile captors would know of my escape by now. They would have strode rudely into my room, whirled the blinds open, perhaps noticed the sheets hanging out of the window, turned around confused – yes, I had stuffed pillows under my covers to make them look like a body, just for amusement, because it felt like the appropriate thing to do, dash it all, because I wanted to! They would have pulled the covers back, realised what I had done and been so very angry, complaining and fretting as they raised the alarm. Then what? I had no idea, but I could only guess that, at some time shortly thereafter, the authorities would have been informed. We faced anxious moments as the officials checked our documents, our photographs; peered closely at us, eventually smiling and ushering us through. Oh, the relief! As we drove into the bowels of the ship we had entered a different world.

And there we were, standing on deck, our journey finally, truly underway. I watched as the land slipped so very slowly into the horizon, until there was nothing left but the grey churning sea, the shrieking and diving of gulls following in our wake, a sky that threatened a serious turn in the weather. A cold wind had picked up and was hurling itself relentlessly against our rather ill-prepared, inappropriately clad selves. Exhaustion soon took hold, neither of us having slept for some twenty four hours, and we gratefully retired to our cabin. Despite the rolling and heaving of the boat in the heavy swell, perhaps soothed by the peculiar constant hum of its engines, I had fallen almost immediately into a restless sleep, Albie breathing softly against my chin. He had been frightened, shaking, and I had gathered him into my arms. Bless him. He must have wondered what had happened to his previously pleasant, and mostly predictable world.

As I came to I forgot, momentarily, where I was; that I was free, and here, and doing this. How wonderful! The sea had calmed and the sun was breaking through soft summer clouds, glinting off the chrome of the porthole, sending shards of light splintering their way across the cabin.

I could hear Angie having a shower. She was singing. How delightful. I imagined that she must be feeling good about this whole adventure at last. I had worried that I might be asking too much of her, as our journey down had been quiet and somewhat tense, and then that conversation we had had about love and leaving one's dear ones behind. I had listened, but I didn't want to expand too much on anything for fear of saying the wrong thing; having her change her mind. Selfish? Perhaps. But I did think that this would do her the world of good. A completely fresh start. New beginnings. She could now do with her life as she pleased. At least, so I hoped.

'Oh, hiya. I didnae wake ye did I?' she said breezily, as she stepped out of the shower cabinet, her hair wrapped in a towel, another tied around her body. I had never seen her bare arms before and I caught myself staring at the scars. There were the remains of awful, ugly track-marks on her veins – those were to be expected – but there were also angry white scars across her wrists, up her forearms. Row upon row of them.

'No, no. Good morning dear,' I replied, rather too slowly.

'Aye, morning!' she grimaced, embarrassed, catching my stare. She straightened her arms out and looked at them herself. 'I know. They're ugly, eh?' Drugs an teenage angst! Anyway...'

'I had no idea.'

She shrugged. 'It was a long while back. Just something I did. Something someone else did. Aw history now. Eh, are you okay, like?'

'Yes dear. Quite splendid in fact.'

'Aye? It's just that you were greetin. In yer sleep.'

'Oh dear, was I really? I...I don't remember. How very peculiar.' And suddenly I did. As dreams can creep out at the strangest of moments, so this one did. An awful sadness had washed over me, only it wasn't me – someone else, but in my dream I was them – I was alone in the darkness with a dreadful melancholy. It was as if I were suffering a bereavement, but I couldn't understand for what, for whom. I was terribly, terribly lonely. Then as quickly as it had come the dream left me.

I was determined that this journey be positive, exciting. It had to be. I was finding me. I had no room for sadness, or whatever that was. I would dismiss it. But should I? Again I was caught in that place of almost having a memory, almost knowing, but it was painful. So painful. I desperately wanted to find my memory, but if I had left behind such pain, such sadness, could I stomach it were it to show itself to me? After a lifetime of not knowing, of course I could! *Buck up Maria. Pull yourself together. This will be magnificent!*

Angie peered out of the porthole as she slipped a sweatshirt over herself. She smiled. 'Have you looked out the window? There's land!'

'Oh, how very exciting!' I peered out alongside her.

'I know, eh!'

Once we had both showered and dressed and made ourselves presentable we popped Albie up to the Dog Deck and allowed him to do his business. Poor little fellow. It was rather ghastly, the smell frightful, and he wasn't in the least impressed but needs must! Somewhat guiltily I left him in the cabin and headed up to the dining room where breakfast awaited.

There was a rather splendid Scandinavian buffet of smoked salmon and herring and hams and cheeses along with fresh crusty rolls, croissants, and black bread. I surreptitiously slipped some into a napkin for Albie's later enjoyment; a salve of my conscience. There were no tables left beside the windows. I imagine most of the other passengers had the same desire to watch our destination slipping more and more into our reality. Instead we took our breakfast back to our cabin and peered out of the porthole as we ate. Albie scoffed his delicacies down in a second, as if I had made some wonderful mistake and they weren't really his for the eating! I did wonder how any enjoyment could be had in

309

wolfing something down like that. No pause to savour, to relish. However he licked and licked at his mouth ensuring not a trace escaped him.

The distant indistinct forms of grey grew into dotted islands, heavy with trees, then a large unending stretch of land. Buildings revealed themselves on the skyline. The water narrowed to a wide river rather than the open sea. People began to make their way to the exits and we followed suit. I was very appreciative of our decision to travel light – really, how much does one actually need? – as I watched others struggling with too many cumbersome bags. Over-excited children scurried around whilst their parents tried in vain to get them to calm down. Tempers became frayed and smiles turned into exasperated frowns. I had scooped Albie up, not wanting him to get trodden on, tripped over, or scolded. He was only too happy to escape from the mayhem and take up his rightful place in my arms.

'It won't be long now, Albie,' I whispered at his neck, nudging it with my nose. 'Land ahoy!'

The ship had jolted and shuddered, the engines cut. The groan and squeak of heavy doors opening could be heard above the clamour of impatient passengers all vying to be one of the first out. Hurry, hurry. I hung back initially, not wanting to get involved in such a fracas but found myself swept up in the tide of people. It was easier to go with the flow than to stand aside and be polite. We made our way through the rows of cars and found ours. It was done. We would soon be on foreign soil.

# Chapter 58

Angie
June 1993

I wasnae that sure about her being the driver. She'd been weird aw journey. Sort o distant an no aw there. An that greetin she was doing the night before, that wasnae right. But it was her car, her journey an she said she was fine. We got through customs nae bother. A wee check for Albie; aw smiles an sweet words frae the guards an we were off. Fuck me! There I was in Gothenburg, Sweden. Me! Everything was different. The buildings, the smells, the sounds. Everything. I had to remind her to stay on the wrong side o the road on more than one occasion. Heart in mouth. "Look out!"

'If it feels wrong, it's right, and vice versa,' she kept saying to herself.

Aye well, fingers crossed an aw that!

Once we'd made it out o the city it wasnae so tricky. I was navigating so that she only had to look at the road, no the signs, no the map, just the road. We had about three hundred miles o a drive. We'd stopped for lunch an switched drivers an made good time. Once we'd got past Jönköping and onto the E4 it was easy. Just the one road aw the way to Stockholm.

The boat to Helsinki wasnae until the next day so we

found a wee hotel out in the sticks, aw polished wood inside an out, like a chalet only bigger. Everything was clean an sparkly; even the people wi their long legs an sun tans an blond hair. So different, man. So different.

We took Albie for a decent long walk in the woods. He was desperate to get off the lead, tugging an tugging away an looking back as if to say, "Come on!", but Maria was feart that he'd catch a smell an run off an get lost, so, despite his best efforts, he was stuck to us. Dinner was meatballs for all o us. No like any meatballs I'd ever had but tasty enough. Albie fair enjoyed his! After eating we just sat on the balcony, aw quiet, watching the trees, listening to the birds, catching bits o conversations frae folk that walked by that we didnae understand a word o. It was a switching off. No need to listen. No need to be on guard. Nothing to understand, nothing to fear. It was surreal an I struggled no to pinch myself. This wasnae a dream.

The next morning we were off sharp. Didnae need to be. It was only about an hour's drive, or so we'd guessed, an we'd given ourselves another hour to find the docks. Aw good. Nae bother. The boat left at two. Another twenty four hours an there we were in Helsinki. It was only two hours across the Baltic Sea frae there to Tallinn. Estonia man. Estonia! Christ's sake. Hadnae even heard o the place a couple o years back, an now it might become home. She'd said if I liked it I could stay. She was so sure now, even though she hadnae remembered anything – at least no as far as I knew – she was sure that she came frae there. That she was Estonian. That she was going home.

I'm no gonnae lie, then it was exciting. It was like I'd left aw that being edgy an stuff back there somewhere. Back in a place that didnae belong to me any more; a person that wasnae me any more. I had no clue o what to expect; what it'd be like, an as for her, Maria, I could feel it in her. So excited on the outside, but I could tell that inside she was crapping herself. This was pretty massive, wasn't it? I mean, this could make or break her. This could be absolutely brilliant or a total nightmare.

She'd stopped speaking about it an it kinda worried me. Was she hiding something? Was she losing it? Was it just the sickness? She never spoke about that either. Said if she didnae gie it space in her head then it wouldnae keep a hold o her body. Cancer was a word she wouldnae use. I got that. I agreed wi that. Made sense, eh? Anyway, I had no clue what was going on, but I was here an it was happening, whatever it was.

There was music an dancing an some serious drinking going on in the ferry across to Tallinn. I'd've been in there giving it laldy no so long ago. No any more. Naw! The new me was this companion – is that what they're called? – to a posh auld woman who'd lived wi'out her memory nearly aw o her life. Jeez!

# Chapter 59

Maria
June 1993

So this was it. The final leg of my journey was upon me. In a matter of some two hours I would be stepping on to Estonian soil and I would know. Not that I had any doubt any more, but this would cement it; dot the i's of my nationality, as it were. I couldn't bear to miss any of the crossing, so from the moment we had left Helsinki I had taken my place at the bow of the ship and I sat and stared at nothing but the calm blue sea, the diving and soaring of the gulls, the odd cloud drifting by, an endlessness that felt somehow painful, but altogether beautiful.

At last I thought I could see something begin to take form far away on the tip of the horizon. I stood, as if that might somehow make the journey quicker, our route shorter, my vision clearer. I blinked, stared, rubbed my eyes, stared again. It could have been a cloud; a dark storm building. It could have been nothing more than a hallucination. I felt myself clutch Angie's arm.

'Aye,' she said, knowing at once that my clutch was a question. 'I see it too.'

It seemed to take an interminably long time for us to draw any closer; for any form to begin to take shape, an identifiable feature, anything that might confirm that the growing shadow was something solid, substantial. Land. Home. Yes, home! I could taste it in the air I was breathing, feel it on every pore of my body. I was going home.

As the land finally began to take shape, rising slowly out of the sea, we sailed through a peculiar collection of old rusting vessels. Some sort of ship's graveyard it seemed. Beyond them tall elegant towers stretched into the sky.

'Oh my lord...I...Oh.'

I knew the outline. I knew the towers. I knew. My legs buckled beneath me and my breath caught as tears flowed down my face. But this wasn't what I had been expecting at all. This was awful. I felt awful. A terror had filled me.

Angie caught me. Straightened me. Pulled me up. 'Are you aw right?' she asked.

I couldn't speak, but simply nodded. My eyes were fixed on the tower of Saint Olaf's. Yes, I knew its name. The tower of Saint Olaf's church, rising tall and thin above all of the other towers of Tallinn. That outline, all of it, was known so intimately to me. And from that very perspective. But the one that my memory was finally releasing was aflame; the night sky behind it was orange; smoke twisted grotesquely, the sound of gunfire, the thud of falling bombs, an awful wrench to my heart.

But what was before me now was beautiful: soft, gentle and beautiful. I began to sing. I think it was a whisper, but I couldn't be sure. It was the strangest of moments; such a turmoil of emotions. '*Mu isamaa...*' (My fatherland) I sang. There was nothing else I could do. Another voice joined mine, and we sang, but when I looked in their direction there was no-one. Perhaps I was losing my sanity with imaginings, visions? I didn't know. I turned back to the direction in which we were headed. The outlines on the horizon grew closer, more defined, and we would soon be there. On the land. A part of it. How incredible.

'Are you returning as well?' a stranger who had appeared alongside me asked, his eyes also moist with tears, a soft smile lifting his face.

'Yes,' I smiled in return, wiping the tears from my cheeks. 'Yes I believe I am.'

'It's quite something, isn't it?'

'It most certainly is.'

I hoped that he wouldn't reply. Pleasant though he appeared to be, conversation was a struggle. All I wanted to do was take it in, wrap myself in it. Keep it. When we reached the dock I was caught in the most peculiar of dilemmas. Of course I was desperate to set foot on the land, but equally I couldn't bear to have it leave my sight even for an instant.

'Come on,' Angie called above the clamour of the juddering ship, her eyebrows raised in anticipation. Albie was equally anxious to disembark, to be free to be "dog" again. I gave in to their pleadings and we hurried down to the car deck. We settled ourselves in the car and drove through the gaping hole that opened onto Estonia. Estonia! I could hardly believe it.

The border guards took a cursory glance at our documents, a check of the car registration, a look through the windows, a smile at Albie who was bark, bark, barking at their intrusion!

'Hush now, Albie,' I said, knowing full well that it would have little or no effect, but feeling the need to show willing!

The border guard lady just smiled and shook her head in a pleasant, friendly, kind of a way.

As soon as we were clear of the docks I pulled up,

stepped out of the car, took a deep breath of this new air. Everything about it was different. The smell, the taste, the way it climbed into my lungs and filled me with such awe.

'*Eestimaa!*' (Estonia!)

As I stood there, taking it all in, looking around, I came to the awful realisation that I recognised nothing.

'I don't know. I don't know any of it now. Where to go, what to do. Nothing.'

'Aye, well it's been that long. Forty odd years, eh? It's aw gonnae have changed,' Angie said, encouragingly.

'Yes. Yes, of course. Or perhaps my memory is just going to fail me and refuse to resurface after so very long? Oh, I don't know, dear. One would imagine that after so much time I would be patient, but I am simply desperate. I have to know. I have to remember. Please let me remember.'

Angie took my arm. 'Come on. Let's get away. I'll drive, aye?'

'Oh...yes. Of course. Just drive, dear. Just drive.'

I glanced around at the strangeness, the concrete buildings, tarmacadam roads that really could have belonged anywhere. The odd structure that I thought, perhaps, I recognised, but there was no sense of belonging. We came to a park on our right. A decent enough expanse of open space for Albie to have a trot around. I felt he deserved that much at least.

'Why don't we find a parking spot and stretch our legs. It's always a good way to make decisions, don't you think? A walk amongst nature.'

'Aye, right ye are.'

# Chapter 60

## Jaak
### Estonia June 1993

He had barely slept that first night. There were simply too many ghosts. When he awoke the following morning he resolved to smarten the place up; to decorate, rejuvenate, make it as close to how it had been when he had first built it and made it ready for Maarja and him to live in. Some of the furniture was even the same. Things he and his father had made, others they had bought: the kitchen table and chairs, the oak cupboard in the sitting room, the book case. How remarkable that they had lasted so long, endured a generation of children. They should have been his children. They would have been so loved. This house would have been so loved. He found himself imagining games of chase in the garden, cosy nights by the fire, tucking them up in their beds, kissing them goodnight, ready to see the day out with Maarja; to spend the night with her wrapped up in his arms. A whole lifetime denied. How very unfair it had all been.

'Enough!' he chastised himself for wallowing in pointless dreaming. Imaginary reminiscing.

He hadn't thought to bring food with him, supplies,

anything really, and the cupboards were bare. Most of what he had in Tallinn he had left behind. He had decided that everything should be bought in Pärnu. That seemed fitting somehow. It didn't do to waste and he had perhaps been foolish, but it was done now. After a quick check of what he needed, what he wanted, he was about to head back into town when there was a knock at the door.

'Sven! What the devil? How did you even know I was here?'

'Ah, it's a small town. You were spotted yesterday sitting outside Georg's. I guessed you might have taken the plunge and moved back in here. Mighty glad you have old man. Mighty glad! But you should have said. I would have met you.'

'It wasn't...I wasn't sure how I'd feel; if I'd want to stay.'

'And?'

'It's the place where my heart feels at home. I was just about to go and find some things I need to make it more...habitable. Food and suchlike.'

They returned with enough groceries to last a few days, paint, and tools. Sven stayed and helped prepare the walls, sand the woodwork, and whilst Jaak was glad of the help and the company, he was quiet, thoughtful. Every stroke of sandpaper, scrape of metal across plaster, was attached to a wish, a deep, deep longing that the purpose of this wasn't for him alone. One day she would return and their little house would be ready; he would be ready. He didn't dare to voice any of this. His friend would worry about his sanity. And anyway, his feelings were so personal, his dreams so secret, they weren't for sharing.

Unbeknown to Jaak, Sven had more that an inkling

about what was going on in his mind. The delicacy, the choice of colour, the precision, were all new – behaviour he hadn't witnessed in Jaak before. He knew about the depth of feeling; the love that had survived decades with no return. He would help his friend achieve what he had to, regardless of the implausible reasons for their labour. They worked on into the night, until everything was ready for painting the following day.

'Are you sure you wouldn't rather come and stay at my house until it's all ready here? You know you're more than welcome. It'd be a squash, but a happy one! The boys, I call them boys, but they're men now.' He laughed at himself. 'They're always pleased to see you.'

'Kind of you, lad, but no. I can crack on at first light if I sleep here. Get more done.'

'Is there a rush? Something that I don't know about?'

'You know me; can't settle until a job is done. And I have set myself a time. It will be ready for *Jaanipäev*.'

'Are you having a party then?'

'No, no,' he smiled softly. 'Quite the opposite.'

'You should come and join us. We will be on the beach, as usual.'

Jaak smiled. 'Perhaps.' But he knew he wouldn't be going. Not this year.

They parted with their customary strong handshake. Jaak sat on his doorstep looking out at his garden, as he had all those years ago, before heading off to become a Forest Brother. Such a long time ago, but somehow so very close. He pulled a blanket out onto the grass and lay, looking up at the stars until sleep finally took him.

He awoke with the birds a few hours later – their song so overwhelming, filling every corner of the garden, of the sky – not fully rested but keen to work on. His back ached, his limbs likewise, such were the accompaniments of old age. Nevertheless he pushed on through the pain. The kitchen became yellow, like the early spring daffodils, the sitting room the gentle green of the leaves of the lime tree, the bedrooms the soft pink of the roses that were blooming in their garden, the bathroom the blue of the cornflower – Estonia's national flower – all exactly as they had planned.

'This would please you,' he whispered. Satisfied.

# Chapter 61

Angie
Estonia June 1993

The place just wasnae what I was expecting at aw, though I didnae hae that much to go on. First off, it was roasting. Aw blue skies an sunshine an leafy trees.

'So where does the term Baltic come frae? Doesnae fit wi this one bit.'

'You know, I was just thinking something rather similar. It is simply glorious, isn't it?'

'Aye. I didnae think to pack suntan cream!'

She laughed. That was good. It had been too serious an sad frae her for a bit now. No what she'd hoped for. No instant memories, places she knew, apart frae that church steeple. We were in this big stretch o open space, aw trees an grass. No a park really, but nice enough. We walked dead slow cos Albie was just sniffing an peeing, sniffing an peeing. Couldnae blame him, eh? He'd had a few days o being locked up, travelling in strange places, no getting much time to be a dog.

We came to a wee cobbled street, dead narrow, that went through an archway in this ancient building – a massive round tower wi tiny wee windows, aw different shapes an sizes. A smaller one on the other side. That church spire was poking out in the background behind aw the red tiles on the roofs. She'd seen it an aw, though she wasnae saying anything, just staring.

We walked on through the archway. She stopped, looked aw around, stared up the wee street o pointy houses wi their crumbling paintwork. Faded pink, auld yellow. Pretty enough but a bit run down, like they hadnae been looked after right.

'You know I don't feel as if I know this place at all. Not one jot!' She sighed. 'I, I think we should return to the car and journey on.'

'Aye. Right ye are.' I'd've been happy going on a wee wander, but she was boss, so back we went.

We drove off, clueless. It was dead quiet. No that many cars about, an most o them looked ancient – like out o the sixties. Names I'd never heard o: Lada, Volga, Gaz, Moskvich. The odd black Mercedes, shiny, new an posh.

'Mafia!' she whispered knowingly, eyebrows up, as one went speeding by.

'Ye reckon, aye?'

'Oh yes dear,' she said wi this serious, knowing look on her face.

Weird! Just aw weird! Trams rumbled up an down the middle o the road; sparks flying out frae the wires they went along. When they stopped an folk got off, they just trotted across the road, no looking up or down, left or right. Took me a while to get to grips wi what was going on. To work it aw out. Tram stopping equals cars stopping. Okay. Just another thing to worry about, as if being on the wrong side o the road wasnae enough! Jeez!

We were on this big wide road, two lanes each way. That suited me fine. I didnae fancy wee twisty turny streets. No the now.

'Just keep going, aye?' I asked.

'Yes. I think so dear,' she said, her voice changed, weak, so quiet I could hardly hear.

I took my eyes off the road for a wee sec just to check on her. Her face was drawn an she didnae look that good. What the fuck would I do if she got really sick? I didnae speak a word. No clue as to where to take her, what to do. Nothing. When we were planning aw o this we hadnae even talked about medical insurance. You'd have thought, considering, health would've been right up there, but naw, it had just slipped on by. I thought maybe I should try an be more like her; no worry about it. Easier said than done, but I'd give it a go. Aye. Let it be. Ditch the thought along wi the fear. Just keep going.

Whatever, I wanted to get somewhere. It didnae matter where. Just some place we could stop an make a base. Lock a door. Feet up, brains down. No stressing for a while. Get to know a bit about the place. Feel like we knew what we were doing. Course we didnae, other than her hoping something would happen. Her memory would wake up an say "Hi!" Christ, I wished it would, an aw, an quick!

Anyway, we drove on; trees aw the way up the sides o the road, auld buildings hiding behind them. No that I could see much. Didnae dare look away frae the road. Pay attention! This big tower block o a hotel shouted at me frae the corner o the road just ahead, poking up above the trees. Hotel Viru, the sign on its roof said.

'What d'ye reckon? Maybe stop for a bit, aye?' I asked, hopefully. 'Get a room, unpack, look around, get to know the place. Maybe things'll come back easier if you take it slow?'

She took a deep breath. 'You know dear, I think that

324

might just be wise.'

But before we got to the hotel I had to work out how to get round this weird looking roundabout that had sprung up in front o us. Aw confused an complicated, it was, an...jeez...going the wrong way, doing the wrong thing! I was scared o messing this up big time! She was looking at the road for me, being co-driver frae the place where the driver should've been. I'd stopped where I thought I should've stopped. Other cars were driving on through, but there was a line, a dotted line, and in my mind that meant stop!

'On you go, dear. It's all clear.'

I wasnae so sure, but I couldnae see right. Hesitating. Neck stuck out like an ostrich, straining to see what was happening. Crawling out dead slow.

'Go, go, go!' she called. 'Put your foot down!'

I did as she said, eyes peeling this way an that, panicking like fuck! I was that nervous I drove right the way round, missing the turn off for the hotel, right the way round again, sure folk were staring. Well, they were, just cos o the car. Foreign plates, the wheel on the wrong side. Worthy o a stare. An there I was making a great show o my dodgy driving skills! Third time lucky, eyes on the turning, got in the right lane, almost drove into a tram that was shouting away at me. Well, how was I to know ye stop in the middle o a roundabout to let a tram through? Finally made it. Note to self. When you see a tram stop. Doesnae matter where ye are, what's going on, just stop!

'Well done, dear!' she said.

I wasnae entirely sure if it was genuine or just a wee bit sarky. Anyway, white knuckled, shaky, an nerves shot to shit, but, aye, made it!

There was a parking bay at the front o the hotel. I guessed it was okay to stop there. Wasnae caring that much. I was stopping, getting out. End of! Wobbly legs took me through the automatic doors as they swished their way around an we were inside. Suddenly it was dead quiet. A big open space, high ceilings, shiny marble floor, wee spot lights reflected in it, pot plants, massive mirrors, a row o clocks up on the wall just in case ye wanted to know what time it was in Moscow, or Sydney, or London, or Berlin – aye, well, ye get the idea. It was nice enough, twenty odd floors high. Sort o seventies look to it but clean an shiny. Folk that looked like they were there on business. Smart, suits, money, foreigners, that kind o thing.

Maria asked for a room wi a view. The woman at reception smiled. No a grin, just a soft wee kind o a smile. She looked like she belonged on a catwalk, no behind a desk. She was aw cheek bones, blue eyes an long blond hair.

'Very beautiful,' she said, as she slipped the keys across the desk at us wi perfectly manicured nails too long to be any use to anyone. 'Best views in Tallinn. Enjoy!' A wee hint o an American accent.

She wasnae wrong about the view, but!

'Oh my dear, just look at that,' Maria said, peering out o the window. 'Just look!'

It was gorgeous, right enough. We were on the eighteenth floor an we could see right across the city. That church she'd recognised – Saint whatever it was, loads more auld looking towers, red roofs, trees everywhere, an the sea we'd just sailed across, aw blue an sparkly. A magic view, so it was.

Albie was jumping on an off the beds, frae one to the other an back again. Wee nutter! I sat down for a bit, let my legs an my head settle. Maria just stood an stared at that view. Ten minutes later an we were on the move again. So, no rest then! The folk at reception gave us a wee map o the Old Town. We changed some money an set off to explore. We both forgot which way the traffic went. Again! After one false start, nearly getting squished by a car, a quick leap back onto the pavement, embarrassed giggles, we looked up the road an saw a pedestrian crossing. Folk waiting. Okay. Good. Behave like the locals an it'd be fine. We just had to cross that one big road an we were there, in the Old Town.

The streets turned aw narrow an cobbled an there were no cars. Right up one side, sort o cut onto this wee hill, there was a row o kiosks. Most o them selling flowers. Gorgeous smell, like. The kiosk at the end sold cigarettes an such like. Bought myself some Camel Lights. Stupidly cheap, they were! Gave the woman a twenty five Kroon note an got some change. Less than a pound. Couldnae believe it! I was choking on one an wondered for a minute about lighting up. The place was spotless. Clean, clean streets. Nae litter, nae fag ends, nothing stuck in the gutter. To smoke or not to smoke? Were there rules? I had no idea. Then I spotted two men in uniform, police type uniforms, an they were smoking, strolling up the street aw casual like, puffing away. No like the bizzies back home, that's for sure! Weird no to be feart o them, needing to run, to hide. I even smiled at one o them. He gave me a weird look, sort o smiled back, sort o didnae, if ye get my drift. I lit up an blew out a big puff o smoke, watching it twist away into the blue.

There was a mood about the place. Quiet an old an just so different frae Edinburgh, frae anything I knew. All o us – me, her an Albie – just walked dead slow. Albie sniffing, us just looking around. Pretty wee buildings, pink an yellow, an blue. An a smell. An auld, auld smell.

We wandered up this wee narrow street called Viru

Tanav until we came to this big open square, aw cobbles an quaintness, an ancient, but grand. Posh buildings that looked like rich folk would've lived in them way back when. Ye had to stop an stare, spin around, take it aw in. There were plastic tables wi umbrellas stuck in the middle o them, folk sitting at them drinking beer. Could've gone one myself, right enough. Settle the nerves. Chill. I'd been warned to be careful though, best for me to stay clear o any addictive substances, alcohol included, but that was never my poison. Never felt I had a need or a problem wi the drink. No really. It was circumstance. It was drugs. It was that auld me frae back then. I wasnae her any more.

I could smell a curry house an suddenly felt really hungry. She'd smelled it too. It was tucked away right on the corner o the square an had tables an chairs outside. I didnae like to suggest things like eating out.

I was glad when she piped up wi, 'You know, I've never eaten Indian. I rather fancy sampling it. How about you?'

'Aye! Scabby horse an aw that!'

She looked at me like I was the one speaking the foreign language.

'Aye! I'm starving!' I clarified.

She smiled, whispered, 'Scabby horse,' nodded an smiled again.

We sat down. The waiter spoke English an was fussing about chitty chatting away. Funny that, there we were in a place that had been in the Soviet Union for the past fifty years or so an the good old Indian waiter was just the same as back home! Bizarre!

'And to drink?' he asked.

I was about to order a beer, just cos that's what ye do, aye? Curry, beer, right? But I stopped myself. Naw, I wasnae going down that road. I wasnae about to do anything that could fuck this up. Fuck me up. Best be safe, aye?

We both settled for fizzy water. Local stuff called Värska wi an odd salty taste to it, but I quite liked it. Different.

Anyway, the food was really good. I sucked the sauce off o a piece o my chicken an gave it to Albie. How could I no? Wee soul had been sitting staring for the past half hour. A wee stare at her, a wee stare at me, a wee drip frae his nose, a wee lick o his lips.

Maria was quiet most o the time, listening to what was going on. I guessed trying to understand, make sense o something.

# Chapter 62

## Maria
### Estonia June 1993

To say that I was disappointed would have been a monumental understatement. I was quite devastated. As I walked along the cobbled streets, desperately trying to trawl back memories from the depths of my brain, spark recognition, nothing came. I didn't know this place. Lovely though it was, Tallinn was not my home. The language however, that was familiar. Snippets of overheard conversations began to make sense and then drifted away again around corners, up alleys, into the air. That was all right. I could wait. At least it gave me that confirmation. Yes, I am Estonian. But who? From where? Of that I still had no idea, and, I realised, I should reconcile myself with the fact that I might never know. But at least I was now home. That was some consolation.

Of course, Angie was right; now that we were here we should take the time to explore. The Old Town was very beautiful and intriguing. It truly was like stepping back in time. After a rather delicious lunch – oh, what I had been missing – we headed away from the square and twisted our way around some alleyways, through arches, and onto a pleasant little side-street called Pikk.

Through another ancient archway a cobbled lane, Pikk Jalg, where rough uneven little stones of pinks and greys – rather pretty – drifted up a hill that had been worn down, smoothed, by the passing of centuries of feet, leaving the stones slippery, precarious. One had to walk as if one were stepping on ice!

Walking along in pleasant solitude, we passed a couple of remarkably old buildings, that were crumbly, dishevelled, three and four storeys high, then immense ancient stone walls that rose tall on either side, bedecked with a variety of wild plants that had taken hold in the rock and clung on. Quaint little wrought-iron street-lights protruded from the walls. The climb was steep and rather a challenge was placed upon my legs, but they stood up to it nonetheless.

Near the top of the lane a Russian Orthodox church stood with its swirls and curls, onion domes, peculiar crosses, and ornate decoration. It was quite beautiful! More twists and turns led further up the hill and onto a cul-de-sac where one thought one perhaps shouldn't enter. It felt somehow private, but there was nothing blocking our way, so we tentatively walked on until we reached a low wall, beyond which there was the most magnificent of views. It was akin to that from our hotel only closer, more intimate, open. Yet still, I had no recognition whatsoever. If it hadn't been so breathtaking I would have felt bereft, but whatever else might transpire, this in itself was simply stunning and I would enjoy it. Life, my life, was precarious. I might not have much of it left and it would be a sin to waste it in sadness and regret.

We had spent the whole afternoon and evening exploring, finding little cafes and resting places, discovering hidden courtyards and alleyways. By the time we returned to our hotel, I'll confess, I was quite exhausted! Yet restless.

'I think tomorrow we should travel on,' I suggested to Angie as we sat looking out at our spectacular view. Colours faded with the setting of the sun, but the place still sparkled in its own unique way; something about the light, the air, the quality of the colours.

'Aye, fine, if that's what ye want, but where to? Any ideas?'

'Oh, I don't know. It's all rather frustrating, isn't it? What if I never find out who I am, where I'm from? What if this is all a waste of time, an old woman's fantasy?'

'Less o that you! We're here an we're gonnae keep searching. It'll happen. I know it will. Something somewhere will just click an ye'll know.'

'Do you really think so?'

'Aye. Aye, I do!'

She spread the map of Estonia out on the table between us. I stared at it, as I had done so many times before, just praying for something to leap out at me. Something to say, "Here!"

I followed the coastline with my index finger, wondering what lay in each twist and turn of the land. I was convinced that I had lived by the sea. I was also quite determined that a bay, a gracious sweep of sand akin to the one at Gullane, had played a major factor in my early history. There were many, of course – Estonia being coastal to the north and the west – inlets, islands, bays, it could have been any one of them. But my eye kept coming back to settle on a place called Pärnu. It was on a bay in the south-west of the country and it felt...it felt somehow right.

'I think here,' I said, pointing to where it sat on the map. 'Pärnu.'

'Aye. Nae bother. There's a nice straight road. Should

be easy enough.'

She took a pen and a piece of paper and wrote the directions down as I read them out.

'We follow the E67 the whole way down, and we pass through, some small-looking places; Laagri, Saue, Jõgisoo, Kernu, Varbola, Märjamaa.' I paused on that one, played it around on my tongue. 'Märjamaa. That has a rather lovely lilt to it, don't you think?'

She smiled up at me. I carried on reading until Pärnu, our destination, perhaps my home. My excitement was such that my heart was beating faster than was good for it. I had to keep reminding myself that nothing might come of this. I should prepare myself for that and not leave room for the disappointment I had felt earlier on that day at not knowing Tallinn, but it was so very difficult. Sleep did not want to come. Fitful tossings and turnings ticked away the night and I was up and raring to go by six o'clock the following morning.

I took Albie for a little trot outside as Angie showered and got herself ready for the day ahead. It looked as though it were going to be another glorious day, the sun rising in the clearest of skies – a pale suggestive blue – a slight chill to the air, but the surety that it would soon enough be sweltering again. We walked around a pleasant little park of grass and trees. There was a scent clinging to the dawn air. Beautiful, heady, familiar. I breathed it in. A picture. A memory. Withering lime blossom flitted to the ground and sat in little circles of pale yellow, green, and orange. Someone stretched up and snipped a piece of blossom from a tree. Tucked it behind my ear. The smell. The beautiful, beautiful smell. And suddenly it was gone. I picked some blossom, held it to my nose. Nothing more came, but it had been there. I had remembered! My face was wet with tears, but these were joyous. It would come.

Little by little, it would come!

There was barely a soul around, the sound of birds carrying on the gentle breeze with little else to interrupt them. The odd rumble of a tram, a trolley bus. Albie had done his business and had a decent sniff so we headed back to the hotel, the blossom clenched in one hand, his leash in the other. I could sense his disappointment.

'Never mind, Albie, there'll be wonderful walks soon enough, of that I am quite sure! Wonderful walks!'

Who knows what they understand, but he wagged his little tail at me in reply.

We had checked out and were on the road by seven.

# Chapter 63

## Angie
### Estonia June 1993

I'll confess I could've done wi a decent long-lie, but we
were up an on the road dead early. I almost forgot which
side o the road to drive on. Again! She was way too
excited to drive, an she had to look out, eh. See
everything. Of course she did! Anyway, it wasnae hard
to find the way. I'd studied it last night, memorised it.
Easy enough, Estonia Street then left onto Pärnu Street,
then straight on aw the way.

It wasnae long before the buildings changed frae
blocks o flats to houses wi gardens, wooden fences, wee
wooden houses, an then countryside. Trees everywhere.
That was what struck me the most about the place, apart
frae the heat. Trees. We had left the city well behind. I
wasnae a country kind o a person, but I'd started getting
used to it in Aberlady. This was something else though;
just quiet, quiet countryside.

'Ye ready for this, aye?' I asked.

'Aye,' she replied wi a smile.

We both laughed. She looked better again. That
sparkle in her eyes was back – that excitement. Maybe
she felt something. Maybe she knew. Anyway, we drove
on down, though the road was that straight an empty,

there was hardly any driving to do. Nothing but trees on both sides, their leaves making shadows dance all ower the road in front. I had to blink every now an again to keep my focus, to stay awake. It was dead easy to drift off wi the shadows. Dream a little.

She was doing the navigating, but I was checking too, marking off each place in my head as we passed by. Sometimes all there was to see was a signpost, a wee village maybe, but ye wouldnae know it. I took it slow so as we both could see. It was aw new for me. Aw different. For her? I hoped no. I hoped it was starting to register, wee bits falling in to place like building up a jigsaw puzzle.

Funny that, her trying so hard to remember her childhood, me trying so hard to forget mine. Wash it aw away like the nasty stain that it was. The nuns, the dormitory, the wickedness o the place. Never anything anywhere near love. That first night I'd been that scared I'd curled myself up into a tight ball, hugging my knees, wishing it would aw just go away, that I'd wake up back home. Okay, home wasnae that great. Any money we had she'd spend on the drink. Men would come an go – uncle this an uncle that – tempers were short, times were hard, but it was home. My home. An I knew I belonged there. It didnae matter who else was around, who said what, who did what, it was mine.

I had slept in a teeny wee room – just enough space for my mattress on the floor, an a cupboard – a wee window that looked out onto someone else's wall, a door that locked frae the outside, but it was mine an I felt safe in there, even when I was locked in, I felt safe. But that first night in the orphanage it had aw gone. Everything. I wet the bed cos I was that scared. Too scared to go to the toilet even. The nuns shrieked at me. Told everyone else. Made me carry the wet sheet through the other beds as they called me names. 'Dirty little girl. Utterly shameful! We'll have none of that disgusting behaviour in here, will we girls?' 'No,' they chorused back as I cried my way out the room. I toughened up quick enough. Nae choice.

And then there was Deke. What was that? Had that ever been love? I thought so back then. He said so. But now? Now I'm no so sure. Whatever it was in the beginning it had aw gone bad. So bad. Just the thought o it made me feel dirty, an wrong, an someone else. Something else. There was no need to cling on to any o it any more. It was like I was just this different person, an I guess I was really. Back then I was a wee lassie wi no clue, just doing what she had to do. Just getting by.

I glanced ower at her. Her wee dog sat on her knee, his head following her eyes. Wherever she looked, he looked, like they were one, an it was dead cute, an I was a part o it. I was crapping myself at the thought o it no lasting long. Aye. Terrified about that. But, for just then, it was aw barry. It was great, an that's aw I could think about. Right then, that day was a very good day, an I was happy. Really, really happy. Who'd've thought, eh? All I can say right now is, 'Cancer, thank you, an screw you, aw in one go!' Life-changing. Aye. That's for sure!

The drive only took a couple o hours an we hit Pärnu outskirts well before lunch time. I was already starving, though. Even if there had been anything close to a service station, which there wasnae, I doubt she'd have been up for stopping anyway.

# PART IV

# Chapter 64

Maria
Estonia June 1993

I knew as soon as we were leaving Tallinn that it was the right thing to do. Sometimes one just knows, doesn't one? A sixth sense, a feeling, some higher knowledge – something that stands beyond our comprehension but is unquestionably real. It had been awfully disappointing not to sense any belonging to Tallinn. Any feelings I had trawled up were negative. Fear and anxiety. Not what I had been expecting nor hoping for. Perhaps it had been naïve of me to imagine that I might set foot in this country and suddenly have everything fall into place and for it all to be like a fairy tale; memories of happiness and enchantment.

The leaves on the trees fluttered in the gentlest summer breeze, as if a million butterflies were dancing just for me, their shadows trickling across the tarmac. It was all very pretty, mesmeric. The odd nesting stork interrupted the view. An unruly, seemingly random mass of twigs precariously balanced on a surface that seemed too small, too tall, too narrow – a telegraph pole, a rooftop, a chimney. Peculiar how they chose to nest on man-made structures. Perhaps that's what gave rise to the fable?

There was the odd junction, tiny side-roads that didn't look as though they led to anywhere other than a small farm, or steading, or some such, perhaps even a village, but we had chosen not to explore that day. Best to keep to the major thoroughfare. After almost two hours we reached the outskirts of Pärnu. The sign lifted my spirits and I smiled. My soul smiled. We drove through little wooden houses of all descriptions and a multitude of colours. And a feeling. A warm gentle feeling. I turned to Angie.

'Well, whatever else happens, I do believe we have come across a rather lovely little town.'

'Aye. It's no bad, is it?'

I leaned my head out of the window and took a deep breath. Albie followed suit and I held him close. A tingle ran through me and it felt simply glorious. Everything felt glorious.

'I think we should find a hotel or some such and make our base. Get settled. Does that sound agreeable?' I asked, turning back in to face Angie.

'Oh aye, an the rest!'

The houses soon gave way to small tenement type buildings and then we came upon a sizeable river that stretched out into the sea. As we drove across a rather quaint little bridge, the water below sparkled fiercely in the sunlight, as if diamonds had been strewn upon the river, small yachts bobbed around in a harbour. It was quite breathtaking. We reached the town centre. Trees everywhere.

'I think we should park up and walk,' I suggested.

We pulled in and parked in the shade of some trees on a street called Vee near the junction with Rüütli. As I stepped out it hit me full on like an express train and I had to steady myself by clutching onto the car door. Good God! This was it. I absolutely knew this place. I really knew it!

'Are you aw right there?' Angie asked.

'Oh, my dear, I am so much more than all right. I am home!'

She grinned at me and threw her arms around me.

'You're sure, aye?' she said, stepping back a pace, holding me by the shoulders, looking me in the eye.

'Oh yes.'

We walked along Rüütli – which sufficed as the high street – arm in arm, not just for companionship but also for support. My legs felt that they might give way at any second as I stared at what I knew. The precious cluster of small buildings that lined the narrow pedestrianised street, the clock jutting out of the wall, the archways and balconies, the Gothic red brick building on the corner of Rüütli and Hommiku. It had always fascinated me. I knew that. I know that. Opposite it sat Georg's cafe. It felt prudent to stop and have a bite to eat. Inside there was a counter with a glass cabinet full of local food. We filled our tray with egg and herring with black bread, coffee and orange juice, and *kissell* – sweet and sticky and delicious – and sat at one of the small tables on the pavement. The heat of the sun was almost too much. Almost uncomfortable. But the gentlest of breezes fluttered by every now and again, bringing just enough relief.

The moment that first spoonful of *kissell* entered my mouth I remembered. I remembered my mother stewing fruit that we had picked from our garden. I was small, perhaps nine or ten, fingers stained a deep red, waiting patiently for my bowl to be filled. A boy sat opposite me. Not a brother. No. A friend? I think he was a friend. We were grinning at each other conspiratorially. Such a closeness.

'Maria?' Angie's voice broke through my reverie.

'Oh,' I sighed through watery eyes, clutching at my heart. 'Another snippet. I remember!'

'That's magic. How much? Your name?'

'No. No, not that. My mother. A little piece of my childhood. Such happiness. Oh my dear, I do believe that it is all going to come back. All of it!'

I was caught between wanting to sit there for hours, just taking it all in, bathing in it – the people, the smells, the familiarity – and wanting to move, to explore, to find out more. We eventually decided on the latter.

I asked the lady behind the counter if she knew of a hotel. At first she looked quizzically and tilted her head, not understanding. I tried again, just saying hotel, slowly, clearly.

'Ah. *Hotell*!' she replied. '*Jah, jah*. No *Inglise*!' she added shaking her head, waggling her finger back and forth.

I shrugged in helplessness. She held a finger up. '*Üks hekt.*' (One minute)

She returned with a small square of paper and a pencil. Laying it on the counter she sketched directions for us. It looked straight forward enough. I smiled and thanked her.

'*Aitäh!*' (Thank you)

'*Palun!*' (You're welcome!)

# Chapter 65

## Jaak
### Estonia June 1993

Content with what he had done to the interior, it was now time to work on the garden. The task didn't appear to be too great as the garden had been looked after and only fallen prey to weeds that summer. He enjoyed the feeling of earth on his fingers; being in touch with nature, tending it, an integral part of it. He worked on through the rising heat of the morning, filling his basket with weeds, emptying it into the compost heap, turning over the soil, clipping back overgrown fruit bushes and trees.

Allowing himself a break at midday, he hoisted a bucket of water up from the well, tipping some over his hands before taking a drink from it. It tasted of the ground, of the earth, of life itself. He had placed some black bread, cheese and sausage on the wooden table in the garden. He added some freshly picked tomatoes and berries and sat on the bench satisfying his hunger and reflecting on what he had done and what still needed doing.

There was an abundance of colour: roses, daisies, geraniums, and the scent of honeysuckle and jasmine,

345

but he felt that something was missing. Cornflowers. Of course! There had to be cornflowers. He would plant seeds for next year, but he felt he had to have some now. He would finish up this afternoon then tomorrow he would search out one of the women who stood at the side of the road with their baskets full of freshly picked strawberries, mushrooms, and cornflowers for sale. If there were none he would take a walk up to the market.

Sven dropped in on him that evening and they sat drinking beer, in the shade of the apple tree, sharing memories and dreams. They had their independence now, but times were still hard. Sven was impatient for things to improve for his family. He wanted his boys to grow up in a prosperous Estonia. A land of opportunity and freedom. Jaak? Of course he shared Sven's hopes for his country, but there was only one thing he truly wanted now. Just one more chance to see her. To touch her. To have her smile at him. Maarja.

# Chapter 66

Angie
Estonia 1993

We drove along Ranna Puiestee which means Beach Avenue – chufftied at myself for finding that out an remembering it. Might as well try an learn a bit, eh? Didnae learn shit at school. What was the point? Much more fun just to piss the teachers off an be a pain, so that was what I did. But now, well, I had a reason, aye. No idea how it would aw pan out. No idea at aw, but so far I was feeling good about the place. It was weird an kinda like stepping back in time. Dead simple like. Quiet. Uncomplicated. I kinda liked that.

There were just trees everywhere. All the way along the road you couldnae see a thing but trees. No wee manicured things either, but great big pine trees an stuff. I almost drove on past the hotel, but noticed the gap in the trees an a turn off just in time. A quick slam o the brakes – no a problem cos the roads were as good as empty – a sharp turn right, an there it was, the Ranna Hotel. I'm no gonnae lie, the hotel was a stunner! No what I was expecting frae a place just out o the Soviet Union. I didnae know much about that either, but I did know it was aw meant to be shite. This just wasnae! It was super posh, wi arches an swirls an marble an glass.

347

Just gorgeous, so it was!

She'd asked if I'd wanted my own room. I'd said naw. To be honest I wanted to make sure that she was okay. I stood well back as she checked in cos we were a bit worried about wee Albie in a place that posh, see – no sure about if he'd be allowed in or no, an no wanting to take the chance – so he was in my bag, being really quiet, as if he knew. He made a wee excited yelp when Maria came back, the key in her hand, a smile on her face. I coughed loudly to try an disguise the noise, an we hurried on up, no looking back, hoping we'd got way wi it. Seemed we had. Either that or they werenae bothered. We carried on up the stairs, aw wide an white, an sleek an shiny. Our room was at the top o the hotel, on the third floor. Low an exclusive, this place, no like the tower block o the Viru. Totally different ball game! I was sitting bouncing up an down on the bed, checking it out, as she was walking across to the windows.

'Oh...' she said, aw softly. 'Oh my lord.'

She opened up the balcony doors an stepped out. I joined her. What a view! Albie's wee nose was up, catching aw the smells. A wee bit grass an some trees (course!) then the beach an the sea, aw golden sands an calm water an just pure beautiful!

'Wow!' I said. 'No bad eh?'

She just stood there, leaning forward against the railings o the balcony. It was kinda like being on a ship; guess that was the point! Her head was high an she was breathing big deep breaths, sighing, like it was filling up every bit o her, filling up her soul.

I leaned ower the railings wi her an was thinking a wee rest; sit for a while on the chairs out there on the balcony, take it easy, maybe even a wee snooze, but naw. She wasnae having any o it.

'Oh, I need to go down there. Come on.' She patted

her leg an Albie trotted happily up to her. She picked him up an carried him in her arms, her jacket covering him. An that was that. We were offski! No even a quick seat, a shower an a change o clothes, just offski! No a nice leisurely stroll down the grand stairway like posh folk do. Naw. Hurry down, hurry out, nash around the side o the hotel, an we were on the beach. She let Albie down but kept him on his lead. Then she was taking it slow. Dead slow. She took her shoes off an wiggled her toes in the sand an stared out at the sea, then up an down the beach. Miles o it. Folk lying down, folk exercising (weird!) kids playing an screeching, folk swimming an paddling an just being aw things beachy.

She took my hand an squeezed it an didnae let go, an we walked through the wide stretch o sand down to the water. I guessed folk'd think I was wi my gran. Normal enough, I guess. Wouldnae really know, never having had one, or at least no one that I knew. We walked along the edge o the water, just our feet in it, our shoes in our hands. The water was dead warm but sort o orange, like it was a wee bit rusty, which was a bit weird, an I wondered if that was aw right, but the locals were in so I guessed it was.

'Do you remember that beach?' she asked. 'The one I took you to in between Gullane and Aberlady?'

I thought for a bit, trying to picture it in my head. 'Aye. Your favourite. I remember.'

'Look dear...do you see? Do you see why?' she asked, spreading her arm out at the beach, like she was stroking it.

She squeezed my hand again.

'Eh, aye.' I could see what she was getting at. The big long sandy beach. The same curve. Aye.

'I think it might be the feeling of the place. The beauty of it. I always knew I'd lived somewhere like this. The connection I had with that beach. It all makes sense now.'

She wasnae looking at me as she talked, but out to sea, out at the water.

'Shall we maybe head back? Get rested? Come back out tomorrow?' I asked hopefully.

I could see she didnae want to, but she sighed an agreed. Who knew, maybe sitting up on that balcony, or in the restaurant listening to Estonian voices, maybe bits would come back. Bits o her. Whatever, I knew that she was meant to take it easy, to look after herself. I could at least do that much for her.

# Chapter 67

Maria
Estonia June 1993

It had been the most marvellous of days. From the disappointment of not knowing Tallinn to the jubilant realisation that I was from Pärnu. Such a beautiful little town. Everything about it felt right and the beach simply cemented it. I had a home and Pärnu was it.

There was a rather magnificent dining room in the hotel, it's frontage entirely windowed, looking out at the sea, and a very tempting patio. However pleasant it might have been, I decided to err on the side of caution and order room service. It wouldn't do if we were to leave Albie and he barked his protestations for all to hear. No. This evening we would eat in our room. It was hardly a chore after all, with the view that it had!

So there we sat, a warm breeze in our faces drifting in from the sea. The water sparkled in the most magical of ways, from the sand to the horizon, alight with an iridescent shimmering. As my eyes caught a young couple strolling along, arms entwined around waists, eyes only for each other, I imagined having walked along there as a young woman, perhaps with a lover, just like them. I could picture it. Feel it. A product of my imagination or a memory? I couldn't quite tell.

I would have played there as a child, picnicked with my parents. Family? Did I still have family there? Someone who remembered me? I desperately hoped so, but I had read of Stalin's purges; of mass killings and deportations, tens of thousands of them, and from such a tiny population. It was simply devastating with every family having been touched by it in some way or another. Of course mine would have been as well. I could only hope and pray that someone had survived.

As the sun began to sink the beach emptied, leaving only a few stragglers, a group of youngsters laughing, a lone elderly man, staring out to sea. He was far off so I couldn't be entirely sure, but his stance spoke of age. A shiver ran across my shoulders. I wanted to run down and call, "Do you know me? Does anyone know me?" It seemed I had allowed my internal words to voice themselves.

'What's that?' Angie asked.

'Oh, I didn't mean...I was just daydreaming, dear.'

She looked oddly at me. A touch of concern clouded her eyes.

'Maybe we should turn in, aye? Get up early an hae a good wander about the place? See if anything jumps out at ye?' she suggested lightly.

'Yes. Yes, I think we should.'

As I felt myself falling asleep, pictures filled my head, but nothing that made any sense. It was like the fragmented playing of an old film. Scenes were missing. Nothing stayed, but it was a beginning. I now had images alongside feelings and even some concrete memories. My mother. Picking berries. Yes. Those were real memories. Those were a part of me.

By nine o'clock the following morning we were off. We left the car and walked. It felt as though it were going to be another blisteringly hot day as there was no breeze and barely a cloud in the sky. I had taken my drawing of the house out and rather sheepishly shown it to Angie. The one that I had started away back in that awful place and finally completed in Aberlady. No-one else had set eyes on it and even I had hidden it away – buried it – until I had left Glenbirrie. It didn't do to hanker, to dream about one's past when one's present was so fragile. But since I had begun this search; since I had met Angie really, I had pored over it regularly, dreaming, hoping, wishing, and now? Now I could search for it. That little house. It really could have been anywhere, but it was worth a shot. One just never knew.

'I drew this when I first arrived in England all those years ago. I don't know if it is even a true memory, but it is all I have.'

Angie took the drawing, studied it politely, cocked her head and said cheekily, 'Aye, well, that narrows it down then!'

We both laughed.

'But seriously though, yours has a wee shed thing an trees right at the front o its garden. And most o these places look like shared houses o some kind. Yours, well, it doesnae.'

'You know, I do believe you're right.'

We had been walking all morning, up and down one street after another, peering as inconspicuously as possible into other people's properties, other people's lives, feeling somewhat impertinent, and had just turned into a street called Karja. The name of it immediately jumped out at me. My heart was pounding. We walked along the quaint little street amongst a splendidly peculiar assortment of properties, mostly small wooden affairs of a multitude of colours and shapes. Nothing was uniform. There were some single storey bungalow type places with steep roofs, others were two storey

353

with odd little diamond shaped windows. Some were set back in lush gardens full of fruit bushes and trees, others on the roadside.

The heat of the sun had set off the most peculiar smell of what I can only describe as toasting wood. Yes. Toasting wood. As my eyes flitted from one property to the next suddenly, there in front of us, was my house! The drawing. It was almost identical. I clutched on to Angie's arm.

'Aye,' she said. 'Looks like it, right enough.'

'What now?' I stammered.

'We walk up an we chap the door an we say hi!'

'Oh my dear, I couldn't possibly!'

'Aye, ye can. Come on.'

As brazenly as you like she opened the little wooden gate, strode up to the front door and knocked! I could have died. Simply died on the spot. Perhaps no-one was home. Did I want there to be? Of course I did. Of course. *Buck up. Pull yourself together.* I chastised myself. I heard footsteps. The door opened. A peculiar smell of old wood, of time passed, escaped with its opening. Little flecks of dust danced in the streak of sunlight that broke through the window behind it. A young woman smiled and looked quizzically at us.

'English? Do you speak English?' I managed to blurt out.

'Little. Yes.'

I showed her my drawing. 'I think. I think I may have lived here a long time ago. The nineteen-forties?'

There was no connection between us. At least none that I could feel. One would know, wouldn't one? If one met family, loved ones from one's history? One would know.

'Moment,' she said and retreated into the house. '*Vanaema*' she called.

'Perhaps her grandmother will know something?' I whispered hopefully to Angie.

'You understood her?'

'Oh my lord! Yes I did.'

An elderly woman shuffled to the door, her face wrinkled and suntanned, a wisdom to her, a floral housecoat wrapped around her ample frame, worn slippers on her feet, a heaviness to her breath.

'*Tere!*' she said.

'*Tere!*' I replied.

With the help of her grandchildren we managed to hold the most basic of conversations. No, she didn't know anything about the people who had lived here before. She had only been here since 1950, but there was a neighbour, two houses down. If her memory served her right they had been friends somehow, the families. She had heard something like that. At least, she thought she had. She was old, her memory perhaps not what it used to be. We should try asking there.

The neighbour's property was very different. It sat in a large well-manicured garden, its walls were of brick, and it boasted a balconied upstairs. Floral curtains had escaped from a window and fluttered gently in the welcome breeze. Again I hesitated, nerves snatching at me. Confound them! Once again Angie took the lead and walked purposefully up the path that cut through the grass of a well-sized lawn. It suddenly struck me how little resemblance she bore to that girl I had first met.

'*Zdravstvuyte!*' (hello!) a voice called from a figure kneeling down tending to the rose bushes. I was sure that she wasn't speaking Estonian and was somewhat taken aback. I assumed that she must have been Russian. I had learned that around one third of the population was now Russian. Thankfully this woman understood what we were trying to convey as we repeated our story, our questions. She informed us that there was no-one at home just now who could help, but we should return the following morning. Her husband might know. He had lived here as a boy, but he was away until tomorrow. '*Da, da, vernut'sya zavtra.*' (Yes, yes, come back tomorrow) she repeated as we left.

So, that was that. There was nothing more for us to do but wait until the following day. Mindful of the hour and my need for sustenance and medication we returned to our hotel.

Back at the hotel I couldn't settle. There seemed so much to do, yet nothing! It was most unnerving. There I was, sitting on the cusp of, well, of everything, and yet able to do nothing. We sat on the balcony and chatted about what the next day might hold.

As evening drew in we took a stroll along the beach. The mosquitoes were beastly, but the place heavenly, and I did my best to ignore them, but it was a challenge. The devils could even bite through clothing!

'I think we should seek out some insect repellent tomorrow,' I said, flapping my hand across my face as we walked through a swarm of the beasts!

'Aye, an some! Seems they like you more than me though, eh!' she answered, laughing, as she swiped one off my arm.

I decided that Albie should be allowed some time off-leash. The poor little chap had endured so much over the past few days and he had behaved so very well. He began with a jolly little bark and run around but quickly came back and remained close. That was splendid. I could relax and he could have fun.

We were sauntering along, our toes in the sand, a slight chill to the air, when it suddenly struck me how frightfully selfish I had been. This was all about me and my journey, my history. How Angie might be coping with everything, might be feeling, simply hadn't crossed my mind. I now worried that she might feel unsettled, anxious about her future. That wasn't advisable for her recovery. I had said this before, but I felt it had to be confirmed. No doubt could be left.

'You know, dear, that whatever the outcome of this, you are well provided for. The house in Aberlady is yours to do with as you will; my savings will become yours once I have slipped off this mortal coil, and there is quite a tidy sum.'

'Dinnae talk like that. There's years left in ye yet.'

'That's as maybe, but one never knows, and I want you to be confident in your future. Do you think you'll return? Or might you stay here?'

'I hadnae really thought about it, ye know? Going back there? Well, too much bad shit, aye. An this place? Well, I'm getting a feel for it. I like it, right enough. But, ye know what they say, one day at a time an aw that. Best no get too tied up in the past or the future. Right now, I'm enjoying myself.'

'That's splendid, and rather sound advice!'

'An ye know, I can never thank ye enough for it aw. Wi'out ye, well, Christ knows. I sure as hell wouldnae be here!'

'Likewise, Angie, likewise!'

I squeezed her arm and she smiled. Yes. She looked happy and relaxed and I felt good about it. I felt good about life!

We had reached a track at the far end of the beach. It was barely visible as such, but it was there. A path barely trodden, perhaps secret, or private. Beyond it stood forest.

Albie began to follow the track, his little nose picking up interesting trails to follow. We hesitated, almost followed, called him back and returned the way we had come. The light had faded sufficiently enough for us to be drawn back to places we knew.

Tomorrow.

# Chapter 68

## Jaak
## Estonia 1993

He awoke with aching limbs and a stiff back but a feeling of contentment. The decision to move back here – to reclaim what was rightfully his – now felt like the correct one. He belonged. As was now his custom, he took breakfast in his garden, sitting in the shade of the apple tree, drifting off into the fluttering of the leaves, the singing of the birds, as he ate bread and fruit, and drank coffee.

By the time he was finished with his garden he should have plenty of supplies, which would leave him almost self-sufficient, as was his intention. The garden now looked as it should, beautiful, but there was still much to do. The vegetable plot, although hidden out of sight behind the raspberry and gooseberry bushes, was weed ridden and in dire need of tending. He could see it in his mind's eye and it bothered him, as he wasn't one to settle when there was still work to be done. That sign from the labour camps flicked into his mind and he found himself repeating it.

'Labour is a matter of honour, a matter of glory, a matter of valour and heroism.'

He allowed himself a sardonic laugh as he thought back to Siberia and the hollow emptiness, no, the bitterness of those words that held absolutely no meaning to him and his fellow prisoners; that reflected nothing of the regime, of the camps. Now his labour was indeed glorious, to him at least.

He decided that he would buy some chickens, and perhaps some ducks, for eggs and amusement. 'Yes!' he confirmed to himself. Once the vegetable plot was done he would build a pond; nothing grand, a simple affair for his ducks. But his thoughts were drifting. Today he had to buy his cornflowers.

He straightened up his protesting body to clicks and groans and headed off towards the shop, outside of which, if he were fortunate, he would find some sellers and be able to return with his hands full of flowers.

There were people selling strawberries in little handmade paper tubs and the smell itself was tempting him to buy some, until he reminded himself that he had his own supply at home – that was a word, a feeling to cherish, home – but there were no cornflowers on offer and he would have to journey on. That was no hardship as he loved this little town and its quiet streets, the air heavy with the perfume of nature. It was a place to wander, to amble, to enjoy, and he did just that. He found himself outside Johann's house. What a fool he had been to allow history to come between their friendship. He was glad that reparations had since been made; that finally they felt that old kinship again. Yes, he would call on him. Perhaps they would share a drink, a walk, a memory.

'Jaak, you old dog! I was wondering when you would call. I was going to give it one more day before turning up on your doorstep, and here you are!'

'Here I am!'

They shook hands firmly and slapped each other's backs, both grinning broadly.

'I was just on my way to the market to buy some cornflowers, passed your house and thought, why not?'

'And I'm glad you did. You could pick some if you want. I have a few in the back.'

'I doubt you'll have enough for my purposes. I need a bucket full!' Jaak held his bucket out in confirmation.

Johann pulled a questioning face. 'Old age has got to you then?' he joked.

Jaak laughed. 'Perhaps. I just want the house full of them.'

They clicked the gate behind them and headed towards the market.

'Johann! The foreigners!' Tatiana called after them from the kitchen. But they were out of earshot.

'Oh well,' she mumbled to herself. 'I doubt they'll return anyway.'

Jaak thought he could hear two female voices speaking in English. That was peculiar. He turned to see who it might be – English wasn't a language heard here and worthy of note – but they had turned the corner into Karja and disappeared. A peculiar feeling swept over him and sent a shiver down his spine. He shook it off as he wondered if that would become common – foreigners, Westerners, walking their streets – and if so, would it be a good thing? Perhaps it would keep them safe; protected from their dangerous neighbour? Yes, he decided, it was a good thing.

At the market they found a flower-seller with a large supply of cornflowers. She laughed when Jaak asked how much for the entire bucket-full, assuming he was joking. Her eyebrows raised when she realised that he was indeed serious. A good day's work had been completed in a few minutes. She could treat herself to a little something, perhaps some chocolate. Yes, a small bar of *Kalev* chocolate. She smiled at the thought.

When Jaak returned to his house he took all of the empty jars out of the kitchen cupboard where they had been stored in readiness for pickling, and jam making, and preservation of all that his garden would offer him. They would be a valuable source of food over the long winter months when snow took hold of the land once again. He carefully spread his cornflowers out on the kitchen table and arranged them one by one in the jars that were filled with water from his well. Twelve jars in all.

He decided on two for each room and four for the sitting room, but something wasn't quite right. Of course! They needed poppies amongst them to look complete. He hurried outside and tenderly picked what he needed – such fragile things, poppies – and arranged them just so, with the precision of a seamstress. Yes, he nodded to himself in satisfaction, that was perfect. He was tired and should sit down to rest for a while, but he couldn't settle. Instead he paced around the rooms, the garden, again, and again, before leaving to take his late night walk along the beach.

# Chapter 69

Angie
Estonia June 1993

We'd gone back the next day to that house at around about the same time, like the woman had said, but there was no-one there. At least no-one answered the door. I could've sworn I saw a shadow creep back frae the window. Didnae say anything, cos, well, I wasnae sure, an what good would it have done anyway? None that I could think o.

'Oh well. Perhaps we should come back later, or tomorrow. People have busy lives after all!' Maria said, an smiled, but it was tight, forced, an I could see through it.

She just stood there an stared at the house for a minute. A couple o wee clouds had built up an drifted across the sun, spreading a shadow ower us. It made me shiver. Weird, cos it wasnae cold.

'We should move, aye? Maybe explore a bit more. Have something to eat at Georg's. Check out the other side o the town?' I slipped my arm through hers an nudged her on.

'Yes, yes we should.'

The same woman was serving at Georg's. She smiled

at us. '*Tere!*' (hello) she said. That was nice. '*Hotell?*' she asked.

'Aye, ehm, *jah, aitah!*' (yes, thanks!) I said back, wee words settling in, making me feel good. Making me feel like I could do this. I could be somebody else, some-place else, an it could work. It really could. I'd been warned against the geographical cure before. Told it doesnae work. But, hey, here I was, doing grand. Aye. Doing grand. Exceptions to every rule. I quite liked that thought. Aye, I'd be an exception.

There were wee glass bowls o ricey stuff in the chilled bit (I guessed fish but thought better o picking a bowl up an having a sniff to check!) an some hot stewy type stuff, an some things in batter in these big metal dishes, hot plates, but I had no clue what any o it was so I kept to what I knew. Eggs are eggs, eh! That kirsell jelly stuff is barry, so it is, so I got more o that too, wi a wee dollop o something white on top that wasnae cream, but it was okay. Tasty enough.

After we'd eaten we wandered down to the end o Rüütli, through a bit o a park, an on to a weird archway called Tallinn Gate. It was dead ancient. Just stood there aw on its own making a tunnel through the grassy hill on either side. Inside was dark an damp an a wee bit creepy. Cobble stones on the ground, peeling plaster on the walls, an funny wee doors that you'd have to duck down to walk through, an massive big ones at either end. Huge chunky things! Wouldnae fancy getting locked up in there o a night!

Through it was a bonnie park, a pond wi ducks, an trees that big their leaves hung down an trailed in the water. We walked through it an down to the harbour. Wee yachts tied on to wooden walkways jiggling away on the water, posh folk being loud like posh folk can be. She was dead quiet again – slow an quiet – an I just let her be, let her lead the way, go where she wanted to go. It wasnae just that though. There was something about the place – about Pärnu – that just made being quiet feel right. It was weird, but good. Aye. Good.

We ended up back at the beach, but the far end where we hadnae been before.

'Should've brought our swimmies. I'm roasting, so I am!' I said, pulling at my top to try an make a bit o a breeze against my skin.

'Not to worry, my dear. Not to worry!' she replied, squeezing my arm, like she does when she's excited, when she's remembered something. 'The women's beach is just along here.'

I wasnae sure what she was on about, but I found out soon enough. There we were in about aw these women an children that were starkers, an I mean completely, bold as brass, swimming, sunbathing, playing, free as ye like. No giving a shit! I tried no to stare, but I couldnae help myself. No at first anyway. Maria stopped an just stripped off, just like that. I couldnae believe it!

'Are you coming?' she called, as she headed off towards the water, her white flesh jiggling an wiggling away!

What could I do? It was weird, it's no as if I've hidden my body frae strangers, but this was so different an I came ower aw self-conscious an stupid! I know, eh! Then I thought, *oh, what the hell?* I stripped off an followed her, an I'm no gonnae lie, it was pure bliss. Such a brilliant sensation. Liberating. Aye. That was it. Liberating. Albie had been told to sit on the sand, on our clothes, an he wasnae so impressed! We swam an messed about a bit before heading back for dinner.

# Chapter 70

Maria
Estonia June 1993

I knew Tallinn Gate, the park, the harbour, the *muul*, and the women's beach. I knew them, but I didn't yet have memories of them. Not really. I knew that I had walked along the *muul;* the strip of enormous boulders that stretched far out into the sea. I knew that I had swum in that water, played on that sand. But knowing and remembering, how different they are. How close, yet how different. The feeling was most peculiar.

Perhaps it was simply because I had spent a lifetime suppressing memories, being someone else, and it was all just that little bit too distant, too difficult for my brain to claw back. I imagined many people of my age might have only a scant memory of their childhoods, but I was worried. For me this was more than simply remembering. It was a bigger thing than that, of more importance. So, yes, I was worried that I would never find out who I really was; the person behind this façade that I had built. But at least I had this, I was here, and it was so very beautiful. I tried to convince myself that I could accept just this – I could settle for it – I suppose, if I had to.

As we walked back along the beach in the peculiarly

orange water of the shallows, Albie trotted alongside us, quite the thing, taking a little swim every now and then, but not going far; not even in chase of some poor unsuspecting bird. I imagined he would be after them soon enough, once he had found his feet in this strange land, assuming of course that dogs are aware of such things, foreignness. Did he understand distance? The distance we had travelled. The countries we had crossed. I would like to think he did. When we returned to the hotel another guest walked down the stairs with her little dog proudly in tow. Splendid! Albie need no longer be kept a secret!

We ate dinner on the terrace, overlooking the sea. Once again, as the sky changed its colours to the soft hues of evening, my eyes were drawn to an elderly gentleman walking slowly along the water's edge, looking out to sea. I think it was the same one I had seen the day before. He felt sad and lonely and my heart went out to him. But on that night he wasn't a solitary figure. The beach hadn't emptied as before as it seemed something was happening; some celebration or other. Dotted along the beach there were bonfires and groups of people being quite boisterous! The smell of cooking sausages and meat. Shrieks and laughter and merriment.

After dinner, as we left the hotel for our night-time walk along the beach, the receptionist called something to us. She had a lovely tiara of flowers on her head. Cornflowers and daisies. Quite beautiful.

'*Head Jaanipäeva!* Happy Saint John's Day!' she called.

'*Aitah!*' I replied.

*Jaanipäev!* I knew this. The word, the celebration. This was a special day – mid-summer – but also a personal one. This was highly significant to me. A time of great happiness. We walked along the beach, pausing to admire the odd bonfire, the revellers, but not intruding. I was a tad concerned that Albie might chance his luck and run in to steal some tasty snack if we were to get too close. His nose was certainly anticipating the taste and I could read the intent in his walk. Much to his disgust I clipped his leash on until we were at a safe enough distance for him to be set free again.

We reached the far end of the beach where the trees met the sand. Albie now ran ahead, confident in where he was leading us to. That little track seemed to attract his attention again and he decided that we were going to follow it this time. Perhaps a hundred yards or so on stood a beautiful, ancient, weeping birch tree, its hanging branches creating a cavern of leaves, its heavy foliage rustling in the whisper of the gentle night breeze. Albie had run on in, perhaps chasing after some poor unsuspecting rabbit, or some such, and we had followed, pushing twigs and leaves aside to allow our entry. It was rather magical and somehow familiar. I held my hands out to the trunk, stroking it, my fingers flitting over its bark, pausing at indentations. Letters. It was too dark to see properly; to read them. But I knew. Initials. Initials in a heart. ML JS. I pressed my hand hard against them, searing the imprint on my palm. I had to feel it, have it cause me pain. My face once more awash with tears.

'Are ye aw right there?'

I tried to compose myself enough to speak.

'That is me. ML is me. Maarja! JS is...is Jaak. My Jaak! And, oh, I loved him so.'

I could see it. I could see me and him. We were young, teenagers, as one. Yes, as one. I remembered walking this path. I remembered the feel of his hand over mine, his breath on my neck as he whispered to me. And I remembered many years later a terrible sadness. Oh, this was just so very difficult. So many emotions. So much confusion. Angie hugged me as I wept on her shoulder.

'Shall we go on, aye?' Angie asked once I had calmed down again, composed myself again.

'I am so scared. So very scared!'

'Ye're aw right. I'm here,' she said, linking her arm through mine and squeezing it reassuringly.

We followed the little track through the grasses and the trees, the revelry of the beach parties now a distant hum of indistinct sound, until we came to a clearing. I could smell the evocative scent of a bonfire, hear the crackle of burning wood, see a twist of smoke drifting up into the night sky. I worried that we might be intruding. A private party, or some such. I hesitated. Listened. There were no voices.

'Should we turn back?' I whispered.

Angie simply shrugged in reply.

Albie was trotting on ahead, taking no heed of the fact that we had stopped.

'Albie,' I called softly.

He ignored me, picked up his step, the little monkey, and carried on, caught by some irresistible smell, I imagined. He disappeared around a corner.

We hurried after him, the crackle of dry grass under our feet. As we rounded another corner, there, right there, a little house stood all on its own. Candles lit up the path through the garden. More candles stood in each of the windows. It was quite simply the most beautiful thing that I had ever seen. I stared, dumbfounded, my hands drawn to my face. It was mine. I was quite sure it was mine. A small bonfire burned in the garden. The figure of a man stepped out from the shadows.

'Maarja,' he whispered.

We walked towards each other and the years fell away. He smiled at me and held his arms open.

'Jaak, oh Jaak.'

He wrapped me up in himself. We slipped into one and nothing else mattered.

# EPILOGUE

It's been five years now an I'm still here. I've just been to their funeral. Jaak an Maria's. Cannae quite get my head around her name. Still call her Maria, no Maarja. Shit. Still called her Maria. Past tense. Christ that's hard. She was like my family an my best friend aw wrapped up in this great wee bundle, an now she's gone. An I miss her like hell. Aye. Closest thing to family I've ever had, but better, cos it was a choice. We chose each other in a weird kind o a way.

She did well though, aye. Defied the odds an hung on, like she said she would. The two o them went awmost together; hours between each other. She died first, then him. It couldnae hae been any other way. No after that. Aw o that. Christ, what a love story, eh? It was pure magic seeing them together. They couldnae keep their hands off o each other. Strokes an squeezes an hugs an kisses an such. Ye could see just how much in love they were. I felt awkward at first, wanted to leave them alone, but she insisted that I stayed wi them, at least for a while. So I did, trying to keep myself to myself as much as I could; trying to close my ears to the banging o their headboard – aye, at their age!

Everything's cheap as chips ower here an what she paid me was way more than what I needed, so I saved. A year later I had enough to buy myself a wee flat in one o those wooden houses. It only cost me a couple o grand. I know, eh! Mental. So, I had my own wee place, an I'd go an see them every weekend. It was just dead nice to be around that – that magic, that love they had – an to know I'd helped. I'd done something decent.

Even though I could survive well enough – more than

371

well enough – it wasnae good for me to be idle, to maybe let demons sneak back in to fill up spaces, so I thought about what I could do to keep me busy, make a wee bit o my own money, make me feel just normal, working an aw that. So, I started offering English lessons. What a laugh eh! Turns out there were a good few folk interested. Clever folk, these Estonians, aye wanting to learn an do well. Course I tone the accent down a bit when I'm teaching, aye. Well, I tone down the accent most o the time now, cos folk just werenae getting it otherwise! Anyway, there's a few folk walking around here now wi a bit o a Scottish accent, an that was me. Aye. That was me too.

Jaak's mate Sven had a son called Marko. Me an him hit it off right away. Friends like, nothing more. We'd chat away wi a dictionary to help us. I tried to teach him English an he did the same wi me an Estonian. It was a laugh. It was easy an comfortable an, well, just nice, ye know? Turns out that after a couple o years we sort o slipped into being more than just friends. No because he was a really nice looking guy, no because I needed something frae him, no like it was wi Deke. Naw. Just because we fit, me an him. He's like my biker's jacket, soft an comfy an something I wouldnae want to be wi'out. So, aye, I'm staying. I speak a fair bit o Estonian now; enough to get by. I get their ways. Way different frae ours, like, but I get them, an I like it, an I'm staying. Oh, an wee Albie? Course, he's wi me. My wee pal. My wee bit o her; my wee bit o them.

# LÕPP

If you enjoyed this story you can help other people find it by writing a review on the site where you bought it from. It doesn't have to be much. Just a few words can really help spread the word and make a big difference to its visibility. Thank you!

## Author's Note

The story of the Soviet occupation of Estonia is a true one, as is the remarkable struggle of Estonians to reinstate their independence through the Singing Revolution. Whilst the characters involved in this section of the story are fictitious, I have done my utmost to keep the historical events as factual as possible. I have drawn upon stories I was told about those times when I lived there, as well as carrying out my own research through books, personal narratives, newsreel archives, videos and film. The most noteworthy of these being:

*Carrying Linda's Stones – an anthology of Estonian women's life stories – Tallinn University Press*

*Man is Wolf to Man – surviving Stalin's gulag – Scribner*

*The Singing Revolution – Docurama Films*

*In The Crosswind (Risttuules) – Martti Helde*

All quotes I have added from bystanders and political leaders are verbatim.

## Also By This Author

## Don't Get Involved

**Ukraine, 2001**
**Three street-kids**
**A Mafia hitman**
**A deadly chase**

Dima, Alyona and Sasha, three street-kids with nothing but each other, stumble on a holdall full of cocaine. This could be it. A way out.

Leonid, a Mafia hit man who will stop at nothing to achieve his goals, is sent to retrieve the cocaine and dispose of the children. Failure isn't an option.

Nadia, a naive expat is looking for a new beginning. She wasn't expecting this!

As their paths get tangled up in the biting cold of a ferocious winter in Kyiv all of them will need to find more strength and courage than they ever imagined they had if they are to survive.

What do you call on when you have nothing left to give?

# Dan Knew

**A puppy born to the dangers of street life
A woman in trouble
An unbreakable bond**

Wee Dan, a Ukrainian street dog, is rescued from certain death by an ex-pat family. As he travels with them through Lithuania, Estonia, Portugal and the UK he learns how to be a people dog, but a darkness grows and he finds himself narrating more than just his story. More than just a dog story. Ultimately it's a story of escape and survival told in his voice.

The world through Wee Dan's eyes is a story that will stay with you long after you turn the last page.

# To Retribution

## He thought she was dead
## She wasn't

Suze, an idealistic young journalist, is used to hiding as her cell tries to keep their online news channel open. They publish the truth about the repatriations, the re-education camps, the corruption, the deceit.
New Dawn, the feared security force, is closing in, yet again.
Suze runs, yet again.
This time, however, she is pursued with a relentlessness; a brutality which seems far too extreme for her "crimes". This is more. This is personal.

When her death is finally confirmed, he is celebrating it.

Big mistake.

Retribution will be hers!

# Writing as Fiona Curnow

## Before the Swallows Come Back

**Perfect for fans of *Where the Crawdads Sing* by Delia Owens, *The Great Alone* by Kristin Hannah, and *Sal* by Mik Kitson, with its celebration of the natural world, its misunderstood central characters living on the outside of society's norms, their survival in the wilderness, and the ultimate fight for justice.**

**Before the Swallows Come Back is a story of love, found family, and redemption that will break your heart and have it soaring time and time again as you sit on the edge of your seat desperately hoping.**

Tommy struggles with people, with communicating, preferring solitude, drifting off with nature. He is protected by his Tinker family who keep to the old ways. A life of quiet seclusion under canvas is all he knows.

Charlotte cares for her sickly father. She meets Tommy by the riverside and an unexpected friendship develops. Over the years it becomes something more, something crucial to both of them. But when tragedy strikes each family they are torn apart.

Charlotte is sent far away.

Tommy might have done something very bad.

377

# About The Author

Fiona worked as an international school teacher for fifteen years, predominantly in Eastern Europe. Seven of those years were spent in Estonia – a little country she fell in love with. She now lives in East Lothian, Scotland, where her days are spent walking her dog, Brockie the Springer, and writing.

The Unravelling Of Maria is her fourth novel.

## Contact with the author
Twitter http://twitter.com/@FJCurlew
Facebook http://facebook.com/FJCurlew
Website https://fjcurlew.wixsite.com/author

Made in United States
Troutdale, OR
09/28/2024